# PRAISE FOR VICTORIA LEE'S
## *THE FEVER KING*

"A standout. Diverse characters, frank discussions about sexual and mental abuse, and reasonably plausible science-based magic elevate this above many dystopian peers."

—*Kirkus Reviews*

"Lee thoughtfully gives the subject of refugee and immigration policies center stage . . . The setup of this new world and planned series is genuinely compelling, and it's filled with striking moments . . . Readers will be absorbed as the book melds fantasy and action with psychology and political intrigue."

—*The Bulletin of the Center for Children's Books*

"This fast-paced, issue-driven thriller will collect readers who will eagerly anticipate the sequel. With references to the Holocaust as well as present-day issues of immigration, deportation, martial law, and racism, Lee has worked philosophical and current-day realities into a promising series opener."

—*Booklist*

"Adults and older teens who appreciate stories with close ties among magic, science, and political machinations will find this first novel appealing."

—*Library Journal*

"This is a book for teens of today wrestling with the political unrest in the United States. Written from the refugee perspective, it explores topics of abuse, suicide, intergenerational trauma, mass plague outbreaks, and more. Lee's writing is advanced, sophisticated, and full of emotion. This is for true lovers of sci-fi and dystopian [fiction] who enjoy deep character development mixed with a little romance. Fans of Neal Shusterman and Veronica Roth will be drawn to this novel. Highly recommended."

—*School Library Journal*

"A plague as scary as Stephen King and a romance as complicated and compelling as all my favorites."

—Sarah Rees Brennan, award-winning author of *In Other Lands*

"My kind of sci-fi: sharp, smart and political, with something important to say about our own world. Lee offers a fresh twist on magic that makes *The Fever King* feel totally new and unique. I was absorbed in Noam's world from the first page—and was dreading leaving it by the last."

—Natasha Ngan, *New York Times* bestselling author of *Girls of Paper and Fire*

"Deliciously fierce and unforgiving, Victoria Lee's *The Fever King* is a merciless story that fans of V. E. Schwab's *Vicious* should not miss. I will never be over this book."

—Ashley Poston, author of *Heart of Iron* and *Geekerella*

"Brutal yet thoughtful, *The Fever King* is a nuanced, unblinking study of the complex structures of power in a world where magic itself is a disease that few survive. Lee's science-based, gritty world and sky-high stakes meld perfectly with the timely political intrigue of this book's twisting, devastating plot."

—Emily Suvada, author of *This Mortal Coil*

# THE

# ELECTRIC

# HEIR

# ALSO BY VICTORIA LEE

*The Fever King* (Feverwake: Book One)

# THE

# ELECTRIC

# HEIR

## VICTORIA LEE

**SKYSCAPE**

Text copyright © 2020 by Victoria Lee

All rights reserved.

No part of this book may be reproduced, or stored in a retrieval system, or transmitted in any form or by any means, electronic, mechanical, photocopying, recording, or otherwise, without express written permission of the publisher.

Published by Skyscape, New York

www.apub.com

Amazon, the Amazon logo, and Skyscape are trademarks of Amazon.com, Inc., or its affiliates.

ISBN-13: 9781542005081 (hardcover)
ISBN-10: 1542005086 (hardcover)

ISBN-13: 9781542005074 (paperback)
ISBN-10: 1542005078 (paperback)

Cover design by David Curtis

tes of America

*For the survivors*

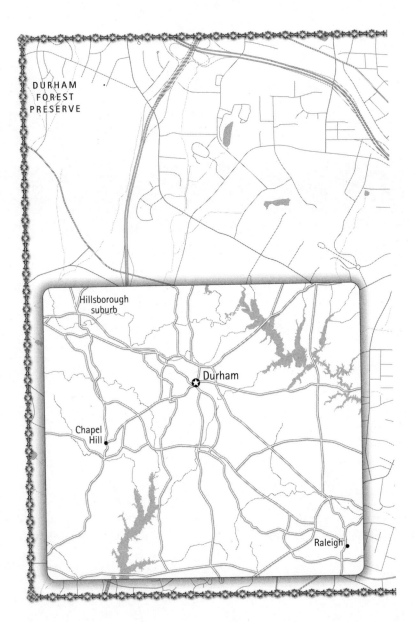

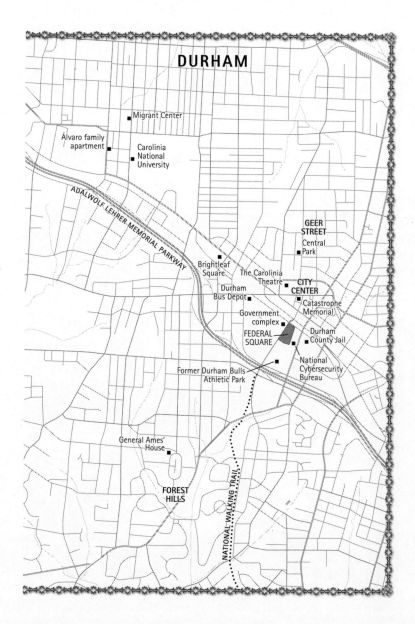

# NOTE

This book contains content that might be disturbing to some readers. For more details, please see the content notes at the back of the book.

*Digital copy of a filmed interview dated May 2019, stolen by Noam Álvaro from the apartment of Calix Lehrer.*

The video opens onto an image of a young man, recognizable as Calix Lehrer. He's about twenty or twenty-one years old, wearing a dove-gray suit that reflects its color into his eyes, making them appear steady and slate. He wears a slim gold circlet atop his brow; he was recently crowned king.

INTERVIEWER: "Thank you for meeting with us today, Your Majesty."

LEHRER: "Of course. Thank you for having me."

INTERVIEWER: "This is the first private interview you've granted since your coronation. There have been rumors about why you've been so relatively reclusive."

LEHRER: "As one might imagine, it has been rather time consuming to build a solid foundation for this country to stand on. I have taken a great deal of that responsibility upon myself."

INTERVIEWER: "And of course, you are still mourning your brother."

Lehrer is still for a moment, unspeaking, then—

LEHRER (steadily): "We all miss Adalwolf very much."

INTERVIEWER: "He was a great leader."

Silence follows.

INTERVIEWER: "So tell me, Your Majesty, what is your vision for Carolinia as a young nation? With the war over, where do we go from here?"

LEHRER (smiling again): "I'm glad you asked. Carolinia itself was founded, of course, on resistance: against fascism, against tyranny—most particularly, against the persecution of those who managed to survive the magic virus."

INTERVIEWER: "Yes—I believe many have reclaimed the term *witching* to describe survivors."

LEHRER: "I suppose it's better than some of the alternatives."

INTERVIEWER: "At any rate, I'm sorry for interrupting—please continue."

LEHRER: "At the Boulder Summit, when our neighboring states demanded we exterminate eighty percent of the Carolinian witching population as a gesture of goodwill, I refused. Shortly thereafter, I publicly declared Carolinia as a witching state—and I stand by that to this day. Above all else, Carolinia should model itself as a haven for witchings. When the rest of the world aims to destroy us, witchings will know that in Carolinia, they will be safe. Our borders might be closed now for security reasons, but an exception will always be made for witching refugees fleeing persecution in Texas, or York, or England, or anywhere else."

INTERVIEWER: "A laudable goal. However, some have expressed concern that the positioning of Carolinia as a witching state will come at the expense of baseline citizens. Do you have a statement on that?"

LEHRER: "I understand the concern. However, it is unfounded. Carolinia will continue to protect all its citizens, baseline and witching alike."

*End of tape.*

*Transmissions received in Dallas, July 2123.*

07.13.2123. SACHA DEAD. LEHRER'S FORCES VICTORIOUS IN CAROLINIA. MILITARY JUNTA HAS TAKEN POWER.

07.14.2123. ATLANTIAN REFUGEES IN CAROLINIA GRANTED CITIZENSHIP.

07.16.2123. SACHA SUPPORTERS PUBLICLY EXECUTED. AWAITING EXTRACTION ORDERS.

07.17.2123. PRO-SACHA RESISTANCE RIOTS QUASHED. HUNDREDS DEAD.

07.20.2123. JUNTA HAS ANNOUNCED SPECIAL ELECTION CYCLE. LEHRER LIKELY TO BE

ELECTED CHANCELLOR. STILL NO WORD ON EXTRACTION ORDERS.

07.22.2123. ANOTHER SKIRMISH ENDS IN BLOODSHED.

07.24.2123. SPECIAL ELECTION TO BE HELD IN ONE MONTH. WILL AGENTS BE EXTRACTED PRIOR TO THAT DATE? PLEASE RESPOND.

08.09.2123. AGENTS DESCRIBE AN OUTBREAK OF MAGIC IN GOLDSBORO THAT HAS NOT BEEN REPORTED IN CAROLINIAN MEDIA. CAN YOU CONFIRM?

08.15.2123. EARLY POLLS SUPPORT LEHRER. IS ANYONE RECEIVING THESE MESSAGES? PLEASE RESPOND.

08.24.2123. LEHRER IS CHANCELLOR.

# CHAPTER ONE

## NOAM

The trees grew dense and close together in the quarantined zone, magic humming through their branches and stretching in their roots beneath soil and snow. At dusk everything was shadow, shifting shapes merging and diverging on the forest floor—near impossible to tell which were human and which were tricks of the light. Magic shivered through the ambient air. Noam felt it like a physical thing all around him, connected to his own power somehow, the virus infecting everything it touched. It crystallized on his breath and prickled his skin like static.

The target hid behind that copse of trees at Noam's four o'clock; electromagnetism eddied and tugged around him the same way it did everything else, betraying his location. Noam sensed the iron in the target's veins, his magic a silvery glimmer that nearly bled into the snow.

It would be tempting to think this was an easy kill, but Noam knew better. This target was strong. He'd drawn Noam's blood twice already— still sticky on Noam's face, although the cuts were healed.

But he couldn't wait forever. Noam counted his heartbeats and closed his eyes, feeling along the wires of that electromagnetic tension and looping it like fabric around the target's body. He heard the whump of weight hitting the ground, air displaced from lungs.

That didn't last. A burst of energy, plasma-like, exploded through the trees, cutting through branches and trunks. Noam pulled up a defensive shield just in time, twisting gravity and magnetism as he deflected the magic away to crackle like fire through the deadwood overhead.

Which, fuck, exposed his position. Noam stepped out from behind his tree and sent lightning across the space between him and the target, who huddled in wet snow with sweat turning to frost on his hair.

The bolt made contact. Finally. Noam wasn't tired, but he certainly was cold. Better to end this quickly.

He pushed harder, another burst of force behind the lightning, drawing as much as he could from static and electromagnetism. The target was deflecting some of Noam's magic, but not all. He dropped to his knees with a grunt, body shaking with the effort of holding Noam off.

The man was almost out of energy. Noam could tell. A little longer and Noam would exhaust the last of his resources, have him seizing on the ground as chaotic electrical impulses swarmed his brain.

Then he'd die.

Just not yet. Noam moved closer, ice crunching beneath his boots and magic swarming round his ankles like white water.

The vessels had burst in the target's eyes, whites shot through with red, mouth slack and drool smearing his chin. His muscles twitched uncontrollably as their nerves misfired, thousands of volts searing through his brain. When he lost balance, crumpling onto his side—when Noam felt his magic falter—that was when Noam let go.

In the absence of power, the forest was too silent. The animals had fled; all that was left were the sound of tree branches cracking in the ice and fire—and the heavy, arrhythmic gasps of the target struggling to breathe.

No—not breathe. Speak.

Noam moved closer, but he kept one hand on the butt of his gun and his power near. Just in case.

The target fumbled over his own tongue, gargling on spit. With veins bulging out of his neck, he looked like a caricature of himself. Noam crouched in the snow at his side.

"I know this isn't the only lab left. Where are the rest?"

The target made a convulsive movement; it took Noam a second to realize he was shaking his head. "No. You . . . listen." He could barely move, but he managed to grab the leg of Noam's pants anyway.

Noam drew his gun quicker than humanly possible, his magic doing half the work, pointing the barrel at the man's head as he clicked off the safety.

"Take your hand off me." The man let go, but Noam kept the gun where it was. "Answer the question."

"You can't . . . trust him." A garbled noise, and the man spat out a mouthful of blood. Then: "Lehrer. Don't. Trust him."

Noam tapped the gun against the man's temple. "Thanks for the advice. Now tell me about the labs."

The man pressed his lips together hard enough the skin blanched around his mouth. He glared at Noam with all the heat he could muster—which wasn't much, at this juncture. *Fuck it,* Noam thought. He was going to have to start yanking out fingernails, which was fucking disgusting—

Suddenly the color drained from the target's face. Noam didn't need telepathy to feel the man's terror—it bled out of him like a sickness—and he didn't need to turn around to know why. But he did anyway, twisting to track the target's red gaze as Lehrer stepped out from between the trees. He was tall, nearly blending in with their shadows. A specter dressed in black.

Their gazes met. Lehrer gestured with one gloved hand. "Let me finish this, Noam."

Noam got to his feet and made room.

Lehrer knelt at the man's side. There was something gentle about the way Lehrer rested his fingers along the curve of the man's neck, thumb skirting the windpipe. He could've been human, almost, if it weren't for the strange colorlessness of his eyes—and the fact there was nothing behind them.

"What is your name?" Lehrer said.

The man stared at him and didn't speak, trembling visibly under Lehrer's touch. Of course the target was afraid. How could he have predicted that Lehrer would come into the quarantined zone and do his own dirty work? Noam holstered his weapon and clasped his hands behind his back, watching and feeling nothing—not even when Lehrer smiled, the expression thin and sickly insincere on his face.

"Your name," Lehrer said again.

"M-Michael."

"Michael, why don't you tell us where the other labs are?"

The sounds Michael made were pathetic. Wet, snuffling noises, like a wounded animal. Lehrer's thumb rubbed against his skin, a soothing motion.

Noam wondered if Michael felt Lehrer's presence in his mind the same way Noam had: like a shadow version of himself tangling its fingers up in the threads of his thoughts, twisting and braiding them into new patterns. Or maybe that was the wrong metaphor.

*Stain,* Noam thought. Lehrer's persuasion left a stain.

At least Michael wouldn't be unclean for much longer.

Noam saw it in Michael's eyes the moment his will snapped, the humiliation and self-loathing Michael felt when he opened his mouth and the information spilled out like sea bursting past stone.

When it was finished, when Michael was finally left wordless and sobbing in the snow, Lehrer unfolded back to his full height and looked at Noam. He didn't have to say anything. Still, Noam waited until Lehrer had stepped out of spatter range to draw his gun again and pull the trigger.

He hit the target right in the skull: a clean kill shot that sent blood and brain matter bursting out across the white ground like a brilliant red star.

For a moment Noam was reminded of Brennan, the scarlet mess on the wall behind his desk. That first kill was half a year ago now—long enough that Noam had started to forget the details. Had Brennan's tie been gray or blue? Had Noam been able to smell the gunpowder? The memory was like water in cupped hands.

Lehrer waited ten feet away, already impatient by the time Noam holstered his gun. "Get the samples," Lehrer reminded him.

The samples were in the satchel the target had looped over his head and shoulder, a black leather construction pinned beneath dead weight. Noam had to push the corpse out of the way, rolling him over to lie facedown in the snow while Noam tugged the bag's strap over the ruined skull and slung it over his own shoulder instead. He checked its contents, just to be safe.

There they were: Six vials of blood swarming with the virus. Two of its milky vaccine.

Noam pulled a vial free and turned it over in his palm, the thick fluid contents slipping along the glass walls. Was that really all it would take? Just a few centiliters of this strange substance would protect someone from the same death that had killed Noam's father. One injection could take down even the strongest witching.

"Noam."

He startled, badly enough he almost dropped the satchel—and its precious contents. Telekinesis caught the vaccine vial before it could hit the ground. "Shit—sorry."

Lehrer's gaze was sharp when Noam looked up again. "Be more careful. Let's go."

Noam tucked the vaccine back into its case and zipped up the satchel, clutching a protective hand around the strap. He fell into step beside Lehrer, who was checking his watch with a frown on his face, probably already late for some meeting or another. Ever since his election as chancellor, Lehrer had been busier than ever. Noam was surprised he found the time to sleep.

After a few steps, Lehrer held out one hand, palm up. Of course. He didn't trust Noam, not even now. Not even with every horrific thing Noam had done to prove his loyalty.

Noam passed Lehrer the bag. His frozen fingers ached when he let go.

"We'll deal with the next lab this weekend," Lehrer said once they reached the ancient car they'd requisitioned, parked in an abandoned lot a mile from where they'd killed Michael. Not driverless—Lehrer didn't want anything with GPS, anything that might raise questions when the car went for maintenance and they realized Noam had falsified location records. They were supposed to be just five miles outside the Carolinian border, where the worst magic one might encounter was a two-headed rabbit or a nomadic tree—not fifty miles.

Lehrer opened the passenger-side door and held it there for Noam to duck under his arm and slide onto the leather seat, then pushed it shut.

*I'm okay,* Noam told himself. *I'm in control.*

*I'm in control.*

Noam sat in the silent interior of the car, shivering in the cold and watching Lehrer walk round the front to the driver's side. Only when Lehrer had opened the door and sat down did Noam use magic to start the engine.

Lehrer gave him a sidelong, approving glance, then pulled the shifter into gear and started them off down the decaying road back to Carolinia.

"I'm working Saturday," Noam told him.

"Then we'll go on Sunday."

Noam tilted his head away, brow pressed against the cold window. The gray landscape rolled past, bare trees and bombed-out shells of old buildings. Lehrer seemed to hit every single pothole, the chassis of the car jolting each time and jarring Noam against his seat.

"You seem to have taken a liking to that Beretta."

Noam glanced back at Lehrer, who flicked his gaze down toward the gun holstered at Noam's hip. Noam's fingers skipped down to graze the textured grip.

"I'm glad," Lehrer went on, smiling slightly before he looked back toward the road. "There's a reason I chose this model for you last year. It's the perfect size and weight for your hand."

Noam curled that hand into a fist. "What did you do with the original one?"

"Disposed of it. Don't worry—I told you they'd never trace that gun back to you. The Brennan case is closed."

Right. No one cared about the assassination of a refugee liaison when there was a coup to contend with.

Four hours later—on the other side of decontamination showers, after a thousand tests to be sure they weren't bringing virus particles over the border and another long drive back to Durham—Lehrer walked side by side with Noam across the government complex courtyard.

"You did very well today," Lehrer said at last, as they passed a manufactured waterfall on the stream, the crash of water loud enough to drown out their words for passersby. "It won't take long, now. That's good. We can't afford for Texas to get their hands on the vaccine."

"I know." Noam tugged at the hem of his sweater, self-conscious of the Beretta—now tucked into the back of his jeans, the holster safely sequestered in the QZ car.

"Carolinia would be left defenseless."

"I know."

Lehrer was still looking at him when Noam glanced up; Lehrer's expression was unreadable. "I hope that you do," he said as they approached the atrium, the noise of the stream fading. "I'm relying on you."

When Noam returned to the barracks, heading past the empty common room and the generic framed wall art—which still struck him as bizarre, even though Noam had lived here over a year—Ames was waiting for him. She sat in the boys' bedroom on an empty bunk, a dark figure silhouetted against the window. "Where were you?" She kept her voice low, but Taye—who occupied the bed across from Noam—didn't stir. He always slept like the dead.

"Work."

Ames had a bottle of vodka clutched between her knees. She held his gaze as she took a long swallow. "No, you weren't. I went by the store, and you weren't there."

"Not the store. The computer repair place."

"I thought you quit that job."

Noam shrugged one shoulder. He pointed at the vodka. "Give me that."

Ames rose to her feet. He couldn't make out the expression on her face, not in this light—not until she'd already stepped closer, and closer again, near enough he felt her breath on his skin. Her face was all tight lines, eyes narrowed and lips thin. She pressed the bottle into his hand. "You don't need to adopt all of Dara's old habits."

"Dara didn't even like vodka."

"You know what I mean."

He did, but he was never going to admit it.

She left the bottle, although there wasn't much left. He stared down at the vodka, clear liquid sloshing around like the contents of Noam's stomach—sickly, intoxicating.

Noam poured the vodka down the sink. Better wasted than back in Ames's hands—she'd been drinking as much as Dara these days. Noam could count on one hand, probably, the number of times he'd seen her sober since her father had been murdered. Murdered *by* Dara, although that seemed like the kind of detail Ames didn't need to know. What good would it do her now?

Even though Noam hadn't drunk any of the vodka himself, when he lay down—curled up in Dara's old bed under Dara's old blanket— the room tilted and swayed before stabilizing. Noam pressed his face into the pillow and breathed in his own humid air, eyes clenched tight shut.

It had been six months. Dara was dead by now. Noam knew that. Still.

The room rocked again, dizziness rippling in waves through Noam's mind. Or maybe that was the effect of the sleeping pills.

When he closed his eyes, lately, too often it was to see Dara's face. The way he'd looked when Noam put him in that car and sent him over the border into the QZ. The way he'd grasped at Noam during the coup before Lehrer's soldiers dragged him away. The way his body would have decayed out there in the forest, rotting into the magic-infested soil until only his bones remained. One of these days Noam would be out there on a mission with Lehrer, and they'd find Dara's skull half-buried in a tangled root system.

*No. Don't think about that.*

Noam turned away from the bones. He imagined instead that he was on a small boat with Dara out in the middle of a vast and empty sea, dark and lifeless below them as above. It was snowing. The white flakes glittered in Dara's hair and melted before they could touch the surface of the ocean. Dara's fingertips, where they brushed Noam's hand, were cold. Noam watched him, the silence of his mouth and unreadable eyes, until Dara went blurry, the whole scene tilting sideways and smearing out of sight.

After that, the night was dreamless.

# Chapter Two

## Dara

Midwinter hung over the city like a blade waiting to fall, the streets silent as a held breath, the night Dara returned to Carolinia.

He didn't know what he'd been expecting. Asphalt slick with blood, perhaps, the virus like a viper snapping at passing heels. But Durham was perfect as a postcard, glittering with fresh snowfall and holiday lights that still hadn't been taken down. The air smelled like pine and cold. And no matter how far Dara reached, all his mind met was void.

"Your name is Daniel Holland," Claire said. She passed him a federal ID card. The photo had been taken when he was still fevermad, too much magic burning him from the inside out. Dara's gaze stared up at him from the laminated plastic, sharp with mania. "You're twenty-two. You just moved here from Beaufort, and you're looking for work."

"Not looking very hard," Dara said.

"Well, yeah. Can't have anyone recognizing that pretty face of yours." Claire smiled and thumped him on the shoulder with her fist. "Come on. This is the place."

They'd rented out an apartment on the second floor of a run-down old tenement just north of downtown. The building was sandwiched between two bars and across the street from a suspicious-looking burger joint. A man in an apron loitered in front of that door, puffing on a cigarette and giving the pair of them dirty looks from twenty feet away as they fumbled with the rusty lock. The air inside was musty and worse when they got to Dara's new apartment. A thin layer of ice crusted the windowsill.

Claire kicked the radiator, which emitted a weak stream of hot water against the wall, then shuddered and died.

"We'll get you a space heater," she reassured him.

Dara sat on the narrow bed next to his duffel, tucking his hands under his thighs. His breath clouded in front of his face every time he exhaled. "It's fine. I can put up with anything for six days."

Claire hitched herself up onto the dresser on the other side of the room, legs swinging through empty space. "Sure. Of course you can. Focus on that—in less than a week, this'll all be over. We'll be sleeping pretty in the government complex, and Lehrer's head will be up on a spike."

Dara tried to match her optimism, but his smile felt weak.

Claire noticed, of course—she didn't miss much. But she didn't mention it. Just tapped long painted green nails against the dresser and said, "You got the plan down?"

He nodded.

"Want to repeat it to me? Sorry. I don't think you're an idiot. But I gotta be sure."

"I'll sneak into the Sunday gala at six thirty. You and Priya will be there, disguised as serving staff. I'll wait until you've confirmed Lehrer's been given the suppressant. Then." He tipped two fingers against his temple and mimed pulling a trigger.

Claire gave him two thumbs up. "Great. Good. Now, is there anything else you need from me before I go back to Priya's? Food? There's that burger place across the street."

"I'm not very hungry. Thanks, though."

"You sure?"

"Positive." Anything he ate would come right back up. His stomach was a sickly mess of bile and adrenaline.

Claire pursed her lips. "Listen . . ."

"Please don't," he said before she could start in on him again. He'd heard it all before—from her, from Priya, from the doctor back at base who monitored him as he struggled to make it through alcohol withdrawal. "I'm fine. Really. I can keep it together for six days."

"It's different out here," Claire said. "You didn't have any other option in the QZ; we ran out of booze back in 2043. Are you sure you—"

"I said I'm fine. Stop asking."

She raised both eyebrows at him, then held up her hands in a gesture of surrender. "Okay, whatever. Just let me say one last thing. I'm here. Yeah? If you need to chat. It's not every day you're plotting to assassinate a head of state."

"I've killed people before."

"Not your own guardian, you haven't." She slid off the dresser and tugged at the hem of her shirt, straightening out the wrinkles. He reached for her mind before remembering, *Oh*. He couldn't anymore. The Claire who looked back at him from across the room might as well have been a corpse, thoughts quenched out.

"It's not gonna be the same," she said. "I don't need you losing your shit on me day of."

"I won't."

She left, eventually, but only after giving him one last look, like she thought she might read some reluctance from the set of his mouth or the way he had his arms crossed over his chest. He thought about saying, *I want him dead more than all the rest of you combined*, but didn't.

He wasn't even sure that was true.

The room seemed even smaller with Claire gone. Dara could pace from one end to the other in four strides, touching fingertips against the frigid window glass and those same fingers, a beat later, against the grimy wall opposite. He unpacked his duffel, folding his clothes into the dresser. They were the same clothes he'd left Durham with, now ill fitting and weak at the seams. He toed off his shoes and pushed them into the corner. There was a vanity mirror over the dresser; Dara avoided his own gaze as he slid the drawers shut. He was darkly, dreadfully certain that if he looked, he wouldn't be the only one reflected there.

This room was full of shadows and distant noises: cars on the street, the burble of laughter from the apartment down the hall, a door slamming shut. It was all so much louder than he remembered, like the absence of telepathic voices in his head was a void that sucked in more sound than usual. This dead city reverberated inside his skull.

Not just the city. This whole country felt like a graveyard. Like every single body populating it was a corpse—an empty shell, reanimated and going through the motions but not *real*. Not really.

Dara sucked in a breath, made himself exhale slowly. Then he looked at the mirror.

There was no one reflected in the room behind him. Just his own face, cheekbones more pronounced than they used to be—he'd lost weight in the QZ. His eyes were wide, whites showing around the irises.

He made himself keep looking: another second, one more.

He took off his wristwatch last. It was an expensive piece: mechanical, with a leather strap and a white face. Lehrer had given it to him for his fifteenth birthday. Back then Dara had been able to sense the cogs turning inside it, the hand ticking away the seconds of his life. Now it was as dead as everything else—but it was the only nice thing Dara had.

He set it atop the dresser at a perfect right angle to the outer ledge.

Six months since Dara left. Five since Lehrer had been elected chancellor. The news they got out in the quarantine zone had been sporadic and vague, enough to make Dara wonder if Lehrer had tightened restrictions on the press. He'd let himself start imagining some horrific dystopia, soldiers in the streets and the bodies of traitors hung from the walls of the government complex.

But if anything, things in Carolinia seemed better. They'd repaved Mangum Street, which had been full of potholes for as long as Dara could remember; the drive through downtown had been smooth. There was new construction, the tenements replaced with safe, affordable housing and schools. No more beggars, at least that Dara had seen. No breadlines or Atlantian refugees rioting for equal rights.

Lehrer, damn him, had his utopia after all.

And this time he hadn't even needed to declare himself king.

Dara had to remind himself of the truth: no matter how many social programs Lehrer implemented, no matter how efficiently he used taxes or how much the people seemed to adore him, Lehrer was a killer. A mass murderer. Every one of Lehrer's adoring citizens had lost loved ones to the virus. Every Carolinian feared the infection Lehrer had released on his own people.

It was Dara's job to make sure they knew the truth. It was Dara's job—the Black Magnolia's job—to free them.

Dara turned off the lights and lay down on the thin mattress, staring up at the cracks that spindled across the ceiling like spiderwebs. His chest felt tight when he inhaled. His fingers curled into fists atop the sheets.

This apartment was one mile from the government complex.

It was ten minutes past midnight. Noam might still be awake, sitting cross-legged in his barracks bed with a magic-cast light floating overhead illuminating the pages of the book in his lap. His hair a little messy, as if he'd tried to sleep but given up early. The cap end of his pen stuck in his mouth. His mind a glowing ember in the sleepy darkness.

When this was done . . . when Lehrer was dead . . . Dara might see him again.

He almost didn't dare imagine it.

The Black Magnolia wasn't interested in suicide missions, generally speaking. This was an exception—and only because Dara had insisted he be the one to pull the trigger. Even if Dara managed to kill Lehrer, he wouldn't make it out of that gala alive. Not without magic—and he'd given up magic four months ago, when he finally gave in and accepted the vaccine. He'd waited as long as he possibly could, until he was barely coherent with fever. He kept thinking, maybe, maybe he'd be the exception. Maybe he'd hold on to his sanity. His life.

Dara hadn't even planned on coming back to Carolinia at first. That was all Claire. *You have to face him* and *we need what you know.*

At last he shut his eyes and rolled over onto his stomach, pressing his face against the pillow and breathing in the smell of mildew. He already knew he wouldn't be falling asleep tonight. He'd lie awake and flinch when the radiator finally rattled to life, certain every shifting shadow was a tall figure slipping out from the dark.

After all, Noam wasn't the only person who was just a mile away.

# CHAPTER THREE

## NOAM

Late Tuesday, the Atlantian Center for Pathogen Control declared a state of emergency as the number of victims of a magic outbreak in Birmingham rose to 143,000. This latest outbreak was first identified on December 28. Officials originally stated the epidemic had been successfully contained in southwest Birmingham; now, victims are being diagnosed as far north as Ensley. Carolinian minister of defense Amelia García confirmed several units of Carolinian infantry have been dispatched to Atlantia for aid.

Noam scrolled farther down the article on his phone with technopathy, slumping a little lower against the pillows. The *Herald* had included a particularly gruesome photo: a man curled on his side, his spine like railroad tracks beneath bruised skin, bloodstains on his clothes. Dead, probably.

The man might've had a family. A husband who loved him—a daughter who thought he could do no wrong.

Now he was combustion fuel outside a red ward, him and the virus both burned like trash.

The vaccine Noam and Lehrer had found in the quarantined zone three days ago wouldn't do the dead man any good. Wouldn't do any of those people—those Atlantians—any good. How many would survive this outbreak? Would Lehrer find himself with a new crop of witchings ready to be trained and shaped into perfect Carolinian soldiers?

Or maybe, for once, magic would kill every one of them. Maybe it would burn through their blood and bone, and instead of rising from those ashes with incredible powers, the infected would just be dead.

The shower cut off in the adjoining bathroom. Noam let out a small breath and shut his eyes, wondering if he should pretend to be asleep. Better than answering questions like *What were you reading?* and *When are you planning to get out of bed?*

Probably he *should* get out of bed. It was almost dinnertime. Probably he should finish writing that paper for Swensson's class, start his physics p-set.

But instead he lay there, quiet, too conscious of the rise and fall of his chest as the bathroom door opened and footsteps padded across the room. The mattress dipped beneath new weight.

"Are you awake?"

Noam opened his eyes. There was no point pretending. Lehrer could sense Noam's heartbeat, probably ever so slightly too fast. Lehrer had his wet hair combed back from his face, but a droplet fell onto Noam's cheek anyway. Lehrer's long fingers swept it away. He kissed him softly, as if Noam were fragile. As if he'd never put a gun in Noam's hand and ordered him to shoot.

"Are you all right?" Lehrer murmured. He kissed Noam's throat next.

Noam hummed out something wordless and closed his eyes. When he tipped his head back against the pillow, Lehrer's lips shifted against his skin, smiling.

At last Lehrer drew away, pushing himself up and heading to the closet. Noam disentangled himself from the sheets and swung his legs off the edge of the bed as well. He half expected Lehrer to say something, change the subject to schoolwork or their next trip into the QZ—but there was nothing.

Noam went into the bathroom and shut the door.

The air was still humid, marble counter damp beneath Noam's hands as he clutched the edge. When he rubbed away the fog on the mirror, the Noam reflected there was flush-cheeked and glassy-eyed, hair tousled. A bruise had formed above his collarbone where Lehrer's teeth had caught the skin. He looked crazed.

Fevermad.

Noam flipped on the faucet and hunched over the sink, splashing cold water on his face. When he closed his eyes, he still felt Lehrer's hand on his thigh, Lehrer's breath hot against his ear. But the whole time Lehrer was touching him, all Noam could think about was that look on Dara's face, the last time Noam saw him alive.

Noam pressed his face against one of Lehrer's plush towels. Breathed out.

When he straightened, his reflection had reclaimed its composure. Noam dragged his fingers back through his hair and practiced smiling.

Lehrer was waiting when Noam returned. He'd changed into a plain shirt and trousers, incongruously casual—and when he reached out, Noam went to him, kissed him with both hands slipping into Lehrer's still-cold hair. "Are you leaving?"

"Not tonight," Lehrer said, gaze half-lidded. He rubbed his thumb against the hollow beneath Noam's hip bone. "I thought you might like to stay until morning. I'll even make you dinner."

"Depends. What are you cooking?"

"Whatever you want."

Noam tipped his head back, pretending to consider. "Pancakes."

"Pancakes it is."

Lehrer left Noam there to throw on fresh clothes from the selection he kept in Lehrer's bottom dresser drawer. He wasn't sure precisely when that had happened—when Noam started storing clothes here, a spare toothbrush in Lehrer's medicine cabinet and his laundry mixed with Lehrer's in the hamper. They'd started sleeping together two months after Dara disappeared into the quarantined zone—right around the time Noam realized that Dara was probably dead. Dara's fevermadness had already been advanced, inflaming more organs than just his brain. So for all Noam gave Dara what he wanted by helping him leave, Noam had killed him in the same stroke.

Lehrer was the only person who understood that guilt.

Lehrer had lost Dara too.

Noam sat at the kitchen table as Lehrer cooked. Lehrer had rolled his sleeves up to the elbows; every time he tossed the pan's contents, the muscles in his forearms shifted and drew taut. If Lehrer were to activate his power now, the handle of the cast-iron skillet would crumple in his grip easy as scrap paper. Noam's gut twisted into a warm knot.

"Here you go," Lehrer said, nudging a stack of pancakes onto Noam's plate. "And butter."

The pat of butter he smeared on top melted fast, leaving a slimy trail as it slipped off the pancake and onto the platter. Noam tried to feel hungry.

Lehrer took the seat adjacent to Noam's, legs long enough his knee unavoidably bumped against Noam's thigh beneath the table. He folded his hands and fixed Noam with an even look. "I'm going to ask you a question," he said, "and I want you to tell me the truth."

Noam picked up his knife. "All right."

"Why can't I read your mind anymore?"

Noam had just put a bite of pancake into his mouth. He practically choked, grabbing onto the table edge with one white-knuckled hand as he forced himself to chew once, twice. Swallow. "You can—what?"

Lehrer tapped one finger against the back of his hand. "No dramatics. Answer me. What happened to make you feel so distant from me that your mind would block itself off from my telepathy?"

Noam stared at him, wide eyed.

Well. Thank god for *no dramatics*, anyway. He'd never been very good at faking surprise.

Even so. It had been a month now since Noam figured out the second secret of Faraday. Since Noam managed to create an electromagnetic shield around his own mind, sustained by magic, preventing Lehrer's persuasion from influencing the electrical signals inside his brain just as Sacha's crown had protected Sacha. Noam had developed the shield after a fight with Lehrer. They'd been out in public, arguing over something inconsequential, and Lehrer had used his power to make Noam stop talking. He'd apologized later, of course, but the damage was done. And that night Noam had sat cross-legged on his barracks bed and wondered if he'd made a mistake, if he had gotten in over his head, if Lehrer was too powerful to be trusted.

Trying the Faraday shield had been impulsive, a flash-fire effort to keep Lehrer from persuading him again. Only then it had worked.

Using the shield had other, unanticipated effects as well.

A whole month, and Lehrer never asked him why Noam's mind had gone silent. Not once.

"I don't know," Noam said, trying to look stunned all the same. Even if Noam didn't have a Faraday shield—even if Lehrer's persuasion still worked on him—*no dramatics* wouldn't mean *don't act surprised.* "I've been thinking a lot about . . . what happened."

"What happened with what?" Lehrer pressed.

"With Brennan. When I . . . killed. Him."

"You did what was necessary. What was *right.*"

Noam had prepared this response the night he made the shield, shaking and terrified on the bathroom floor. Now the excuse felt stale in his mouth . . . outdated, unlikely.

"I'm not so sure anymore," Noam said and finally let his gaze slide down toward the pancakes. The dough was starting to look soggy from the syrup. "I'm reconsidering things. I'm starting to wonder if I would have done that if you didn't . . . if you hadn't asked me. I keep thinking about your power and how you said it wasn't mind control—that it's *persuasion*—and . . . that scares me." A soft breath. "You've used persuasion on me once already, at least that I know of. You broke your promise. You . . . lied to me."

"I see," Lehrer said. When Noam stole a glance up, Lehrer had one hand propped against his chin, assessing Noam almost musingly—as if Noam were a work of art he considered purchasing.

Noam wasn't an idiot. So far, Lehrer hadn't realized Noam was using a Faraday shield to keep him out. But if Lehrer knew he couldn't control Noam, if he knew Noam had taken efforts to make it that way . . . Lehrer seemed to like Noam well enough now, but all this— the mentorship, the sex, the soft smiles and lingering touches—was provisional.

"Very well," Lehrer said at last and sighed. He reached for his water glass and took a small sip. "Forget we discussed this."

The shock and confusion faded from Noam's face in a single instant, closed away behind a neutral mask. He picked up his fork and cut into his pancakes. "What's the plan for Sunday?" he asked and popped a fresh bite into his mouth.

Lehrer leaned back in his chair, gazing fondly at Noam as if he hadn't just tried to wipe Noam's memory. "We'll need to leave for the quarantine zone no later than four thirty or five. You might as well sleep here Saturday night."

"Do you really think it'll take that long?"

"I'm attending a gala that evening, and I can't be late. It's hosted by the Keats family. You remember the Keatses; they were one of my campaign's biggest donors."

Noam did remember. Everyone in that family was a witching—in the same suspicious way that everyone left alive in Ames's family had been a witching.

Lehrer sat forward again and began cutting into his pancakes. "I'd like you to accompany me."

Noam blinked. Lehrer's attention was on his food, his fingers warm around the steel handle of the fork as he speared a piece of turkey sausage.

"Aren't I a bit young to be your date?"

It was deeply gratifying to watch the way Lehrer's expression changed, a ripple of something unreadable flickering beneath his eyes as Lehrer looked up. He put down the fork. "I didn't mean to make you uncomfortable," he started, very slowly, as if testing the words on the tip of his tongue before saying them.

Sleeping with a 124-year-old immortal was the very least of what made Noam uncomfortable nowadays. "No, it's fine. There is a problem, though."

"What's that?"

"I don't have anything to wear." Noam pressed a smirk to one corner of his mouth and picked up his water. He watched Lehrer over the rim of the glass as he took a sip, then added, "Unless you're telling me you prefer the cadet uniform."

"My tailor will make you something." Lehrer's gaze didn't waver from his. "Are you coming?"

Noam wanted to ask why. Why did Lehrer need him there, when Noam was still a seventeen-year-old student? Only he thought he already knew the answer. Lehrer was still fielding suspicion from certain corners over Dara's disappearance, even six months later. He wanted Noam there as a distraction: Lehrer's new, improved protégé.

After a beat, Noam nodded. "All right. But only because I want an expensive shirt."

Lehrer laughed, the tension of a moment ago breaking like pond ice.

He refilled Noam's glass with water from the pitcher, and when they were done eating, they took Wolf for a walk, then ended up on the living room sofa, tangled together as Lehrer drew heat to Noam's skin and lit him up like an electrical fire. That night Noam lay awake next to Lehrer, in Lehrer's bed, staring at the back of Lehrer's neck and the single freckle next to his third vertebra usually hidden by shirt collars. And he wondered if Lehrer ever tossed and turned till dawn consumed by the same guilt: the deep and unwavering knowledge they both shared, that Dara was what had really brought them together—and that they, together, were the reason he died.

Noam counted his sins.

First sin: he let himself become vulnerable.

It took a month after Dara left before Lehrer called him into his office and sat him down on the velvet-upholstered sofa. Said, "I promised you I wouldn't go looking for Dara, and I've kept that promise. But it's been three weeks, Noam. I would like to send a team to retrieve his body."

And even though Lehrer was in his military uniform—this had been before the special election—even though he was as strictly formal as Noam had ever seen him, not one hair out of place . . . somehow, Noam could still tell he hadn't been sleeping. It was a tension to his features, perhaps, or the way the area under Lehrer's eyes looked bruised.

He'd brought that image back with him to the barracks, replaying those moments in his mind as he tried to fall asleep: the twitch of muscle in Lehrer's cheek when Noam agreed. The quiet way Lehrer said thank you, and how the following silence felt like a net ensnaring them together in unspoken sorrow.

Four days later, Lehrer made Noam stay after lessons. Invited him back into his apartment for tea, even. Noam had sat clutching the mug between both hands while Lehrer stood in front of him, said, "I'm worried about you."

Noam couldn't remember the exact moment when he started to cry. But he remembered Lehrer on the sofa next to him, Lehrer's hand warm and heavy on the back of his neck.

"It's my fault," Noam had said. "I shouldn't have helped him leave. Or I should have gone with him to make sure he was okay. And now he's dead."

Lehrer's fingers pressed harder against Noam's spine, just for a moment.

"I might have been able to save him," Lehrer said. "If he had stayed."

Something sharp lanced through Noam's chest. He shuddered and rocked forward, dragging a hand into his hair. *Of course. Of course. Suppressants, and steroid therapy, and maybe he—maybe he would've—*

Only then Lehrer went on. "But if you had gone with him, he would have died anyway. And probably you would have, as well. You can't blame yourself for that."

His hand smoothed down Noam's back, a steadying weight as Noam's shoulders shook through his sobs. It had felt like something breaking inside him, the wall he'd built to hold back his misery finally crumbling and spilling all that grief like oil into the sea. Lehrer took the teacup away with a curl of telekinesis and just . . . let him cry, until at last the pain had receded to a low throb in the pit of his stomach.

"I feel guilty too," Lehrer murmured eventually. His voice was quiet enough Noam almost didn't catch the words. "It's my fault. I wasn't a very good father, I'm afraid, and Dara . . . well. I was so focused on making Carolinia better—on fighting Sacha, trying to bring this country back to its roots. I didn't have anything left for Dara, after that. I didn't pay attention to him."

"You loved him," Noam said.

"Not enough."

When Noam finally stole a glance at Lehrer, Lehrer's gaze was fixed on some spot across the room, shoulders pushed back and taut. For the first time, Noam glimpsed a shadow of what this really was—as if he were watching Lehrer construct this façade in real time, hollowing himself out bit by bit and blotting out the pain until he was all cold logic and utilitarian restraint. Lehrer didn't become who he was passively. He *built* this.

And maybe that was why Noam kept coming back. Those days, he'd been . . . well. He'd been fucked up. Constantly. Hungover in class, vomiting between sprints during basic, him and Ames slowly killing themselves with every kind of substance Ames could get her tattooed hands on.

But even when the rest of Noam's teachers were sick of it—of him—Lehrer was always there. Lehrer always had time to talk or to serve him a cup of tea, even after the election passed and he was officially made chancellor.

And he was there on the anniversary of Noam's mother's suicide, when Noam showed up at midnight, trashed off god knows how many tequila shots and swaying on Lehrer's doorstep as he said, "I kill everyone I know."

Lehrer had hesitated just a moment, standing in the shadows of his study. "Noam—"

"I killed Dara," Noam insisted, head spinning and heat prickling against his eyelids. "I killed my dad because I never got him out of that neighborhood. I made my—I made my mother kill herself, because I . . . I . . ."

Lehrer grasped his shoulder, and Noam couldn't finish. His throat was too swollen to speak. He let Lehrer draw him into the apartment, flicking on lamplights as they went. In the narrow hall past Lehrer's front door, it felt like someone had struck a match and consumed all the oxygen in the air. Noam couldn't breathe. And Lehrer didn't say anything, just let Noam go, just *looked* at him. Looked at him until Noam couldn't stand it anymore, dizzy from staring into those creepy fucking eyes.

Finally, Noam managed to choke out the words. "I hate myself."

"I know," Lehrer said quietly. "I hate myself sometimes too."

For a moment all Noam could hear was his own heartbeat. Lehrer's gaze hadn't fluctuated—didn't, even when Noam took a step forward and put his hands on Lehrer's face, pulled himself up onto the balls of his feet, and kissed him.

Second sin.

They'd had sex that night, and Noam woke up in Lehrer's bed the next morning with the sheets tangled around his legs and Lehrer already in the kitchen making breakfast. Noam had tried to apologize to him, awkward in sock feet while Lehrer cracked an egg over the frying pan.

"It's fine," Lehrer said. "Let it go."

So what other choice did Noam have? He tried to let it go. He took a shower in Lehrer's bathroom, standing on Lehrer's stone-tile floor, used Lehrer's pine-scented shampoo. Got dressed in the same clothes he'd worn the previous night. Lehrer walked him to the door, and they both stood there, uncomfortable silence stretching out until at last Noam couldn't resist filling it.

"Okay," he said. "Bye."

Only Lehrer didn't say anything, just nodded, and Noam still didn't leave. Couldn't.

He took a half step forward and stopped.

It was Lehrer who closed the rest of the distance between them, Lehrer whose hands found Noam's hips and pushed him back against the shut door, Lehrer's body hot and firm where it pressed against his.

And it only occurred to Noam later that Lehrer wasn't drunk the first time, or the second. And he hadn't hesitated.

It was a little weird, but at the time it'd been reassuring in its own way. Especially in those intervening weeks, when Lehrer barely acknowledged what had happened. They still had their lessons every day, but Lehrer scarcely seemed to glance twice at him. Lehrer's apparent disinterest threw Noam's own desire into sharper relief: every time Lehrer had touched him—their fingers grazing when Lehrer handed him a book, the paternalistic pressure of Lehrer's hand on Noam's shoulder

32

when he introduced him to another politician—Noam had tallied up the contact in a sort of mental reckoning. Those touches were suddenly imbued with meaning: *He wants me, he wants me not.*

So when Lehrer's restraint finally broke, three weeks later, Noam didn't hesitate. He threw himself into the affair with all he had.

Third sin.

After Faraday—after all Noam's memories had come rushing back, blood welling to fill the wound—Noam had wondered if Dara had craved Lehrer's affection the same way Noam had. As if Lehrer was the most intoxicating drug in the world and everyone else just addicts scrambling for another fix. And every time Lehrer pulled away, you wanted him more, and more, until you would happily strip your dignity down to the bone if it meant Lehrer wanted you back.

*Now look where we are,* Noam thought as they both got dressed for the Keatses' gala—in the same room, wordless, the only sound that of rustling cloth and the spritz of aftershave.

But whatever other lies Lehrer might have told, his grief was real.

The two of them built this hell together, and together they were damned to it.

# CHAPTER FOUR

## DARA

They'd bought the suit secondhand in west Durham, untailored and sewed from cheap cotton, but it fit surprisingly well. Well enough, at least, that the man in charge of checking invitations didn't give him the once-over the old Dara would have given someone walking up to a high-society gala in anything short of bespoke.

Then again, the invitation was a *very* good fake.

So good a fake, in fact, that it wasn't a fake at all. Lehrer really should have done a better job sniffing out Sacha loyalists in his new administration. Not that being *Grayson Heath, Minister Holloway's nephew*, was going to get him very far at a party full of people who'd known him since he was a terrifyingly telepathic four-year-old.

Dara smiled at the invitation checker all the same and let the footman take his coat.

The last time he'd visited the Keatses' home, he'd been thirteen. Their daughter, Eleanor, took him up to her bedroom and tried to kiss him against the floral wallpaper. He'd spent the rest of the evening avoiding her and reading trashy novels in the toilet while pretending to have food poisoning.

Eleanor wouldn't be here, of course. She'd been a year older, and last he heard, she'd graduated Level II and promptly married the Norwegian ambassador to avoid military service. She lived in Oslo now.

He didn't miss Eleanor, but he missed a lot more than he'd have thought about being thirteen. For one, the ability to go hide in a bathroom.

If Dara still had magic, he could have draped an illusion over himself like a cloak and looked like anyone. A grizzled old war vet, maybe, dripping with medals of honor and scowling at the world through filmy cataracts. Someone no one would mess with. If Dara still had magic, he'd have every thought in this room at his fingertips. He could dip his hands into the mind of the minister of finance, sifting through emotions like glittering jewels, and sense the precise moment Kurt Langley recognized him.

"If it isn't Dara Shirazi," Langley said, clearly delighted with himself for having spotted Dara first. He reached forward with both hands, and Dara had no choice but to let him clasp one of his between them. Langley's palms were moist with lotion. "My dear, dear boy . . . I thought . . ."

Dara smiled back at him, waiting as Langley fumbled for the correct words.

"Weren't you," Langley managed at last with a delicate little cough, "missing?"

Dara patted his hand. "Hardly. And as you can see, I'm back now. Didn't Calix tell you?" He detached himself before Langley could answer, drifting toward the refreshment table and leaving the man to wonder why, in fact, Lehrer *hadn't* told him.

Although something about the way Langley had said *missing* kept itching at him. Dara rather suspected Lehrer hadn't said he was missing at all, but hidden away in some clinic in a foreign allied nation, kept comfortable as fevermadness ate away at his brain and his life.

Even Dara had to admit it was a deft move. No one would expect Lehrer to lie about such a thing, as Dara's behavior reflected upon his own reputation. The story was just embarrassing enough to be believed. And that explanation would cast in new light anything Dara had ever said to suggest he was less than enamored with Lehrer. The promiscuity. The drugs.

*What a shame,* they all used to think—always with that mental note of comingling disappointment and delight, pleased that their own children, at least, were not so fundamentally broken as Lehrer's. *What a waste of talent.*

Dara might have chosen to take on this mission, but he hated being here. He hated that this was that kind of party, filled with the kinds of high-society people who would recognize Dara Shirazi even if Lehrer had kept Dara's face hidden from the rest of the world.

Still, he was glad he'd be the one holding the gun when its bullet tore through Lehrer's brain.

Now that Langley had recognized him, though, it was only a matter of time before that knowledge made the rounds. Dara had to find Lehrer before Lehrer heard that Dara was here.

Lehrer was taller than anyone had any right to be, but in this crowd picking him out was impossible. Too many military uniforms, too many fine suits and fair-haired heads. After watching a moment, though, Dara noticed a pattern to the way people moved through the room. It was as if they were all asteroids in orbit around a knot of people at the far end, by the fireplace. And—

Yes. There. Just a glimpse was enough, just the sharp line of a cheekbone and the neat part of Lehrer's hair, and god, but Dara would recognize him anywhere.

He wanted to reach for the gun strapped to his right hip. He wanted to start shooting right now, damn the consequences. He was nauseated down to the marrow of his bones, sickness seeping like venom into his blood. Even breathing was difficult, like his rib cage was constricting round his lungs and squeezing all the air out.

He couldn't do it. He—he couldn't, he couldn't walk over there and look Lehrer in the eye again, hear that soft voice twisting reality with every syllable he spoke. Not even to shoot him.

*You have to.* Think about Noam, still in Carolinia, still trusting Lehrer and blind to what Lehrer really was. Maybe Lehrer's persuasion would break when Lehrer died, every thread of that lethal magic snapping at once and freeing the nation from its bonds. Maybe Dara would miraculously manage to get out of here alive. And Noam would remember.

That only happened if Lehrer died. Which only happened if he drank the suppressant first.

Dara took in a sharp breath and made himself exhale slowly.

All right. Where was Claire? He had to wait for the signal.

He felt people's eyes on him, gazes snagging on his face and dragging after him as he walked deeper into the room. They were thinking about approaching him. Dara didn't need telepathy to know that. And if they weren't thinking about approaching him, they were thinking of approaching Lehrer, waiting for a break in conversation to say, *Dara looks well. You must be so relieved.*

He scanned the faces of the passing servers, meant to be unobtrusive in their plain black uniforms. What if something had come up with Claire's papers and she hadn't been able to get past security? He should find Holloway, perhaps. Make sure.

Only—no. There she was, tangled up in a knot of giggling socialites who'd clearly already had enough to drink. She had a tray in hand, little glasses of schnapps. Which one was meant for Lehrer? Or had she poisoned them all?

Their gazes met. He arched a brow. She shook her head, however minutely.

Not yet.

Maybe Dara could go hide in that bathroom after all.

He started off in that direction, slipping his hands in his pockets and trying to look like he was headed somewhere in particular so he wouldn't be interrupted. He made it about ten feet before the crowd shifted, a knot of partygoers departing toward the refreshment table, and Dara could see clear through to where Lehrer stood. He was facing away, toward the hearth, momentarily free from sycophants. But he wasn't alone.

Dara froze in place.

He'd spent eight months memorizing the shape of that body, the long limbs and narrow waist now flaunted to great effect in a tailored suit. How his hair looked almost red in the firelight, neatly trimmed for once and swept out of his beloved face, briefly visible in profile as he glanced toward Lehrer and said something inaudible.

Dara's pulse roared in his ears.

And Lehrer.

Lehrer's hand rested on the small of Noam's back like it belonged there, as Lehrer leaned over and murmured into Noam's ear, then smiled.

Dara spun on his heel, gasping for a breath that felt like it wasn't coming. The rest of the party seethed on around him, loud voices wordless and incomprehensible, someone's laughter, the distant shatter of a dropped glass.

No. He was . . . this wasn't. He must have imagined it.

Only he hadn't imagined it, and he hadn't misinterpreted it. Because Dara had once been the one standing at Lehrer's side while Lehrer touched him and told him exactly what he planned to do to him later tonight once they were alone. He knew what that looked like.

And he knew what he saw.

He squeezed his eyes shut.

He never should have left. He should have stayed, locked up in Lehrer's apartment drunk on sedatives and suppressant, because at least then Lehrer would have been somewhere Dara could see him.

In the QZ, Dara used to imagine Noam realizing the truth and escaping—showing up at camp dirty and exhausted but *alive*. After all, Noam had believed Dara—he'd worshipped Lehrer just like the rest of them, but at the end of it all Noam still *believed Dara* when no one else would, and so why not? Why not hope that was still true, that the bright-burning kernel of *goodness* that existed at Noam's core could somehow overwhelm even Lehrer's magic—that he'd come back to Dara?

But it turned out all Noam wanted was to stay here, with Lehrer, and relish his temporary victory while Lehrer tied a rope around his neck.

Only . . .

No.

That wasn't right.

Noam was a lot of things, but Dara refused to believe he would let Lehrer drag him down into this prison so willingly.

Dara turned around again, and when he inhaled this time, his breath was even.

He pushed forward, evading the sparkling socialite who tried to get his attention, ignoring the irritated grumble of the man whose champagne he plucked from his hand as he passed. The fluted glass fit perfectly against his palm, chilly and slightly damp. All Dara could see was *them*; all he could hear was the white noise buzzing in his skull.

Lehrer must have heard him approach or sensed him somehow, even though Dara doubted they were close enough now for Lehrer to read his mind, because he began to turn when Dara was still two steps away, and their gazes met. It was like being shot in slow motion, adrenaline ricocheting through his chest and leaving him raw and bloody in its wake. Lehrer's gaze was . . . *exactly*, it was exactly how Dara remembered it, that odd crystalline quality, the patternlessness of his irises. *Dead eyes*, Sacha had said once, but that wasn't true. If anything they were too alive, lit from their own internal electric circuit that never shut off.

There was that brief moment of recognition, shock flickering across Lehrer's features, before it was subsumed by the still-water surface of Lehrer's usual placid mask.

"Lovely party," Dara said. And that was when Noam turned too.

He looked both completely the same and yet not at all. The same features, same height and skin color and brownish hair. But he looked too perfect somehow, as if someone (Lehrer) had taken the time to file away the rough edges and trim every loose end. Tall and neat and polished to within an inch of his life. It was worse, now that Dara couldn't read his mind. Noam felt less like a person and far more like a sculpture.

That perfection cracked, though, when he looked at Dara. The color drained from his cheeks, the series of expressions that flickered over his face all tumbling into one another and leaving Noam gaping at Dara like he, Dara, was a dead man.

It occurred to Dara only now that was probably exactly what Noam thought he was.

"Britta always did know how to play hostess," Lehrer said without missing a beat.

Noam was still staring at Dara, still shell shocked. A beat later his gaze flickered down to Dara's hip.

Of course. He sensed the gun.

"You're looking well," Lehrer commented. He lifted his glass of scotch and took a small, controlled sip. His attention never wavered from Dara's face.

Something feral clawed at the inside of Dara's chest. *Run. Run away. Run now.*

"Must be all that fresh mountain air," Dara said.

Lehrer smiled blandly, politely, and stepped forward. Dara moved back just quickly enough, before Lehrer could reach for him. He saw it in Lehrer's eyes, what Lehrer meant to do—the same thing Lehrer did that time at Minister Langley's party, Lehrer's hand on Dara's shoulder: barely touching him, but with enough magic seeping through his fingertips that it felt like being crushed under a boulder. Dara had fought so hard to keep from crying out, from letting the pain flicker across his expression and betray them both. It would be so easy, even now, for Lehrer to close his fingers around Dara's arm and direct him away from here, out of sight, somewhere he could snap Dara's neck like a twig and deal with the fallout later.

Instead, Lehrer's fingertips skimmed empty air.

"Don't you ever," Dara said, his voice low and very, very even, "touch me again."

Lehrer's hand curled into a loose fist, and his arm dropped back down to his side. That mild smile was back. Of course, Lehrer didn't want to cause a scene. Not here. And especially not in front of Noam.

Dara looked back at Noam. Noam's gaze immediately flitted away, staring down at his whisky instead like it was the most interesting thing in the world.

"Why are you with him?" Dara demanded.

Noam sucked in a shallow breath and opened his mouth to answer, but Lehrer was faster.

"I don't know—why *are* you with me?" Lehrer asked Noam, so lightly it might have been a private joke shared between the two of them, and he laughed.

His hand, again, was at Noam's back.

Noam startled visibly. For one moment he looked between Dara and Lehrer like he was waiting for one of them to tell him what to say— how to react—and in that second Dara was so sure Lehrer must have done something. Hurt him, somehow. Electricity—or superstrength.

But that wasn't pain in Noam's eyes.

It was something else.

Dara rotted slowly, standing here looking at Noam not looking back, at Lehrer's gaze burning a hole in the side of Dara's face, Lehrer's small and self-satisfied smile.

What if Noam *chose* this?

Dara's hand was shaking. He put the champagne glass down on a passing tray, quick, before Lehrer saw the liquid sloshing in the glass.

"This has been an illuminating conversation," he said, and it was a struggle to keep his voice steady. Noam still wouldn't meet his gaze. Dara looked at Lehrer instead, and Lehrer arched a brow. "But I'm afraid I have appointments elsewhere this evening." He pushed the corners of his mouth up and inclined his head toward them both. "Please tell Britta it was a lovely party."

He left before he could think better of it. And he didn't look back, not even at Claire, who glared at him as he slipped past her and out the front door. Lehrer must have wasted no time when Dara left—he had a tail on him almost immediately, some baseline in a suit. Pathetic. An insult to all that Level IV training, to every time Lehrer had taken Dara out to the QZ and had him pull a trigger. Even with the man's mind nothing but a smear of silence, outsmarting him was only too easy. Dara slipped his tail in an alley, lurking in the shadow beneath a fire escape until the baseline passed. Dara caught him from behind. Easy. And as he tightened the garrote around the man's neck, as the man struggled to breathe—as, a minute later, Dara lowered his unconscious body to the slick asphalt—he couldn't stop thinking that this was what Lehrer wanted, in the end.

And Lehrer always got what he wanted.

# CHAPTER FIVE

## NOAM

Lehrer led the way into the apartment, Noam trailing a half step behind. In the dim hallway Lehrer was a shadow limned in gold—light? magic? what did it matter—as he slipped out of his coat.

Noam's mouth felt sewed shut. All the words he might have said were dead in his lungs.

"I don't know how he survived," Lehrer was saying, clearly to himself and not to Noam. There was something sharp about the way he moved through the shadows, flicking on a lamp with a twist of his fingers and sparking telekinesis. "He should have died within weeks. Perhaps days."

Noam took off his shoes in the foyer and stood there with his toes curling in the faded rug, wondering if perhaps he ought to go. But Lehrer hadn't yet given him permission to return to the barracks, and Noam knew damn well how Lehrer felt about him leaving prematurely.

"He's sided with those terrorists in the quarantined zone," Lehrer said. A scotch bottle uncapped itself and poured two fingers' worth into a glass. To Noam's surprise a second glass poured as well. Lehrer turned and offered that one to him. Noam drifted forward as if in a dream and took it. Even from a foot away he could smell the peat. "He came to that party to kill me."

"You don't know that," Noam said at last. He held the whisky between his hands without drinking. Lehrer's gaze was sharp on his face, all-seeing. "You've barely spoken to him."

"While I'm not surprised you defend him," Lehrer said, "I should think I know my own child far better than you do."

It was one of the only times Noam had heard Lehrer call Dara his child. Usually it was *ward* or even *student*.

Lehrer sipped at his scotch.

*Kill me,* Dara had said, pale as parchment paper and clinging to Noam with both hands.

The room tilted, surreal and dizzying. "Why would he want to kill you, then?"

That, at least, earned him a pointed glance. "I'm sure he's invented his reasons. Nevertheless, I will have to be careful in dealing with this. He's been seen. Now, quiet; I need to think."

Noam hadn't planned to say anything, but he kept his mouth shut. Lehrer's gaze didn't falter from his, a frown tugging at his mouth. At last, Lehrer turned away and put his glass down on the windowsill, pacing the length of the sitting room with long hands slid into his pockets.

"Perhaps," Lehrer said, "I should consider the possibility he'll move against me openly. In that case, it would be best if I spoke against him early. I could disseminate a warrant for his arrest."

Noam put his full drink down on an end table and moved to the sofa, perching on the armrest. The same sofa, he thought, that Dara might have slept on those late nights he stayed up reading Russian literature past midnight.

"No," Lehrer said, deciding against himself a beat later. He turned at the far end of the room, pacing another lap. "Dara's too skilled at illusion; it would make no difference. He could appear as anyone . . .

unless he'd appear as himself just to make things difficult for me reputationally? But if I issue a warrant, that's a challenge all its own."

Noam's very bones felt sick. The effort of keeping his mouth shut was exhausting. He wanted to lie down on that sofa and press his face into the cushions and suffocate there.

"I think perhaps it's best if I tell a select number of people that Dara has escaped from the clinic and is gravely ill. I'm desperate for any assistance in finding him." Lehrer stopped, there, in the middle of the room. He was positioned perfectly in front of the window, framed like an oil painting. "After all," Lehrer went on, "he could die."

Dara hadn't seemed very sick when Noam saw him. The opposite, in fact. If his eyes had been too bright, it wasn't from fever.

Something bitter climbed up the back of Noam's throat. All at once the room was overhot, sweat prickling the nape of Noam's neck. He dug his nails into the upholstery.

"Don't worry," Lehrer said, and this was directed toward Noam. He even smiled, as if to be reassuring. "I won't kill him. If Dara is connected to these insurgents, it's far better to use him to find out who else is involved. I'm sure he has friends in this administration—I need to know who they are. I need to tear this little rebellion out by the root, not simply trim the weeds."

Noam closed his eyes. He couldn't—all he could think about was the way Dara had looked at him tonight. Like Noam had torn his heart from his chest right there in front of him.

The soft sound of footfalls on carpet, then Lehrer's cool fingertips slid along Noam's cheek. "It's all right," Lehrer said quietly. "You can look at me."

Noam looked.

Lehrer's touch stayed where it was, gossamer-light. Little shivers racked their way up and down Noam's spine. Lehrer's thumb rubbed the corner of his mouth. His gaze was steady, surveying.

Lehrer said, "Thank you for listening. Forget this conversation now."

Noam turned his face away from Lehrer's hand. The shivering kept getting worse. He knew Lehrer could see it, like a death chill.

"Excuse me," he mumbled and ducked under Lehrer's arm. He didn't even make it to the bathroom. He stumbled into the kitchen, gripped the cold steel edge of the sink, and threw up.

The retching felt like it would never end. Nausea kept coming in waves, a salty ocean that closed overhead and threatened to drown. He was distantly aware of Lehrer entering the kitchen, but it was only when Lehrer stroked his spine and Noam's body reflexively heaved all over again that he realized how close Lehrer stood.

Noam vomited up everything he had for dinner, all the champagne, and after that his stomach kept trying to surge up through his mouth even though there was nothing left to come out. Lehrer turned on the faucet, washing away the evidence while Noam shut his eyes and tried to breathe, fighting back each successive gag.

"You're okay," Lehrer said gently. He had his hand on Noam's hip, holding him up—Noam's legs were too weak to manage standing now, Noam hanging on to the counter with both hands to stay upright. Lehrer shut off the faucet with his free hand, then combed water-damp fingers back through Noam's hair. The cold felt good on his scalp. "There, now. It's over. It's all right."

Impossible to say if that was persuasion. If it was, and Noam vomited again, Lehrer would realize Noam had a Faraday shield. He'd realize he couldn't influence him, and then—then . . .

Noam's gut kept clenching around air, but he didn't puke again.

Lehrer helped him away from the sink, half carrying him back out into the hall, down toward the darkened bedroom. He didn't bother turning on the light, just pulled back the duvet with telekinesis and let Noam curl up there fully clothed on the clean sheets.

Lehrer sat on the edge of the bed, his hip against Noam's knee and his hand on Noam's thigh.

"I think you should stay here tonight," Lehrer said as his magic tugged Noam's shoes off one after the other. "I can speak to Sergeant Li about your missing basic tomorrow morning. You've had a terrible shock."

Noam was afraid if he opened his mouth, he'd gag again. So he nodded instead, and Lehrer brushed his hair off his forehead.

"I'll bring you some tea," he said and slipped out of the room, leaving Noam alone in the dark.

Noam pulled the covers up over his head and, when Lehrer returned a few minutes later bearing a mug of chamomile, pretended he was already asleep.

*THE CAROLINIA HERALD*

August 24, 2021

## TRAINING PROGRAM ESTABLISHED FOR WITCHING YOUTH

*Durham*—Calix Lehrer announced yesterday afternoon the formation of a new government-funded training program to educate new survivors of the magic virus. The program will be split into four levels by dynamic ability, with the fourth level reserved for training particularly promising recent witchings as well as witchings who have advanced from lower levels. Level I will be located in Charleston, Level II in Asheville, and Level III in Richmond. Level IV will be headquartered in Durham at the government complex. Major Greta Handsmith has been assigned to administrate all units; Colonels Shawn Wang, Stephanie Gold, Bridget Prinz, and Thomas Singh will oversee Levels I–IV respectively.

"These programs, and the Level IV program in particular, are designed to take advantage of the unique gifts and abilities of witching youth," said Lehrer. "The programs will allow witching children to master their magic in a safe environment and help them develop new strengths with which they can become vital and productive members of Carolinian society."

The first cohort of students has already been recruited. Fifty-six total witching youth will be admitted as cadets, with three to attend Level IV.

# CHAPTER SIX

## DARA

Claire found him in the apartment thirty minutes past one in the morning. He lay on the bed with the sheets kicked down around his ankles and face turned toward the ceiling, and only flinched a little when she slammed the door shut.

"What the hell, Dara?"

He tipped his head enough to see the look on her face: furious, of course, although that consternated expression might be from the cold air. "Hi, Claire."

"Don't you 'hi, Claire' me. I'm waiting for your explanation." She thrust both eyebrows up toward her hairline and folded her arms over her chest. "I can't believe you. You were supposed to wait for my signal, then shoot him—not walk right up to his face and start a casual conversation!"

"I know."

"Now he knows you're still alive. He'll have half the Ministry of Defense out looking for you. We're so screwed. We're *so* screwed."

"I know."

"Stop saying *I know!*"

"Sorry." Dara pushed himself up, even though moving hurt. His bones were like glass, hollow and so, so breakable. He leaned back against the wall and breathed out and refused to think about where Noam was right now. Who he was with. "I do know, though. But it's too late for that. We need to think about what we're going to do next."

Claire jabbed a finger in his direction. "What *you're* gonna do next is sit right here and keep your face out of the public eye until Lehrer's dead in the ground. Got it?"

"Got it."

Claire puffed out a heavy breath and paced the narrow length of the apartment, floorboards creaking with every step. Her hands were clenched into fists. "Okay. Okay, we'll figure it out. I'll call a meeting—we can talk to Holloway and the others in the ministry and figure out how much Lehrer has guessed. Then we'll come up with a game plan." She paced another lap, then shot a glance over at Dara, still on the bed. "Who was that with Lehrer, anyway? The teenager."

"Noam Álvaro."

She stopped pacing. "Really? That was Lehrer's new protégé?"

Dara nodded.

"Huh. Thought he'd be younger."

So she hadn't noticed anything strange about the way Lehrer had been with Noam—or if so, she wasn't admitting it out loud. Was Dara reading too far into things? Was this just paranoia and old grudges clouding his judgment?

Dara rested his chin in his palm, fingers curved just so to hide the set of his mouth.

He questioned himself like this, when he was younger. Used to think if he'd been a little less foolish, hadn't gotten himself involved with Lehrer in games he was too young to understand . . .

It took a long time for Dara to trust himself. He wasn't about to start doubting now.

He knew what he saw.

"What do you think?" Claire wondered aloud, pausing by the window to peer out at the dark street. "Could he be turned? Or manipulated, perhaps? If he's close to Lehrer, he could be a valuable resource."

"I'm not sure." Dara would kill for a drink; he really would. Or seven drinks. "He helped me escape into the quarantined zone—but he also chose to stay with Lehrer. The pair of them are . . ." Dara didn't know how to explain it to Claire, the things Noam thought he owed Lehrer—but also the way Noam didn't trust anyone, not even Lehrer. Certainly not Dara. Eventually Dara shrugged and said, "It doesn't matter. Lehrer probably has him under persuasion, anyway."

"Is there any way to tell for sure?"

"No." Even when he had telepathy, Dara couldn't always tell. Lehrer's power didn't leave a mark in someone's mind—not a visible one, anyway. The mind wasn't a box of thoughts he could sieve through at leisure. He could only read what people were actively thinking about. So unless they were reminiscing on all the nasty orders Lehrer'd given them of late, Dara had been as blind as anyone else.

He drew his hand away from his mouth.

"Claire," he said. "Do you think you could get a message to him?"

"To who?"

"Álvaro."

"Sounds dangerous. Didn't you say Lehrer could read his mind?"

"So we do it when he's not around Lehrer." Dara shook his head. "But believe me, Álvaro's a loose thread we can't afford to leave hanging."

Claire narrowed her gaze at him, like she was trying to pick apart his words and ascertain his real motives. Good thing Dara hadn't gotten chatty when he was fevermad. If she knew the truth about Dara's relationship with Noam—or even about Lehrer—she'd never have brought him back to Carolinia.

He barely remembered most of those months of fevermadness, especially toward the end. Just moments and images, the prick of the vaccine needle sliding into a vein. Then an emptiness as complete as death.

At the time, he hadn't wanted the vaccine to work. That was another secret he'd kept hidden, like a pill under his tongue. He'd wanted to slip into that darkness and never emerge. He was . . . *grateful* for it.

But he did emerge. And then he'd had to figure out a way to go on living—without Noam, without his magic, and with Lehrer just out of reach.

Claire left him, eventually, with promises to get Dara's message to Noam and a series of colorful threats as to what she'd do to him if he left the apartment. Of course, that meant that the moment she was gone, all he could think about was slipping out that door, down two flights of stairs, holing up in the pub, and asking the barman to leave the bottle.

He didn't, of course.

But he wanted to.

For the past six months, when Dara thought of Noam, he'd remember him as he last saw him: a figure diminishing in the rear window, framed by brick and concrete. The heat waves rising off the asphalt had blurred Noam's features too quickly. Dara didn't have time to memorize them.

But that quickly became the least of his worries.

Noam's friend Linda couldn't go into the QZ with him—she'd never been infected; she'd probably die there—so Dara had to continue past the wall and into the woods on foot. It was summer, but the setting sun shining through the leaves was so red it looked like blood on the forest floor. But maybe that was just magic. Or hallucinations, creeping back into his mind as the last of Lehrer's steroid drip metabolized and wore off.

The trees grew close together, root systems tangling up and knotting underfoot. It wasn't the kind of forest one saw in movies. The underbrush was thick and full of thorns, nearly impassable in some areas; a hole got ripped in Dara's trousers fifteen minutes in, and his flesh was next.

*Infection,* Bethany's voice said in his mind, the perennial healer. *You're going to get an infection.*

He'd get worse than that if he didn't put enough distance between himself and the border before Lehrer got an antiwitching unit out here.

He didn't even know what he was running to. Not Atlantia—Atlantia was full of Carolinian soldiers; he'd be caught in no time. York was too far. The quarantined zone, it seemed, was a destination in and of itself.

Dara wasn't under any illusions he'd survive fevermadness. But if he was going to die either way, he wanted to die here—on his own terms—and not by Lehrer's magic. Not anywhere Lehrer could find his body and make a pretense of mourning over it, somehow twisting Dara's death into a political weapon.

He'd walked all day and well into the night, stumbling over fallen branches and angry roots, until the fever rising hot in his veins was smoldering in his mind so bright he couldn't see straight. So he found a patch of ground blanketed in soft and earthy-smelling mushrooms, curled up there, and fell into a fitful sleep.

He'd thought the fever would break in a few hours. It usually did, those waves of sickness coming and going like an inevitable tide.

Only it turned out fevermadness wasn't the biggest threat. Not at all.

Dara woke while the sky was still gray, dawn light not quite filtering down through the branches. He felt like something had seized his chest, a giant's hand clenching around his heart—and he managed to push himself up on trembling arms in time to vomit all over the mushrooms and twigs and rotting leaves.

*Oh. Right.*

He'd been here before, that time—sixteen years old—he'd tried to get sober. He'd spent days shivering and puking in his bedroom at Lehrer's apartment, until at last he couldn't stand it anymore, and he drank down three glasses of Lehrer's best bourbon while Lehrer sat there in his armchair and didn't say a word. At the time, Dara had seen it as a small mercy.

This time, there was no bourbon.

The shaking got worse. Dara tried to keep walking, to put more distance between himself and Carolinia, but he didn't make it far. Better, he decided eventually, to hole up in a defensible spot and wait it out until the withdrawal or the fever finally took him for good.

He'd found a tree with large roots that curved around a sunken trough of earth and curled up on the damp black soil. It was only after he'd been lying there awhile, staring at the sun tracking its way across the distant sky, that he realized he'd never found any water.

*Sooner rather than later, then,* Dara remembered thinking, and that was his last coherent thought before the delirium took him.

Later, he found out that he'd probably only lain there for a few hours at most. It felt like more. He watched the trees come alive and trundle around like giant insects. He saw the ghosts of the dead parents he didn't remember flit between their trunks. And soon he slid into a daze, color and light bleeding into a muddy blur that darkened to black.

He was unconscious for four days. When he woke, he was still sick. Still fevermad. But the withdrawal had faded to a dull throb in his temples and a lingering queasiness. And he was no longer in the forest. He was in an unfamiliar building, a blank concrete ceiling staring down from overhead, and when he tried to get up, found he was strapped down to the bed at both wrists and ankles.

"You're awake," a voice had said, a voice with a thick Texan accent. The speaker, when she stepped into view, was a slim black girl with close-cropped hair and sharp eyes.

Her name was Claire.

# CHAPTER SEVEN

## NOAM

For three days, Lehrer flat-out refused to let Noam leave his apartment.

He had plenty of good reasons: *You're still in shock. You're ill. We don't know who might be looking for you. Dangerous.*

It almost didn't even matter where Noam was. He barely even got out of bed. He spent his hours curled up under the blankets with his eyes closed, trying to pretend he didn't exist.

The morning Lehrer finally relented, he stood there in the foyer with both hands on Noam's shoulders and looked at him like he thought he could still strip back the layers of Noam's mind if only he tried hard enough. His pale gaze flicked back and forth between Noam's eyes, tiny saccades that sent a strange flutter down Noam's spine.

"I don't want you leaving the government complex," he said. "And you're not sleeping in the barracks. You'll come back here tonight when your classes are through. Understood?"

Noam nodded.

"What's that?"

"Yes."

Lehrer shook his head, however minutely. "This isn't a request. I am your commanding officer."

"Yes, sir."

Lehrer's hands fell away from Noam's shoulders, and he straightened the cuffs so a perfect quarter inch of white sleeve showed beneath his suit jacket. "Better." A brief pause, then something in Lehrer's expression softened, and he added, "I'm sorry to be so strict about this, darling. But we have to be careful now—I don't want anything to happen to you."

"I know," Noam said, and Lehrer tipped forward, resting his brow against Noam's for a moment and closing his eyes. Noam had the odd urge to lift his hand and slip his fingers into Lehrer's hair, keep him there.

"I'll cook something nice for dinner," Lehrer told him. "I'll make this up to you. I promise."

He left, and Noam waited the obligatory ten minutes there alone in the apartment, sipping his lukewarm coffee and watching people meander through the icy courtyard below the window, before he finally grabbed his satchel from the armchair and headed out in Lehrer's wake.

He always left when the hall was empty, mornings like these, but he didn't have Dara's skill of illusion—he couldn't make himself look like anything but an out-of-bounds teenage cadet wandering through the government complex on his way back to the barracks. At least people recognized him. They knew he was Lehrer's student. They assumed he had reason to be here.

Over these past three days, Noam had barely spoken to Lehrer. Before Dara's return they'd existed in the same small spaces, circling each other in their shared guilt over a death that never even happened.

Noam's guilt, perhaps, more than Lehrer's.

Now, after Lehrer had realized Dara was still alive, he hadn't . . . he'd been so *cold*. He'd stood there in his apartment debating the merits of putting out a warrant for Dara's arrest, hadn't even considered the possibility of inviting his own son back home. Maybe Noam had been lying to himself thinking Lehrer's grief was real.

Lehrer sure as hell wasn't grieving now.

Noam got back to the barracks at nine and slid into his seat for Swensson's class three minutes after the lecture had already started. Swensson paused midsentence to give Noam one long, meaningful look before proceeding with his discussion of inflammatory cytokines. Great. Now Noam was back on Swensson's shit list. Not like he ever *wasn't*, considering he barely attended class anymore thanks to Lehrer's extracurricular excursions into the quarantined zone—

"What the fuck, Noam?" Ames hissed, leaning halfway out her seat and across the aisle.

Swensson's sharp gaze swung over to fix on her instead. "Silence."

Ames's expression was murderous, her lips twisting in a painful-looking knot, but she didn't speak again. Just grabbed her pen and scribbled something down on a sheet of scrap paper. She at least waited until Swensson had turned toward the holoboard to toss it onto Noam's desk.

*Where the hell were you?*

She was still glaring when he looked back over.

He shrugged.

The scowl deepened.

He picked up his pen and wrote, *Would you believe me if I told you it was classified?*

Ames practically snatched the note out of his hand when he offered it across the aisle.

*Fuck no. Where. Were. You?*

Noam sighed. He almost didn't write back at all, but Ames would probably find a way to kill him with malevolent thoughts alone if he didn't, so. *Tell you later.*

Ames didn't waste time, once class was out, in grabbing him by the arm and dragging him past a very befuddled-looking Bethany and Taye and into the boys' bedroom. She kicked the door shut and rounded on him, arms folded over her chest.

"Three days, Noam," she said. "That's how long you've been gone. So what the hell were you doing?"

"It really was classified," Noam said. In hopes of seeming casual, he added: "I can't tell you. I'm sorry."

"You *were* with Lehrer, then?"

"Of course. I told you. It's fine."

But that was the wrong thing to say; color flooded Ames's cheeks, and she jabbed one tattooed finger in his direction. "I'm not putting up with this bullshit from you too. At least Dara—" She broke off, then scrubbed a hand over her scalp, mussing her hair.

"What about Dara?"

"Nothing. Never mind."

Noam lifted both brows. *"Tell me."*

"If Dara wanted you to know, he'd've told you himself." Ames shook her head. "Nope. Although I'll be shocked if you can't *guess*, at this point."

She narrowed her gaze at him, as if trying to track every little shifting microexpression that crossed his face.

He should tell her. It would be so easy. *Dara's still alive.* He'd get to watch the relief dawn on her face—he could bring her to him, smudge out the misery that lined her eyes and mouth.

But if he told Ames that Dara was alive, that'd be one more person Lehrer could take advantage of.

"You're being cryptic," he said instead.

"No more cryptic than you," she shot back. "But I guess that's what happens when you get tight with Lehrer. You start keeping secrets."

"Oh, fuck off, Ames," Noam said. "You don't know what you're talking about."

Ames shifted her weight from foot to foot, her jaw clenched hard enough Noam could practically hear her teeth grinding together. "Listen. I do know what I'm talking about. Okay? I do."

"Why don't you enlighten me, then?"

She looked like she would rather peel her own skin off slowly. But she said: "I know you don't want to think of yourself as a victim, Noam, but—"

Noam had heard enough. He shoved past her, stripping his shirt off over his head and tossing it into the hamper. When he glanced around again, she was staring at him, color high in her cheeks.

"I have to shower," he said and jerked his thumb toward the bathroom door. "Do you mind?"

She left, but not before throwing her hands up and making a sharp, exasperated noise between her teeth.

He rinsed off quickly—there wasn't much time between Swensson's class and Adebayo's—and ran his fingertips over the skin on the underside of his wrist. The same place Lehrer's fingers had touched, tracing the lines of Noam's veins. The same place Dara's lips had kissed as they lay in bed together, Dara's hair sweat-damp and his body bare.

Where was Dara now?

When Dara had looked at them, at Noam standing so close to Lehrer, listing toward him as if Lehrer were the only light in the dark—had he known? Could he tell? Did he look into Noam's eyes and see all those memories of how Noam had felt after Dara left—the day he realized Dara was probably dead, had died alone and feverish in Atlantia like so many of Noam's old friends? This whole thing with Lehrer had seemed so horribly inevitable: Noam and Lehrer, shipwrecked by the same grief.

Now Dara was back.

Something sickly reached long fingers down into Noam's gut and tangled him into a hot, pulsing knot.

He barely paid attention in the rest of his lessons that day, even though they were doing demonstrations with Adebayo, and he usually loved watching the other Level IV witchings put their presenting powers to work. Instead he sat in the back row, saying nothing, while Ames shifted water from liquid to gel state and Taye exponentially shrank Adebayo's desk down to the size of a pinhead. Their magic washed over him in strange oceanic waves, incomprehensible. Lehrer had canceled their private lessons, in the interest of catching up on some work he'd missed while watching Noam that first day after the gala. That meant Noam spent his afternoon bouncing around the barracks and wishing he had a power he could stretch out over the city—the kind of power that let you *find* people. Probably Lehrer would have wanted Noam to go straight back to his apartment now that classes were done, but he couldn't bring himself to obey. It felt worse, somehow, to spend these hours staring at the same walls he'd stared at for three days, waiting obediently for Lehrer to come home like Lehrer's . . . like Lehrer's goddamn trophy wife.

No. He wasn't doing that.

So Noam didn't leave the barracks until six, an hour before he knew Lehrer would be leaving work himself. Plenty of time to get back, to seem like he'd kept himself busy reading *Lolita* while Lehrer shook hands with all the self-important diplomats and signed treaties Noam knew damn well Lehrer had no intention of honoring.

As he walked through the government complex, he dragged his technopathy through the passing mobile phones, tablets, laptop computers—by force of habit more than anything else. The data poured through his mind and then slipped from conscious awareness just as easily. Noam realized only as he was passing the atrium that any of these people could be Dara. With Dara's illusion ability . . . he could be here, even now—the black-suited man scowling at Noam as he headed for the doors, the woman chatting away into her phone. Noam still remembered how complete the disguise had been when Dara pretended to be Minister Holloway. That same dark-haired man walked toward Noam now, absorbed in his phone, typing away into the notes feature—

Wait.

Noam, Holloway typed.

Noam stared—but Holloway didn't even look up, just kept typing.

I have a message from Dara. He wants you to meet him in apartment 304 above that dive bar on Rigsbee Ave, near the original athletic park. Go now. Make sure you don't run into Lehrer on your way. Right now.

Holloway brushed past Noam, close enough Noam could have reached out and trailed his fingers against Holloway's jacket sleeve. He left the distinct scent of bergamot cologne in his wake.

Noam felt as if his body had suddenly been emptied of all organs, nothing left but a yawning void.

Right.

Right, okay.

Noam was five steps from the door into the west wing when he diverted track—not for the front door, of course, as he didn't doubt Lehrer had instructed the guards not to let him leave. He went back into the east wing instead, climbed the stairs to the second floor, then jumped out a hall window using magnetism to break his fall. He landed soft on the pads of his feet, right between the dumpster and the recycling bin. There was a security camera watching, but these days it took next to no effort to ensure it didn't register his presence.

Noam knew what bar Holloway was talking about. It was a mile or so away—easily walkable, but if Dara was there—if Dara was waiting for him—then seriously, *fuck that.*

He grabbed the first northbound bus and stood there crammed in with all the government complex employees commuting home from work, staring at the back of someone's conservative haircut with someone else's briefcase bumping against his thigh. The ride felt as if it took ten years, each second dragging on into the next. Noam's body buzzed with adrenaline, and he realized he was clenching his teeth only when his jaw started to hurt.

He shoved his way out of the crowd when the bus stopped three blocks from the bar; there were closer stops, but he had to be sure he wasn't being followed. He was too anxious to try and lose a tail or try again another day. Likely he'd have just killed whomever it was and dumped the body in a convenient alley.

Noam's breath froze in front of his face as he tramped through the snow that still hadn't been shoveled off the sidewalk. Jesus, he should have at least gone back to the barracks and grabbed a coat and gloves. Instead he was going to show up on Dara's doorstep, the first time after six months' separation, teeth chattering and nose red and runny. He tried to adjust his satchel so the strap fell over the cadet star on his sleeve; drawing attention was the last thing he needed.

Hopefully it was dark enough nobody would notice him at all.

The bar was beginning to fill up, even at six thirty. The orange light glowing through the windows looked warm and welcoming from where Noam stood out on the sidewalk trying to decide which door was the right door to go up to the apartments. His fingers were frozen in fists.

Whatever. Left door looked good enough.

Noam opened it with telekinesis so he didn't have to take his hands out of his pockets, leaning in with his shoulder to block the obvious magic from passing gazes.

A narrow stair led upward, lit only by a single bare bulb screwed into the ceiling. Noam sucked in a shallow breath and started up. Each step jarred him down to the bone, spelling out a familiar rhythm: *Da-ra. Da-ra.*

Apartment 304 was right at the end of the hall. Noam loitered on the stoop, staring at the peeling fake-gold stickers that numbered the door.

It took several moments for him to muster the courage to lift his hand and knock.

Footsteps, on the other side of the door. The creak of a loose floorboard. The heat of someone's skin on the opposite knob. It turned, and the door opened.

Dara looked as if he had just stepped out of Noam's own memories. Well. His hair was shorter, unevenly cut, like it had been chopped off at some point and grown back wrong. But that face was the same. The expression on that face, too, as if someone had taken a snapshot of him as he was before the fever turned his eyes overbright and his cheeks too pink, and given it life.

Noam's next breath hitched in his throat. Somehow he hadn't anticipated that seeing Dara again would feel like *this*. Without shock to cushion the blow, it was like being shot with a bullet he hadn't sensed coming. He said Dara's name, his voice coming out strangled and wrong.

Dara took a step back, and Noam moved forward to fill the emptied space. He slid a hand into Dara's hair, kicked the door shut with his heel, and kissed him hard on the mouth.

He expected Dara to taste like whiskey and cigarettes the way he always used to, but this Dara tasted like nothing but himself. He felt the same, though. Same warm body, same firm chest pressed against Noam's. Same slim fingers on Noam's cheek. Same heartbeat pumping iron through his blood, tangible to Noam's sense of all things ferromagnetic.

A part of him thought Dara would push him away—braced for it, even, his veins all live wire crackling with electricity. But Dara didn't. And when Noam drove him back, Dara went, the pair of them stumbling across the narrow space of Dara's one-room apartment until Dara grabbed Noam by the collar, turned him around, and shoved him back onto the bed. He climbed after him, kissing Noam's throat, the corner of his mouth, teeth catching Noam's lower lip. Noam's hands on Dara's waist slid down to curve over his ass.

God, how had Noam lived these past months without this—without *him*?

Dara's weight was heavy against Noam's lap, and Noam wanted more of that, more of Dara touching him like he couldn't get enough.

"I can't believe you're alive," Noam said, breathless and between kisses. "I can't believe you're here—"

Dara broke the kiss but he kept his head there, brow tipped against Noam's and his breath hot and humid between them.

"I missed you so much," Noam said and touched Dara's cheek, Dara's skin warm but not feverish, not anymore.

Dara's fingers curved around Noam's wrist, and after a beat, he pulled Noam's hand away. When he leaned back and met Noam's gaze, his eyes were too serious. His thumb still pressed in at Noam's pulse point as he said, "You're with Lehrer now."

It wasn't an accusation, not quite—but it struck like a thrown dart, a sharp and sudden pain lancing through Noam's chest. He wondered if Dara could feel it against his thumb, the way Noam's heart raced.

"It's . . . complicated," Noam said. The words were lame and awkward on his tongue, even as he spoke them.

Dara sat back. The light cast strange shadows on his face, making his expression unreadable. "Why don't you explain it to me?"

God. There was no way to put this that wouldn't make Dara hate him.

"We . . ."

Noam's tongue felt wrong in his mouth, too dry.

Dara raised an expectant brow.

Noam swallowed and forced himself to go on. "We're sleeping together, yeah. Or we were."

"Were?"

"Not since I realized . . . not since you came back."

Dara said, very calmly, "Was it consensual?"

The sickness in Noam's stomach swelled toward his throat. He wanted to reach for Dara with both hands and kiss him on the lips, pushing that question back into Dara's mouth, silencing it.

"Yes."

Dara slid off the edge of the bed, onto his feet. He had his face turned away from Noam. Noam couldn't see his expression, couldn't tell if Dara . . . if Dara hated him now, truly this time, or if he . . . if he . . .

"Dara," Noam said, shoving the rumpled sheets out of the way until he could sit on the edge of the bed and gaze up at the back of Dara's head. "You have to understand—I thought you were dead; he was—he was the *only* person who understood what that meant, who'd lost you like I had. He—"

Dara paced to the far end of the room, then back again. Both hands lifted to drag back through his hair, twisting dark curls in his fingers. When he rounded on Noam again, there was a hardness to his face that hadn't been there before, like a thin layer of frost had crystallized beneath his skin. When he spoke, his voice trembled. "Lehrer raped me."

Noam wanted to die. He wanted to strip off this body like dirty clothes, toss it aside, and disappear. He could barely stand living with himself. Living in this skin, which Lehrer had touched—

"I know."

He was crying; he was . . . he couldn't help it, couldn't hold it back. Noam scrubbed the heels of his palms against his damp cheeks, for what little good it did. Tears didn't make it any better, not to Dara anyway—who had lived like this with Lehrer for years, and not because he chose to.

Dara looked at him for one long, horrible moment. Then he spun on his heel, lashing out with one arm to hurl the lamp off the bedside table. It crashed onto the floor in a mess of pewter and shattering glass that spun out across the hard wood toward the far corners of the room. Noam startled where he sat, but he didn't dare launch to his feet. Dara was a storm cloud blackening fast, a terrible energy pulsing off him that Noam felt in his very blood.

"And when did you figure this out?" Dara flung the question at him like a grenade—there was no right answer there; Dara had to know that. His cheeks were bright with anger. "Last time I saw you, you didn't remember a goddamn thing I told you about him. When did you figure it out? *Before* you slept with him?"

Noam couldn't answer, couldn't say a word. Everything he might have told Dara was jumbled in the back of his throat, too many excuses, too many hollow apologies. He couldn't keep looking at Dara either. Looking at him meant imagining a younger version of Dara, all wide eyes and baby fat—imagined how vicious you'd have to be to ever want to *hurt* him. Fuck. Noam pressed his face into his hands instead, eyes clenching shut against his overhot palms.

"After?" Dara pressed.

"I swear I didn't know when we started—when I—" *When I threw myself at him.* "But I figured out—I put a Faraday shield around my own mind so he couldn't influence me anymore, and that must've done something, because then I remembered what you told me about Lehrer, and—"

"And you *kept sleeping with him*?" Dara's voice spun higher in pitch. Noam didn't have to open his eyes to guess that sound was Dara kicking the dresser.

"Would it help if you—I can take the shield down, you can read my mind, you can see for yourself—"

Dara's footfalls went silent. Noam lifted his head to find Dara standing there in the center of the room staring at him with an incredulous look on his face, lips parted. "Noam. I took the vaccine, in the quarantined zone. I don't *have* magic anymore. I can't read your mind."

Wait, what?

"And even if I could," Dara went on, "I wouldn't want to. Why the hell would I want to see—*god*, Noam!"

Noam almost didn't believe him. The idea of a Dara without magic was—it was—Noam couldn't wrap his mind around it. Magic and Dara were so intertwined as to be synonymous. That was who Dara *was*: the too-powerful, too-brilliant prince of Carolinia.

If Dara didn't have telepathy anymore, Lehrer might be able to read his mind. That was what had kept him from being able to do so before, wasn't it? Dara's telepathy interfering with Lehrer's.

Noam couldn't tell Dara the truth now, not without taking the risk it'd get back to Lehrer.

But if Dara was anywhere near enough for Lehrer to read his mind, they were all dead anyway.

"I had to keep sleeping with him," Noam said. "Don't you get that? I'm trying to bring him down—I remembered everything you told me, about the virus, the vaccines—I'm trying to *kill* him, Dara! If I don't act like everything's normal, he'll know something's wrong!"

"That is such bullshit, Álvaro."

"It's not," Noam insisted. He pushed up to his feet and moved toward Dara, reaching for him—he wanted to touch him, had to feel the solid weight of Dara's body under his hand. But Dara stepped back almost as quickly and shook his head. He was crying, too—the tears hadn't fallen, not yet, but his eyes gleamed with them. "I love you, Dara—I swear, I never meant to . . . to hurt you, I just—I swear to God."

"You *love* me?" Dara's voice cracked, his hands balling into trembling fists. "Forgive me if I find that incredibly hard to believe. First you left me—you sent me off to the quarantined zone alone while you stayed behind with *Lehrer*—then you start fucking him? Were you just *waiting* for me to leave so you could—"

"It wasn't like that!"

"Really? Because it sounds like it was *just like that*."

"I didn't—" he started, but Dara didn't let him finish, just grabbed a discarded book off the end table and hurled it at him.

"I don't want to hear it. I don't. You say you love me, but you're exactly like every other guy I've ever fucked, aren't you? You're not different at all."

"*Dara—*"

"Who started it?"

"I don't . . ."

"It's a simple question, Noam. Even you should be able to figure out the answer to this one. Who. Started. It?"

Dara was practically luminous with rage, limbs quivering ever so slightly. And he was—god, but he was right to be; this was all Noam's fault, Noam's idiocy. His cheeks burned. Still, he owed Dara this much. He owed Dara the truth.

"I don't know," he said. "I was . . . I was *really* drunk, Dara; I couldn't even see straight. I remember kissing him. That's about it."

Dara stared at him like he still thought he could slide between the pages of Noam's thoughts and read the truth there. "Did he *tell* you to sleep with him?"

Noam knew what answer Dara wanted. Maybe not hoped for, but what answer Dara would find more palatable than the alternative.

He even thought about lying. But he couldn't. He'd done enough, hadn't he?

"I . . . don't know. But I don't think so. He . . ." *God.* "He wouldn't have needed to tell me to do anything."

Dara's mouth twisted, like he was going to say something else and then thought better of it. What came out was: "Fine. If you don't remember who started it, perhaps you remember who continued it."

Noam wanted to die. "Me."

The anger was gone, bled out. In its absence Dara was pale and still, his eyes black iron. Noam hadn't seen Dara wear this mask since . . . since before they had sex, when Dara still held him at arm's length. Seeing Dara slip behind that façade once more was like being stabbed. It hurt. Badly.

"I see," Dara said. He crossed his arms, tapping his fingers against the opposite bicep. "I think you'd better go."

Noam stepped toward Dara again, reaching for him—hoping if he touched him, somehow, he could make Dara see . . . see what, exactly, he didn't know, but it didn't matter. Dara knocked Noam's hands away with a quick stroke of his wrist.

"Leave."

"I can explain—"

"I don't think you can." Dara strode across the narrow room to open the door and glare at Noam through narrowed eyes. "I don't even want to look at you. You need to leave."

Dara looked more than willing to enforce that using his fists.

Noam felt sick, the kind of sickness that fermented in his marrow and poisoned his blood. "Okay. Okay." He couldn't meet Dara's gaze as he slipped into the hall, though he passed close enough to smell the cigarette smoke clinging to Dara's clothes. He turned, hoping to say something—*I'm sorry,* maybe, or *Can I come back later,* but Dara slammed the door in his face. A beat later, Noam felt the twist of a metal latch.

He didn't hear footsteps. Dara stood right there on the other side of the door. If Noam tried, perhaps he could have sensed the heat of Dara's skin against his clothes, the movement of his blood. He could have used magic to unlock that door and shoulder his way back inside and *make* Dara listen.

He did none of those things.

Instead he went down the narrow stairs, caught the bus at the corner, and returned to Lehrer's apartment. He made it back a scant five minutes before Lehrer arrived in his slim chancellor's suit to kiss Noam's temple and ask if Gisela had been by with the groceries, thankfully oblivious to where Noam had been. Noam begged off dinner pretending to have a headache and lay alone in the darkened bedroom with Dara's words replaying themselves in his head, long past when Lehrer went to sleep himself. When the first gray light of dawn finally crept through the cracks between the blinds, Noam knew it was already too late to repair his mistakes. Whatever he and Dara had was broken now. And it was no one's fault but his own.

Noam dreamed he stood at the entrance of Dara's bedroom. Not the barracks. And not the room as it was in the apartment now—barren of personality, empty of anything to suggest a boy had ever lived and grown up there.

No. This room had an occupant. An IV pole stood next to the nightstand, its bag filled with a clear fluid. The curtains were drawn. A clock ticked on the wall, counting down the days.

On the bed, a figure curled up beneath the covers. Dara's black hair flared against the white pillowcase. Even bundled up in blankets, it was clear he was too thin. Breakable.

The IV line snaked down from the pole, vanishing under the duvet. Its contents kept Dara alive, but they also kept him powerless.

Noam opened his mouth to speak, but nothing came out. Dara shifted, shivered, the duvet slipping off one shoulder; sweaty skin glinted in the dim light. *He's dying.*

*He's dying.*

*It's my fault.*

Someone was standing right behind him.

"Dara," Lehrer's voice murmured in Noam's ear, his breath hot on Noam's nape. "It's time to wake up now."

Noam lurched upright, his throat burning and someone's hands gripping his arms, Lehrer's hands—*Lehrer*, restraining him—

"You're okay—"

"Don't touch me," Noam gasped, swatting at those arms and shoving at the mattress with both heels. "Don't touch me!"

"Jesus—okay, sorry." The hands let go.

Noam sucked in another agonized breath, and the room slid into focus. Not Lehrer's room. Not Lehrer's hands.

Taye sat at the foot of Noam's bed, eyes wide and gleaming in the darkness.

Right. Noam wasn't at Lehrer's anymore—it was Thursday night. He was in the barracks. Lehrer was nowhere near him.

He was fine.

Taye had both hands twisted up in his pajama bottoms. "You were having a nightmare," he said, like Noam hadn't figured that out yet.

Noam was shivering even though the heat was cranked up high. He scrubbed both hands over his face. "Yeah," he said eventually. "Sorry."

"For what?"

"Waking you up." Noam's hands dropped back into his lap. Taye hadn't moved from his perch, was still watching Noam like he thought Noam might start screaming again any second now.

"It's no problem," Taye said. "You . . . kind of do this a lot, actually. So I figured maybe I should try and help for once."

*You do this a lot.* As if Noam didn't already want to sink into the floor and die of embarrassment. "How often?"

"Um. Pretty much every night you're in the barracks?"

"Great." Noam's head tipped forward to rest against his palms. "Cool."

At least it was just Taye in the boys' dormitory. There was no one else around to witness Noam thrashing and screaming in his bed—in *Dara's* bed—every other night.

Only now Noam was wondering how often this actually happened. If some nights Lehrer lay awake and watched Noam squirm and cringe away from unseen shadows. If Lehrer knew what those dreams were about.

"I can get you some water or something," Taye offered eventually.

"No. I'm good. Thanks." Noam made himself look up again. "Really."

A brief smile passed over Taye's lips. "I had them a lot, too, when I first came here," he said. "It'll sound stupid. I mean . . . my parents are still alive and all. I don't have anything to be upset about. But the red ward . . ."

Noam still remembered the girl's corpse lying next to him in that hospital room, her face locked in an eternal mask of pain. That was in his nightmares just as often as Dara. Just as often as Brennan with his brains splattered all over the wall.

"I get it," Noam said. "It's a lot. Especially if you were a little kid."

"I don't want to make you talk about it if you don't want to," Taye started, "but . . . he was my friend, too, you know."

"Dara." Noam sighed. "Yeah. It's just . . . I helped him get out into the quarantined zone. I don't know if I told you that. So it was my fault he—"

*Died.* Only Dara wasn't dead. He was here, now. And Noam had ripped his heart right out of his chest.

Noam wet his lips. "It was my fault he had to go through . . . all that."

If Noam had never gotten involved in the coup, Lehrer would never have needed to take Dara out of the picture. Dara would never have been locked up in that apartment. Dara would never have seen his future as a choice between suicide and a slower death out there, lost in the wilderness but free.

"I used to imagine . . ." Noam swallowed against his raw throat. "I used to pretend he'd gotten better out in the QZ. That he was out there with all the stars, could see every constellation. Dara never seemed like the type who would like *hiking*, you know? But he told me he did. Once. Or that he wanted to try it, anyway. He said the only thing keeping him from packing up a bag and setting out on a trail for two weeks was the fact that he'd want to bring at least six or seven books, and they'd be too heavy to carry."

Noam laughed a little, the sound surprising him. Taye grinned too.

"Shame he never told me that," Taye said. "I could have made those books weigh next to nothing. Exponents, and all."

"You're gonna have to teach me that trick someday," Noam said.

"Sure thing." Taye paused a moment, drumming his thumbs against his knees. Then: "Dara really liked you, you know. He didn't always act like it, but he did. Dara told me you were the most confusing person he'd ever met. Coming from him—"

"That's a compliment," Noam finished and gave Taye a tiny smile. "Yeah."

Taye shifted back off Noam's bed, getting to his feet. "I'll let you sleep," he said, crossing back to his own bunk.

Noam waited until Taye was under the covers and curled up with his face to the wall before he pushed up and reached under his bed to dig out his satchel. He'd picked up a bottle of sleeping pills from the pharmacy a few months ago when the nightmares about Brennan got bad. He'd been taking them more and more often. And one pill wasn't enough anymore. Hadn't been for a while.

Noam tipped four into his palm and swallowed them dry.

He couldn't keep this up forever. He knew that.

But at least for tonight, it bought him a dreamless sleep.

NATION OF CAROLINIA, County Court, Buncombe County

In the matter of the adoption of

 Dara Shirazi ,

a  4 year-old child assigned  male  sex at birth, by

 Calix Lehrer  and

 [single parent adoption]  , their spouse.

I,  Buncombe County Department of Child Welfare , do hereby consent to the adoption of  Dara Shirazi , born in  Asheville, Carolinia , on  October 25, 2104  , to biological parents  Nazreen Shirazi & Younes Shirazi , by adoptive parent(s)  Calix Lehrer .

My reason for giving this consent is  for the best interests of the child .

Dated at Asheville, Carolinia, this  4th  day of  February , CE 2108 .

(Attach seal of court) __Buncombe County Dept. of Child Welfare__

*Brent Michaels*, __Judge__

*Cx Lehrer*, **Adoptive Parent**

Status of biological parents: __Deceased__

Citizenship of biological parents: __Carolinian__

Citizenship of child: __Carolinian__

*Note appended to record:* Please advise that the child's parents were witchings who died under suspicious circumstances at their home. Despite the adoption of the child, this remains an open investigation. Homicide has not been ruled out.

# CHAPTER EIGHT

## DARA

Given his track record, Dara thought, it wasn't a surprise that he should end up here: draped over the bar in the pub below his apartment peeling the label off a bottle of bourbon, closer to unconscious than sober.

The bartender had been giving him that look for the past hour or so, the look that said *I'm thinking about cutting you off* but simultaneously said *I want you to suck my dick.*

Dara peeled another strip off the bottle label and poured himself a glass. An eighth glass, he was pretty sure. Or maybe eleventh.

"You're out of peanuts," he said, lifting his voice so the bartender would hear him.

"You ate them all." The man was making someone a martini; he barely even glanced up.

"That's not the point."

Dara took a sip of whiskey. What was Noam doing right now?

Probably also drinking whiskey. Probably an old fashioned, complete with imported bitters and a delicate curl of orange peel trapped beneath the ice.

Noam didn't know how to make old fashioneds. Someone else would've made it for him.

Dara finished the rest of his glass in a single swallow.

"What's the point, then?" the bartender asked, humoring him.

"The point," Dara said, setting down the glass with a harsh click against wood, "is that I'm still hungry."

He tried to arch a single brow but wasn't sure how well he managed it. His facial muscles felt slow and clumsy, awkward.

God, had his tolerance really gotten that bad? He'd only been sober for six months. He should still be able to hold his liquor.

To provide convergent evidence for such a hypothesis, Dara poured another drink and downed that one too.

"Don't you think you've had enough?"

Wow, how had the bartender gotten all the way over here so fast? Dara narrowed his eyes at him, searching for signs of a witching tele-port . . . teleportationist? Teleportpath?

Whatever.

"No," Dara said, perhaps more aggressively than warranted.

"I'm going to bring you a water," the bartender said.

"I hate water."

"Too bad."

The man even added a slice of lemon, for garnish. *Pretentious,* Noam's voice said in Dara's mind, and Dara suddenly wanted to throw up.

He took the water and sipped it to push against the bile. The bartender watched with a steady gaze, hands braced against the edge of the bar. How long had Dara been here? There was only one other customer left, a sad old man at the far end nursing a dirty martini. He tried reaching into the bartender's mind, but that only made him dizzy. These days telepathy was nothing more than a thought experiment.

Sickness rolled through his gut, a steady sway inevitable as the tide. He couldn't quite focus his eyes well enough to make out the details of the bartender's face anymore. He was East Asian, with brown hair. Attractive? Maybe?

The bartender reached for the bourbon bottle and pressed the cork back in. "I think you're done."

Dara lurched forward, but he wasn't fast enough. The bartender had already set the bottle on the counter behind him, out of reach.

"I have money," Dara argued. He slapped a wrinkled handful of cash on the counter. "If I'm *paying* for it—"

The bartender snorted. "How old are you, anyway? Seventeen?"

"I'm twenty-two. You saw my ID."

"I saw your *fake* ID, sure."

Dara made a face. "Fine, I'm nineteen. I'm still over age. Give me the bourbon."

"Nope. Drink your water."

Dara obeyed, then hated himself for obeying. The water wasn't settling well in his stomach.

Down the bar, the old man tugged on his coat. When he left, the wind blew a flurry of snow in through the open door. The cold air cut through Dara's clothes too easily, prickling against his skin like hundreds of tiny needles.

"Your bourbon's shitty, anyway," he informed the bartender. He was distantly aware the words weren't coming out right, consonants bleeding together and vowels overlong. "D'you know that? Shitty. Fucking. Bourbon. Do better."

"Oh? And what would you know about it?" The man's brows went up, and he was *smiling*, damn him. "Are you an expert in fancy whiskeys?"

"Maybe I am." Dara jabbed a finger against the sticky bar top. "Look at you. Serving your customers this . . . this high-rye swill. Not even single barrel."

"Some people like rye bourbons."

"Not. Me."

The bartender laughed. "You're a snobby little shit, aren't you?"

Those words shouldn't affect Dara like they did. It was like swallowing a gulp of whiskey too fast, a sudden heat blooming in his chest. "*You* don't get to call me that." He sucked in a shallow breath, one hand clenching in a fist. His heart raced. "Don't."

The man held up both hands. Surrender. "Sorry. It's just rich kids don't come in here that much. Kinda out of their way, you know?"

"Whatever," Dara muttered. He tipped his head forward, pressing his brow against the chilly wood.

He imagined long fingers pressing against the nape of his neck, holding him in place.

Dara jerked upright, for one reeling moment sure—so sure—he was going to vomit. But the moment passed, and the bartender was looking at him with a frown on his lips, and he was gonna kick Dara out, make Dara wander up and down the icy street because he couldn't go upstairs, not now, couldn't pace circles round that tiny apartment for another six hours, couldn't.

"You okay?" the bartender asked. He sounded uncertain. But of course he didn't *really* care if Dara was okay. He had to ask. It was a liability thing.

"Fine." Dara smiled, and it almost felt real. He pushed back his chair and stood, then hoisted himself up onto the bar. Swung his legs over the counter. Dropped back onto his own feet, this time behind the bar, where he could step forward and press both hands against the bartender's warm chest. "I live right upstairs," he said, trying to focus on the man's eyes. His face was blurry, featureless. "Apartment 304. You can come up with me. But you have to bring the bourbon, that's the rules."

The man didn't say anything. He held on to Dara's arms, but he didn't push him back, didn't stop him as Dara leaned in, as Dara slid his fingers into his hair and kissed the line of his jaw. His skin was stubbly under Dara's lips. Rough. The room swayed, and good thing the man had such a firm grip on him, because Dara's legs couldn't hold his weight anymore.

He closed his eyes. Took in a shallow breath that tasted like cheap aftershave. He murmured, "That's my *only* rule."

He stumbled, and the man hauled him up again, had him pinned between his body and the edge of the bar—good, good.

"I'll do . . . ," Dara mumbled, "whatever you want . . ."

He didn't remember anything after that.


Consciousness returned with all the subtlety of a freight train, crashing into Dara full speed, all glaring light and motion sickness. He groaned and kicked the sheets off his sweaty body, but moving sent another lance of pain throbbing through his skull.

"God," he muttered, and wanted nothing more than to burrow under the pillow and pretend the rest of the universe didn't exist. His stomach had other ideas.

He lurched up and grabbed the trash bin next to the bed to spew bourbon and bile into the liner bag. He'd just had time to wonder at the bin's convenient placing next to the head of the bed, between heaves, when someone pressed a cool, wet cloth against the nape of his neck.

"Better out than in," said a semifamiliar voice, and after Dara spat the last of the nasty taste out of his mouth, he looked up.

The bartender from last night perched on the edge of the bed, even more stubbly than he'd been before. It turned out he was, in fact, attractive. So at least Dara'd been right about that much.

"Hi," Dara said when he was finally sure he wasn't going to puke again—or at least, not immediately.

"Hi," the bartender said back. He withdrew the cloth from Dara's neck and offered it to him; Dara took it, wiping his mouth.

*Did we have sex last night?* The question perched on the tip of Dara's tongue, but there was no point asking. He knew the answer.

"You didn't have to stay all night," he said instead.

The bartender's brows went up. "Really? Because last night you kept saying *stay* and *don't leave me here alone* over and over, and I figured I should stick around. Just, you know, to make sure you didn't have alcohol poisoning."

Well, that was embarrassing.

Dara felt color rising in his cheeks and hoped the man blamed it on the hangover. "How considerate of you," he said. "But as you can see, I'm fine now. You can go."

"Fair enough." The bartender pushed himself off the bed, but he didn't leave. He just stood there in the middle of Dara's tiny apartment, both hands stuck in his pockets.

"You aren't going."

"For the record," the man said, "we didn't sleep together. You were trashed. Like, barely even conscious. I wouldn't do that to you. I want you to know that. I only came up here to make sure you were okay."

Dara narrowed his eyes, not entirely sure he believed him. But the man was shifting from foot to foot, uncomfortable but *still here*. And now that Dara thought about it, he was still in the same clothes from last night. The bartender had apparently taken off Dara's shoes, but that was it.

"Okay," Dara said.

But instead of leaving, the bartender turned and paced the narrow length of the studio, from the rickety radiator to the far wall and back again. "Listen," he said eventually, stopping and examining a chip on the corner of Dara's dresser. "So. You got kind of talkative last night. I don't know if you remember."

Dara definitely didn't remember. But he got that sinking feeling in the pit of his stomach anyway.

The bartender abandoned his pretense of being fascinated by the dresser. "I know who you are. You told me. You're Dara Shirazi. Lehrer's son."

Dara kept his mouth shut. He didn't trust himself not to vomit again.

"It was a little bit funny, actually," the bartender went on with a quirk of his mouth. "You kept going on about *do you know who I am* and *you wouldn't be cutting me off if Lehrer were here.* You're like a walking caricature of every minister's kid I ever met."

"What's your point?" Dara snapped at last. Something was smoldering behind his breastbone, dangerous and too hot. He reached for his magic. It wasn't there. Shit. His gun was all the way on the other side of the room, in the drawer of that dresser the bartender leaned against.

"My point," the man said, "is that Dara Shirazi, Chancellor Lehrer's son, has no business being in a bar like mine, staying in an apartment like this, on the north side of town. Dara Shirazi doesn't need a fake ID. So if Dara Shirazi is in hiding, I'm curious why."

Dara stared at him. The bartender stared back. His eyes were black and bright and far too intelligent.

Dara should have predicted this was how it would happen. That he'd somehow miraculously escape Lehrer's clutches, and Lehrer's assassin, only to get arrested because he got wasted at a bar and spilled everything to a handsome bartender too chivalrous for his own good.

"Why is it any of your business?"

"It's my business because you live above my bar, and if you're in some kind of trouble, I at least want to know about it before the MoD firebombs my place of work. So. Are you in trouble?"

*Trouble.* How adorably euphemistic.

Dara pushed himself up off the bed and moved closer to the bartender, close enough the man stepped aside—putting more space between them, like he thought Dara might try to kiss him again. Dara leaned against the dresser and braced his hand near the drawer handle. Just in case.

He had limited options, as far as he could see. And thanks to his rigorous training as Lehrer's erstwhile assassin, he could see pretty damn far.

Option one: Kill the bartender. He could use the gun to threaten him into a more vulnerable position, but then he'd probably have to finish it off by snapping the man's neck or slitting his throat. A gunshot would draw attention. Potential consequences: Messy. Bartender might have friends who'd come looking for him. And Dara would prefer to avoid murdering innocent people as much as possible.

Option two: Make up some story about having argued with Lehrer. Potential consequences: Bartender believes him. Either he drops the issue, or he decides to play hero and sends word to Lehrer to come rescue his wayward son.

Option three: Tell the bartender the truth. Potential consequences: Bartender agrees that Lehrer needs to be taken down and keeps Dara's secret. Alternatively he doesn't, in which case Dara kills him before he can tell anyone what he heard. But at least the bartender would probably give some sign that was his plan—if he was repulsed by Dara's treason, it would show on his face. That kind of thing was hard to disguise.

Dara didn't like the idea of killing the bartender—not at all.

But he liked the idea of letting Lehrer kill *him* even less.

"Okay," Dara said. "To put it bluntly: Lehrer has been infecting Carolinians with the virus for years to create more witchings. His goal is to transform Carolinia into a witching state. A witching majority and a witching oligarchy. He'll invade as many countries as it takes, if it means he gets more witching citizens. Naturalizing the Atlantians gave us, what? Five thousand new witchings? That's not insignificant. I'll bet you a hundred argents Carolinia launches a formal annexation of what's left of Atlantia within a month."

The bartender hadn't moved. Had barely even blinked. He was a fish caught on a hook, and Dara just had to reel him in.

"Well, some of us have a problem with mass genocide. There's a resistance group, the Black Magnolia. We're a mix of Carolinians, Texan outcasts, people who grew up in the quarantined zone. I've been living in the QZ with them for the past six months, and I came back here to kill Lehrer. Is that the kind of trouble you meant?"

He grasped the dresser handle, his whole body alight with adrenaline. The chair by the window—he could get the bartender there, use the wall as leverage against his back when he snapped the neck—

"Sounds about right," the bartender said.

"I beg your pardon?"

The bartender gestured, both hands palm up as if in surrender. "I mean, someone has to do it. If what you say is true."

This wasn't at all what Dara had expected. He didn't trust the unexpected.

He didn't let go of the dresser drawer. "It's true. But why should you believe me? Aren't you . . . shocked?"

The bartender leaned back against the wall, both arms folded over his chest. "Before I was a bartender, I was a soldier. Like you. Only I wasn't a witching. So instead of a cushy Level IV gig, I got sent down to Atlantia." He shook his head, very slowly. "The things they made us do down there . . . Lehrer should be charged with fucking war crimes."

Dara laughed, the sound ripping itself out of his throat before he could stop himself. He rocked forward on the balls of his feet, gripping the dresser for balance now more than anything else. "Right," he said. "You're right. He should."

But that was never going to happen.

Dara looked at the bartender appraisingly now, taking in his untidy white shirt—same one he wore last night, with the sleeves rolled up like Dara might request he make another old fashioned at any moment—and messy hair. If the bartender had been ranting about Sacha's crimes instead of Lehrer's, he'd remind Dara a lot of Noam.

But at least for now, the bartender got to live. Dara's hands could stay marginally less dirty.

"What's your name?" Dara asked.

"Leo."

"Do you have a last name, Leo?"

"Leo Zhang." Pronounced *jong*.

"All right, Leo Zhang. What time does your bar open on Mondays?"

Leo crossed his arms and leaned back against the wall. "We're closed Mondays. Why?"

"Well," Dara said, and smiled. "If you really want to help the resistance, we're in the market for a meeting space."

# CHAPTER NINE

## NOAM

Noam had just swallowed his last bite of Friday-night roast chicken when he realized he couldn't sense his cell phone anymore.

He lowered his fork slowly, glancing across the table at Lehrer, who took a sip of wine and arched a brow. Cold dread shot through Noam's gut, and he twisted his hand in his napkin.

"What the hell did you do?" he croaked.

Noam's magic was gone. He was defenseless.

*He's going to kill me.*

Sudden sweat prickled at the back of Noam's neck.

"Forgive me," Lehrer said. "I had to know if I could trust you."

Noam's gaze snapped down to his own wineglass, sitting so innocuously next to his dinner knife. It hadn't even tasted any different.

Lehrer hadn't stopped watching Noam with those eerie colorless eyes, and Noam was sure, *so* damn sure Lehrer was reading his mind. He could practically sense Lehrer's power tangling up in his thoughts like so many golden threads, snaring him in a net of knots. And the truth would be plastered all over Noam's mind: the truth about Faraday, about Dara. About what Noam had remembered.

Lehrer reached across the table and rested his hand atop Noam's. His fingers were so long, his palm so broad, Noam's hand seemed to be consumed by it. "It will wear off in an hour," he said, almost like an apology. "In my position—you have to understand, Noam, I can't take any risks. I had to be sure you weren't using magic against me."

And Noam was alive. Noam was *still alive*, which meant . . .

Lehrer couldn't read his mind. Not even now, with Faraday obsolete. They weren't close enough anymore—Dara had said Lehrer's telepathy required vulnerability, required his victim to feel like they *wanted* that intimacy. And thank god for that, or else Lehrer would be right back in his mind. He'd know that Noam had used magic to keep him out.

"I'm not," Noam managed to say. Lehrer had to have noticed how his hand trembled slightly beneath Lehrer's own. "I don't understand. How would I use magic against you? I don't—I can't—"

"I know that," Lehrer said quickly. "That's clear, now. This wasn't personal—I have to keep national security in mind."

"I don't understand," Noam said again. That's what the old Noam would have said—the version of Noam who hadn't figured out Faraday and remembered the truth.

"You don't have to understand." This time the words were firm. Lehrer pushed his chair back from the table, legs scraping the tile floor, and picked up his plate. He held out a hand for Noam's, and after a beat Noam passed it over.

All it would take was one order. One twist of Lehrer's persuasive magic, and Noam would be forced to tell Lehrer anything Lehrer wanted to hear.

The world seemed too silent now, blanketed under the weight of an unnatural snow. No buzz of static flickered over Noam's skin, no humming laptop from the next floor down. Even the sound of the dishes clinking as Lehrer set them down in the sink was muted.

Noam braced himself for the order to forget, but it never came.

Because Lehrer trusted them to move past this? Or because he didn't think keeping Noam happy mattered anymore?

Lehrer turned on the faucet. Only then did he glance back over his shoulder. "You should go back to the barracks. You have reading to do, and I'll expect you to be prepared in our lesson tomorrow."

It wasn't an order, not the persuasive kind anyway, but Noam still had no choice. He went.

But not to the barracks.

When they had returned from the quarantined zone two weeks ago, after Noam and Lehrer split in the atrium to head in their separate directions, Noam'd tracked Lehrer through the security cameras as he made his way back out of the government complex. Noam had watched him go out to the barricade and speak to one of the guards there, have a car brought up. Not driverless: Lehrer was paranoid enough to avoid using a computer system.

Even so, Noam had been able to follow him through CCTV up Roxboro Street until he turned onto Main Street and headed west. It had been a struggle to stay on top of the tech. He'd almost lost Lehrer when he turned onto Duke Street, but then his technopathy had caught a glimpse of the car from the high school's security system. Lehrer had pulled in front of the school's main building and emerged into the camera's black-and-white field of view—disappeared into the building itself.

With the school's internal security cameras, Noam had been able to track Lehrer through the empty halls—his tailored suit out of place amid the graffitied lockers and sticky floors—at least, until he disappeared down a narrow flight of stairs and vanished from view for ten minutes. When he finally emerged, it had been to return to his car and drive straight back to the government complex.

It took Noam fifteen minutes to walk to the school and another fifteen for the suppressants to finally wear off. He spent those last minutes sitting on the porch railing of the café across the street, legs dangling out over the asphalt, watching the cars zip back and forth and wondering if this was where he'd have ended up if he hadn't dropped out of school in the eighth grade.

Ninth Street was about a mile from here. They'd started rebuilding. Not tenements, now, but boutique stores and expensive organic groceries. Places where no one who lived there before the outbreak would've been able to afford shopping. And there were expensive apartments right next to the school, right across Duke Street. Maybe students from both neighborhoods had attended, Atlantians brushing shoulders with ministers' kids.

At last, Noam sensed the flicker of tech working in the engines of all those driverless cars, and he pushed off the railing to land in the parking lot, electromagnetism slowing him down before impact.

The school was dark as he darted across Main Street, the cars' AI forcing them to decelerate and let him pass. Someone honked, irritated, but Noam just held up a hand and kept running.

The security cameras saw nothing but empty space as Noam approached the main building. A twist of telekinesis was enough to unlock the front door—still analog; the school board clearly hadn't apportioned the money to buy digital security yet—and Noam slipped inside, flicking on the overhead lights.

It looked remarkably like Noam's old middle school. There was the same off-white tile floor, same student art on the walls and shitty composite-wood classroom doors. Noam followed in Lehrer's footsteps down the hall, descending the staircase into the basement.

The corridors were narrower down here, as if the building was smaller underground than it was above. Or maybe that was Noam's imagination. But here it felt like the walls were closing in on him, the air stale and difficult to breathe. It smelled weird too. Like something had died in the heating vents.

Noam inhaled through his mouth and tried the first door on his right.

Just a classroom, albeit a small and windowless one. Lehrer wouldn't hide the vaccine in plain sight like that, would he? High schoolers were intrepid. If there was a bag of mysterious vials hidden in a regular classroom, they'd have found it in days.

Noam realized after a moment that he thought of *high schoolers* like he wasn't one of them. Like there was something different about teens who went to public school than teens who went to Level IV. Maybe that was true—he doubted any of these kids had hunched over a sink to rinse someone else's blood off their hands.

Or maybe that was Lehrer's influence: *You're so much older than your age . . .*

The smell was really getting to him now. Noam swallowed hard against the urge to gag and stepped back out into the hall, pulling the classroom door shut.

He ruled out the other classrooms on the hall, but the last door on the left was locked. Noam frowned and tried the knob again, like it was somehow supposed to turn on second attempt.

He glanced toward the stairs, half expecting to see Lehrer standing there gazing down at him with shadowed eyes. The landing was empty.

Noam sucked in a shallow breath, anxiety hot in his blood as he drew on telekinesis and turned the latch. The door swung open by forty-five degrees and caught on something heavy, wouldn't go any farther. He edged through the gap, shoving against the door with his shoulder and forcing it against whatever was blocking the way—just an inch of give—and he squeezed past, stumbling into a dark, dusty space.

His magic caught a sense of electricity above the ceiling; he tugged on it, and a single bulb lit overhead. The light was grayish and weak but still enough to illuminate a large room full of . . .

Noam had no idea what all this shit was, actually.

The room looked like it was used as a general storage space for anything that didn't have a better home elsewhere in the school. Cardboard boxes overflowed with sequined theater costumes and polyester wigs; a stack of student art projects towered on a nearby table, the top canvas displaying abstract splatters of paint and what looked like discarded buttons. There was even a toilet abandoned in the middle of the floor, black mildew creeping over the trap.

Noam was starting to get why Lehrer chose to hide the vaccine at a high school. No way would he find the bag hidden among all this *crap*.

Still, Noam crept forward—carefully, as there were boxes everywhere, the floor littered with general detritus—and tried to figure out where the hell to start. Swensson had told them something about this. Not about *searching for illegal magic vaccines the chancellor hid in the basement of the local high school*, but about organizing searches more generally. You were supposed to create a grid over the search area and rule out each zone in sequence.

So he'd start at the beginning, the corner nearest the door.

He turned back where he came from and met his own gaze reflected in a large ornate mirror. That was what had been lodged behind the door, gilt edged and age spotted—and over Noam's right shoulder, a pale figure stared out of the darkness.

Noam yelped and spun around, magic snapping to his fingertips.

But it was just an old mannequin sticking out from an open box. Probably something the art students used for figure-drawing class, blank faced and nude. Harmless.

Even so, it took several seconds for adrenaline to stop flicking between Noam's nerves like static.

At last he exhaled an unsteady breath and moved forward, dragging the mirror out of the way to search behind it. All he found were cartons of markers and ancient printer paper. And even when Noam moved on from that grid and searched another three-square-foot block—and another, and another—he found nothing but junk.

Noam's phone buzzed in his back pocket. He drew it out and glanced down at the screen. Sighed.

"What's up, Ames?" he answered.

"Where are you?"

"I'm downtown. Why?"

A beat of silence. He imagined her drumming her fingers against her thigh, could perfectly envision the frown on her face. "Is that the truth?"

"Yes. What the hell?"

"Not like you haven't been telling a whole lot of stories lately," Ames said brusquely. "So if you're really downtown, you want some company? Bethany keeps trying to get me to help with her math home-work, and honestly, I'm fucked up right now, and I don't want her to notice. Bad influence."

*Of course you're high. You always are.* Noam bit his lip to keep from saying it aloud and turned his gaze toward what was left of the room— another forty feet, easily. This place was massive, probably covered the whole area beneath the cafeteria. "No," he said. "I'm actually about to head back. If you're still up, I'll take over Bethany duty, though."

Although he wasn't sure why Taye didn't help out. Taye was the math prodigy.

"So says the guy who was in remedial math this time last year," Ames pointed out dryly—and now that he was looking for it, Noam could detect the slur to her words. "Besides. Aren't you like . . . too *good* for tutoring now?"

"I'm not sure what that's supposed to mean."

"You're the new Dara. You're Lehrer's protégé. That makes you *cool* to people who don't know any better."

Noam grimaced into the darkness. "You're saying it's gone to my head?"

"Has it?" There was a sharper edge to Ames's voice now. The implication: *If you really understood, you wouldn't be where you are right now.* Or where she clearly thought he was, at least—with Lehrer, despite everything.

"I'm heading back," Noam said again. "I'll see you in a few minutes. Okay?"

But when he got back, Ames barely even spoke to him, just took one look at him, then snorted and shook her head, like she knew something he didn't. And he supposed that was exactly what she thought.

So Noam lay awake in Dara's narrow bed until four, staring across the room—past the clothes on the floor, past the lump-under-the-covers that was Taye—at the bed where he'd kissed Dara the first time. Where they'd discovered each other's bodies, that one perfect set of moments fractured again minutes later. Dara was on the other side of the city, maybe even lying awake himself right now thinking how much he loathed Noam for the choices Noam made.

And he was right. Everything that happened now Noam had chosen.

He had no one to blame but himself.


The next day, after Lehrer had finally dismissed him from their private lesson by lighting a cigarette and waving him off, Noam skipped his next class and headed to the second floor of the west wing instead.

By now, Noam was such a fixture in the government complex that no one even glanced twice at him—not unless it was to tilt their head in recognition. Or sycophancy, given his connection to Lehrer; Noam wasn't quite clear which.

No one asked if he had someplace better to be.

So when Noam knocked on the door to Holloway's office, he knocked like he had every right to disturb the home secretary in the middle of a workday.

The receptionist who opened the door was the same one he ran into last year, when he pretended to be Dara and stole emails off the very computer he sensed in the adjoining office now. This time, though, the computer was actually in use.

"I'm here to see Minister Holloway," Noam said. "He's expecting me."

This time, the receptionist didn't bother asking his name.

Noam lingered there in the anteroom while the woman announced him to Holloway. Noam could barely hear the murmur of muffled voices through the closed door.

This was it, moment of truth.

But when the receptionist emerged, it wasn't to tell him to leave. Instead she ushered him past the heavy mahogany door, into a broad window-lit office and the presence of Minister Maxim Holloway, who rose up from behind his desk even as the door fell shut.

"I hope you're here to discuss the outbreak in Atlantia," Holloway said dryly, "and not anything incriminating."

"Sorry to disappoint."

Noam stepped deeper into the room, far enough to rest his hands atop the back of one of Holloway's guest chairs. Holloway himself hadn't moved, sharp gaze tracking Noam as if he thought Noam might be liable to pull out a gun and shoot him in his own office the way he shot Tom Brennan.

*Don't think about Brennan.*

"Are you involved?" Noam asked.

Holloway lifted one black brow. "That's very bluntly put. But, yes. I am. I have been, since the beginning."

Both of them were carefully stepping around the words that mattered, the ones that felt like pinned grenades: *Resistance. Rebellion.*

Noam's grip tightened on the chair.

"I want to help," he said.

Holloway sighed. He placed his fingertips lightly atop the surface of his desk, as if that would ground him. "Dara said you might."

So Dara *did* want Noam involved, after all.

"Your position is precarious," Holloway went on. "You might find it difficult to escape the complex to make meetings. I suffer the same problems. We're both very visible—to Lehrer, among others."

*To Lehrer.* That was delicately put. Did Holloway know the truth?

"I'll figure it out."

"I'm sure you will." Holloway tipped his head to one side, considering. And for a moment, Noam worried this had been a mistake. He'd assumed Holloway was with the resistance because he delivered a message from Dara. But he might be a double agent. All of this could be fed right back to Lehrer the moment Noam left.

And by now Noam ought to know: there was no one he could trust. Not really.

He'd paid attention to Holloway's political rise following Lehrer's coup. Holloway had taken a bold position in government, hard on crime and harder with punishment. He was a member of Sacha's party, the Republican Democrats. Most of the legislation he supported was far right of center. In fact, he took the opposite stance from Lehrer on almost everything—only Noam got the sense that was exactly how Lehrer wanted it. If Lehrer truly saw Holloway as a threat to his power, he could easily put him under persuasion.

Lehrer and Holloway might be enemies on the public stage, but in the shadowy wings of the political theater, they were allies.

Just how deep did that alliance run?

Noam had to decide. The only thing worse than the wrong choice was complacency.

Holloway was still watching with that same suspiciously penetrating gaze. "We could use your help," he said. "Now that Lehrer is aware of our existence, we're hamstrung. He expects an attack."

"I know exactly what Lehrer expects," Noam said grimly.

Holloway's lips twitched, almost a smile.

"There's a meeting tonight," he said. "The bar on Rigsbee next to the barbecue joint. Nine o'clock."

Noam's heart leaped toward his throat. Holloway wasn't wrong about the challenges of getting away. At nine, he'd be expected to be one of two places: in the barracks, getting ready for bed, or in Lehrer's apartment. And he didn't think Ames was gonna buy *it's classified* as an excuse much longer. But.

"I'll be there."

*What a fucking mess,* he thought all the same that night when Lehrer texted him 8:00 p.m. and Noam hurled his phone onto the opposite side of the sofa.

"That's aggressive," Bethany commented from her position in the armchair by the window.

"Sorry."

"Ex-girlfriend?" Taye said, smirking.

Ames was conspicuously silent. She had one of her curriculum books open on her knee, looking down at the page, but her eyes weren't moving.

"Work," Noam said after a beat. "Emergency meeting in two hours."

"Dude, tell them you have basic in the morning and make them fuck off." Taye spread both hands to either side, half a shrug. "You're Level IV. You can't spend *all* your time liaising, or whatever else it is liaisons do. You have, like, homework."

"Believe me. I know."

Noam glanced at Bethany, who was watching him over the edge of her holoreader with steady, unreadable eyes. She hadn't said much on the subject, although she must have noticed Noam was gone as often as Ames and Taye had. But she was also probably the only reason Ames hadn't publicly and violently lost her shit at Noam yet—she didn't want to make a bad impression on a fifteen-year-old.

"You can do *my* homework for me, if you're looking for extra work," Taye added, lifting his geology textbook and wiggling both eyebrows.

"Definitely, if you don't mind failing Bennett's class."

"I'm already failing Bennett's class. Too many rocks, not enough numbers."

Bethany hid behind her holoreader again, and something twinged in Noam's chest—an odd guilt he couldn't quite place.

"It'll be okay," Noam said, mostly for Bethany's sake. "I signed up for this, after all. It's important. I won't ever be as good an Atlantian liaison as Brennan was, but . . ."

He couldn't finish that thought. Was he seriously using Brennan's memory as a shield to justify having an affair with the man who made Noam kill him? Vile. The bar for basic human decency was *underground* at this point, and Noam still couldn't clear it.

"We can all go out this weekend," he ventured. "Catch a movie in Raleigh . . ."

"You gonna be free this weekend, Noam?" Ames said idly, and popped her gum.

"Should be," he said. He forced a smile when Ames looked at him. "What do you think, Bethany?"

Bethany slapped her book shut and dropped it on the floor with a loud thump. "I think you should both leave me out of it."

She shoved herself up and stalked out of the room. The girls' bedroom door slammed shut behind her, a painting rattling on the wall.

"What's up with her?" Taye said.

Ames's cheeks had flushed red. Noam knew exactly how she felt.

"I'm going for a run," he muttered and pushed up from the sofa, heading back into the bedroom to change—although not before grabbing his phone from the other cushion. The last thing he needed was someone bringing it to him, staring at the screen right when Lehrer inevitably texted again.

It was six miles from the government complex out west, past Noam's old neighborhood, then north—carefully evading the whole Geer Street area, just in case—then back again down side roads and residential streets, cutting past the catastrophe memorial to return home. He always did the same loop, always tried to run it faster than the previous time, until his muscles burned and his lungs ached from the frigid winter air, until he couldn't see for the sweat dripping into his eyes. When he ran, there was nothing. No thoughts. No fears. Just the crunch of the snow under his feet and the pounding of his own heart in his temples.

He hunched over his knees when he finally made it back to the government complex, sucking in a series of sharp shallow breaths and fighting a wave of light-headedness. His clenched fingers were pale and bloodless with cold.

But he'd beat his personal best time by thirty seconds.

And—more importantly—he'd figured out his next move.

Lehrer didn't notice him come in.

That much was obvious as Noam toed off his running shoes in the hall—he could hear Lehrer in the kitchen, the sizzle of a frying pan, and Lehrer's voice narrating out loud: "The most difficult part is folding the dumplings. It helps to use an egg glaze, like this, to glue the edges of the dough together . . ."

*He's finally lost it,* Noam thought as he moved across the living room on sock feet. *Lehrer has finally, actually lost it.*

But when he came into the kitchen, he found Lehrer standing with a little pat of flattened dough in one palm. Wolf sat by the table with his amber gaze fixed unblinking on Lehrer's hand.

"He seems very attentive," Noam said.

Lehrer glanced up, a smile quirking his lips. "I won't flatter myself. He's far more interested in the ground lamb, I think."

It shouldn't be endearing. It really shouldn't. Nope.

"You have a little something," Noam said, gesturing toward his own cheek. "Here."

"Well, why don't you come and get it off?"

Wolf huffed, clearly frustrated that he wasn't going to be offered raw meat tonight, and slouched down to the floor. For his part Noam drifted closer, oddly transfixed by the smudge of flour dusting Lehrer's cheekbone. He slid his hand along Lehrer's flat stomach and rose up onto the balls of his feet, Lehrer leaning over enough for Noam to reach as he kissed the mark away.

When he drew back, they were still too close, Lehrer's free hand having found the small of Noam's back and the tip of his nose grazing Noam's own.

"I missed you today," Lehrer murmured. "During all those meetings, I kept thinking how much I'd rather be talking to you."

Noam's breath caught and Lehrer laughed, his eyes crinkling at the corners.

"Still blushing, even after all this time?"

"Sunburn."

"It's January, you know."

"Yeah, I'm still gonna go with *sunburn*," Noam said, and Lehrer—grinning—swooped in to kiss him on the mouth.

Noam's cheeks were still warm when Lehrer finally let him go. He felt embarrassingly like he was sixteen again, light headed at Lehrer's touch. He gripped the edge of the counter and nodded toward the bowl of spiced meat.

"Do you need any help with this?"

"I think Wolf and I have it under control," Lehrer said wryly. "But you should go and take a shower. I don't mean to cause offense, but . . ."

Right. Noam was still in his running clothes, sweat-streaked and disgusting. Even so, Lehrer's hand trailed along his back as he moved away, escaping out the kitchen and to the cold mercy of Lehrer's shower. There, he reminded himself once, twice, a dozen times: It didn't matter if Lehrer played nice. Lehrer's gift was persuasion—he was really good at *playing nice*. Just because his feelings appeared genuine didn't make them so.

Lehrer was a monster. He deserved to die. He *did*.

And Noam had to play this pitch fucking perfect if he was getting out of this game alive.

"Dara contacted me again," he told Lehrer later, still wet haired but full of lamb dumplings and sitting in Lehrer's living room.

Lehrer looked up from the paperwork he'd been reviewing, pen still in hand. He hadn't tried to get Noam in bed after dinner—had brushed a quick kiss to Noam's mouth when he handed him a drink and then retreated to the opposite side of the room. They'd been sitting in relative silence for the past fifteen minutes, reading.

"I see," Lehrer said. He put down the pen. "And what did he have to say?"

"There's a meeting tonight. Of insurgents." A careful term; the word *resistance* had been on the tip of Noam's tongue, swallowed back just in time. "I'm invited."

He wasn't quite sure what he'd expected from Lehrer's reaction—for Lehrer to be annoyed, maybe, that Noam waited so long to tell him— but all Lehrer did was lean back in his chair, setting aside the paperwork on an end table.

"You should go," Lehrer said.

"Yes," Noam agreed. "I think so." And this was where he had to be careful. Lehrer wouldn't believe Noam wasn't at least tempted to switch sides, if just for Dara alone. He drew a leg up into his chair, clutching his knee toward his chest with both hands. "I don't . . . obviously, I want to protect Carolinia. And maybe . . . I might be able to convince Dara to leave them. Maybe not to join *us*, but—I don't want him to get hurt."

Lehrer sat in silence, the tips of his fingers steepled together. He'd had 124 years to perfect his ability to read facial expressions, to tell when someone was lying—Noam just hoped he decided the risk of letting Noam go was worth it. That he trusted his own ability of persuasion.

All of this only worked so long as Lehrer believed he was still in control.

"There's still hope for Dara," Lehrer said at last, tone even and completely uninterpretable. "He hasn't committed a crime against my government. Not yet. But if he turns to treason, even I won't be able to protect him."

"I have to try," Noam insisted. "I can't—I won't let him do this. And I'll report everything back to you. Whatever they're planning."

"Yes," Lehrer said, one elegant brow going up. "You will."

Right there—that *had* to be persuasion. Lehrer, accounting for the element of risk.

Noam swallowed and nodded.

Lehrer drew up an arm, tugging back his sleeve far enough to glance at his wristwatch. "Well then. I suppose you'd better be going. You wouldn't want to be late on your first day."

It was remarkable Lehrer couldn't hear Noam's heart pounding all the way from the other side of the room as Noam pushed himself up from the chair, draining the last swallow of scotch. Lehrer had spent so much time training Noam how to appear calm, even when he wasn't.

Could he see the threads of his own design stitching Noam together?

Noam grabbed his satchel off the floor. "Okay. I'll see you, then."

He was almost at the door to the study, already halfway down the hall and outside Lehrer's line of sight, when Lehrer said:

"Oh, and Noam . . . you'll come back here tonight. To debrief."

Noam shut his eyes, one hand pressed flat against the wood of the door. "Yes, sir."

*So the game begins,* Noam thought. But he got the feeling it was a game Lehrer invented—one where only Lehrer knew the rules.

# CHAPTER TEN

## DARA

Empty of people, the bar seemed larger than before, even though it was still just a narrow strip of space, hardwood floors and bar top both gleaming thanks to Leo's vigorous deep clean. Dara sat at the end of the bar farthest from the liquor shelves, nursing a club soda and watching Leo scrub out a glass that already sparkled.

"You sure you don't want any peanuts?" Leo said. "I bought more."

"I'm good. Thanks."

He glanced at his watch: three minutes till nine. What if no one else showed up? What if they were all too paranoid Leo was a traitor, what if they didn't trust Dara's judgment, what if they didn't want him anymore since he ruined the gala plan—

But then the door swung open. In spilled Claire and Priya and a flurry of snow; Claire rubbed her gloved hands together and declared, "It's cold as a frog's behind out there."

Dara turned his face toward his club soda—quickly, before they noticed his relief.

"You must be Leo," Claire said, waltzing forward and thrusting a hand toward the bartender. "Claire. You have an admirable record."

"Oh good," Leo said, "you've researched me."

"Don't take it personal. We research everyone. This is Priya."

Priya, busy examining the windows and back exit to make sure they weren't bugged or watched, lifted a hand in acknowledgment.

The door opened again, this time depositing Holloway and still more snow on the welcome mat. "I hope I'm not late."

"We're glad you could get away," Claire said.

Dara was the only one, it seemed, who noticed how Leo's expression had gone rigid. He'd stopped cleaning the bar, both hands white knuckled where they gripped the edge of the counter.

Of course. Leo didn't know Holloway like Dara did. To Leo, Holloway was the draconian new home secretary, an old guard Sacha loyalist. In his previous position as attorney general, Holloway pushed for the death penalty more often than all his predecessors. He'd charged army deserters with treason.

And perhaps that was something Leo had fantasized about, those darker nights down in Atlantia—packing up a rucksack and just *walking away*.

*It's all fake,* Dara wanted to tell Leo. *It's an act. Just politics.*

Somehow he doubted that would change Leo's opinion much.

Dara was about to ask for another lemon slice, to distract him, when the door opened a third time.

Noam.

Dara pushed to his feet, the legs of his barstool scraping against the floor. He was dizzy with the change in posture, sick with it, but god, *god*—

"Why are you here?" he said, too sharply.

Did Lehrer know? Oh god, was—was Lehrer coming right on Noam's heels, had he *followed* him here? Would the door open one final time, Lehrer's figure a shadow against the streetlights, his magic a snap of gold and glitter as he crushed all their hearts in their chests?

But maybe Noam came here on his own, because he knew, because he finally *understood*, because he was leaving Lehrer and joining the resistance and fighting at last to bring Lehrer down.

Vertigo crept in black waves through Dara's vision. He clutched the bar for balance. *Relax. You have to be in control.*

Noam stared back at him, unspeaking. Damn it, why didn't he answer? Why was he looking at Dara like that, like—

"I invited him," Holloway said, settling himself down on an empty stool and leaning one elbow atop the bar. He looked so out of place in his bespoke suit next to the recycled wood counter and the dirty glass ashtrays, like an actor who'd walked onto the wrong set.

"Noam Álvaro," Priya said flatly. "Lehrer's student."

"And Dara's old friend." Holloway's expression was calm as a shallow sea. "Isn't that right, Dara?"

Everyone was looking at Dara now.

Dara ignored Holloway. "Are you here to stay?"

But he knew the answer, even before Noam opened his mouth. It was written all over Noam's face, the furrow between his brows and the way he braced his shoulders, tilting his head back to stand a little taller.

"No," said Noam. "And that's exactly why you need me."

Dara wished he could reach for magic, twist it into something electric and painful that he could snap against Noam's skin. This was Noam's problem: he was too good, too *agonizingly* good, which meant he couldn't see further than the end of his nose.

Noam and his goddamn hero complex were going to get them all killed.

Claire shot Priya a sidelong glance. "He could be under persuasion. Do you think . . . ?"

"I'm not." Noam stepped farther into the room, and Dara recognized that glint in his eyes. *Stupid, stubborn boy.* "He can't read my mind, either, before you ask. I found a way to keep him out." His arms folded over his chest. "If Lehrer thought I knew about his psionic abilities, he'd kill me. Or make me forget. That's how you know I'm telling the truth."

"Lehrer could still be controlling him," Priya said. "This could be Lehrer's script. A gambit. I don't like it."

But Claire was looking at Dara now. Her long spiky nails drummed an arrhythmic beat on the counter; it set Dara's teeth on edge. "Can we trust him?"

It was so damn tempting to say no.

Only, if Noam walked out of here—if he wasn't allowed to come back—Dara might not get to see him again.

Noam's gaze was still steady and fixed on Dara.

Dara sat back down, gripping the seat of the barstool hard enough it hurt. He felt like he'd swallowed acid. "Yes. We can."

For better or for worse.

Noam's mouth tipped into a smile, almost like he was trying to show *gratitude*. Dara shot back his best withering glare and looked away.

He kept his attention fixed on the condensation building at the base of his club soda, one droplet cutting a quick path down to dampen the napkin tucked underneath, as Claire said:

"All right, then. Take a seat. And a beer, maybe—you're serving, right, Leo?"

"He's seventeen. He'll have water," Leo said and grabbed a glass, holding it under the tap. His movements were still stiff, mechanical.

Noam slid onto one of the stools nearer the door. Dara wished the bar weren't quite so small after all. Even on the other side of the room, Noam was close enough Dara caught the way he glanced sidelong at him. Close enough to make out the tightening to his lips and the tension in his cheek.

And really, how dare Noam play the victim? How dare he sit there with that sad, wounded look on his face, like *he* was the one who got hurt?

Dara tugged his napkin out from beneath his glass and smoothed it flat on the bar in front of him.

"Tell us what you're offering, Noam," Priya said, laser focused as ever. "You're Lehrer's protégé. How close are you, really?"

"Close enough," said Noam. "I see him almost every day. For lessons. And he's taken me into the QZ before, looking for vaccine samples. He . . . relies on me."

Slowly, carefully, Dara began tearing his napkin into strips.

"Do you have access to his apartment?"

"Yes. Lehrer trusts me. I know how to get past his wards."

Not that he needed to most of the time, surely. Lehrer was probably there, always, to take them down himself. To tug Noam over the threshold and deeper into his web.

And now that they had Noam, probably Black Magnolia wouldn't even need Dara anymore. What use was he now? His face was too recognizable. He'd blown his cover at that gala. Lehrer was looking for him. He didn't have any magic. Yes, he was trained in physical combat, but he'd have to get past so many layers of security to use it.

Essentially, he was useless. Dead weight.

"I've been collecting material from his apartment," Noam said—and this, at last, made Dara look up.

Noam had his water held between both hands, undrunk. At least he wasn't still staring at Dara; he was focused on Claire, back straight and his feet hooked through the rungs of his stool.

Not for the first time, Dara was struck with the thought that Noam seemed so . . . different from how he was six months ago. He didn't think he could blame all of that on the clothes or Lehrer. But Dara missed the version of Noam that wore clothes he got from the thrift store—or, on one memorable occasion, from a dumpster. Dara had fallen in love with the Noam who drifted off surrounded by calculus books and made terrible decisions in the name of what he thought was right, who read Karl Marx and trusted himself more than he trusted anyone else.

The old version of Noam didn't have this Noam's eyes—wary, watchful. Dara could never have imagined *his* version of Noam killing Tom Brennan.

Killing whomever else Lehrer had made Noam murder since.

"Dara started that, back when he was working with Sacha," Noam went on. "I don't know what he did with the stuff he found"—he glanced toward Dara, briefly—"but I've been trying to find anything I can that might help undermine Lehrer's reputation. Because that's the thing, right? We can't just assassinate him or put him on trial. We have to turn public opinion against him. The same way we turned public opinion against Sacha to bring Lehrer into power."

He faltered on the *we.*

"Do you think no one's ever tried to dig up dirt on Lehrer before?" Dara interjected at last, dropping the final clump of ruined napkin onto the bar. "Like you said, I tried. But it takes a lot to sway public opinion. And even if you do, you really think Lehrer will care? He'll just declare himself dictator and *make* them obey."

"It's better than nothing," Noam said. "And maybe that's why I haven't released any of the shit I've collected yet—I don't know. You're right. We need to do more."

Claire and Priya exchanged glances. Whatever the new plan was— the one to replace the gala plan—they weren't sharing. Not until they'd vetted Noam better than this.

Noam clearly noticed, because when he finally took a sip of his drink, he watched them over the rim the whole time. When he set the glass down again, he said, "We don't have much time. If I'm going to play both sides of this, Lehrer will catch on eventually. Especially now that he knows Dara is back. I'd give us about four weeks, if that."

Dara's next breath hitched in his chest, but he didn't get a chance to respond.

"But I can do better than find dirt on Lehrer," Noam barreled on. "I told you we've been going into the quarantined zone. There are labs out there developing a magic vaccine. I'm sure all y'all know that already. And you also know Lehrer's been collecting it. Studying it to find a way to prevent it from being effective."

Of course they knew. Dara had been there, in the QZ, when Priya stumbled into camp bloody and covered in dirt. She'd been one of those lab techs working on the vaccine. One of thirty at the location near Asheville.

Lehrer had razed it to the ground.

After that, the labs fell like burnt kindling. There was no vaccine left. Lehrer had stolen it all.

"We know about the labs," Claire said coolly. "I have friends who died in those labs, thanks to him."

More than just friends. Not everyone in the quarantined zone survived birth—the vaccine wasn't ubiquitous yet, and with magic grown deep into the land, it infected everyone who lived there. A baby was born while Dara lived there—born, and infected, and sick, and dead: all within a week. They'd buried its corpse outside town, deep in that soil still teeming with old magic from Lehrer's dirty bombs, scraping away at the earth with shrapnel. No one in Carolinia ever talked about that. Winning the war back in 2018—defeating the United States—came at this cost.

The quarantined zone was more Lehrer's child than Dara had ever been.

"I can find the vaccine," Noam said. "I'll steal it. We'll inject Lehrer with the vaccine, and then we'll kill him."

Dara could practically taste it in the air. He knew they all did too, sharp and pungent: *possibility.*

No matter whether they trusted Noam yet, this was a hard offer to disregard. All their plans revolved around suppressing Lehrer—and that had always been a long shot, Dara knew. Lehrer healed so quickly.

He might metabolize the suppressant before it could bind to the proper receptors in his brain, the same way he couldn't get drunk, no matter how well he liked that expensive scotch.

They held out hope, still; suppressant was fast acting, and Lehrer couldn't heal if he didn't have magic. But that was probably unrealistic. Their best bet was, had *always* been, discovering some weakness of Lehrer's to exploit.

And the vaccine . . . that might actually work.

Holloway was the first to break the fragile silence that followed Noam's words, slipping off his barstool and slinging his satchel strap over one shoulder. "Although this has been productive, I'm afraid I must be getting back. I'm expecting a late conference call."

"Of course," Claire said smoothly, interjecting before the conversation could tilt back toward Noam and his suggestion. A suggestion Dara felt certain they'd all be discussing quite seriously in Noam's absence while Priya drew up a cost-benefit analysis of trusting him. "I'll be in touch. Thank you, Maxim."

Holloway tipped his hat as he left, letting in a fresh flurry of snow.

Claire's dark gaze fixed itself on Dara's for a moment, then slid over to look at Noam again. "We can't assume suppressants won't work," she said. "We have to test it. You said you have access to him."

"Ye-es," Noam dragged out the word, like he worried where this line of inquiry was headed.

Claire drew a small vial out of her coat pocket and slid it down the bar. Noam caught the glass before it could roll off the counter and shatter, lifting it so the light glittered off its clear contents.

"Suppressant," Claire confirmed before Dara could say it. "Completely tasteless. Dose him with it; see what happens."

"I've tried that," Noam said. "I bought a few vials off the dark net and poured them in his scotch. It didn't work."

"Did you test them first?" Priya asked.

A pause, and then Noam shook his head. "No. I didn't dose myself, if that's what you mean."

"Then how do you know they were even the real deal? People sell anything on the black market. It was probably sugar water."

Noam's lips pressed into a thin line; Dara could see a muscle twitching in his jaw. He didn't want to take the risk.

And why should he? Why would he give up his cozy little slice of domestic bliss?

Dara downed the rest of his club soda in one swallow and wished it were something stronger.

"Fine," Noam said. "Okay. I'll do it tomorrow."

"Excellent. You have Dara's number, I presume. Text him when you're done."

Noam nodded, and it took Dara a second to realize—of course. Noam was a technopath. Dara didn't have to tell Noam his burner number for Noam to know it.

Claire adjourned the meeting, and they all followed Holloway's lead, chair legs scraping against the floor and glasses clinking against wood as they were set on the countertop. Leo snapped his towel a little too violently against the bar before he tossed it over his shoulder and started washing the dishes. *I sympathize,* Dara wanted to say.

But Noam lingered back, a still figure in his olive drabs as the others shrugged on coats and looped scarves around necks. Dara turned away, pretending to care about rolling his shirtsleeves down and doing up the cuffs. His thumb kept slipping on the button.

"Dara."

Dara clenched his jaw and forced the button through its hole.

"*Dara,*" Noam said again, almost pleading this time.

Leo met Dara's gaze from across the bar and arched a brow. It was a message Dara had seen telegraphed by a dozen bartenders over the years: *Need me to get rid of him?*

Dara exhaled and twisted around to face Noam at last, arms crossed over his chest. "Álvaro."

Noam was closer than he'd expected. Close enough Dara nearly flinched back on reflex—damn it. Another instinct he'd lost with his telepathy. He had no sense anymore of how close people were if he couldn't see them. He'd become like prey, nervous and jumping at the slightest sound.

Noam had noticed Leo, too; his gaze flickered over to him twice. But if Noam had hoped Leo would get the message and retreat to give them privacy, he was out of luck. Leo just wandered a little closer under the guise of putting away a clean glass.

"You know I'm right," Noam said eventually, tacking onto a neutral subject. He met Dara's eyes again. His expression was steady. Would be unreadable, if not for the muscle tic at his jaw.

"Why should anyone trust you?" Dara said, carefully noncommittal. "You're with Lehrer."

"And you were Lehrer's son," Noam said. He leaned on that last word, perhaps just to see Dara tense up—but if Noam was pleased to hit his mark, it didn't show. "I should think, of everyone, the two of us know very well what Lehrer is capable of."

Dara was too conscious of his own breath, how his shoulders rose and fell with each shallow gulp of air. He pressed down against the hiss of anticipation seething in his chest.

"So that's your plan," Dara said softly. "You'll stay with him. You'll play along with his games—don't think I don't know how you're here, Noam; I know you told him you were coming."

Because when Dara had thought about it, it was the only real explanation. The only gambit with any hope of paying off. Noam's reaction—a sharp breath and an upward tilt of his chin—told Dara he was right on target.

Dara smiled, the expression grim and forced. "It won't work. Not even for four weeks. Do you really think you can outsmart Lehrer?"

This time Noam's cheeks flushed red, and it was anger that glinted in his eyes as he glared back at Dara. Noam took a half step forward—Dara's pulse leaped into his throat—and Dara knew he'd gone too far. He'd pushed too viciously at a wound that still chafed.

He held up a hand to stop Noam before Noam could open his mouth and say whatever cruel retort was on the tip of his tongue.

"I mean it. Not because I think you're stupid but because I know *him*. No matter how good your hand, his is better. And no matter how well you plan your play, Lehrer will *always* be two steps ahead."

He grabbed his jacket from the other barstool and fixed Noam with one last look. Then he headed past him, stepping sharply abreast to stay out of Noam's reach, leaving without looking back.

10 DOWNING STREET
London SW1AA 2AA
The Prime Minister
24 August 2123

Dear Chancellor Lehrer,
On behalf of the British government, congratulations
on your recent election as chancellor of Carolinia.

The United Kingdom has great respect both for
the nation of Carolinia and for yourself as its former
monarch and once-again leader. We are confident that
Carolinia will flourish under your leadership and hope
this election signifies the beginning of a renewed peace
between our countries.

Despite our great pleasure at hearing news of your
election, I must also freshly inquire as to the matters
we discussed on the 30th of July regarding the swift
and unfortunate demise of Carolinia's former govern-
mental administration. I feel as if we left that conversation on the wrong foot, as it were, and I would very
much like to revisit the subject. I hope you did not
take our distaste for the junta's methods as reflecting

the United Kingdom's general opinions of Carolinia or of yourself.

One hundred years ago, you met with British leaders to discuss the possibility of a peace treaty. I am not so bold as to expect you to offer me, now, what you would not agree to offer my predecessors. But I hope you will at least consent to meet for tea. London is lovely this time of year.

Sincerely,
James Mehta
Prime Minister of the United Kingdom

# CHAPTER ELEVEN

## NOAM

The morning after the first resistance meeting, Noam woke to an empty bed. For a moment he just lay there, stretching a hand out over the sheets and feeling for body heat—but there was none. Lehrer had been up for a while.

Noam could hear him out in the apartment, the creak of floorboards under Lehrer's step, a faucet turning on and then off. Felt him too. Weight pressing down on the nails in Lehrer's handmade leather shoes. Cuff links. The shimmer of Lehrer's magic.

He exhaled and tried to convince himself to stay there, in bed, until Lehrer left. But now that he was awake, he couldn't stay still. Tension prickled beneath the surface of his skin, Noam's toes curling, legs stretching out long under the covers. At last he threw the sheets back and got up.

When he padded out into the apartment, still in pajamas, he found Lehrer sitting in his usual armchair by the window with a book perched in hand.

"What time is it?" Noam asked, even though he could have looked at the clock, could have *felt* it, even, the ticks of the second hand and the inevitable turning cogs.

Lehrer glanced at his wristwatch. "Ten thirty. You missed basic."

"You should have woken me."

"I thought you might prefer to sleep in." Lehrer readjusted his cuff, tugging it down over his wrist once more. "You haven't been well lately."

It was true. Lehrer had already been in bed when Noam got back last night. The vial of suppressant had been burning a hole in his trouser pocket, Noam's nerves alight with anticipation—already trying to figure out how he'd distract Lehrer long enough to dose him, if he even had it in him to keep a straight face when Lehrer took a sip. Only the apartment was dark, Lehrer a formless shape beneath the duvet. Noam had considered going back to the barracks to sleep, but Lehrer had explicitly said . . . and so Noam crawled in between the sheets slowly, worried too much movement would wake him. He'd curled up on his side facing the wall, so focused on pacing his breaths and keeping his eyes squeezed shut that he didn't realize Lehrer was moving until his hand was already on Noam's hip.

*Not tonight,* Noam had said and tried not to flinch away. *I have a headache.*

This morning, Lehrer watched Noam with an even pale gaze.

*Always two steps ahead.*

"And . . . don't you have work? It's Tuesday."

"I canceled my meetings to stay here with you," Lehrer said, and he finally gave Noam a slim smile. "I told you—I've been worried."

Two months ago, that statement would have landed very differently. Today, Noam just wished he had more clothes on.

"I'm gonna get coffee," Noam said, jerking his thumb toward the kitchen. "Do you want any?"

"Why not," Lehrer said, and it was that easy—it really was *that easy,* it seemed, to dart back into the kitchen and pour two mugs from the carafe. To pop the cap off the vial with shaking fingers and stir a dose of suppressant into Lehrer's drink.

For a moment Noam stood there doing nothing, staring down at the black liquid swirling in Lehrer's cup—imagined Lehrer in this same kitchen, pouring a vial of his own into Noam's drink.

That was enough to make Noam pick up the cups and carry them back into the living room, passing the dosed mug into Lehrer's expectant hand.

Noam sat down on the sofa, gripping his own cup between both hands. He couldn't bring himself to drink—felt certain the moment the coffee hit his stomach, it'd come right back up again.

"Tell me what happened last night," Lehrer said, and as Noam watched, he lifted the mug to his lips.

Noam stared. He didn't know what he expected. There was no change in Lehrer's expression, no dawning realization. No fear.

"We met in a bar off Geer Street," Noam said at last.

"You and Dara," Lehrer said and waited for Noam to nod. "Who else?"

"Two women named Claire and Priya, both from a terrorist cell in the quarantined zone. The bartender—first name Leo, I don't know the surname. And . . ." He hesitated, long enough for Lehrer to lift a brow. "Minister Holloway. The home secretary."

Lehrer's expression didn't change, but he did put aside his book. His hand lingered a moment on its spine, thumb stroking the embossed letters of the author's name as he took another sip of coffee.

"I've suspected Maxim for some time," Lehrer said at last, almost musingly. "But I always assumed if he moved against me, it would be within the political sphere. This is quite the departure."

Noam's mug felt slippery against his palms. "He seemed to be deeply involved."

"Mmm."

What if this was a mistake? What if Lehrer changed his mind about his plans to wait and see, let the grassroots rebellion make a honey trap of themselves, drawing in would-be revolutionaries for Lehrer to crush under his heel?

But Lehrer didn't reach for his phone, didn't call the Ministry of Defense to have Holloway taken into custody.

Instead, Lehrer tapped his armrest: *one-two.* "What else?"

"Oh. Um." Noam fumbled for something else to say, something that wouldn't damn them all. "They had planned to assassinate you at the Keatses' gala. Obviously that failed, but there's no decisive new plan." Except for Noam's plan. *Undermine Lehrer's command. Find the vaccine. Kill him.* "Suppressant came up a few times."

Lehrer's laugh was bone-dry. But the smile that curled around his mouth was benign, even indulgent. "Good. For now, your orders are to carry on as you have been. Attend their meetings, and report back to me. We should gather more information before we decide what to do about this situation."

"Yes, sir."

I can't tell if it worked, he texted Dara, technopathically accessing the phone in his satchel. He hasn't tried to use magic.

And if he did . . . the moment Lehrer tried, if the suppressant *had* worked . . . he'd know Noam betrayed him. Noam wouldn't have another choice—he'd have to kill Lehrer right then and there.

But how? Just . . . electricity, the same way he killed Brennan? Maybe that was appropriate.

Or maybe Noam should use the Beretta Lehrer thought fit his hand so very well.

*For Dara. For Dara, and Brennan, and my father, and anyone else Lehrer ever hurt.*

Lehrer rose from his chair; his book tumbled off the armrest to fall forgotten in the vacant seat. Noam was still, so still—still enough his back ached. But when Lehrer touched his shoulder, trailing fingertips down Noam's arm, he didn't flinch.

"Thank you, Noam," Lehrer said softly. He sat, this time on the sofa next to Noam, one leg tilted in so his knee pressed against Noam's thigh. "I know this hasn't been easy. Doing what we do . . . it will *never* be easy. But it is necessary."

"I know." He let his shoulders relax slightly, in case Lehrer had used persuasion there. It was, as always, impossible to tell. "And I know . . . I know you might not trust me entirely. Because of Dara." His gaze flickered up, meeting Lehrer's. "But I promise. I won't betray this country."

Lehrer nodded. His gaze was curiously soft, tender in a way Noam hadn't seen in a long time. It was more than the fondness with which he looked at Noam sometimes, when Noam did well in class or the QZ—when Noam woke up that early morning three weeks ago to Lehrer brushing a lock of hair away from his face.

This was different.

"I need to discuss something with you," Lehrer said.

Noam took in a shallow breath, and Lehrer reached for his hand. His thumb moved in a slow pattern against the backs of Noam's knuckles, soothing. Noam wondered if he could tell how clammy Noam's palms felt.

Last time Lehrer said *I need to discuss something with you*, it ended with Noam standing over a corpse in the quarantined zone, a gun in his hand and blood on his clothes.

"Let me guess," Noam said. "Another crime in the name of the greatest good."

Lehrer's mouth did twitch at that, although hard to say if it was a smile or something else. "It's about Atlantia. The outbreaks. You know they're getting worse—Atlantia is no longer a functioning nation. They rely on us for all their resources, for contamination protocol, for defense against a potential Texan invasion. If we withdraw, Atlantia will not survive on its own."

Noam did know. He was the Atlantian liaison—he knew better than anyone how bad it was down there. He'd spoken to the refugees, the ones fleeing the latest outbreaks. Some of them brought photos. He'd seen the bodies.

And he knew where this was going.

How long ago did you dose him? Dara's response pinged against Noam's technopathy. Noam silenced his phone's alert noise just in time.

Five minutes, he sent back.

"I want to help," Lehrer said, leaning in a little closer to Noam. Close enough Noam would've been able to see the striations in his irises, if he had any; Lehrer's eyes were patternless as glass. "But I can't justify the expense, not when we're already spending so much to support the new citizens here in our own country. Atlantia is still, after all, a foreign nation."

A horrible thrill shot through Noam's heart. "You want to annex Atlantia."

"It's their only chance at survival," Lehrer said softly. "They have no defenses left—against the virus, or against Texan greed."

"So we invade them before Texas does."

Lehrer looked grim. "You know that's not—"

"Do it."

Lehrer faltered. His grip on Noam's hand tightened.

Noam knew what his father would have said. He could imagine the disappointment written all over Jaime Álvaro's face. The way his mother would have turned away, unable to look at him.

But saving the Atlantian people was more important, right now, than saving a nation in name alone.

"You'll give them all citizenship," Noam said, holding Lehrer's gaze. "You'll protect the old Atlantian borders with the same technology we use in Carolinia."

"Of course."

"Then you should do it." He took a breath. "You're right. It's necessary."

He tugged his hand out of Lehrer's and stood. Lehrer rose as well, but he didn't reach for Noam again—just stood there, with the firm and commanding posture of someone who has always known he'd get his way. Who never really worried Noam might say no.

Was that Lehrer's magic Noam still sensed, glittering gold about him like an aura?

Noam stepped past him, telekinesis grabbing his satchel from the hook by the door. "I have to go to class," he said. "I'll tell you if the insurgents contact me again."

Lehrer nodded and let him leave.

*Let.*

It was Noam's turn to cook lunch. He'd managed to expand his repertoire from cold pasta to include stir-fry and salad, which probably ought to be embarrassing, but Noam figured it was in everyone's best interest if he never tried to fix anything more complicated than spaghetti bolognese. Ames had offered to help, but that seemed like it mostly involved her sitting on the kitchen counter by the stove and swinging her heels against the cabinets while pointing out everything Noam did wrong.

"Maybe there's someone out there whose presenting power is the ability to make a perfect meat sauce every time," Noam said, prodding the sizzling onions with his spatula. "Sorry that's not me."

Ames laughed and kicked one of her feet against his ribs. "Christ, can you imagine? You'd never even know you were a witching. You'd think you were, like, the first person *ever* to survive the virus without magic. But hey, at least you'd have a future at Italian restaurants."

"Mmm. I think the award for most useless power would go to somebody with the ability to . . . I don't know, speed up iron oxidization by a factor of two. Everything rusts, but only twice as fast as it normally would."

At least she was talking to him. Noam had started to think she wouldn't. These past few months she'd grown more and more distant—and that was Lehrer's fault, of course. They might not talk about it, but Ames knew.

Presumably she knew about what Lehrer did to Dara too. But Dara was another thing they didn't talk about.

The urge to tell her shot through him like a sudden bolt of lightning: *Dara's alive.* Noam could imagine her reaction so clearly, how shock would dawn on her face—giving way to incredulity, happiness, relief.

Only then she'd want to see him, and Noam couldn't allow that. Bringing Ames into the fold would introduce one more weak spot for Lehrer to exploit. One more potential victim.

He dumped the ground beef into the skillet too; the oil hissed and spat, violently enough Noam had to turn down the heat.

"Oh, I got it." Ames grinned. "Jesus tricks. You know, water into wine, that kind of thing. Or—no, that's actually the best power ever. Okay. How about . . . carbonation. Your power is that you can *carbonate* anything."

"That has military potential, though. You could carbonate someone's blood."

As soon as he said it, he wanted to take it back. Carbonate someone's *blood?* It was exactly the kind of idea Lehrer would have come up with. Always looking for the martial application of a given power. Always twisting magic to his own ends.

He could tell Ames was thinking the same thing; she'd stopped kicking the cabinets. For a moment she sat very still, both hands gripping the counter ledge.

"Anyway," Noam said, voice coming out strained. He grabbed the saltshaker, only his hand wasn't steady. He poured too much. Shit. "What about talking underwater? That's pretty useless."

"I'm gonna go watch TV," Ames said flatly. She pushed off the counter and disappeared into the living room, leaving Noam alone to push browning meat around the skillet and wish he wasn't such an asshole.

Maybe he should stay in the barracks the next several nights. He'd tell Lehrer people were getting suspicious—not that Lehrer cared; every time Noam had said something to the effect, Lehrer had laughed and said, *The rules don't apply to people like us.*

He was right.

Still, Noam would come up with some excuse. It would be good to spend more time with Ames. The others too. How long had it been since Noam spent an entire weekend here? Before Faraday, he'd been consumed by his obsession with Lehrer—with winning Lehrer's affection scrap by pathetic scrap. After, he'd had a different obsession entirely.

And while Noam was busy with Lehrer, every last one of his friendships had burned to the ground.

The less time Noam spent around Lehrer, the fewer chances he had to mess up and say the wrong thing. Maybe that was enough reason to avoid him. Only avoiding him was suspicious—more so now that Dara was back. It wasn't like Lehrer wouldn't guess why Noam had the sudden change in heart.

Noam had just finished making the sauce, straining the noodles through the colander over the sink, when he heard Ames speak up from the other room, voice sharp.

"Noam. Noam, get in here, right now."

Noam dropped the colander and dashed into the living room, where Ames and the others all huddled around the television set. The news was running—and at first Noam didn't know what he was seeing; they kept showing the same clip of a crowd of people and a sidewalk splattered with blood, antiwitching soldiers setting up a perimeter.

Then he saw the ticker marquee running beneath the images, white text on a bright-blue strip:

# BREAKING NEWS: CALIX LEHRER ASSASSI-NATION ATTEMPT

Noam felt like he'd swallowed gravel, stomach heavy and sick.

"Shit," he muttered.

Taye made a soft noise against his teeth. "Idiots."

Normally Noam would be inclined to agree. Right now all he could think about was whether those idiots had gotten caught.

"I have to go," he said and pushed past Ames and Bethany. Ames called after him, but he didn't hear what she said, didn't care.

He tangled his magic up in the radio signals that carried wireless internet through the training wing, traced them back to the router—and then he plunged that power down deep into wires, cording through the walls all the way down to the server room. A buzz of electromagnetism bypassed the Faraday shield meant to protect that data from technopaths like himself.

Only there was nothing. *Nothing*—nothing useful, anyway. Either that meant the MoD didn't know who was responsible for the attack, or they were intentionally keeping it off the grid. And if they weren't storing that data on their servers, it was because they knew the antitechnopathy ward was compromised.

There was only one person who could have told them that . . . and only one reason he *would*.

But if Lehrer had made Noam, he would've sent someone to arrest Noam in the barracks, right? He wouldn't let Noam run through the halls of the training wing, cutting across the atrium—wouldn't still have Noam's ID plugged into the biometric readers to let him into the west wing of the government complex. And he wouldn't let Noam's technopathy find his cell phone: in his office, the official one on the third floor.

Because of course it was too much to hope that Lehrer had at least been injured in the attempt.

People got out of Noam's way, stepping aside when they saw him coming down the hall. He tried not to overanalyze the way they tilted their heads toward each other, murmured secrets whispered in listening ears.

Lehrer's secretary let him in past the anteroom without a word.

The office was crowded with bodies, gray-uniformed military officers and two men in black suits who Noam could only surmise were the state police. Lehrer stood a head taller than them all, stripped down to a bloodstained white dress shirt with his magic crackling barely restrained beneath his skin.

A doctor kept trying to get close enough to press her stethoscope to Lehrer's chest; he waved her away. "I'm fine."

"We need to check your vitals again, sir," the woman said in a strained voice. "Your pulse was 144."

"A mistake, I'm sure." Lehrer's words were all cold edges and blunt consonants.

"But your temperature—"

Lehrer's gaze fixed on Noam at last.

Was Noam imagining it, or did relief flicker across Lehrer's face? Just for a moment, just briefly, before it was subsumed by careful neutrality.

"Good, you're here," Lehrer said. "All of you—leave us."

There must have been a snap of persuasion beneath that, because this time everyone obeyed. One by one they filtered past Noam and out the door to the anteroom. Lehrer watched them go with narrowed eyes, silent, until finally the door shut behind the last of them.

"I hate doctors," Lehrer muttered with an acidity that was shocking coming from that mouth. He stepped out from behind his desk, and with the room emptied now Noam could get a better look at him. His bloodied shirt was torn right over the heart—and when Lehrer turned to face Noam properly, there was dried blood plastered against the other side of his face.

A sharp jolt struck through Noam's core, and he sucked in a tight breath.

Although the bullet must have hit its target, tearing through flesh and bone and brain matter, Lehrer's skull was as whole and unblemished as it had been last night.

"They shot you," Noam choked out, and he took a half step forward before he managed to stop himself. Both hands knotted into fists. "Calix—"

Lehrer's answering smile was bitter and disparaging. "My own fault; I didn't deflect the bullets in time. This will be a public relations nightmare."

Lehrer's hands rose to the collar of his ruined shirt, and he started pushing the buttons free—manually, not by magic. When he'd stripped the sticky fabric away, Noam gave into the urge. He moved closer until he was half a step away. He lifted both hands and pressed his fingertips against Lehrer's flesh, half expecting . . . he didn't know what he expected. Lehrer's blood was still warm, slippery beneath his palms.

He'd never seen Lehrer bleed.

Lehrer's stomach shifted beneath his touch as he took in a breath— and then Lehrer drew him in, one arm around Noam's waist, one hand cupping the back of Noam's head like a child's. "I'm fine," Lehrer said, more gently. "You don't have to worry."

And.

*What the* fuck *am I doing?*

Goddamn it. He couldn't stop seeing the expression on Ames's face, right before she stalked out of the kitchen this afternoon. The contempt curling her lip.

Too late to pull back now; he had no choice but to stand there and let Lehrer comfort him. As if Noam were actually *concerned*, as if Noam cared about *him* and not the fact that he still. Wasn't. Dead.

Eventually, though, Lehrer let Noam go—although not without pressing a chaste kiss to his brow first.

Noam glanced down at the gore smearing his hands.

"Here," he said and used a wave of magic to clean the blood off them both.

Lehrer nodded approvingly, already back to playing the role of mentor. "Good."

He tugged open a drawer on his desk, retrieving a clean shirt—packaged in plastic, as if it had only just been returned from dry-cleaning. Lehrer dressed with quick, efficient movements, looking back over to Noam as he knotted a fresh tie around his neck.

"You'll find out who was behind this," he told him. "I can only imagine it's Dara and Holloway and all your other new friends."

*There's still hope for Dara,* Lehrer had said. *He hasn't committed a crime. Not yet.*

Noam sucked in a shallow breath through his nose. "Yes, sir. I'll look into it."

And he would. He absolutely fucking would.

*Video file stolen from C. Lehrer's personal records.*

INT. CALIX LEHRER'S OFFICE

Lehrer—approximately twenty years old—sits behind an oak desk positioned before large windows, sunlight streaming through. He holds a file in hand, reading with a pen tapped against his lower lip. He wears the king's gold circlet atop his head.

A knock comes at the door; Lehrer lifts his gaze from the papers.

LEHRER: Enter.

The door opens. A man pokes his head inside: Lehrer's aide.

AIDE: Dr. Gleeson for you, sir.

LEHRER: Show him in.

Dr. Gleeson enters. He is stocky and white, with auburn hair threaded through with gray and the drawn, gaunt look of a man who has aged a great deal in a short amount of time. He carries his worn leather satchel over to one of the chairs before Lehrer's desk, and—when Lehrer gestures—he sits.

LEHRER (without looking up from his file): You're tired.

GLEESON: I haven't been sleeping well.

LEHRER: What a shame. Can I get you anything? Tea? Whisky . . . ?

GLEESON: No. Thank you.

LEHRER: Suit yourself.

Lehrer uses telekinesis to pour himself a dram of scotch. He slips the papers he'd been reading into the top drawer of his desk and leans back in his chair, surveying Gleeson over the rim of his glass.

LEHRER: So. Where shall we begin today?

GLEESON: I thought we might discuss your brother.

LEHRER: Adalwolf is dead. There's nothing to discuss.

GLEESON: He's been dead for over a year, and we still haven't talked about it. You need to process what happened to him, come to terms with—

Lehrer arches a brow.

GLEESON: —how he died.

LEHRER: He died in the battle for DC. He was a martyr to Carolinia. A hero.

GLEESON: You told me . . . you said there was a note.

A pause.

LEHRER (eventually): Yes.

GLEESON: What did the note say?

LEHRER: He wrote that he was going to DC. He . . . made it clear he did not expect to return.

GLEESON: But there was no reason for Adalwolf to be in DC, was there? And he was ill.

LEHRER: No. He should have stayed in Durham. Nevertheless . . . nevertheless, I'm not convinced this was suicide. I told him to release the virus on DC. I used persuasion. If he misinterpreted the order—

GLEESON: Is that likely?

LEHRER: I don't know. Possibly. Yes. But on the other hand, Adalwolf was sick. He'd gone fevermad. It's not outside the realm of possibility that he would have elected to take matters into his own hands.

GLEESON (patiently): And why do you think he would do such a thing?

LEHRER: I told you, he was—

GLEESON: Fevermad, yes. But there's another reason. You thought it, just now.

Lehrer's gaze sharpens, and for a moment it's Gleeson's turn to sit a little taller, both hands gripping his own knees. Then:

LEHRER: In the letter . . . he said something. He said he wanted me to abdicate power. To—move on with my life.

Gleeson says nothing, although Lehrer is clearly expecting him to finish the thought. At last:

LEHRER: I suspect he saw his death as a way to instill grief in me.

GLEESON: Why would he want you to grieve? Why would anyone—

LEHRER (flatly): Because he wanted me to feel something. Those were his words. He wanted to use his own death as a weapon to cut me back into the image of a mind and character he found acceptable. Even after he was gone, he wanted to control me.

GLEESON: Is that how you see it? That Wolf wanted to control you?

LEHRER: Am I wrong?

Gleeson elects not to answer that question.

LEHRER: From the moment I left that hospital, Adalwolf saw me as a tool. I'd always been intelligent. Once Wolf realized he could use me to craft his strategies—to win the war—that became my purpose, in his eyes. Of course . . . (Lehrer smiles coldly.) He didn't anticipate that I might just as easily use my power against him.

*Video file is incomplete.*

# CHAPTER TWELVE

## DARA

The room was featureless and yet familiar, less a setting than a set stage—or maybe that was just how Dara felt, as if the furniture and walls and windows had all fallen away, the world a void beyond the patch of floor where they stood. Dara's eyes were barely closed, breath shuddering in his chest with every inhale. His lashes fluttered against his cheek—*don't open your eyes, don't.* A light touch skimmed down his upper arm, dropped to his hip. *Don't open your eyes.*

Only Dara did. And suddenly he wasn't him anymore, was outside his body—and his body was Noam's instead, Noam's hip under that grasp, Noam's lips kissing that mouth. Then the hand that had been on Noam's hip slid up, under the hem of his shirt, and Lehrer said—

Dara lurched upright into humid darkness. For a moment all he could hear was his own heartbeat, fingers twisted in damp bedsheets and lungs aching.

When he reached for the clock on his bedside table, it read 2:03 a.m. Bass thumped through the walls—a car parked outside—punctuated with the rising-pitch laughter of a drunken undergrad.

A shadow shifted against the wall. Dara's gaze snapped up, and he lifted a hand, half prepared to reach for his magic. Only there was no magic, and the shadow was just the glow of passing headlights filtered through the window blinds.

He couldn't stay here.

Dara shoved the blankets off his legs and staggered out of bed, grabbing his wristwatch from the dresser and buckling it on, shoving his feet into his old scuffed-up shoes. He clattered down the stairs, fear prickling the nape of his neck. That feeling of being watched—of a presence following just out of sight—didn't diminish until he was stepping into the gold light and low music of Leo's bar.

"Three drinks, max," Leo said when he caught sight of Dara, holding up three fingers to underscore his point.

"Just club soda, thanks," Dara said, sliding onto one of the stools.

A few patrons clustered at far tables, and two older men were deep in conversation at the other end of the bar, but it was a bit late for crowds. Not that crowds would have stopped Dara tonight. He'd have preferred the risk of being recognized to staying up in that room alone with nightmares scratching at the windows.

Leo inclined his head, something almost appraising in his gaze before he went to get a glass. Dara dug the side of his thumbnail into the table grooves, tracing the grimy wood grain through the damp spots left by previous drinks.

"Have you heard from Claire?" he asked when Leo returned.

Leo set the soda down on a coaster by Dara's right hand. He'd stuck a lime wedge on the rim. "No. Why? Should I have?"

Dara glanced toward the television positioned in the far top corner of the room. Judging by the closed captions, they were still talking about the failed assassination attempt. But if they'd caught someone . . . if they had a suspect in custody, that would be reported. Right?

"No reason."

He sipped at his club soda. It was a little clubbier than normal; Leo's spigot must've added too much carbonation.

Leo drummed his fingers against the bar top. "Are you okay? You seem . . . off."

*Diplomatic.* "Fine. Couldn't sleep."

"You don't look fine."

"Glanced in a mirror lately, Zhang?" It came out more snappish than Dara intended, but he didn't take it back.

Leo just rolled his eyes and propped both elbows atop the counter, leaning in. His hair was messy now, at the end of the night; it hung lopsided over his face in that kind of carefree fashion Dara used to spend ages trying to achieve every morning.

So irritating.

"I used to know kids like you," Leo said musingly. "Brash, arrogant. Vain. Bullies who started making fun of other people hoping no one would notice how broken they really were."

"I beg your pardon?"

"Lashing out to hide your own insecurities? Please, Dara. At least try to be original."

Dara opened his mouth to retort but immediately clamped it shut again. He wasn't going to prove Leo's point. Instead he narrowed his gaze and picked up his soda, swallowing venom down with the water.

Leo laughed. "Here," he said. "Have some peanuts. I need to check on the other customers."

The bar was emptying out, bit by bit, but with Leo gone Dara felt far too visible sitting here alone nursing a sparkling water and wearing this ugly, too-large sweater. He pulled out his burner phone and pretended to be texting. Of course, he didn't know who he'd text. The only numbers he'd memorized were Claire's and Priya's. He didn't dare contact Noam.

Noam, who was probably in Lehrer's apartment right now, lounging on Lehrer's sofa and drinking Lehrer's scotch, his phone screen perfectly in Lehrer's view.

On second thought, maybe he *should* text Noam. Something incriminating. Something dirty. Something Lehrer would see that would—

Only, no. God. Of course he didn't want that. He felt guilty even thinking it. He didn't want Noam to get hurt.

Unless . . . there was a chance Lehrer was totally different with Noam. The bond they shared might be different, more affectionate, less violent and—

Dara scrubbed the heel of one hand over his face and made himself exhale hard. *Stop it. This is unproductive.*

"Dara."

Dara lifted his head. Claire stood right next to his chair, arms crossed over her chest and brows raised.

"You're alive," Dara said, the words coming out all on one breath. "I thought—when we didn't hear—"

"Yeah, I'm alive. And you're out of your room."

Oh, right. "Sorry. Couldn't sleep." But that was rather beside the point, of course.

He pushed at the legs of the stool next to his, dragging it out for Claire to sit. And, after a frustrated beat, she did.

"What happened?" he pressed.

Claire lifted a hand to get Leo's attention. He dropped the dishcloth he'd been using to wipe out a cocktail shaker and came to join them, both hands braced against the edge of the counter.

"Lehrer," Claire said in low tones, "is far more powerful than he lets on."

"I could have told you that," Dara said.

"Yeah? Well, you didn't tell us he could heal a goddamn *head shot.* I blew his brains out. He was *suppressed.* How the fuck did he survive?"

Both she and Leo were looking at him expectantly. Dara shrugged. "I don't know. You should ask Álvaro."

He had to admit he was surprised himself. He'd known Lehrer could perform magic so quickly that it seemed instantaneous—all those decades of knowledge so well engrained in his memory as to become intuitive—but this . . . this was something else entirely. Inhuman.

But more than that, he was surprised Lehrer let himself get shot at all.

"Are you sure your friend actually dosed Lehrer?" Leo asked, something almost apologetic lacing his voice. "If he's Lehrer's new favorite, he might have chickened out."

"He didn't chicken out."

"You can't possibly know that," Claire said. "I'm not necessarily saying he betrayed us, just . . . all kinds of things could have happened. Maybe he never got a chance."

"Noam told me he dosed him," Dara insisted. "And if he said he dosed him, he dosed him. End of story."

Claire and Leo exchanged glances, and Leo sighed. "I hope you know we're taking your word on this. It better not backfire."

Dara couldn't bring himself to reassure them.

"Well, Álvaro was right about one thing," Claire said grimly. "We're definitely gonna need that vaccine."

Dara lost track, sometimes, of the fact it had been over a year since he first met Noam Álvaro.

November 2123—that was the month, even if Dara couldn't remember the precise date. But he remembered everything else with the kind of crystalline clarity that accompanied the most formative events in one's life: first kills, first kisses, first fucks.

First loves.

He'd hated Álvaro so much at first. He'd hated Álvaro's stupid ill-fitting clothes, his gratingly southern accent, his penchant for eating crunchy pork rinds during the sad parts of movies. Hated the way

Noam tilted toward Lehrer as if Lehrer were the only light source in the universe.

But Dara couldn't stay out of his mind.

Past that angry, devil-may-care façade, Noam Álvaro was . . . *more*. Dara could have spent hours listening to him internally debate the merits of communism versus anarcho-syndicalism, changing his mind every two seconds, it felt like, only to get distracted because someone brought up the Velvet Underground (which, as Dara had learned, was Noam's favorite vintage band).

Dara knew he was a selfish person himself. But he'd been in a lot of minds—selfishness was a universal trait. Unless you were Noam Álvaro. Then your thoughts were a mess of anger and idealism, tilted so sharply toward *the greater good* that anything else, everything else, became ephemera. It was one of the things that made Álvaro so frustrating, so impossible to talk to. It was a naivete that couldn't be shattered by anything Dara said. Worse, Dara wasn't sure he wanted to shatter Noam. He feared Noam would put himself back together all wrong, the pieces mismatched, his mind taking on the same dingy patina as everyone else's.

Besides, Noam didn't see Dara the way other people did. He had no idea who Dara was, politically speaking—he didn't know Lehrer had adopted Dara as a child or what that meant. Therefore, he didn't see Dara as someone to be *used*. In fact, he spent most of his time thinking Dara was insufferable.

Noam thought about Dara quite a lot, actually.

One time Ames had dragged them all out to a club, and afterward they'd sat in a little twenty-four-hour diner on the outskirts of town that served floppy waffles drowning in corn syrup and shriveled-looking strawberries. Dara had eyed his plate and promptly asked the waiter to bring him a bowl of lemon slices, which he ate plain while Noam bloody Álvaro stuffed his face with 1,020 calories worth of preservatives and carbs.

"Shall we order you a second serving?" Dara had said dryly once Noam had consumed the last bite of waffle—although not without smearing it around to soak up all the extra syrup first.

Noam had glanced up, his amber eyes meeting Dara's across the table. Dara ignored the little thrill that rolled down his spine.

"Not all of us can survive on lemon slices and sour grapes, Shirazi."

And then Álvaro'd reached over and picked up Dara's plate of waffles and eaten them too.

"Don't worry," Ames had added, her elbow poking Dara in the ribs. "Dara gets plenty of calories from bourbon."

A comment perfectly crafted, of course, to make Dara want to crawl under the table and disappear.

They walked back from there, even though it was two miles from the government complex through what Taye informed them all was a *bad neighborhood*. Dara could tell from the bitter twist to Noam's thoughts that he'd interpreted the comment to mean *Atlantian*.

"It seems fine to me," Dara had said. "There's even a playground. It's probably a lot of families."

Ames snorted. "You grew up in the government complex, Dara."

"And you both grew up in Forest Hills. What's your point?"

Noam just kept walking, his gaze fixed on the broken concrete of the sidewalk a few paces ahead. And suddenly Dara was irritated—with all of them, including himself. Because Noam clearly wasn't going to point out that he'd grown up in a neighborhood a lot worse than this one. That *worse* just appeared to be a synonym for *poor*. And even if there were violent criminals lurking in the bushes, they'd hardly stand a chance against four Level IV cadets at the height of their powers. The damage that a single word from Dara Shirazi could do against someone from this neighborhood was a whole lot worse than anything they might do to him.

"Whatever," Ames said. "I'm calling a car."

The cab met them at an upcoming intersection. Ames and Taye piled into the back seat, but Noam held back, shaking his head.

"It's a nice night," Noam said. "I think I'm just going to walk the rest of the way back."

"Are you sure? It's our treat," Taye offered, which was of course the stupidest thing he could possibly have said.

"Pretty sure. Thanks."

"I'll walk with you," Dara said abruptly, taking a step back up onto the curb.

Noam grimaced. "You don't have to. I don't need protection."

"Don't worry—I'd just as soon let the serial killer have you." Dara shoved his hands into his pockets. "I'm feeling queasy, that's all. I need the fresh air."

And of course there was nothing Noam could say in response to that. He'd shrugged and let Dara fall into step beside him as the cab peeled away, taillights vanishing over the dark horizon.

"I'm sorry I stole the rest of your food," Noam said after a while.

"It's okay."

"I'll buy you another waffle."

Dara snorted. "Oh, I'm counting on it."

Noam laughed and kicked half a broken beer bottle into the grass. There was a warm quality to his mind all of a sudden. Dara wanted to curl in closer to that heat, let it sink from Noam's skin into his.

"So you really like lemons, huh?" Noam said.

"Shut up, Álvaro."

"Well, at least we know why you're queasy."

"Shut *up*."

"You might as well have swallowed a glassful of battery acid."

"I happen to like battery acid."

Dara could tell Noam was trying not to laugh again, sensed him purse his lips to hold back a smile. Noam was unable to come up with a response; Dara relished his temporary victory. He had the sudden urge

145

to bump his shoulder against Noam's and knock him off the sidewalk, half hoped that if he did, Noam might retaliate and bump him back. Then maybe they'd walk the rest of the way back to the government complex like that, elbows brushing, Dara's heart in his throat.

Upon reflection, Dara had loved Noam since the moment they met. But this was the night he always thought of as the night he first *knew*, down in his soul, that he'd never feel this way about anyone else, ever again. Noam had crawled his way into Dara's mind and planted himself there, a root system tangled into Dara's thoughts and Dara's telepathy.

Inextricable.

# Chapter Thirteen

## Noam

It snowed again the evening of the second meeting Noam attended of the Black Magnolia.

He was soaked to the core as he let himself into Leo's bar, hair plastered cold to his forehead. The umbrella he'd borrowed from Lehrer had done little to preserve him from the snow when the winds were blowing practically at gale force. The weather had been terrible ever since Carolinia's only meteorpath died in Lehrer's coup; according to the news anchors, this was the worst storm in half a decade.

But that hadn't stopped the Black Magnolia from holding their meeting at the regularly scheduled time. No way to communicate a change in plans, after all—Noam and Holloway both couldn't be contacted on their government-issue phones. All communication happened in person, always, and "in person" relied on a steady schedule.

Holloway was already there, at least, perched on a barstool and nursing a gin martini. A tiny bead of relief burst in Noam's chest—part of him had worried they'd decide involving Noam was too great a risk. That he'd show up here to a locked door and a **CLOSED** sign in the window.

That he'd never see Dara again.

So although Noam never thought he'd consider *Maxim Holloway* to be a familiar face, he smiled as he sat down in the seat to Holloway's left.

"You look dry."

"I took a car." Holloway's gaze dropped down the length of Noam's form, taking in his sodden sweater and squelching boots. "Can't Lehrer at least spring for a bus pass?"

Noam made a face. "Buses aren't running. Blizzard conditions—old fashioned, thanks," he added when Leo approached.

Leo's gaze narrowed. "I told you. I'm not serving you if you're underage."

"Somehow," Holloway drawled, scrolling through emails on his phone, "I think losing your liquor license should be the least of your worries, Mr. Zhang."

"Not happening. Besides. All I have is bottom-shelf rye, which I'm told isn't good enough."

Noam made a face. "Honestly, I can't taste the difference."

Leo laughed, even though Noam didn't see how that was funny. He slapped a coaster down in front of Noam and headed down the bar to pour Noam a soda.

"So," Holloway murmured, still not looking up from his phone; Noam resisted the intense urge to reach into the cell drive with technopathy and read along with him. "I hear this whole Atlantia annexation plan of Lehrer's was your idea."

"Is that what Lehrer said?"

Holloway turned toward Noam at last, gaze steady and curious. "Certainly. In fact, I wouldn't be surprised if he asks you to collaborate with me to construct a palatable way to present it to the public."

Noam's chest was overtight, ribs restricting around his lungs. He took his drink from Leo as soon as the man returned, covering up the twist of his lips with a long swallow. A mistake—the soda settled odd in his stomach, made him queasy. But when he lowered the glass, at least, he was in control.

"Then we'll have an excuse to meet in private," Noam said, turning his gaze back to Holloway, whose mouth twitched in half a smile.

"That we will."

The door opened again. Noam felt the gust of cold air at the back of his neck and reached for his collar, tugging it up to cover his nape. Dara swept into the room like a black storm cloud—and with an expression to match.

"Probably my fault," Noam muttered to no one in particular.

As predicted, Dara headed straight across to the bar. He slapped something down on the counter between Noam and Holloway—a folded-up newspaper. Noam twisted round in his chair to look.

Front of page six: a half-page photo of Noam and Lehrer, in color, captioned *Chancellor Lehrer Makes Time to Mentor Level IV Protégé.*

The worst part was Noam remembered exactly when this was taken: a week ago, on their way back from the grocery store. Lehrer had a bag in hand. Noam was . . . god, Noam was even wearing one of Lehrer's old vintage Rolling Stones shirts. They'd gone home afterward and baked lemon cake, laughing in the kitchen, Lehrer singing along to AC/DC on vinyl. It was sickeningly domestic. It was—

Holloway picked up the paper to take a closer look, but Noam was already looking for Dara, who was down at the far end of the bar sipping a club soda and chatting with Leo. He didn't even glance in Noam's direction.

"Let's get started," Claire announced, clapping her hands to get their attention.

Silence fell, punctuated by the clink of drinks glasses and the flick of Dara's lighter as he held it up to a cigarette.

"So clearly we have a problem," Claire said. "Don't know if you've all seen the news, but it seems our immortal friend is even more immortal than we all were led to believe. Álvaro was right; suppressants won't work on Lehrer."

"Thanks for the heads-up, by the way," Noam said bitterly. "If Lehrer had realized I dosed him, I'd be dead right now."

"Sorry about that," Claire said, although she didn't sound all that sorry. "Name of the game. We didn't know we could trust you. But now we need a plan B."

Yeah. And they were going to spend the next thirty minutes dancing around the obvious, too, if no one stopped them.

"The vaccine," Noam said. "I don't see what other option we have. No single one of us is powerful enough to match Lehrer."

Maybe Dara, maybe once. But that was a long time ago.

"A plan that relies on you finding said vaccine," Priya interjected, her odd accent—some hybrid of Atlantian and Texan, perhaps unique to those who had grown up in the quarantined zone—as smooth as butter.

"My odds are better than most. Unless you have another idea?"

Noam let the question hang in the air, Priya and Claire trading glances—then Priya glanced toward Dara, one brow raised. Dara stabbed at his club soda with his straw.

"We have to," Dara said. "The vaccine should work." The words *I think* tagged along on the tail of that sentence, unspoken but still heard. "But we can't just inject him and kill him and hope for the best. You've seen how everyone's reacted to the assassination attempt. The people adore him."

"We need to fix public opinion," Holloway confirmed. "It's as you said last time, Dara. We have to undermine his entire administration. We can't let him become a martyr like his brother."

Dara nodded slowly. "And we can't move too quickly either. Even if we were to release all the material I collected last year right now, it wouldn't be enough. People will be confused. Ambivalent. And in ambivalence, people will always choose to maintain the status quo. It's simple loss aversion—" Dara must have noticed the way they were all looking at him, flat-expressioned. "Tversky and Kahneman, 1991," he added impatiently, like that was supposed to clarify anything.

"So we start leaking what we have now," Claire said. "Noam gets us more. We leak that too. And then, when people are finally starting to realize what a shitty person Lehrer really is, we find a nice and public way to kill him."

"He's speaking on Independence Day," Noam said suddenly, the realization dropping into his mind perfectly packaged. "At the catastrophe memorial, in March. They haven't announced it yet, but he'll be there. That's an unsecured location—only Lehrer won't have bodyguards. He's too proud for that. It'll be internationally televised."

Priya set down her beer, a clink of glass on wood. "Perfect. Noam, making sure Lehrer is injected with the vaccine will be up to you. You'll have to do it when he's already onstage, in front of the cameras, or he'll cancel. We'll have snipers in place."

Noam had the brief vision of the look on Lehrer's face when he sank the needle into his neck. Lips parting with surprise, anger already rising up behind his eyes like a storm. And maybe there would be betrayal, too, just a hint of hurt.

Or maybe Noam was lying to himself again. Lehrer didn't care enough about him for that. He didn't care about anyone.

"Two months," Dara interjected flatly. All gazes swung back to him. He put his cigarette out on the ashtray and arched a brow. "You're saying we have to wait *two months* to kill him."

Noam frowned. "Dara, you said yourself—"

"It's not that. But we're planning on two months with you and him. Together. Wasn't it just the other day that you estimated four weeks at most before Lehrer realized what you're really doing?"

Claire had been watching Dara, but now her gaze swung around to fix on Noam instead. "What have you told Lehrer? Where does he think you are right now?"

Shit. Noam had hoped he'd get away with just *not* telling the whole of Black Magnolia how thin the line he walked really was. He should have known they were smarter than that.

On the other hand, if she was asking, then Dara had kept Noam's secret.

That had to mean something.

Even so, Dara's expression was as tight and angry as it always was nowadays; when Dara met Noam's gaze, his eyes glittered with malevolence.

"Presumably he thinks I'm in the barracks," Noam said, drawing both hands up at his sides in an open gesture, as if to say, *You can read me like a book.* "It's not as if he tracks my every move."

He wasn't sure how good they were at reading faces. Wasn't sure how good his face was at hiding things, for that matter.

He turned toward Leo so all Claire and Priya could see was his profile, pushing his glass across the counter for Leo to refill. But if Noam hoped his expression was uninterpretable, Leo's was a blank sheet. Nothing moved behind that gaze as he handed Noam a fresh drink.

How well did Dara really know this guy? Noam frowned back at Leo, attention skimming down from Leo's face to his arms, braced against the bar top. They were still well muscled, like he'd just gotten off active duty yesterday. Not the arms of a man whose only exercise was using a cocktail shaker.

"But you're within his sphere of influence," Dara said. "Isn't this plan extremely dangerous? Not just for Noam, but all of us. Lehrer wouldn't confront Noam—he'd track him here. He'd have us all dead in half a second."

"This whole fucking plan is dangerous," Noam snapped. "Going into that gala with a gun in your trousers was dangerous. Trying to dose Lehrer with suppressants was dangerous. At least I have the magic to defend myself."

Dara's posture went wooden, but Noam didn't take it back. It was true. What the hell had Dara thought would happen, walking into that party like that—with his face, with his weaknesses? Lehrer might not be willing to kill Dara right in front of all those people, but he easily could have used persuasion to trap Dara in place. Would have, if he'd realized Dara was powerless.

"It's the best plan we've got, Dara," Claire said with an unexpected gentleness. A muscle twitched in Dara's jaw.

Noam straightened his arm, tugging the sleeve of his shirt high enough he could glance down at the face of his wristwatch. "I have to go," he said. "It's late. I have basic in the morning."

He half expected Dara to lob another sharp comment after him, but he didn't. Noam made it to the door and onto the whiteout street, Dara's gaze burning a hole in his back the whole way.

Claire caught up with him before he made it to the corner.

"Hey, Álvaro," she said, fumbling to get her coat hood up against the gale winds. "Thought we could talk."

"About what?"

She grimaced and gestured one gloved hand toward his whole body, his soaked sweater clinging to his shoulders and his umbrella tangling up in the wind. "Didn't you bring a jacket?"

"Nope. What's up?"

"We didn't get a chance to go into much detail about the aftermath of the assassination attempt, back there," Claire said, falling into step alongside him with both arms hugged around her middle. "But now that we've made such a visible move, I expect things'll get complicated. Lehrer will be upping his security, I'm sure. You'll need to keep an eye out for that, or any other changes he makes to his plans."

"I'm not actually sure he *will* up security," Noam said. Claire grimaced and shook her head. It took Noam a second to realize she meant she couldn't hear him over the shrieking winds. He raised his voice and repeated himself, then added, "There's a reason you don't see Lehrer walking around flanked by the Chancellarian Guard all the time. He hates having bodyguards, thinks it makes him look weak. The very fact you managed to shoot him at all makes him look weak, actually. He'll probably be working twice as hard to remind people how omnipotent he is."

"I hope you're right," Claire said grimly. "Have you . . . has he done anything like this before? I mean . . . surviving a *head shot* . . . it's a little bit extra, even for Lehrer."

"You're talking about the same guy who single-handedly destroyed DC. I don't think we should assume there's anything he isn't capable of."

They walked in silence a few more paces, Noam squinting against the snow that blew into his eyes. His lashes were already freezing. He tried to focus on making the air molecules closest to him speed up, but he clearly didn't understand the science behind heat well enough, because it made absolutely no difference.

"You saw him very soon after it happened," Claire said eventually. And if Noam wasn't mistaken, there was a lilt of suspicion to her voice—which made sense, really. For all she knew, he'd never dosed Lehrer in the first place. "Did he summon you personally? A . . . Level IV cadet?"

Awkward. Because . . . no. Lehrer hadn't summoned Noam. He hadn't needed to.

But Noam couldn't just be like *Nah, I dropped everything and ran to his side, but that doesn't mean anything, I swear.*

"No-o," Noam said, dragging the word out. Not that stalling did him much good. "But when I saw the news, I was worried about . . . I wanted to know if he'd realized who was responsible. So I went to him."

Claire didn't immediately respond. It was impossible to tell if her eyes were narrowed because she didn't believe him or just because of the wind.

"And did he?" Claire said. "Know who did it?"

Noam shook his head. "No. But I'll have to tell him it was you. He won't trust me if it looks like I'm keeping secrets."

She snorted. "That's fine. Yeah. You know what? I *want* him to know it was me that shot him. I want him to know some crazy Texas bitch with a sniper rifle shot Calix Lehrer right in the skull."

"You're Texan?" he asked, latching on to that with a slight sense of desperation. He couldn't escape the sense that if they kept on this track, she'd see him too clearly—take a good long look at Noam and see how much touching Lehrer in that office, Lehrer's skin bloody but his skin warm, had felt like heartbreak.

"Yep. Studied engineering at Austin. I was going to get a master's degree, only then I got drafted and spent the next three years playing sniper for the army."

"I thought Texas exiled all their witchings to the QZ."

"Oh, they do," Claire said bitterly. "I was two months out from discharge. Someone broke quarantine protocol after a QZ mission, and my whole unit got sick. I was the only survivor. Woke up in the hospital and realized I could move things around with my mind. I didn't want to wait for the police to come for me, so I did their work for them and exiled myself."

"I'm sorry."

Claire shrugged. "It wasn't so bad. I ran into one of the communities out there a few weeks in. I was able to have a life, sort of. I met Priya."

"But then Dara showed up?"

"Nope. Then Lehrer destroyed the vaccine lab Priya was working in, and she barely got out with her life. It was six *weeks* before we were sure she was even gonna make it. Lost a lot of friends in that attack—a lot of good people trying to cure the worst plague this world's ever seen. *Then* Dara turned up."

Noam had spent a lot of time trying to imagine what the QZ was like for Dara. He knew what the QZ was *generally* like, obviously—he'd been there plenty of times with Lehrer or on Level IV training mis-sions—but living there was something completely different. Before he and Lehrer had started searching out the vaccine, he'd had no idea people had settled out there. Or not really. They'd all heard rumors of squatters in the wilderness, surviving off mushrooms and wild animals, half-feral with fevermadness. But he hadn't imagined whole communi-ties. Whole labs high tech enough to develop vaccine research programs.

"So," he said, once they'd turned onto the street that would take Noam almost all the way back to the government complex if he stayed on it, "y'all had like . . . a whole town? Or what?"

"Yeah," she said. "There are lots of abandoned cities out in the QZ. A lot of them are uninhabitable—they got all grown over with magic and plants, or they're all irradiated still—but there are a few that are just a little crumbly. People have been living out there since the catastrophe. Some never left. They just hunkered down and stayed put—and were lucky enough to survive the virus when they inevitably got infected. It's a town like any town you might have in Carolinia. Only all witching. And maybe a little more communal, I guess. People do what they can."

"It's amazing no one knows about these towns."

"Not really. I mean, passenger jets have a minimum height they have to fly over the QZ to avoid getting caught up in magic. Governments probably have satellite data on us, but for the most part we're harmless. They let us be."

"Till now," he said.

"Till *Lehrer*."

There was no arguing with that. They parted ways close to down-town; Claire couldn't risk being recognized on CCTV, had to head back to the apartment she and Priya had rented on the east side.

And maybe Noam was personally complicit on some level for the destruction of Claire and Priya's way of life out there. After all, he'd helped Lehrer do his dirty work. Before Noam had figured out Faraday, he'd even *believed* in it. He had convinced himself that the threat of letting the vaccine fall into the wrong hands—Texan hands—was great enough to justify destroying those labs. Lehrer was a lot of things, but he was right about the threat the rest of the world posed to witching survival. Lehrer knew that much from personal experience.

Noam had seen how those labs affected Lehrer. So many of the facilities were built in old hospitals—and there was always something particularly vicious about the way Lehrer destroyed those. The nights following, Noam would wake up to find Lehrer upright in bed beside him, staring blank faced into the darkness like he could see something in the shadows that Noam couldn't.

*I hate doctors,* Lehrer had said in his office, still covered in blood, and . . . god. Noam should have realized the moment he stepped into that room, the moment he saw how Lehrer flinched back from the stethoscopes and gloved hands. He should have—

*Don't sympathize with him,* Noam ordered himself.

Another voice answered: *Too late.*

Lehrer was still awake when Noam returned. He'd made it halfway to the barracks before his phone buzzed in his pocket with a text from Lehrer—Come back to the apartment when you're done—and he'd had to turn around in the middle of the atrium to take the stairs up to the west wing instead.

Lehrer was in the living room, reclining on the sofa with Wolf curled at his feet and a book open in his hand. He put it down when Noam entered, resting its pages open atop his stomach.

Noam glanced around the room—an empty mug of tea sat on the floor by Lehrer's hip, the lights dimmed so low he was amazed Lehrer could read the words on the page. Wolf's pink tongue flicked out to lap at Lehrer's ankle; the dog didn't even look at Noam when he came in.

"Is everything . . . okay?" Noam said, because Lehrer didn't look well. He was paler than usual, his usually neat hair messy like he'd been raking his fingers through it. Fingers that trembled, however minutely, where they rested atop his book.

"Sit down," Lehrer said instead of answering.

Noam paced over to the empty armchair nearest the sofa, perching on the edge of the seat and gripping the cushion beneath him. He couldn't stop looking at Lehrer. He felt—concern, maybe, but something else too. Wariness.

An injured predator could be lethal.

Lehrer's cool gaze drifted over Noam's face, as if cataloging it. "I met with my personal physician," he said. "As you might imagine, I lost a lot of blood in the assassination attempt."

Noam's mind flashed back to the images he'd seen on the TV—all that blood black like tar on the sidewalk. Soaking Lehrer's shirt as he stripped it off in his office.

Lehrer seemed to be waiting for a response. Noam nodded.

"Unfortunately," Lehrer began, and that unsteady hand curled into a fist. "Unfortunately, my body has not yet been able to recover on its own. And I spent too much magic healing myself in the moment; I can't risk using more."

"Oh." Noam bit the inside of his lip, fingertips pressing harder into the seat cushion. "I . . . you know that I don't know healing magic. Maybe Bethany . . . ?"

"Not that," Lehrer said, a humorless smile passing over his mouth. He drew the book aside and pushed himself up. Slowly, like his joints were stiff and painful. He swung his legs off the sofa to plant his feet flat on the ground, facing Noam. "I was rather hoping I might convince you to loan me your blood."

Noam was so used to thinking of magic as the solution for everything, these days, that for a moment he almost laughed—almost said, *What, are you a vampire now?*—and Lehrer must have recognized the look on his face before he arched a brow and interjected:

"A transfusion, Noam. I need a blood transfusion."

A dull heat rose in Noam's cheeks, one he tried to push away by folding his arms over his stomach and lifting his chin. *Right.* Of course.

"So . . . ," he said, not really sure where he was going with this but needing to fill the awkward silence that had welled up in the wake of Lehrer's words. "You need . . ."

"We have the same blood type," Lehrer said. "I checked your records from the red ward. You can understand why I want to keep this as discreet as possible. There are ways to track who receives transfusions delivered through the usual donation system. I can't afford to seem weak right now."

That much was true. Especially after an attempt on his life—Lehrer was right, it was a PR shitshow. Lehrer was supposed to be untouchable, and now there was video footage of his blood all over the ground. Witnesses who could say they'd seen him with a bullet in his head. It wasn't exactly Lehrer's *brand*.

"Okay," Noam said. "Sure. I mean . . . yes. All right."

He didn't know what he'd expected—that Lehrer might make him an appointment at the hospital the following day, perhaps, send him to some clinical office with white walls that smelled of antiseptic—but an hour later he was sitting on the edge of Lehrer's bathtub, Lehrer's personal physician kneeling at his feet as she scrubbed his forearm with an alcohol wipe.

"This might sting," she murmured and slid the hollow needle into his vein.

Noam's blood was dark as garnet as it slid out of his arm and into the clear tubing that snaked down past his knee toward the bag on the floor. He squeezed the rubber ball she'd given him to hold.

"I suppose it's a good thing I've never been afraid of blood," he said and attempted a grin she didn't return.

Lehrer stood in the doorway, a silhouette watching in silence. He met Noam's gaze when Noam lifted his head, then turned away. His footsteps retreated through the bedroom and down the hall, toward the living room.

Lehrer sent him back to the barracks when it was done. Noam kept his shirtsleeve rolled down to cover the gauze taped to his inner elbow; he couldn't explain this to Ames. Couldn't even really explain it to himself. It was harmless, it was—it wasn't like Noam could have said no.

But still.

He went to bed early, curling up under the sheets and clutching his arm to his chest; his skin throbbed where the needle went in, and he felt . . . tired, drained, like that doctor had drawn more than just blood. But he couldn't sleep. He kept twisting under his blankets, sweat beading at the small of his back, until finally he kicked the duvet away and grabbed his bottle of sleeping pills, swallowed five with his head stuck under the sink faucet.

When he finally slept, his dreams were haunted by shadows and beasts.

# Chapter Fourteen

## Dara

Sometimes, Dara missed the quarantined zone.

Not the social life, of course—there were about 150 people total living in the little commune Claire and Priya and the others had built up. Not that being back in Durham was much better, given Dara couldn't even leave this damn apartment without seeing his face plastered on every missing person poster from here to Raleigh.

But the rest of it. The way it felt to be *no one*. To live somewhere that his identity didn't matter—no one respected him more because he was Lehrer's ward. No one heard him say *Level IV* and raised their brows. He didn't have to overhear the endless monologue inside people's heads: always either *Will he tell Lehrer about this?* or *Can't get over how pretty that boy is.* Like Dara could be reduced to those two attributes: Lehrer and looks. Nothing more.

If people still thought of him that way, at least he didn't know it. But these weren't the social-climbing, prestige-obsessed sycophants of Carolinian high society. These were the anarchist terrorist motherfuckers who would tear that whole hegemony to the ground. If Dara knew Lehrer, well, that was an unfortunate piece of background information to be politely ignored, like having a parent who'd been convicted of murder.

And once Dara had shuddered and vomited and hallucinated his way through the worst of alcohol withdrawal, it had been easier not to drink. No booze in the quarantine zone, as Claire had reminded him so astutely. Not since forever.

No temptation.

Unlike here, where Dara quite literally lived right over a bar. Leo had taken a habit of going straight for the club soda whenever Dara walked in, sliding it across the counter and ignoring the way Dara's gaze inevitably drifted toward his top shelf. He somehow managed to be both a twelve-step program and a judgmental parent all rolled into one convenient package.

Today, he was cutting Dara's hair.

"I don't understand how you managed to screw it up this badly," Leo said, dragging his fingers through Dara's uneven curls and tugging his head to one side. Dara could see Leo's expression reflected in the mirror over his dresser: baffled but amused. "Were you using a hatchet?"

Dara hated the way he looked when he blushed, which wasn't often. Blushing always made him look younger. "Just scissors. Those scissors."

"Those are kitchen shears, Dara."

"Well, that's what I could find on short notice, considering I'm not allowed to leave this building."

"I would have gone out and got you something better, if you'd asked." Leo tugged one of Dara's curls almost straight, then let go, watching it bounce back toward his head.

Dara made a face at him in the mirror. "Stop playing with my hair."

"Sorry. It's just *really* bad, you know."

Dara did know. He had eyes. He could see how he looked, hair longer on one side of his head, cut far too close in other patches. But he'd woken up this morning and looked at his reflection and decided he couldn't live one more day like this. His hair was too long, messy—and *not* in a good way—sweater overlarge with a hole in the sleeve, designer but two seasons out of date. He didn't recognize himself. The boy in the mirror lived in a tiny one-room apartment off Geer Street, uneaten takeout rotting in the sink, his magic decayed and blown away with the last of his dignity. The boy in the mirror wasn't killing Calix Lehrer anytime soon.

"Can you fix it?"

Leo picked up the kitchen shears, snapping the blades together twice. "Think so. It's probably still not going to look good, though—I'll be honest. This isn't exactly my wheelhouse."

He went slowly, at least, considering for several seconds before he clipped. Dara had his teeth gritted so hard his jaw hurt, almost flinching each time the shears snapped shut.

"I used to go to a specialist," Dara said a few minutes in, as Leo frowned at the side of his head. "Someone who knew how to do curly hair. They used some new fancy technique from France. I don't know how much it cost—I always put it on the card—but it was a lot."

He held his breath, braced for the inevitable reaction: for Leo to look up or stiffen with anticipation, waiting for Lehrer's name. Not *the* card. *His* card. But Leo just clipped another lock of hair and didn't even glance away from his scissors.

"Lucky you, then," Leo said. "I'll give you the friends-and-family discount."

Dara clasped his hands together in his lap, digging the edge of one thumbnail into flesh. He wished he had telepathy. He wanted to dip his fingers into Leo's mind and trail them through all those thoughts, opaque now and hidden behind Leo's skull. It used to be so easy to know what people wanted. To give them what they wanted.

He'd thought he'd known, with Leo. He'd tried. And he'd been mistaken.

Now, there was no way of telling if Leo was thinking about what Dara said—thinking about Dara using Lehrer's card, Dara having the kind of life that meant he *could* use Lehrer's card.

And maybe Leo didn't want to hear any of this . . . but the confession rose in Dara's throat all the same. Like bile.

A black apprehension rippled through the pit of Dara's stomach. He gripped his fists tighter and held the words on the tip of his tongue, heavy as coins. Leo snipped another curl and ran his fingers through Dara's hair, mussing it enough to check his progress.

"I want it short," Dara said at last, because it was now or never. Now, or he didn't think he'd ever muster the nerve to say it. He lifted a hand and touched one of the longer ends of his hair, twisting the strands around his knuckle.

"How short?"

*Now or never.* And Dara was tired of staying silent.

Dara wet his lips. "When I was fifteen, I started getting drunk early. I'd open my first bottle around three in the afternoon. It meant I was wasted by the time he got home."

Leo's gaze caught his in the mirror, his hands frozen with scissors still in grasp. Dara looked back at him.

"Well. Eventually, he got sick of waiting for me to sober up. So one night he grabbed me by the hair"—Dara tugged at that lock twisted round his finger, tugged until it hurt—"and he dragged me into the bathroom, and he held my head under in a sink of cold water until I couldn't breathe. Until I was choking. He only let go after I stopped fighting, that moment right before I would've passed out." Dara lifted one shoulder, dropped it down. "But I guess it worked. I wasn't drunk anymore."

Leo was still staring at him. He didn't say anything. Dara's lips curled in a bitter smile.

"Cut it short enough he couldn't do that again."

He heard Leo inhale, deeply enough his shoulders visibly shifted. His knuckles had gone white around the handle of the scissors. The current running through Dara's body felt lethal—but he stayed where he was, sat there in the chair, holding Leo's gaze, until Leo looked away first.

Dara shut his eyes, just for a moment. And for once, the black undersides of his eyelids weren't painted with images from old memories. It was soft and quiet. When he opened them again, this small room didn't feel quite as suffocating as before.

At last, Leo lifted the scissors. Said, "I'll cut it short."

Afterward, Dara ran his hand over his close-cropped hair and stared at his reflection. He wasn't recognizable. Without the fall of curls to soften them, his features were sharp and dangerous looking, the line of his mouth like the first fine cut from a scalpel. This wasn't the foolish child so desperate for affection he'd almost killed himself seeking it. This wasn't the fragile boy who broke so easily under Lehrer's touch.

No.

The boy in this mirror was steel and frost and a bloodied knife. And he wasn't afraid of anything.

# Chapter Fifteen

## Noam

They formally annexed Atlantia on January 31. The change in power was immediate and absolute. After all, the Carolinian military already dominated the region; what was left of the Atlantian government was in shambles, decentralized and impotent. The headlines ran in all Carolinian papers, big block letters framed in past tense, a fait accompli.

The reaction from the Atlantian diaspora was just as immediate.

Pamphlets went up in Little Atlantia, posted on all the same walls and windows as the ones Noam had printed the previous year. Protests spilled into the streets, people shouting at faceless and silent soldiers, the red star that had once represented Atlantia as a nation now representing nothing more than a movement: Atlantian nationalism. Atlantian anger.

And this time, there was no Tom Brennan to quell the outrage.

The whole process was planned out in conference rooms and offices: Noam and Maxim Holloway plotting contrasting speech points from leather armchairs, Lehrer frowning at Noam in the foyer of his apartment before a rally, reaching out to untuck Noam's designer shirt: *Dictatorship of the proletariat, remember.*

It was for the greater good. Noam kept telling himself that, the whole time he stood on an overturned shipping crate in front of the Migrant Center, yelling to be heard over the raucous crowd. It was for the greater good.

And so for every speech Holloway gave, flatly opposed to the Atlantian annexation, Noam was there to remind Atlantians of their real enemy: Holloway, and Sacha, and people like them—people who would have rather Atlantia burned into dust, a thousand square miles of corpses and quarantined zone. He stirred that anger, *directed* it—and by the time Lehrer spoke on the subject, all *ultimate goal of Atlantian independence* and *temporary measures*, the people were too busy calling for Holloway's resignation to question Lehrer's motives.

After all . . . if Maxim Holloway wanted something, it was evil by default. Opposing him—opposing Sacha's party—was more important than principle.

It was for the greater good. And yet Noam went to bed sick with himself every night, lying awake and listening to the soft susurration of Lehrer's breath an arm's reach away. A sickness that swelled again every time Lehrer reassured him: "In two years, when we have repaired the damaged infrastructure and restored Atlantian independence, they'll understand. History will write us as heroes."

Only Lehrer had no intention of restoring Atlantian independence. This was just another crime Noam would have to reckon with after Lehrer was dead.

"Texas is going to be a problem," Lehrer murmured one evening, presiding from his favorite chair in the apartment, papers spread over his bent knee and the accent table at his side. "I predict they'll pull their ambassador any day now. They see the Atlantian annexation as a threat."

Noam glanced up from Wolf, who'd sprawled across the sofa to let Noam scratch him behind the ears. "Really? They would have invaded Atlantia, too, if you hadn't gotten there first."

Lehrer's mouth twitched. "Good, you're paying attention. However, you'll find would-haves matter very little in foreign affairs."

Wolf twisted his head in Noam's lap, pushing his nose against Noam's hip bone, clearly peeved by the shift in Noam's attention. He let his hand drop back to the top of the dog's skull.

"This might be a stupid question," Noam said, "but how much does it really matter what Texas thinks? Our military outstrips theirs, any day. They can't threaten us."

Lehrer put down the memo he'd been skimming and stacked it together with the other papers in his lap, setting them all aside on the end table. His gaze lifted to Noam's, and he propped his head against the heel of one hand. "It matters," he said, "because the rest of the world will sympathize with them, not us. They might be wary of declaring outright war—but they can impose trade sanctions that could be crippling. Carolinia is a small country. We rely extensively on foreign trade for oil, certain metals . . . not to mention that scotch you're drinking."

So. Definitely a stupid question, then.

At least Lehrer was being indulgent about it—which, actually, that was a bit strange. Lehrer never had much patience for naivete.

"Besides," Lehrer went on, "Texas has advanced antiwitching technology. Even if our military is generally stronger thanks to our witching soldiers, Texas has their own defenses in that regard. All the Level IV–trained assassins in the world will be little good against Texan science, if it comes to that. And that same technology makes their servers impenetrable even to your power, Noam. I will admit it worries me."

Noam picked up his glass of expensive imported whisky, took a small sip. Lehrer was right, of course. If Texan tech was as good as Lehrer suspected, even Lehrer's many abilities would be rendered useless.

And Texas wanted nothing more than a witchingless world.

"What are you going to do?" he asked after a moment.

Lehrer was silent for a beat, one crossed leg swinging idly and his quartz-like gaze fixed on Noam's. Then, at last, he looked away—picked up the memo again, and a pen. "I don't know yet."

After Lehrer had gone to bed, Noam slipped out and back down the hall to the sitting room. He flicked on a lamp with electromagnetism, casting the empty room in shades of amber and gold. The memos had been put away, stacked in the top drawer of Lehrer's desk with all the other artifacts of a head of state. Noam arranged them on the desk surface and used his phone to take photos of every page.

He shuffled them back into the drawer quickly, glancing over his shoulder toward the dark hall leading back to Lehrer's bedroom. Empty. Some part of him had expected Lehrer to be standing there watching—Lehrer was a light sleeper, after all; he frequently woke just from Noam rolling over in bed.

He shut the drawer with his hip and glanced through his phone with technopathy. Noam doubted these pictures were anything they could use . . . but it was better than doing nothing.

*Nothing* had become a slow poison in Noam's veins. The kind of poison that would eat away at his organs and soft tissue until there was no part of Noam Álvaro left to fight.


Noam's fist collided with Lehrer's shoulder, the lead jab quick and forceful enough to make contact before Lehrer could block it. Lehrer didn't reel back—he'd increased his own weight, the vinyl floor cracking underfoot like thin ice—and when he returned the blow, it was with enough strength Noam staggered, power dragging against metal pipes in the walls to keep from falling over.

"Too low," Lehrer said. "Aim for my face."

"I can't reach your fucking face," Noam got out through gritted teeth. Sweat dripped down his brow, stinging in his eyes as he blinked it away. His rotator cuff ached—not torn, not yet, but agonized from throwing off Lehrer's clinch.

"Then play to your strengths. I'm much taller than you. How can you use that?"

Noam sucked in another breath, lungs straining with the effort. Then he lunged forward with a rear kick, aiming for low on Lehrer's stomach, under his center of gravity. This time it was Lehrer's turn to stumble, magic glittering in waves over his torso as his cells repaired themselves.

Noam had been feeling sick for two weeks, ever since the assassination attempt, the subsequent annexation—stress, he didn't doubt. But this morning he woke up alert again, alive, adrenaline hot in his veins like magic. And it felt good to fight.

It felt good to fight Lehrer, in particular.

A grin cut across Lehrer's mouth. "Better. But what—"

Noam didn't let him finish. He'd pushed forward into Lehrer's space, drawn close enough he could smell Lehrer's cologne even over his own perspiration. His right fist punched upward, under Lehrer's jaw; he felt the snap of bone on bone reverberating against his knuckles as Lehrer's teeth crashed together. He'd used superstrength, enough to break Lehrer's mandible.

Healed instantaneously, of course, but it was still immensely satisfying to imagine the bolt of pain that would have shot through Lehrer's nerves in that split second.

As far as Noam was concerned, Lehrer didn't feel nearly enough pain.

This time, Lehrer dispensed with the instructional remarks. He just retaliated, several strikes with his magic in quick succession; Noam blocked them all and gave up none of the ground he'd gained. He could practically taste all that magic buzzing in the air, vibrant and humming with danger. Only Noam wasn't afraid. That was reckless, probably—foolish, even, with Lehrer standing opposite him with errant strands of his tawny hair fallen over his brow and the first buttons of his shirt undone, power burning under his skin.

But Lehrer's cheeks were flushed, and there was a faint sheen of perspiration along the exposed line of his neck. Noam was so used to seeing him as Calix Lehrer—legendary, effortlessly omniscient. But this . . . it was intoxicating. Noam wanted to push more, harder, until he fractured Lehrer's defenses the same way Lehrer's magic had cracked the floor. Until Lehrer paid for everything he'd done. Until Noam stopped seeing Atlantian faces—stopped seeing *Dara's* face— every time he shut his eyes.

He looped his power into the hum of the earth's geomagnetic field and used it as leverage to lift his whole body off the floor, to propel himself forward so both feet collided with Lehrer's sternum. Lehrer's body absorbed the shock, bones breaking and healing all in the same instant. Which, fuck, was probably how Lehrer survived the bullet wound. If whatever part of his brain that controlled his magic hadn't been destroyed, it would have repaired the rest on reflex.

They needed that vaccine. Of course, Lehrer would never let them find it.

Electricity came next—easily, because Noam was already using magnetism. It struck out from his body like lightning, white hot and blinding in the small room. Lehrer's responding blow missed, skirting off the edge of Noam's shields and exploding uselessly against the far wall in a crash of smoke and light.

Maybe Lehrer had gotten back into sparring too quickly after the assassination attempt. Right now . . . right now, Noam felt like it would be only too easy to tear Lehrer's defenses apart like paper and burn them into ash. Lehrer felt it too. Noam saw it in his eyes, when they were close, in that second before Lehrer parried Noam's next punch: pupils dilated, sweat beading on his temples.

Noam drew back, magic still held at the ready but putting space between them. Lehrer pressed the heel of one hand against his brow, wiping away the blood from an injury he'd already healed.

"We can stop," Noam offered, his own breath coming in uneven little gasps. But for once he wasn't dizzy with exertion—he was illuminated by it, ebullient. "If you're tired. We can just end it."

Lehrer exhaled again, and when he stepped forward, Noam saw something else in his eyes—not exhaustion this time. A shadow, dropping like a curtain onstage.

Noam saw it coming a blink before Lehrer moved. He threw up an arm, blocking Lehrer's hook before it could crack against his cheekbone. Adrenaline reared up in the back of his mind, all animalistic reflex—*fight, flight*—but too slow; Lehrer was faster than reflex. Faster than any human should be.

Lehrer's magic barreled into him with the force of a hurricane, blasting Noam off his feet and sending him flying across the room. He smashed into the wall hard enough he cried out, pain searing through his vision bright as a magnesium flare. His body dropped broken to the floor, Noam's breath shallow and shuddering against his shattered ribs. The pain was too much. It had chased his magic away, electricity just a flicker at his fingertips, sparks from a frayed wire.

Lehrer approached on silent feet, steps surer now than they had been when Noam was all power and euphoria and impossible strength. When he crouched down in front of Noam, the sweat on his skin had evaporated, his hair already slicked back and his shirt collar rebuttoned like he'd just come from his office: chancellor of Carolinia again.

He reached out a hand and healed Noam's broken ribs.

But he left the bruises. He always did. *Cause and effect, act and consequence.*

"You're right," Lehrer said at last, pushing to his feet. He glanced at his wristwatch. "I think that's enough for today."

He held out a hand to help Noam up, his grip firm and forceful. The exhaustion, the way Lehrer's magic seemed to falter in his grasp—it was as if Noam had imagined it all. Instead Noam, heavy-limbed and dizzy, was the one who felt as if all the life had drained from him over the course of several seconds.

Noam let Lehrer pull him to his feet, once more the fond mentor, always in control, always alert. Noam swayed on his feet, and Lehrer carded his fingers through Noam's hair, a flicker of gold magic against Noam's spine keeping him upright as Noam laughed, said, "Guess I should have paced myself."

It was only later, as Noam was washing the sweat off in Lehrer's shower and rubbing his thumb against the burns on his wrist, that he knew.

He hadn't imagined it.

On that sparring floor, Lehrer had been weak. Noam could have killed him. But he hadn't. He'd chosen not to.

And that choice said far more about Noam Álvaro than he'd like to admit.

It wasn't enough.

The next day, when Noam woke up sore from sparring and Lehrer was still there, still alive—the protests in response to Lehrer's annexation of Atlantia all over the front page of the *Herald*—Noam called in sick to class and took the bus back to the high school.

It was a Thursday afternoon. The campus teemed with students migrating from one class to the next, all of them in knots of friends or staring at their cell phones or listening to music. Noam mingled unseen among them.

The basement hallway was crowded now; even so, with Noam's power they didn't notice him shouldering open a small door at the end of the hall and slipping inside. The room was as dusty as he remembered—the mannequin still peering eerily out from the shadows, the age-spotted mirror reflecting a yellow glow from the narrow windows high on the walls and the misshapen edges of rotting cardboard boxes.

Noam resumed his search per the grid he'd laid out earlier. This time, without classes to worry about—Lehrer, if he heard Noam was missing, would assume he was in the barracks; the teachers would all assume he'd gone to Lehrer's—he was able to take his time. It didn't look like anyone who worked at the school actually came down here, after all. That meant Noam wouldn't be interrupted . . . by Ames or anyone else.

He had no idea where the school got half the things he found in these boxes—ancient ballet shoes, about seven thousand copies of a printed-out script of *The Lottery*, outdated textbooks, art supplies—but none of it resembled a vaccine. None of it seemed like it had Lehrer's fingerprints stamped all over it.

Noam was on the last grid, had just finished digging through a carton of old theater costumes and shoved the box aside, when he saw it. The black leather bag he'd taken off Michael, the dead man in the quarantine zone—still speckled with Michael's blood, the strap gone stiff with it.

Noam's chest abruptly tightened. All he could hear was the roar of his own blood in his ears, louder and louder, his hands shaking as he undid the buckled front.

*This is it.* Noam would take those vials, fit them to a syringe—fit the syringe's needle in Lehrer's neck. Flood his veins with something far more powerful than suppressant.

And then he'd kill him.

The strap slipped free, and Noam shoved open the bag, blinking against the dim light—

The bag was empty.

Empty—except for a single vial shattered at the bottom, spilled blood. Lehrer had been here already. He'd taken the vaccine, and he'd left the bag behind because he knew Noam would come, wanted Noam to know that Lehrer knew—

*Maybe he just moves the vaccines often,* Noam told himself, trying to believe it was paranoia, but . . .

Noam was gripping that bag in both hands now. Why would Lehrer leave the bag if he was moving the samples to keep them from being found by a curious student or teacher? Surely bringing the bag with him would make transport easier.

*He knows.*

Noam's technopathy felt clumsy, but he managed to send a text to Dara all the same. Found where Lehrer's been hiding the vaccines, but he's already moved them.

He paused a moment—could already imagine Dara's response. So he sent another message on the heels of the first:

I'll just have to figure out his next hiding spot. If I can find one, I can find the others.

*I hope.*

Because now that the adrenaline of the initial shock was wearing off, it was obvious Lehrer hadn't discovered Noam's game. Couldn't have. Why would he have let Noam live—let him keep going to those meetings—if he suspected?

Noam dropped the bag back where he found it, under all those piles of petticoats. Wiped sweaty palms against his thighs. The air seemed thicker in here now as he made his way back across the basement room, nearly stumbling over the boxes he'd dislodged during his search. He pulled open the narrow door and edged back out into the hall, tugging the door shut and locking it telekinetically in his wake.

"You're not supposed to be in there," a voice said over his left shoulder.

Noam spun around and found himself face to face with a thin-lipped woman wearing a security guard's uniform. She was standing too close, arms folded over her chest.

Dry mouthed, Noam managed to push aside the initial panic—*what if she recognizes me from the papers, that article with Lehrer—what if she tries the lock, I used telekinesis, can't unlock it again—she'll hear—know I'm a witching—did Lehrer send her?*—in favor of forcing a weak smile onto his lips. "Sorry," he said. "I was just . . . curious."

"Get to class," she said, jerking a thumb over her shoulder, and Noam didn't wait to be told twice.

By the time he burst out onto the sidewalk in front of the school building, breathless in the icy air, all that brief comfort had vanished, because he remembered what Lehrer had said when he first realized Dara was involved with the resistance:

*I need to tear this little rebellion out by the root, not simply trim the weeds.*

If Lehrer knew Noam betrayed him, he wouldn't kill him. He'd leave Noam in place. He'd let Noam go to those meetings, let Noam prove what a traitor he really was.

Then . . . and only then . . . would he crush them all.

THE DURHAM HERALD

*April 23, 2020*

## NEW ADALWOLF LEHRER STATUE UNVEILED AT CATASTROPHE MEMORIAL

*Durham, Carolinia*—A statue of catastrophe war hero Adalwolf Lehrer was revealed today at the catastrophe memorial, located in the square between Chapel Hill Street and Main Street. King Calix Lehrer was present at the unveiling, although he did not make a statement.

The catastrophe memorial was erected in winter last year as a symbol recognizing the deaths of innocent witchings who lost their lives during the former United States' genocide. The addition of the statue acknowledges the unique contribution of one of those witchings—Adalwolf Lehrer—to the end of the genocide and the establishment of the Carolinian state.

The statue was designed by renowned artist Emily Martin. The monument represents the first Carolinian historical figure to be thus memorialized.

*[Attached: a photograph of Calix Lehrer at the statue's unveiling. He wears a gray suit and stands with his head tipped down and one hand lifted as if to block the camera's view of his face.]*

# Chapter Sixteen

## Dara

"We're going to have to meet more often than this," Claire muttered to Dara that next Monday night, sitting at the bar with her leg jiggling up and down and her gaze flicking toward the door every three seconds. It was ten minutes past start time, and neither Noam nor Holloway had shown up yet.

Dara squeezed his lemon slice into his club soda and nodded and didn't say anything. He didn't think he could open his mouth without his fear spilling out, black and tarry all over the floor. The radiator had broken in the bar two hours ago, and it was starting to get cold, the tips of Dara's fingers numb no matter how close he stood to the space heater.

*Three weeks.* It had been three weeks since Noam showed up at that first meeting and said he was staying with Lehrer, undercover. Three weeks since Noam told them he could last four weeks under Lehrer's gaze.

Even right now, Noam could be lying dead or dying in that apartment, his blood seeping into the antique carpet and that beautiful mind of his gone silent forever.

Leo kept pacing back and forth behind the counter with a gray dishrag in hand, occasionally scrubbing at an invisible spot only to start pacing again. Priya watched him with shuttered eyes, her vodka tonic left untouched.

At last the door opened again and Noam entered the bar, pink cheeked and scrubbing gloved hands together. But he wasn't alone.

Dara leaped to his feet, heart surging up into his mouth; beside him, Priya's hand was already on her gun.

"Shit," Ames said, eyes wide when they met Dara's. "Shit, you really are—"

Dara put his soda down and was at her side a beat later, wrapping both arms around her body and tugging her in tight. She smelled like smoke and snow, her fingertips digging into the nape of his neck and his brow buried against her hair. She'd grown it out since he saw her last. It was almost chin length now.

After a moment she pushed him back, holding him by the shoulders as her gaze traversed his face, like she was checking to make sure he really was himself and not some kind of clever simulacrum. It took him a second to recognize that expression she was making—the same look she used to get when she was thinking something really loud in his general direction that usually meant she wanted him to read her mind.

"I can't anymore," he said, and his pulse still skipped a beat every time he said that. "I took the vaccine."

"So it's true. You don't . . . you're not . . ."

"A witching? No. Not anymore."

Noam hovered at Ames's side, both arms crossed over his chest now with a muscle twitching in his cheek. "She kind of made me let her come," he said, more to Claire and Priya than to Dara. "Ames—she's an old friend."

"Wouldn't take no for an answer," Ames said, but it wasn't in the tone she'd usually take. No levity, no edge of self-deprecation. All flat vowels and clipped consonants. "I'd have followed him if he hadn't given in."

"I guess we have open membership now," Priya said dryly.

Ames snorted. "Yeah, well. Hi. I'm Carter Ames. And I've been hating Lehrer since some of y'all were in primary school."

It was true. She'd hated Lehrer even before Dara did. Back when Dara still made excuses for him, still covered the bruises and told himself pride was a small price to pay for Lehrer's affection. The first time he confessed to Ames that he and Lehrer had slept together, grinning, cupping that secret close like it could keep him warm—she was so repulsed. And he'd been angry with her. Thought she didn't understand, didn't *get it*. Wouldn't speak to her for months.

But when that paper castle burned to the ground, she'd been there. She didn't care he'd pushed her away. She just hugged him tight and said, *We'll fucking destroy him.*

Dara didn't see that now. When she looked at him, he could see her flinch every time—if not outwardly, then inside. Invisibly. He didn't need telepathy to know her. He'd always known her.

"Come on," he said quietly, reaching for her hand and tugging her deeper into the bar. "It's okay. Sit wherever. Leo will make you a drink."

He led her to the counter, made her take the stool by him. She showed Leo her ID and ordered a beer, but her hand lingered on Dara's wrist, fingertips brushing right over the pulse point.

"You look thin," she murmured.

He met her gaze, but there wasn't a right answer to that. It wasn't even a question. He shook his head, very minutely, and drew his hand out of reach under the guise of drinking his soda.

Noam was watching them both. Dara felt his eyes burning like twin coals at the nape of his neck. He dragged a self-conscious hand through his hair, but it was too short now, the gesture not nearly as satisfying as it once was. He kept forgetting.

"Let's go ahead and get started," Claire said, clearly making the executive decision to let Ames stay. Maybe it was the combined endorsement of both Noam and Dara—or maybe it was just impatience.

Less than two months left until Independence Day.

"We need to talk about Texas," Noam said immediately, voice gone flat. "That's the real threat. If they attack before we're ready to make our move, Lehrer won't hesitate to use war as an excuse to consolidate his power. And then even if we leak all this info me and Dara have been collecting from Lehrer's apartment, it won't matter—fighting Texas will make Lehrer look even better. Between Texas and Atlantia, public fear will be strong enough everyone will be only too happy to sacrifice liberty in the name of national security."

"That's why Lehrer was made king in the first place," Dara said. "When Carolinia was founded. In uncertainty, people want centralized power—even if it's dictatorship."

Noam nodded, visibly relieved to have Dara agree with him about something. He shifted in his chair, facing Dara a little more fully. "He hasn't said so explicitly, but I know him well enough for that. It's the same play he made last year during the coup." Noam shrugged. "At least he's predictable."

Only Lehrer wasn't predictable. Dara frowned, gaze drifting toward Ames—who still watched Noam, as fixated on him as if he were the only person in the room. If Lehrer seemed predictable, that just meant they weren't paying attention to the right things.

"What's his plan for Texas?" Leo asked, grabbing Noam's empty glass to refill it at the sink. "Invade first, ask questions later?"

"I don't know." Noam shrugged. "I asked him last night. That's what he said."

"He's lying," Dara said.

"Oh, you think?" Noam snorted. "Of course he's lying. But he does have reason to worry. Texan antiwitching tech is really fucking good. If we aren't prepared when they come for us, then Calix is right—we're screwed."

That name shot through Dara's chest like a bullet. He saw the exact moment Noam realized what he'd said: the color drained from his face, and their gazes met, Noam's wild and wide as a trapped deer's.

Dara's mouth twisted in a macabre grin, and he put out his cigarette with one sharp jab into the ashtray.

"We need those antiwitching tech schematics," Claire said, and if she noticed the sudden tension in the room, she barreled right past it. "I'm an engineer; I can probably build a prototype. Of course, maybe we won't have time to use it before—" She broke off, gaze flicking over to Ames; even with Noam's endorsement, Ames clearly hadn't yet passed the test. "Anyway," Claire said after a beat. "Enemy of our enemy is our friend. We gotta talk to Texas."

"I don't know if you've noticed," Leo said, "but all of you are witchings. Except me. Any envoy Texas sends us is gonna come with six bullets—one for each of us."

"Then we control the terms of engagement," Noam interjected, finally tearing his gaze away from Dara. "Meet somewhere public. It doesn't even matter if they trust us or not—if I can get ahold of a Texan phone, one connected to Texan servers, I can figure out how to hack them the old-fashioned way."

"Hopefully it won't come to that," Priya said—it was the first time she'd spoken all night since Ames came in. "Claire was born in Texas; she has contacts down South. We'll get in touch, see if we can arrange a friendly rendezvous. They know us. They'll take it serious."

"Too right," said Claire with a short nod. "Okay, that's settled. Noam—we'll be in touch once something's planned."

Ames turned back to Dara almost immediately, finishing off her beer in one long swallow. "So," she said. "You gonna show me where you're staying now, or what?"

A small, weak smile flickered across Dara's mouth. "You don't want to see it. Trust me."

"It can't be any worse than mine. Every time I go back home, I'm just rattling around in this massive fucking house by myself. If you thought that place was depressing when my dad was alive, well, somehow it got worse."

Dara shook his head and slid off his barstool. "I need to talk to Noam."

Ames let out a low laugh. "What," she said, "haven't you heard? Noam has a new boyfriend these days."

"He told you?"

"No. But I'm pretty good at recognizing patterns lately. And Lehrer obviously has a type."

"Excuse me?"

She arched a brow. "Young, powerful, desperate for a father figure. Or am I missing something?"

Dara grimaced. "No, that pretty much covers it."

A flicker of guilt crossed her face like a shadow, and she reached out—then faltered, like she was going to grab his arm and then thought better of it. "I'm sorry," she said. "I didn't mean . . ."

"It's fine," Dara said. "It's true, anyway. Or it was."

"Still. Sorry. I'm not trying to ruin our joyous reunion, or whatever. You know . . . you know I'm glad to see you."

She was chewing on her lower lip, the skin already gone red and chapped. A thread of regret unspooled down Dara's spine, tangling in his stomach. *There's nothing I can do. Nothing.* He rested one hand on her shoulder and squeezed.

"I know," he said gently. "I'm glad to see you too."

He left her there on the barstool, catching Noam's gaze somewhere near the back door. Noam followed three steps behind as Dara headed out into the back alley. The snow was deep enough now to be cold around Dara's ankles, melting down into his socks. He pulled his pack of cigarettes out of his back pocket and cupped a hand over his mouth to light one. His hands were numb; his thumb kept slipping on the lighter, each spark quickly eaten up in the cold air.

"God*damn* it."

"Here," Noam said. "Let me."

He tramped through the snow, closing the distance between them. He snapped his fingers and lifted a flame to the end of Dara's cigarette. Dara inhaled smoke and the scent of Noam's aftershave—since when did Noam wear aftershave?

Noam's hand lingered a beat too long on Dara's, his fingertips still warm with pyromancy.

"Thanks," Dara muttered and exhaled his smoke away from Noam's face. It had the added benefit of turning his cheek toward Noam—Dara had the distinct suspicion Noam had thought of kissing him, just then. He fixed his gaze at a spot on the brick wall of the opposite building until finally Noam stepped away.

"So," Noam said eventually. "What's up?"

Dara turned back to him. Noam still managed to look *hopeful*, even with Lehrer's watch on his wrist, even wearing Lehrer's taste in clothes with Lehrer's touch written all over his skin.

"Ames is under persuasion," Dara said. "She's a spy for Lehrer."

He watched Noam process that information in waves: each shifting emotion a ripple across his expression—skepticism, realization. Horror.

Dara set his mouth in a grim line—it shouldn't be so satisfying. It was terrible. It was Dara's best friend with her mind caught in Lehrer's puppet strings. But. Noam believed him. And that wasn't nothing.

"How do you know?" Noam said in lowered tones, like he thought Ames might have her ear pressed to the bar door.

"I know *her*," Dara said. "I know how persuasion victims look. How they act. And what's more, I know Lehrer." He fixed Noam with a steady look. "You keep making the same mistake, Álvaro. You keep assuming Lehrer will act as you would act. It would never occur to you to enslave the will of a girl you've known since her childhood. But Lehrer doesn't have your conscience, and he isn't stupid. He doesn't trust you, no matter what he says. He has to make *sure*."

Noam's throat shifted as he swallowed. There was snow caught in his hair, dusting the lines of his shoulders. He looked like a statue slowly frosting over. "I know he doesn't trust me," he said slowly. "He put me under suppressants. Questioned me. But then I thought . . ."

"You thought that would be enough for him," Dara finished. He arched a brow. "Like I said. Maybe it would be enough for you, but—"

"But, Lehrer." Noam sighed and scrubbed one hand through his snow-damp hair. He had his eyes squeezed shut, mouth twisted in a knot. Dara didn't need telepathy with him; Noam wore his heart on his sleeve. But when Noam finally looked back to Dara, his gaze was even. "Okay. Ames is under persuasion."

"Anything we say in front of her will get right back to Lehrer," Dara said.

"Right. And I think we should leave her in place." Noam shrugged. "Better the devil we know."

It wasn't what Dara expected him to say. It was exactly the kind of thing Dara himself might have come up with, but Noam wasn't like that. He'd never seen his friends as weapons to hone and use. The Noam that Dara knew would have insisted on some harebrained rescue mission, would've tied Ames up in Dara's apartment until he could figure out how to break the spell.

Dara's Noam wouldn't say things like, "It'll help my cover if Ames only reports back the same things I report. We can feed her misinformation to lead Lehrer off track."

Dara let out a breath. Well, Noam wasn't wrong—and if he was finally thinking like Lehrer, Dara had no right to complain. This was what he said he wanted. "I agree," he said at last. "But it does mean we'll have to find other times to meet too. Times that Ames and Lehrer don't know about."

Noam nodded. "I can make it work." And from the set of his jaw, the fierce gleam in his eyes, Dara almost believed him.

He glanced toward the door, still shut. Ames was still in there, probably getting suspicious. And whether she wanted to or not, she'd have to report those suspicions to Lehrer. "We should go back inside."

"Wait," Noam said. He reached for Dara's arm—almost grasped, but instead his fingertips awkwardly grazed Dara's shoulder, then dropped toward his elbow.

Dara's fingertips were numb. He pressed his hands against his thighs, for what little good that did. "What?"

The snow was falling more heavily now, blanketing the alley and making the street seem oddly silent, or maybe that was Noam, building a ward. Without magic, Dara couldn't tell.

Noam blinked, a few flakes of snow falling from his lashes to dust his cheeks instead. "We need to talk about the bartender. Leo."

"What about him?"

Noam bit his lower lip, an expression he used to make all the time back in the barracks, usually when he was considering how to say something he knew Dara didn't want to hear. Dara frowned.

"*What?*"

"I don't know if we can trust him," Noam said, thrusting his hands into his pockets and locking his elbows in against his sides. "I mean . . . how well do you really know this guy? Who's to say he won't turn us in as soon as he has enough information to make a case?"

"Lehrer already knows about the Black Magnolia. Or have you forgotten?"

"I'm not worried he's working for Lehrer. I'm worried he might turn us in to the police." Noam's voice was firmer now, like he was talking himself into it even as he spoke. "If we get arrested by the Ministry of Defense, Lehrer isn't gonna intervene. We'll all get guillotined. Just like Sacha's supporters."

Dara's eyes narrowed. "I should think I'm a better judge of character than you are."

"Or maybe you think he's good looking."

That hit Dara like a poison dart shot between the ribs, knocking the air from his lungs. It came out in a breathless sort of laugh. "Is that so?"

Noam visibly recoiled, shaking his head once and drawing a hand over his mouth. "I'm sorry," he said. "I didn't—I don't know why I said that."

"I do." Dara's pulse was a drum beating in his stomach, a rhythm that reverberated through his whole body. He didn't even feel the cold anymore, even though ice had crystallized on his shirtsleeves, seeping down into his marrow. A quick and vicious smile cut across his lips. "You're afraid I'll fall in love with someone who isn't you. You don't even distrust Leo—you just want him gone. And you've been around Lehrer enough you'll do whatever's necessary to take back what you think is *yours*."

He didn't let Noam respond to that. He just gave him one last derisive look and headed back inside—into the gold light of the bar, back to the building that would imprison him until Lehrer was dead, and to the girl who was now as trapped in Lehrer's thrall as everyone else.

# CHAPTER SEVENTEEN

## NOAM

It was an awkward walk home through the snow, Ames and Noam trudging along side by side and not speaking. Noam didn't dare open his mouth—he worried he might say something stupid, like, *Promise me you aren't under persuasion* or *Tell me you aren't talking to Lehrer after this*. Every time he stole a glance at her, she was staring at a spot on the sidewalk a few paces ahead of them, a muscle twitching in her jaw.

Dara was right. And now that Noam knew that, it seemed impossible that he hadn't noticed earlier.

She didn't say a word to him until they were back in the atrium of the government complex. Then she turned to face him in the middle of the room, melted snow dripping off her coat and puddling on the marble floor, and said: "Are you sleeping in the barracks tonight?"

Whatever part of Noam hadn't withered into ash in that alley with Dara died inside him now. He tried to keep his posture easy, casual, even though he felt like all his blood had gone dry. "I have a meeting with Lehrer."

Ames gazed back at him unblinkingly. Then she made a rough sound in the back of her throat and shook her head. "Figures. Fine.

Go have your *eleven p.m. meeting*. I guess I'll see you in the morning. Maybe."

"Ames—"

"You know Bethany asks about you, right?" She had her arms folded over her chest, sodden hair plastered to her cheeks. Her eyes were brighter than he'd ever seen them, even those nights she came back from Raleigh dizzy and flush-cheeked with a bloody nose, her pupils gone wide. "All the time. She can't figure out why you don't ever come to the barracks anymore. Or to class. Or basic. I'm kind of running out of excuses to give her."

Noam clenched his jaw so hard he heard his teeth grinding together. "Tell her whatever you want. You're clearly dying to just *come out with* whatever the hell it is you think—"

"What I *think*?" Ames laughed and took a sharp step forward, bringing her close enough Noam had no choice but to move back. "Dara's alive, Noam. He's fucking—he's *alive*. So you have to stop this fucking—this *bullshit*, okay?" She shoved him with both hands, making him stumble back again. She leaned in, bringing her face near his; he couldn't tell if her skin was wet from the snow or if she was crying now. Every breath she took hitched in her throat. "You know what Lehrer did to him. You *know*."

And Noam wasn't—he couldn't deny it, couldn't look her in the eye and . . . there was a strange weight in his chest, heavy and painful as a bullet. He shook his head once, twice, sucked in a shallow lungful of air that didn't do much against the way the room had started spinning.

Ames was right. Dara was right. And Noam was the worst fucking person in the world, because—

"You two, break it up!"

One of the guards was halfway across the atrium already, a hand resting on his comm. Ames stepped back, her mouth twisted in a cruel smile.

"I'll see you around, Álvaro."

She turned on her heel and stalked off toward the training wing, the wet soles of her boots squeaking on the floor and leaving a watery trail in her wake. He watched her go with a dark knot in his throat, one he couldn't swallow down no matter how many times he tried.

"Everything all right, Mr. Álvaro?" the guard asked when he was close, and Noam shook his head—then nodded, quickly, and forced half a laugh.

"Yeah. Sorry. Fine. Just . . . it's fine."

And he tried very hard not to think about when he'd become *Mr. Álvaro*. About when he'd become so much a fixture in this part of the government complex that the night guards knew him by name.

It was a silent walk through the halls and up the stairs back to Lehrer's apartment. He was starting to hate how empty the west wing was in the evenings. The silence made it too clear he wasn't supposed to be here. Why he *was* here.

He hesitated in Lehrer's study, standing there on the plush carpet with his magic already tangled up in Lehrer's wards.

Maybe he shouldn't. Maybe he should go back to Level IV, like Ames said. It didn't have to be a . . . a *thing*. It wasn't like he and Lehrer were together. They just . . .

He could end it all.

Put Dara out of his misery.

But if he did that, he'd give up any chance of finding the vaccine.

Ames was right. Noam did know what Lehrer had done to Dara. And he was going to make sure Lehrer fucking suffered for it.

He tugged down Lehrer's wards, letting himself into the apartment. They re-formed behind him automatically, glittering gold threads knitting together in an impenetrable tapestry. The living room was dark, only a single lamp lit on the table by Lehrer's usual armchair, which was empty. For a moment Noam thought maybe this was a sign after all, but then Lehrer's voice drifted down the hall: "Come here, Noam."

There was no choice but to obey.

191

Noam padded down the hall, damp socks squelching on the hardwood floor. Lehrer was in the bedroom, dressed in the T-shirt and loose flannels he usually slept in, a sheaf of paper held in one hand. He stood somewhere between the bathroom and the closet, like he'd been pacing back and forth before Noam showed up. He was barefoot.

"I was wondering when you'd show up," Lehrer said, cool gaze traversing Noam's wet hair, then dipping down his body—Noam's clothes as sodden as his socks. At last, his eyes flicked back up to Noam's face. His mouth pressed into a thin line. "I take it the meeting ran late."

Noam got the hint. He shrugged off his sweater, peeling the wet fabric away from his skin. "Ames confronted me on my way out," he said. "She made me take her with me. So. She's involved now."

Which Lehrer knew already, of course—not that it showed on his face.

"What else?"

"Well, she definitely figured out about this." Noam gestured broadly between himself and Lehrer. "She made that clear."

Lehrer waved a dismissive hand. "Inconsequential. Carter knows when to keep things to herself. The meeting, Noam."

"I told them you were worried about Texas," Noam said. "Claire and Priya are going to try to get in touch with one of Claire's Texan contacts, see if we can get our hands on their antiwitching tech schematics."

"Good. Play that out. What else?"

"That was pretty much it. Lots of talk about the Atlantian independence protests. Oh—Claire is the one who shot you, by the way. Claire Jackson. Obviously that was a no-go, so they're all fumbling around trying to come up with a plan B."

"And the plan B is . . . ?" Lehrer pulled a cigarette out of the case on his nightstand, holding it up to his mouth with his right, nondominant hand. Noam thought there was something a little rough about the way he lit the flame, a sharp snap of his fingers and an answering spark—but then again, maybe there wasn't. Maybe Noam was getting paranoid, seeing violence even in the mundane.

"There isn't one. I'd tell you if there were."

Lehrer gave him a look, narrowed eyes keen even through the haze of smoke that drifted up in front of his face. "It sounds," he said, "like a very disorganized revolution."

"Well, not everyone can be you and Adalwolf Lehrer." Noam tossed his wet shirt into the hamper with telekinesis.

"Evidently not. In fact, I'm sure you could come up with something better, given your training." Lehrer put down the sheaf of papers he'd been working on and stepped closer to Noam, close enough he could smell the sweet-smoke scent of tobacco. Lehrer tilted his head to one side. "How would you kill me, Noam?"

Noam faltered. He should have seen that question coming. Should have prepped for it—with Dara, maybe, or even on the walk home while Dara's words were still ringing in his head: how he needed to think more like Lehrer.

But not too much like Lehrer, apparently.

"Oh," he said. Shit. The obvious best answer was the one they were actually planning to attempt—could he say that? Would Lehrer think it was an impossible errand and laugh it off? Or would he double down the security on the vaccine, make twice as certain Noam never discovered its location?

Noam moved forward, narrowing the distance between them. Smiled, a slow smile, the kind of smile that has secrets. Lehrer's hand—the one holding the cigarette—drifted down to his side, as if he already knew what Noam was going to do.

"Let's see," Noam said softly, examining Lehrer with an even gaze. "You're too powerful to kill by conventional means. You could block most magical attacks. And I suspect you heal too quickly for suppressants to be of any use." He let the fingertips of one hand skim up Lehrer's chest, drawing a faint line along his sternum. He felt the steady movement of Lehrer's breath as his touch skimmed the skin at the base of his neck.

Noam rose on the balls of his feet and pressed the heel of his hand forward, closing his fingers around Lehrer's throat.

"But maybe," he said, "with superstrength . . ."

He tightened his grasp only slightly. Lehrer's eyes were half-lidded, gazing down at Noam and darkened in the dim light. Noam imagined gripping harder, and then harder still, until bruises bloomed like black flowers under Lehrer's skin. Until he choked and grasped at Noam's wrist, desperate for air.

Noam's smile sharpened, his thumb grazing up along the line of Lehrer's carotid to press over his pulse point.

Lehrer surged forward, one hand finding Noam's hip and driving him back. Noam's shoulders hit the wall, and Lehrer kissed him, leaning his weight in against Noam's body. He tasted like smoke and whisky. The hand that held his cigarette skimmed through Noam's hair, and for one reeling moment Noam was sure Lehrer would burn them both down together.

Noam kissed back, that one hand staying in place on Lehrer's throat, pushing against his windpipe; Lehrer made a soft, low noise, like a growl. Noam shivered.

Lehrer's hand smoothed up his bare ribs, then down, reaching for his belt. "Take these off," he murmured against Noam's lips.

Cold water darted into Noam's veins.

Persuasion? It'd been half a year now, and Noam *still* couldn't tell the difference—

This had already gone on too long. Noam should have stopped Lehrer sooner, should have realized where this would end when he dared to tighten his fingers round Lehrer's neck.

He knocked Lehrer's hand away, but it was just to finish undoing his belt buckle on his own, with telekinesis. Lehrer grinned against

Noam's mouth, clearly pleased with the use of magic, his teeth catching Noam's lower lip as Noam kicked his wet trousers off and away.

He let Lehrer keep kissing him for a moment. But not for long.

Noam turned his face away, suddenly breathless. His skin was cold now, damp and exposed, as he stood there in his underwear with Lehrer the only source of heat.

"What is it?" Lehrer murmured and didn't draw away.

"Sorry," Noam said, blinking against the suddenly too-bright light of the lamp on Lehrer's bedside table. "I just. Headache."

Lehrer's fingers slid along his jaw, tilting his chin so he faced him once more. His gaze slid over Noam's face—although what he searched for Noam wasn't sure. "It's the stress," Lehrer said at last. "Maybe I was wrong to trust you with this."

Noam's pulse stumbled. "No," he said, trying not to argue back too quickly—he didn't want to seem defensive. "It's . . . fine. I'm just tired." He pressed his lips into a tight smile.

"Perhaps," Lehrer said slowly. "I'll admit I've been . . . concerned. You've shown remarkable progress these past six months, since the coup. I was impressed with how you handled the Brennan situation. But surely that was difficult for you. And this winter, especially—" His thumb grazed Noam's lower lip. "You've been drinking too much. It concerns me."

"Not that much." *Not like Ames.* "You're the one who's always handing me a glass of scotch every time I walk into the room—"

"Enough." Lehrer's hand fell from Noam's face and he stepped away, retrieving his papers from the foot of the bed. He paced away from Noam again, reading—and at first Noam thought that was the end of it, that perhaps Lehrer might even order him to change into his uniform and return to the barracks. But then Lehrer said, his back to Noam: "I would hate for you to end up like Dara."

Noam went still. His feet grew roots into the floor, tethering him in place as his breath went cold in his lungs. "What is that supposed to mean?"

Lehrer glanced back at him. "What do you think?" He turned toward Noam more fully, and Noam wondered if he could see how Noam's skin prickled with a sudden chill. "By the time I realized how bad Dara's problem had become, it was too late. When he tried to get sober, he nearly died."

Noam chewed the inside of his cheek. "I knew he drank a lot, but . . ."

"Dara was an alcoholic," Lehrer said flatly. "And an addict. Although perhaps I should say *is*."

"Well, he's clean now. He only drinks soda at meetings."

Lehrer waved a hand, cigarette scattering sparks into the dim air. "It won't take. Believe me, I tried. That boy could barely keep himself alive without my help. Wouldn't even eat unless I forced him. And then he managed to go fevermad—despite my warnings. Despite everything I taught him about the dangers of using his magic in excess." Lehrer tapped his tongue against the backs of his teeth. "Reckless."

There was a lot Noam could have said to that. None of it was likely to help his case, to convince Lehrer he could be trusted to stay in place with Dara and the rest of the Black Magnolia. So instead he nodded and carried his wet trousers into the closet, dumping them in the hamper atop his sodden shirt. He stared down into the basket for a moment, wondering how the hell this had become his life. His laundry mixed in with Lehrer's. His pajamas folded on the bottom shelf in Lehrer's closet.

Only he knew exactly how it happened.

*Reckless,* Lehrer's voice said again in his head.

Noam grabbed a pair of flannels from the shelf and yanked them on with quick, violent motions. Lehrer was still reading those papers when Noam emerged. He didn't look up when Noam walked past, or when Noam crawled into the bed and tugged the covers up to his hips.

Once, a couple months after they got involved—before Noam had discovered Faraday and remembered the truth—he'd sat on the sofa while Lehrer paced the living room holding a similar stack of papers, reading aloud his speech for the next Remembrance Day. It was in many ways a thinly disguised attempt to rally Carolinians against Texas; Texas had just threatened a trade embargo, an issue Lehrer hoped to use to fuel patriotic sentiment.

Noam was idly scrolling through his phone, reading headlines but not much else. Lehrer kept reading over the same phrase again and again, experimenting with different pitches, different gestures to punctuate his words.

"Let me be clear," Lehrer said, with a sharp downward stroke of his hand like the fall of a blade. "These threats by Texas are nothing more than a blatant declaration of antiwitching bigotry—"

"War," Noam said.

Lehrer paused, glancing up from his speech. Noam put down his phone.

"Texas has declared a war on witchings," he said.

A small smile cut across Lehrer's mouth, and he turned away. But when he gave that speech on Tuesday, he said, "Let me be clear—with these threats, Texas has declared a war on witchings," and by five all the news outlets were repeating those words as zealously as if Texas had coined the term themselves.

Noam would like to think that was the start of his moral decay, the night he'd find at the root of all his own evil. But he knew that wasn't true.

It started in a cold November courtyard, his face turned toward the starry sky and Lehrer's marked hand heavy on his shoulder.

It started the moment they met.


The outbreak happened fast.

The first case came from near Atlantia's southern border—or what used to be Atlantia's border but was now Carolinia's border—and from there it spread like fire in dry grass. The response from Carolinian government was just as immediate: quarantines were drawn up, red wards stuffed full of patients, a zone of two hundred square miles sprayed with disinfectant. The images coming out of the south showed crowds of faceless Atlantians all wearing gas masks, wide black glass where their eyes ought to be.

"This outbreak demonstrates that the annexation of Atlantia has come at a critical point," Lehrer said in a speech that Wednesday, filmed in the courtyard of the government complex; the light wind rippled against his coat, the effect framing him against the ancient brick walls like a figure out of legend. "With Carolinian technology and Carolinian medicine, we can control the spread and prevent further deaths. We are confident that this outbreak will remain isolated to the far southern zone."

Noam knew what Lehrer expected from him. He was supposed to get up on his soapbox in Little Atlantia and parrot the same speech. *Better than dying,* he was supposed to say. Remind people to be grateful for Carolinian interventionism. Remind them it could have been worse.

This was just more proof Lehrer didn't know him at all. That despite everything he said—all those soft touches and sharp smiles, all the times he told Noam they were so alike, all those times he said *I trust you*—all of it was in service of *this*. Using Noam's loyalty to Atlantia for his own twisted ends.

Noam ended up on a soapbox, all right. But this time it wasn't out in public where Lehrer's spies could watch and report back, where anyone could film him and upload his speeches to the internet to spread Lehrer's message from Noam's mouth.

No—this time Noam met them in back rooms of old warehouses, in the meal line at the Migrant Center, in Cajun restaurants and barbecue joints. He couldn't tell them the truth—*Lehrer did this; he caused the outbreak himself just so he could play the hero*—but he could do the next best thing.

He could tell them to fight back.

It wasn't like Noam thought this wouldn't get back to Lehrer eventually—he wasn't that naive. But.

This was Noam's fault, really. For not killing Lehrer when he had the chance. For not having found the vaccine yet. For encouraging silence and complacency while Lehrer *murdered his people.*

His rage carried him all the way back to the government complex, one mental finger on social media—his technopathy had become reflexive now; it was easier than ever to hold multiple lines of thought—in case anyone tried to upload a video from today. But the hashtags were clean. No traitors.

Not yet.

Noam was certain if he went to Lehrer's right now, he wouldn't be able to keep a straight face. He'd end up punching Lehrer's, breaking his knuckles on Lehrer's cheek—Lehrer unharmed, of course. So he went back to the barracks instead, climbing the stairs with heavy feet.

Bethany was the only one there, curled up on the common room sofa with sock feet tucked under her weight and a holoreader perched against her knees. She looked up when he came in, a blip of electricity flickering against Noam's senses as she shut off her computer.

"Hey," she said.

"Hey."

"Are you okay?"

Noam frowned. Was it that obvious? "I don't know what you mean."

"You look like you haven't been getting a lot of sleep—that's all." It was diplomatically put; Bethany was a healer. She could probably tell exactly how much sleep Noam had or hadn't gotten. But he couldn't sense her magic right now, characteristically rosy like a soft sunrise glow, so maybe his exhaustion really was written all over his face.

"Curse of working two jobs," Noam said. "I'm counting Level IV as a job, by the way."

"Seems fair." Bethany moved over on the couch and patted the seat cushion next to her; he dropped his satchel by the coffee table and sat, tipping his head back to stare at the ceiling.

"Sorry," he mumbled eventually. "I'm not gonna be very interesting tonight."

"You've been spending a lot of time around Lehrer," Bethany said.

He looked at her, a muscle clenching in his jaw—but she gazed back with an even expression, unruffled.

"What does that have to do with anything?" he asked at last, words coming out tight.

"Maybe nothing," she said slowly. "But . . . you know . . . I can sense when someone's hurt. It's hard to ignore. And I never said anything because I didn't think it was my business, but that doesn't mean I didn't notice."

Noam's breath came quicker now, little sips of air that he couldn't keep in his lungs. He wet dry lips. "Dara."

She nodded. "I healed him a few times. If it was bad enough."

Noam let his head fall forward against his hands, dragging fingers back through his hair and squeezing his eyes shut. "Yeah," he said. "Yeah. I know . . . about that."

"Maybe I should have done something," Bethany whispered, tone curling up slightly at the end of the sentence like it was half a question. "I thought it was right to keep his secrets, but . . ."

When he opened his eyes this time, he saw Bethany had drawn her legs up toward her chest, both arms wrapped around her shins and color darkening her cheeks. She couldn't look at him now—just kept her gaze fixed on the far wall, glaring at it. Her lashes were damp.

"It wasn't your fault," Noam said. He reached over and curled his hand around her wrist, squeezing very lightly. "Listen to me, Bethany. I mean it. There was nothing you could have done. Nothing he would have *wanted* you to do. Even if you had told someone . . . Dara would have denied it, and Lehrer would have buried it, and nothing would've changed."

"I know," she breathed. "I just wish he . . . I wish he'd let someone help. You know?"

Noam nodded slowly. "Yeah. I do." He twisted toward her more fully, sliding his arm around her shoulders and tugging her into a half embrace. She fit her head beneath his chin, her blonde hair tickling Noam's nose when he tipped his face down to kiss her crown. "My mother killed herself. I don't know if I ever told you."

She shook her head against his chest. "No. I'm sorry."

"It was years ago now. It's—" Only he couldn't say it was fine, because it wasn't. Even now. "I blamed myself. I didn't even know she was sick. I had . . . *no* idea. I spent every day with her, and I still didn't see it coming. And I kept thinking there must have been signs. People don't just . . . *do* that, they—"

"Noam . . ."

"There was nothing I could have done," Noam said. "I know. That's my point. There was nothing I could have done, just like there's nothing you could've done. You can't fix everything."

It had the false note of words said to convince himself as much as her, but he needed to believe it. Needed to try.

But even now, Noam wondered if someday someone might say that about him. If whatever infected his mother—his father—lived in his blood as well, and one day it would rise up and consume him whole. And there would be nothing he or anyone else could do to stop it.

"You know what I'm saying, though," Bethany added after a long moment's silence, her fingers twisting knots in the hem of Noam's shirt. "Right?"

"It's not like that," Noam said, leaning into the words more forcefully than he meant to. "I mean—I know, obviously. I know what he's capable of. But I think you have the wrong idea about me and Lehrer."

Bethany leaned back enough to meet his gaze. "Then what's the right idea?"

Noam wasn't sure how to answer that. Later, he couldn't even remember precisely what he said—just that he made up something fumbled about Lehrer being his instructor, Lehrer-as-political-figure, and escaped back to the bedroom as soon as he could.

But once he climbed into bed, the darkness opened up above him—and he knew that if he closed his eyes, the old nightmare would seep in to fill the far corners of his mind: Brennan's body still warm in Noam's arms as he dragged it into the chair, Brennan's eyes staring without seeing. He grabbed for his bottle of sleeping pills but then hesitated with five tablets clutched in hand, breath hitching in his chest. Because . . . because what if he took the pills and he fell asleep and he couldn't wake up? What if he stayed trapped in that memory for hours, circling over it again and again until his alarm rang?

Noam shoved the pills into his pocket and made himself get up, traipsing back into the common room and turning on the fluorescent overhead light. He stayed there all night, pacing from window to wall and back when the fatigue threatened to rise up and drag him under. And finally—after he'd read two whole books and made six cups of coffee, after his body felt like it had been dragged over miles of gravel—the sun rose over the horizon and the night was over, and Noam was safe again.

*Flyer hidden alongside paraphernalia stolen from C. Lehrer's records, concealed under a floorboard beneath Noam Álvaro's barracks bed.*

### Carolinia National Domestic Violence Hotline
### +6 99 182 5555

Your relationship might be abusive if your partner:

- Is jealous and possessive, saying things like "You're the only person who matters to me."
- Isolates you, refusing to let you spend time with other friends and family.
- Is controlling; they might demand to know where you are at all times or read your private messages.
- Becomes angry when you disagree with them or don't follow their advice.
- Pressures or forces you to have sex. This includes having sex when you are too drunk to consent.
- Blames you for their own bad behavior.
- Is condescending and critical.
- Hits you, restrains you, or is rough and forceful in their physical interactions with you.

- Is violent toward other people or has a history of assault and domestic violence.
- Seems to have a split personality; sometimes they are charming and affectionate, but they can become aggressive and angry at the flip of a switch.
- Makes excuses for abusive behavior, saying things like "No one else would understand our relationship."
- Believes they are above the law.

# Chapter Eighteen

## Dara

"It feels like it won't ever stop snowing," Dara said. He tipped his head forward to press his brow against the icy window glass. The street outside was bare and white, emptied of people even though it was only eight p.m. The market lights strung over the outdoor patio of the music hall across the street glimmered like fireflies in a blizzard, made small and weak by the storm. There was a crack in the bottom right pane of the window, tiny branches of ice breaking away from it in fractals; that must be why his room was so damn cold all the time.

"Weather channel said it's going to keep up through Sunday," Priya said from behind him. She was sitting on the floor, leaning back against his bed and toying with the little origami bird she'd folded. "You're not missing much, being stuck in this apartment. It's all traffic jams and frostbite out there."

"Maybe I like traffic jams and frostbite."

Dara pushed away from the window, crossing the narrow room to drop into the rickety desk chair instead. Priya perched her tiny bird atop her knee and stared at it.

"Okay," she said. "Explain this to me."

Dara exhaled. "I'll do my best," he said. "It will be . . . I can't do it anymore, myself. I can't train you the way I was trained."

"I know that. But you're the only one of us who's ever been able to see magic at all."

"Except Álvaro."

"Except Álvaro," she allowed. But from the silence that stretched out in the wake of those words, he got the sense that for all Priya trusted Noam to come to their meetings, she didn't trust him much further than that.

Dara gripped the seat of his chair, splintering wood scraping his palms.

A part of him wanted to tell her. Priya was . . . quiet, she was discreet, she could keep a secret.

Only how much of this was Dara's secret to tell?

"I'm worried about him," Dara said, letting go of the chair and clasping his hands together in his lap instead. "Álvaro."

Priya leaned back against the edge of Dara's bed, gaze lifting from the origami bird to meet his. Dara had gotten good at reading expressions, living with Lehrer. Hers was guarded. She had a hypothesis as to *why* Dara was so worried, but she didn't want to be the first to say it aloud.

That made two of them.

"You know I grew up with him," Dara said, tugging his sweater sleeve down over his knuckles to start picking at a loose thread; when he tugged it taut, the weave bunched up, torqued around his wrist. Not for the first time, he was grateful Lehrer was notorious enough to be referenced by pronoun alone. "Álvaro doesn't understand what he's capable of."

"And what is he capable of?"

Dara gripped the thread tighter until it cut into his skin. He should have known Priya would ask. She was blunt enough it was practically a character flaw.

"Genocide," he said. "Among other things."

Priya's bird wobbled on her knee and tipped off, dropping to the floor. She retrieved it, straightened a bent wing with thumb and forefinger, and returned it to its perch. "I'm sure Álvaro is well aware."

"He thinks he is." Dara's mouth twisted, a sour taste on his tongue. "But he doesn't understand how personal Lehrer can make pain . . . of course, maybe he wouldn't care. God forbid Noam plays any role besides the hero."

"Has a complex, does he?"

"Just a bit." Dara made himself abandon his sweater sleeve, bracing both hands flat against his thighs instead. "Well. It doesn't matter. He'll survive, or he'll realize he can't, and we extract him."

"Right," Priya said. There was a gentleness to her voice now that hadn't been there before. She even smiled at him, the expression small and almost sympathetic.

But it wasn't pity, at least. Dara couldn't stand pity.

"Okay. Magic." He beat the heels of his hands against his knees once, punctuating the change in subject. "Surprise, surprise: just like everything else, understanding how magic *works* makes you better able to see it and manipulate it—to create wards, that kind of thing."

Priya shifted. "So magic is its own thing, then. Independent of the virus."

"No. Well—yes. It's both. People spend so much time talking about the scientific aspects of magic that it's easy to forget sometimes that it still *is* magic. It's still a little bit . . . ineffable. That's why in the quarantined zone we can see things like talking trees and three-headed rabbits and glow-in-the-dark rocks. Trees and rabbits and rocks can't use magic the way witchings do, intentionally, but they can still be affected by it. When magic isn't directed by a witching's knowledge and intention, it's wild. Unpredictable."

"Like in Narnia."

"Not really. But close enough. Think about—okay. Children. Young children who survive the virus and develop their first ability. Yours was pyromancy. Mine was telepathy." Dara arched a brow. "Of course, I was four years old—it wasn't like I was so well versed in neural firing patterns that I could decode them on instinct and develop telepathic ability that way. I was so young I'd only just started storing long-term memory. Tabula rasa: a blank slate. And yet I could read minds. Why?"

Priya opened her mouth, probably preparing to say something packaged and rote—*natural affinity* or *genetics*—but then she clamped her lips shut. "I don't know."

"No one does," Dara said. "After all, you can't test it empirically. Just correlations. And if I'm an insightful adult—or like Lehrer, a manipulative one—who's to say if that's because I was born that way, or my abilities *made* me that way? There have been some studies. We know probability of surviving the virus runs in families, although it's not clear if that's genetic or driven by class differences since wealthy families can afford better medical care. Our best theory right now is random chance. It's arbitrary. A child is infected with magic, and however they first *use* that magic is what they get used to. It becomes a reflex. If they're older, maybe they use magic to do something they're familiar with, like Álvaro and his technopathy. But presenting powers can be anything."

"So you're telling me that magic is magic."

Dara's lips quirked up. "Essentially, yes."

Priya flicked the bird off her knee; the construction flew about four inches before nosediving toward the floor. "All right, what else?"

"Every time someone uses magic, it releases energy. Kind of like how when you move your arm, that's kinetic energy. Do you follow?"

She nodded.

"Well, magic has its own energy signature. Only it isn't kinetic, or thermal, or radiant, or any other energy type you've heard of. But if you can start to recognize it, you can *see* it. You'll know when someone is using magic in your presence." He hesitated. "Of course, there are drawbacks. If you're observing Lehrer, for example—and he constantly uses magic to repair his own body cells—it can get hard to tell the difference between that latent magic use and him using magic to back up a persuasive order."

Priya exhaled roughly. "Then what's the point? That's what we need to identify. *Lehrer's* our ultimate enemy. If he's using magic all the time, we're screwed."

"I said it could be *hard* to tell. Not impossible. You just have to practice . . . a lot."

But even as he said it, he knew she was right. Learning to see Lehrer's persuasive magic was an uphill battle. Dara could, but he'd also lived with Lehrer his whole life. Noam couldn't, not unless Lehrer wanted him to. And Priya certainly wouldn't be capable of catching the subtle spark of gold that betrayed Lehrer's true intentions.

Only if Dara didn't do this—if he didn't at least *try*—then what good was he?

They'd been practicing for a couple hours, Priya doing odd bits of magic—making her origami bird flap around the room, turning the lights on and off—and trying to sense her own energy signature each time. She never could. And it felt like there was nothing Dara could tell her to change that. She'd either ultimately grasp what he meant, how *magic is magic*, or she wouldn't.

A part of him wondered if that was a side effect of growing up in the QZ like Priya had. In the QZ, everyone was a witching—except, of course, a few infants born in the past few months who were vaccinated at birth. To Priya, magic wasn't *magical* the way it was to, say, Noam Álvaro. Or even to Dara, who'd had Lehrer drill the concept into his head over and over until he couldn't forget it.

To Priya, magic was just mundane.

Maybe Dara would have felt the same way if he'd grown up there.

Dara got tired of the exercise early on, but he couldn't quite bring himself to invent a reason to send Priya away. He wanted her here. He liked *having* her here. Having anyone here. The longer he spent in this apartment, the more it felt like the walls were slowly crumbling in on him, threatening to bury him under a mountain of plaster and brick. Priya's presence kept them at bay. If she left . . .

If she left, he'd be alone again.

Still, he was considering asking her to take a break and come back up in a few hours, when Priya's phone rang.

She glanced at him, and he waved a permissive hand. She picked up. "Yes?"

Dara couldn't make out what was said on the other end of the line, but he did mark how Priya's face settled like the still surface of a lake, her hand curled loose in her lap. Whatever it was . . . it wasn't good.

"What?" he said the moment she lowered the phone—although she didn't put it down, just gripped it with tight fingers.

She took in a shallow breath and shook her head, and for a moment he thought she wouldn't be able to speak at all. But then:

"It's Lehrer," she said. "He did it. He declared war against Texas."

# Chapter Nineteen

## Noam

The bar was one of those places you could only find if you already knew where it was. There was no sign, no recorded address—just a black door on the back side of a strip of restaurants and shops along Main Street, nestled between the dumpsters and loading zones, the sidewalk underfoot practically soft with cigarette butts. A man checked Noam's fake ID at the door and barely even looked at his face before letting him in. Noam descended the narrow steps into the basement, the bass throbbing in the walls and up through the soles of his feet to pulse in his bones. Noam chose this bar for that reason: it was hard to find, it only had one exit, and because tonight—instead of the usual acoustic singer-songwriter or piano man—they'd signed a DJ. The flyers plastered on the black-painted walls said *Thursday Night Pride Party!*

Yeah, that was the other plus. Texans fucking hated gay people.

Maybe Claire would've had something to say about Noam intentionally antagonizing her Texas contact, but it was good policy as far as clandestine terrorist meetings went. Noam needed the upper hand, but he had to get it without scaring the contact off. The guy was bound to be on edge already, considering he was meeting a Level IV witching in the capital of Carolinia.

Anger was better than fear. It made people just as predictable, without making them liable to run.

Being here, under these circumstances, was . . . strange. This was exactly the kind of place Noam might've come on his own accord, back before Level IV—underground, tarot themed, queer friendly, with an Atlantian flag hanging behind the bar right next to a painting of a pentacle. Only Noam wasn't here for himself. He was here for Lehrer.

Sort of.

"Good," Lehrer had said when Noam told him the meeting was arranged. "Get the schematics from Jackson's contact. Bring them to me first—I'll make some changes—and then you can forward the altered files to the insurgents."

Lehrer'd been pleased, a twitch at the corner of his mouth that he couldn't quite suppress. Noam had hated the part of himself that still craved that, needed it like vital medicine. Lehrer touched his cheek with light fingers, touch trailing down toward Noam's jaw.

"When you're done," Lehrer said softly, those achromatic eyes holding Noam's gaze, his magic a faint swell of glittering gold—layering persuasion beneath the words? Impossible to say—"kill him."

Noam had gotten used to the weight of the Beretta by now, tucked into the back waistband of his jeans and concealed by the fall of his flannel shirt. The cold shape of that metal was almost comforting to his magic's senses, like a familiar friend.

He ordered a water at the bar—he couldn't get Lehrer's words out of his head, *End up like Dara*—and chose a spot away from the crowd, claiming one half of an antique love seat. A fortune-teller held court at a table a few feet to the left, but she and her clients were so absorbed in her reading of the cards they wouldn't pay attention to Noam. It was the closest thing to privacy you could get in Carolinia. Noam pulled out his phone and pretended to text, technopathy reaching into the feed from the security camera at the door—the camera he'd made sure missed his arrival—and watched the faces of each new person the bouncer let past.

It wasn't that he'd recognize Priya's contact, obviously. But he could record their faces for later—for Lehrer. Even if he checked the guy's ID after he killed him, there was no guarantee it was real. Lehrer would want a name.

*are you okay?*

He typed the message out twice, deleted it. Typed it again. And then he made himself hit send before he could think better of it, the tiny data packet zooming off through cyberspace toward Dara's burner phone.

Noam stared down at his phone, those three words hovering in a green bubble on the right side of the screen. Stupid. Shouldn't have fucking done it. Dara wasn't gonna text him back.

He closed out of the app and shoved his phone into his back pocket, out of sight.

"You got a light?"

Noam lifted his head. The speaker was a burly-looking guy in a robin's-egg-blue shirt and—Noam's gaze dipped down—cowboy boots. Consistent with what they'd asked Claire's guy to wear, but it wouldn't have mattered if he'd come in flip-flops—the M1911 Noam sensed holstered under the guy's jacket would've given him away.

Texans sure did love their Browning pistols.

"Depends," Noam said. "Tobacco or clove?"

"Carolina bright leaf. What else?"

Noam's lighter leaped into his hand with a tug of telekinesis, and he offered it up to the Texan, who only grimaced a little before taking it. Noam smiled. "Take a seat."

The man didn't have another choice. A part of Noam expected him to perch on the very edge of the cushion, just to signal how *ungay* he was, but it turned out the Texan was a professional—he sat normally, one arm slung over the back of the sofa and both feet flat on the floor.

Noam held out a hand for a cigarette, even though he didn't smoke; the man passed one over, along with Noam's lighter. Noam lit the end, inhaling deep.

"Rules of engagement said no weapons," he commented, blowing his smoke out toward the dance floor.

The man gazed back at him with a flat expression. "If you've got your magic, I've got my .45."

"Fair enough." Noam shrugged. "I'm Noam. Don't know if Claire told you."

"Yeah, I know who you are," the guy said, gesturing with his cigarette toward Noam's face. "There's a whole dossier on you back in Dallas."

Noam grinned again. "Wow, I'm flattered."

"I gotta say, though," the man went on, his accent a steady low drawl, "you're about the last person I'd expect to turn traitor on Lehrer. Ain't you his main mouthpiece on the whole Atlantian annexation thing?"

"Sure. And I fuck him too." Noam arched a brow. "Don't know if your dossier mentioned that."

The man was disappointingly unfazed. "They left your personal life off the record. So you're with the Black Magnolia now. Why?"

"I have the same problem with Lehrer that Texas does. Well. Not the witching bit. Just the genocide."

The Texan took another drag off his cigarette and tapped his ash into an empty glass on the side table. "Fair enough. Anyway, if Claire trusts you, I guess I do too. She's a pretty good judge of character."

Noam doubted character had much to do with Claire's judgment. Just utility.

"So," Noam said. "These schematics . . ."

"Yeah, I've got 'em," the guy said. He tilted his hip up to tug a flopcell out of his back pocket. "I gotta say it was a pain in the ass converting these files for y'all's ancient tech. Carolinia planning on joining the rest of the world in 2124 anytime soon?"

"Not as far as I know," Noam said, holding out his hand for the flopcell.

And that was when his gaze caught movement over the Texan's shoulder, a figure descending the stairs into the bar, backlit but recognizable all the same. Noam's breath seized in his chest, tension drawing a sudden wire up his spine.

Dara met his gaze across the room. He still had snow in his hair as he ran his fingers back through the curls, lips quirking in half a smile.

*Shit.*

"What is it?" the Texan said, head swiveling to look—and if he recognized Noam on sight, then he *definitely* knew Dara Shirazi.

"Someone who'll go home with me tonight, hopefully," Noam said, and that was sufficient to make the Texan's attention snap back to him on reflex. Long enough, at least, for Dara to slip into the crowd and vanish beneath the strobe lights.

The man shook his head slowly and stabbed his cigarette out in the abandoned glass. "Y'all really do think we're all backward-ass hicks down in Texas, don't you?"

"Aren't you?"

"I was best man in my sister's wedding to a lady named Wanda." He snorted. "But I guess Carolinian propaganda's a helluva drug."

Noam discarded his own cigarette, even though he'd only taken the one drag. "All that antiwitching legislation y'all keep pushing through isn't propaganda. So you'll forgive me if I'm still a bit prejudiced."

"That's your prerogative," the man said, and when Noam held out his hand again, he finally passed over the flopcell.

Noam's heart was beating too fast, overly aware of Dara's presence as if he'd somehow gotten specially tuned to it.

"I'm sure Claire'll be in touch," the Texan said, rising from his seat and extending a hand toward Noam, who shook it.

Fuck. This was all so fucked.

Dara was here, which meant Dara was *out in public*, only a ten-minute walk from the goddamn government complex like a fucking *idiot* fixing to get arrested, and the Texan guy was heading out the door, and Noam's gun was cold against the small of his back and fuck fuck *fuck*.

Noam threw out his technopathy in a desperate net, and—thank god, Texan guy had a burner phone in his back pocket. Carolinian make, so no Texan wards against Noam's power. Who knew if he'd hang on to it long enough for Noam to actually track him down. But.

Making sure Dara didn't get himself killed was more important right now.

He shoved the flopcell into his back pocket and made his way into the crowd, pressing between the roiling bodies and keeping his magic extended, locked onto the tech of Dara's burner phone.

He couldn't help noticing Dara had gotten his text. Had read it, too; he'd just decided not to reply.

*Because why reply when you can just show up in the middle of a goddamn drop?*

Noam found Dara at the bar, perched on a stool and sipping a club soda, like he had every right to be here.

"Pay your bill—we're going," Noam said without prelude, and when Dara hesitated, he pulled a handful of argents out of his own pocket and slapped them onto the bar. "Dara."

"He's underage, you know," Dara informed the bartender, gesturing toward Noam with his thumb. "Seventeen. He shouldn't be in here."

"We're leaving," Noam said, both to Dara and the bartender, who'd narrowed a suspicious gaze at Noam's face. It took everything Noam had not to grab Dara's arm and physically drag him off that stool.

Dara sighed and put down his soda, sliding off his seat and waving one hand toward the exit as if to say *lead the way.*

Noam's anger seethed inside him as he pushed his way back through the crowd, growing more and more lethal the longer he held on to it.

Dara knew he wasn't supposed to leave the apartment. He knew how dangerous it was—not only for himself but for the entire fucking mission. And he did it anyway.

He barely felt the midnight cold as they stepped out onto the street, even though an icy wind had picked up from the east, tearing through their hair and making Dara's unbuttoned jacket flap around him like black wings.

"How did you get here?" Noam asked.

"I took the bus."

Noam laughed, a bitter sound that tore itself out of his lungs and left his throat feeling raw. "Right."

Of course he did. Of course the one time Dara Shirazi deigned to take the fucking bus was when he had a missing person notice out for him. And they couldn't walk. It was at least forty-five minutes from here to Dara's apartment. That was forty-five minutes to get caught. Noam started off down the alley, cutting back around toward Main Street; he didn't look back, but he heard Dara's boots crunching through the snow in his wake, so at least he was following.

The Texan contact was already halfway across town, per his burner phone. And that was assuming he hadn't done the smart thing and ditched it after meeting with a known technopath.

All so Dara could get some fresh fucking air. God*damn* it.

There was a short line of rental cars parked along the intersection of Main and Market Street; Noam chose the cheapest one, not even driverless, and fed cash into the machine—enough to pay for two hours, just in case. The car beeped benevolently as it unlocked.

"Get in," Noam said, telekinesis tugging open the passenger-side door.

"I'd rather walk," Dara said, still standing there on the sidewalk with both arms hugged around his narrow waist, weight shifting from foot to foot.

"I don't care. Get in the fucking car."

217

At least Dara looked somewhat contrite as he obeyed. When Noam got into the driver's seat, Dara was rubbing his thumb against the fake leather upholstery beneath him like he'd never seen anything like it. He probably hadn't.

"I couldn't stand being in that apartment any longer," Dara said quietly as Noam hit the button on the ignition and put the car in reverse. Noam could sense Dara's gaze on the side of his face; he kept his own attention fixed on the rearview camera as he pulled out of the parking space. "It's—you don't understand what it's like."

"I grew up in a tenement apartment half the size of your old bedroom at Lehrer's place," Noam said. "So yeah, actually, I do."

"At least you could *leave*," Dara insisted. "You weren't locked up there. You could see people, you could—"

He broke off and went silent, presumably having seen the way Noam's grip tightened around the steering wheel.

"We're going back to your apartment," Noam said in a low voice, switching the car into drive and starting off down the street, although he didn't make it far before the light at the upcoming intersection switched to red. "And you will *stay there*, if I have to lock you in myself."

He understood. Of course he did. Dara had spent days locked up in Lehrer's apartment under suppressants—it couldn't be easy to stay in that tiny claustrophobic room after something like that. But didn't Dara get it? Coming out here like this . . . he was gonna get himself shot. He was gonna get himself killed for real, and Noam—Noam couldn't handle losing Dara a second time.

And goddamn it, his gun was digging into the small of his back, the grip twisted just enough to grind against Noam's pelvis; he shifted in his seat, which only made it worse. Finally he swore under his breath and reached back, pulling the Beretta free and setting it on the center console between their seats.

"Why do you have a gun?"

Dara's voice had gone tight. Noam glanced over, meeting his gaze—Dara had one hand braced against the dashboard, twisted fully around in his seat. The remorse of a moment ago was gone, replaced by flashing eyes and a thinned mouth.

"Buckle your seat belt," Noam said.

"Why the *fuck* do you have a gun, Álvaro?"

Noam inhaled a long breath, one meant to steady his anger. It had the opposite effect. And when he exhaled, all that frustration burst out of him with it.

"Because I have to kill that man," Noam snapped at last, jerking around to face Dara properly. "Because I have to get those schematics for Claire, and I had to tell Lehrer what I was doing so he thinks I'm still honest. But now Lehrer wants them too. And *Lehrer* wants me to kill the Texan while I'm at it—so I have to, if I don't want to fuck myself over. Only then *you* show up, because of fucking course. And now I've lost track of the guy I'm supposed to be shooting. It'll take me forever to find him—he might report back. Or he might ditch his phone and I lose him entirely—and then I'll have to explain that one to Lehrer too. Good job. I hope you're pleased with yourself."

Dara stared at him with wide dark eyes, his shoulders rising and falling in quick, shallow rhythm. The light had changed back to green in Noam's peripheral vision; he turned and pressed down on the gas pedal a little too hard, the car lurching forward into the intersection.

"What side are you even on?" Dara said at last. "You were really going to kill our only Texas contact, just to keep your cover with Lehrer? *Really?*"

"Yeah. Really."

The words came out clipped. What else did Dara expect Noam to say? Lehrer would kill Noam if Noam slipped up, even for a second.

And besides, Noam was out of patience for this—for Dara's complete obliviousness, his *selfishness*. Which, really, where did Dara get off moralizing murder? He'd literally stopped the hearts of six people breaking Noam out of Sacha's Faraday cage. He'd stabbed General Ames *sixteen times.*

Dara somehow managed to hold so much fury against Noam in his heart, so much righteous anger, but the second Noam was angry with him in return, Dara shut down. It wasn't fair.

Wasn't fair that Noam had to risk losing Dara over and over again.

"Okay," Dara said, "then I'll ask again. Whose side are you on? Because at this point it seems like you're equally committed."

Another goddamn red light. Noam hit the brakes just in time, the car jerking to a stop halfway through the pedestrian crosswalk and the gun sliding forward along the console to bump against the gearshift. At least the streets were empty.

"I'm on our side," he said. "But there's a lot you don't know, Dara. Like, do you know *why* Lehrer declared war on Texas?" He glanced sidelong, lifting a brow. "It's because Texas got their hands on the vaccine. Lehrer figures it's only a matter of time before they figure out how to weaponize it. It's one short step from that to releasing biological weapons on Carolinian soil. We'd be left magic-less."

"Oh, right. I can't imagine what an abhorrent existence that would be."

"For fuck's—we'd be *defenseless*, Dara. That's what I'm trying to tell you. And I hate Lehrer as much as you do, but—"

Dara snorted.

Noam clenched his jaw so hard he thought he might grind his teeth into dust. "Have something to say, Shirazi?"

When he looked, Dara's face was a mask of bitter amusement, mouth twisted in a tight knotted smile. "You really must hate him a lot," Dara said, "to throw yourself at him like you did."

It was exactly what Noam expected him to say, but somehow it still sent ice plunging into his veins. He swallowed against the bloody taste in the back of his throat. "Are you done?" he managed at last, each syllable rough on his tongue, like speaking a foreign language.

"You're defending him."

"I'm explaining how he *thinks*. Isn't that what you asked for, Dara? You said yourself I needed to understand him."

Dara laughed. "I was wrong. You don't need to understand him—you're just *like* him."

For a moment Noam couldn't breathe properly, as if oxygen had turned to acid in his lungs. He kept his gaze fixed on the road, intently enough the horizon began to blur and wave.

The silence stretched on, long enough it was too late for Noam to fill.

Next to him, Dara picked up the Beretta. He turned it over in his hand, rubbing his thumb against the hammer; Noam felt his heat against the metal as if Dara was touching his own skin.

"How many people have you killed?" Dara said.

"What the hell kind of question is that?" Noam bit out, even though when he clenched his eyes shut to clear his vision, all he could see was the look on the face of that man he killed in the QZ with Lehrer. The fear widening his pupils. The taste of blood and magic in the air.

Noam couldn't even remember the dead man's name anymore.

"A fair question," Dara retorted, and he put the gun back where he found it, dropping the weapon like he found it distasteful to touch. "How many, Noam? Just the one? Or have you been practicing since you killed Tom Brennan?"

"Shut up," Noam said, mouth barely moving.

"Is that how you and Lehrer got so close, *really*? All those little assassination plots—did it turn you on, having so much power?"

"I said *shut up!*" Noam slammed on the brakes to avoid running the next red light, his pulse pounding in his head and his knuckles gone white around the wheel. He turned a glare to Dara, who had gone still, both hands pressed against the flat of his seat. "You don't get it, do you? You don't—I'm doing the best I fucking can, and I'm sorry if that's not good enough for you. But I've been managing pretty well on my own these past six months. I don't fucking—I don't *need* you, Dara."

The silence following those words was brittle as glass. Dara's eyes were wide, glittering with the reflection of the stoplight as it switched back to green.

Noam turned back to the road, jaw clenched so hard it hurt. He still felt Dara's gaze on him, at least for a little while. Then Dara turned away, pressing his brow against the passenger-side window, and Noam finally dared to suck in another breath.

They drove like that for a while, in silence. Noam's heart felt bruised in his chest, twinging painfully with every beat.

Noam couldn't look at him. He glanced into the rearview mirror instead, into the too-bright glow of the headlights behind them. Better to be safe—no way to know if the Texas guy put a tail on them, or ditched the burner phone and followed them himself. Noam took the next left, then the left after that. Dara said nothing, just rolled down the window and draped one arm over the sill, fingers toying with the breeze.

Noam's fault. This was all Noam's fault—the way Dara felt right now, the fact he couldn't leave his apartment, all that anger tangled in a vibrant knot in Dara's mind. If Dara had still had magic, Noam might have *seen* that rage, even, green fractals sparking and splitting off Dara's skin.

If Noam had never gotten involved with Lehrer . . . if he'd killed him when he had the chance, after they sparred, Lehrer's cheeks flushed and his shirt sticking to his sweaty chest . . .

Noam could have finished things then and there. It would have been easy.

He hadn't.

To go back to Dara's apartment, they should turn right at the next light. But Noam didn't even slow down as he approached the intersection, just reached into the cell panel controlling the lights and switched them from red to green.

He was tempted to turn on the radio, drown out their silence with the mumbling hum of talk show personalities and bad music. But then Dara would *stay* silent.

Noam glanced sidelong at him. He had his eyes shut, head tipped back, and the wind was making a mess of his curls—although not as much of a mess as it would have once, before Dara cropped his hair short.

His hand rested on the seat at his side. Noam bit the inside of his cheek, harder and harder until he tasted copper.

*Fuck it.*

He reached over and took Dara's hand, curling his fingers around Dara's palm and squeezing once. And Dara . . .

Dara didn't pull away.

Noam's heart was alive in his chest, wild and beating its way up into his throat. He shifted their hands onto the center console, wrist bumping against the grip of the Beretta, some part of him half expecting Dara to disentangle their fingers the moment he had a chance. But he didn't. He stayed there, his palm warm against Noam's skin, even if he kept his face turned away toward the window.

And Noam kept the stoplights turning green, kept them moving through the neon blur of Durham past midnight. He didn't track their path, just took them on loops through quiet residential neighborhoods, then speeding down Broad Street and turning up Gregson on the return, passing through small pools of yellow lamplight as his pulse finally slowed in his temples.

The digital clock on the dashboard ticked a minute closer to one a.m. Noam rubbed his thumb against the back of Dara's hand and finally turned the car onto Roxboro, heading back to Dara's shitty studio apartment with the lights of the government complex at their backs.

"Don't leave the apartment again," Noam said, hanging out the driver's-side window as Dara stepped up onto the sidewalk outside Leo's bar. "Dara. I mean it. Please . . . for me. Don't risk it."

Dara turned to look at him. In his dark coat he looked like a smudge of coal against the ice. "Don't kill the Texan."

Noam's mouth tightened, but he said nothing.

A soft laugh escaped Dara's throat, and he shook his head before traipsing up the short steps to his apartment. Noam stayed until the door shut behind him, and after, too, staring at the building that had swallowed Dara up.

Then he spread his technopathy throughout the city like a web, into radio signals, catching the Texan's phone signal as it pinged off the nearest tower.

He tracked the man to a seedy neighborhood adjacent to downtown, waited for him in a narrow alley and stayed quiet till the Texan went past. Noam smelled liquor on the man's skin as he came up behind him—the Texan had gone to a bar instead of straight back to his hotel. Foolish. Cocky.

The man had just started to twist around when Noam aimed the silenced end of the Beretta at the side of his head and pulled the trigger.

At least this time, Noam didn't have to see the look on his face.

He kept his gaze tilted away as he crouched down on the street, digging the Texan's burner and personal phones out of his pocket. Just for show, Noam took his wallet too.

He left the Texan's body on the ground, bleeding into the gutter, and tried to tell himself for the hundredth time that what Dara said wasn't true. Noam wasn't like Lehrer.

But he had to pretend he was, just a little while longer.

# Chapter Twenty

## Dara

Dara had thought Noam would get the message after last night—and yet he turned up outside Dara's apartment the very next afternoon all the same, wrapped up in a heavy coat he wouldn't have been able to afford a year ago and knocking relentlessly on Dara's front door.

"What?" Dara snapped as he finally flung the door open after Noam had been banging away so long Dara had started imagining all the creative ways he could chop both Noam's hands off without magic.

"Are you going to invite me in?"

"I don't know—did you murder someone in cold blood last night?"

Noam made a scoffing sound in the back of his throat and said, "Says the guy who killed six people breaking me out of jail."

"I was *fevermad*."

"Oh, so you wouldn't have done it otherwise?"

Noam had one of those infuriating looks on his face, tilting dangerously close to smug. Dara hated him a little for being right. Dara still remembered how easy it had been to kill them—even Sacha.

Sacha, who offered Dara purpose when he'd been ready to put an end to things. Sacha, who, despite knowing about Lehrer—Dara had read his mind; Dara *knew* Sacha knew—had left him in Lehrer's care.

Because it was convenient. Because Dara was more useful in Lehrer's orbit than he was safe.

Those weren't the only men Dara had killed. There was Gordon Ames, of course. He didn't like to think about the others. Those memories were shrouded in shadow, thrust into the furthest corners of Dara's mind along with all the other terrible things Lehrer had made him do.

Dara stepped aside instead of answering, letting Noam move past him into the cramped space of Dara's apartment. And even though Dara knew Noam had grown up places like this, he didn't seem like he fit there anymore. Not with that sharply tailored shirt slanting in toward his narrow hips, not with that elegant wool coat he tossed over the back of Dara's rickety chair.

"Rossini?" Dara said.

Noam's brow knit. "Who?"

Dara gestured toward him, a hand motion that took in Noam's whole figure, from unbuttoned collar to the hem of his trousers. "Giorgio Rossini. The tailor?"

"Oh," Noam said, gaze dropping to his own sleeves, the steel cuff links pinning them closed. "I don't know. Maybe. I just . . ." He trailed off, color lighting in his cheeks, presumably as he realized the implications of what he'd said: that Lehrer gave him these clothes. That Lehrer had him measured for them, dressed him to specification.

"Why are you here?" Dara asked.

"Last night," Noam said. "That was risky—I'm not here to scold you some more," he added, catching Dara's expression. "But every time we meet . . . especially now that Ames is coming on Mondays, it's a risk. Lehrer could send someone to your apartment. Or come himself."

Dara had considered the possibility. But that risk was part of the job; he knew that when he came back to Carolinia.

Noam thrust his hands in his pockets. "So. I thought it might be a good idea if I put up wards in your apartment."

"Wards."

"Yeah. I've been practicing. I'm pretty good with them now, and I think I've come up with a pattern Lehrer won't be able to break easily. It's based off technopathy, right, so—"

"I don't care how it works, Álvaro," Dara snapped. "I won't be able to get past it either. You'll be locking me in."

"I know." Noam at least had the grace to look guilty about it. "And I'm so, so sorry about that, Dara. But we can't risk Lehrer finding you here."

"How am I supposed to get *food*, Álvaro?"

Something brightened in Noam's expression. "Oh, you eat now? I can bring you something—I can teach Claire and Priya how to take down the wards. Don't worry. And I'll—I'll visit you, so you won't be lonely."

He looked so goddamn earnest, weight shifting from foot to foot and gaze fixed on Dara's face like he actually thought Dara was going to be okay with this plan.

It would be endearing if it weren't so annoying.

"I don't want you to put up wards."

Noam shrugged. "Well, I don't want you to die. So it seems we find ourselves at an impasse."

The problem was Noam had a point. If Lehrer came here, Dara had no way of defending himself. And it wouldn't take much for Ames to figure out where his apartment was. But he couldn't just move, either—couldn't be seen out in public again or take the risk of commuting from a new place to Leo's bar every time they had to meet.

He imagined Lehrer stepping in through that door, tall enough to block out the light from the hall outside. The latch would click shut, and Lehrer's voice would be low and soft: *You're not as clever as you seem to think, Dara.*

Both Dara's hands curled into fists.

"How will you even get away from him long enough to visit?" Dara said in lieu of a real answer. He cocked a brow. "Lehrer's going to notice. Don't you practically live with him now?"

Noam sighed, one hand lifting to scrub the back of his head. "Dara . . ."

"It's not just that I'm angry," Dara interjected. He took a step back, dropping down onto the edge of his narrow bed. The room was small enough they still weren't that far apart. He could have lifted one leg and kicked his toe against Noam's shin. "I need you to understand—I need you to see how sick this is. Because you clearly don't."

"I *know* it's sick. That doesn't make it any less necessary."

"Just because he can't persuade you anymore doesn't mean he hasn't brainwashed you all the same. Do you really think all this happened *organically*? That you got involved with Lehrer through a series of accidents—that you *chose* this?" Dara laughed, and it felt like acid in his chest. "Lehrer has been planning this from the beginning. Ever since he met you. After all . . . anyone could have trained you. Anyone could give you remedial lessons. But Lehrer took a personal interest. Didn't it occur to you to wonder why that was?"

Noam swallowed visibly. "I—of course it did. But it was just the coup, Dara. He wanted to use my power to overthrow Sacha."

Sometimes Dara wished Noam were the telepath. Because if Noam could see into Dara's mind—see all the things Lehrer had done, rather than just *hear* about them—maybe he'd finally understand.

"You think he couldn't overthrow Sacha on his own? He wanted *you*. And so he made sure he had you."

But Noam was already shaking his head, and if Dara'd still had his magic, he would have felt those walls going up in Noam's mind brick by brick. "You don't get it," Noam said. "I told you. I haven't slept with him. Not since you came back."

"Wow," Dara said, "congrats, that's a *real* achievement—"

"But he could have made me," Noam cut in. "If what you're saying is true, he could make me. At any time. He could use persuasion to force me. It wouldn't work, of course, with the Faraday shield—but he hasn't even *tried*."

Dara stared at him, all his thoughts temporarily gone to white static.

*He hasn't even tried.*

"I don't know what you're trying to say," Dara managed, the words coming out uneven and full of rough edges. "Are you saying he's—you think he *cares* about you? Or are you saying that I—that if only I'd been more like *you*, if I'd just been more—he wouldn't have—"

The emotion rippled over Noam's face like a sea change, and he lurched forward, a half step aborted at the last second. His hand, which had been reaching for Dara, curled into a loose fist. "*No*," Noam said. "No—Dara, I don't think that at all. I'm . . . god, I'm such a fucking asshole. I'm sorry. I didn't mean it like that."

"Didn't you?"

"Of course not." Noam bit his lower lip hard enough it looked like it hurt; then he gestured toward the bed at Dara's side. "Look. Can I—can I sit? Here?"

He at least waited for Dara to shrug before taking the seat, the mattress dipping under his weight and sending Dara tipping a little closer before Dara braced himself against the bed and shifted away again.

"I'm so sorry," Noam said again. "I want you to know—I . . . I know how hard this must be for you. Or I can imagine. I swear I wouldn't be doing this if I thought there were any other way. It kills me to see how much this hurts you, Dara."

*Clearly it doesn't kill you enough,* Dara almost said, but he pressed his lips together instead and didn't speak.

Noam turned his gaze from Dara's face to his hands, which were clenched tight in his lap. Dara had learned to read every flicker of emotion on Noam's face, had carefully paired every expression with its matching mental state after six months of reading Noam's mind—months of watching him in secret over the edge of books and in late evenings as Noam spread his study materials all over the common room and settled in to work, pencil stuck behind one ear and his brow furrowed.

Noam was upset. No, more than that: *distressed.*

*Good,* a part of Dara thought viciously, and immediately regretted it.

He was a terrible person. A terrible friend. Ames had always said so.

Dara took a shallow breath. "Listen . . . that first night, after the gala, when you told me what happened with Lehrer . . . I didn't respond the way I should have. I acted like any of this was your choice, but it wasn't. I know that, Noam. You were sixteen, and drunk—it was never your choice."

"Dara—"

"Let me finish," Dara said, and Noam shut his mouth. "It's like you told me when you confronted me about General Ames: things like that, when you're a teenager, and especially with people in power . . . they aren't consensual. They can't be, by definition. I know you don't want to hear it, and maybe it's easier to believe you chose this, but that's not how any of this works." He managed a bitter smile. "Take it from someone who would know."

It was more than Dara had ever been able to admit in the past—that General Ames had raped him, that what Lehrer did—to both Dara and Noam—certainly fell under the same category, no matter what lies they'd told themselves in order to maintain some sense of *agency.*

Maybe it was okay to admit helplessness. Maybe it didn't make them weak.

Not at all.

Next to him, Noam had gone a sickly shade of gray, his fingers digging in hard at his own thighs. Dara chewed his own lip and wished with all his heart there was something he could say or do to make that sickness Noam felt go away. But there wasn't. Not without lying to him—and Dara would never do that.

"I'm sorry I lost my temper," Dara said instead. "I was so angry. And . . . scared. I didn't want it to be true either. I didn't want to feel like I'd failed you by leaving you there alone."

"You didn't," Noam said, finally lifting his gaze back to Dara's. "I left you, remember? I sent you out there to die."

"Only because I asked you to."

"Still."

Dara wanted to unravel all those tangled threads of guilt and shame in Noam's mind. He might not be able to read Noam's thoughts directly, but he could still sense those emotions knotted up behind Noam's eyes. It hurt, a visceral kind of pain that Dara had never felt for anyone else. Not before he met Noam.

"Have you had any luck finding the vaccine?" Dara asked, nudging the conversation back onto—somewhat—safer ground.

"No," Noam admitted after a moment. "Not yet, but I've found a lot of other useful material. For the leak. Letters, recordings from after the catastrophe . . . that kind of thing."

"Oh," Dara said. "Well, that's . . . good."

"I know it's not enough—"

"No," Dara interjected firmly. "It's fine. It's a start." He held Noam's gaze long enough to see Noam's expression soften. Dara shrugged one shoulder. "For a long time, that was the most I could do, as well. I felt so . . . inefficacious. But it was better than nothing."

Noam gave him a small, tense smile. He rested his hand on the bed between them, and Dara knew what he was asking, knew . . . knew he should probably make Noam leave. A few PDFs leaked online wasn't enough to justify Noam staying in place. Even the vaccine wasn't worth Noam risking his life.

Dara couldn't imagine a world that didn't have Noam in it. He didn't want to think about living the rest of his life if Noam wasn't out there somewhere talking some poor idiot's ear off about computers and communism. Dara let his hand drift to the side, curling his fingers around Noam's palm. He heard the audible sharp intake of Noam's breath a beat before Noam tightened his grip around Dara's hand in turn.

"Can I visit you tomorrow?" Noam asked.

Dara wanted to say no . . . but after a moment he nodded. Noam's thumb swept a path along the back of Dara's hand. Dara wished that simple contact didn't still send shivers down his spine.

"I'll bring you some things," Noam said. "Food, tea, cigarettes—books, if you want. Is there anything you need?"

"Lehrer's head on a spike."

Noam laughed. "Yeah, well. I'm working on that."

To his surprise, Dara smiled—and although he turned his face away quickly, it was too late; Noam had already seen. Dara felt Noam press a soft kiss to the top of his shoulder—and then Noam drew back, releasing Dara's hand as he rose to his feet.

"Are you okay if I . . . can I put up that ward?"

Dara braced both hands against the edge of the bed. "Fine."

Noam grinned at him, looking far more pleased with himself than Dara thought warranted. He turned his gaze toward the ceiling, performing the necessary magic—not that Dara could sense it.

It didn't take long. "Getting faster," Noam declared smugly when he was finished. "Just a matter of practice . . . listen, I'll show Claire and Priya how to bypass the ward. It's literally a big magic technological lock screen, so all they need is the right code to get in. Easy enough."

"For you."

"Exactly. For me. And not for Lehrer." Noam arched a brow. "You've seen his apartment. He probably doesn't even know what a computer looks like."

Dara had more things to say to that, snappish and cruel remarks that could wipe that smile off Noam's face—but he was tired of it. He was exhausted, and he'd literally *just* apologized.

He didn't want to fight anymore.

"Okay," he said. "Well, then. I'm going to sleep. It's not like I have anything better to do in here."

"I'll bring you books," Noam said again, painfully sincere, and Dara just waved a hand.

"Sure. Tomorrow, then."

Noam took the cue this time.

The room felt smaller with him gone, the bland white walls drawing in suffocatingly close. Dara lay down on his bed, face turned toward the ceiling, and clenched his eyes shut against the traitorous heat prickling there.

He hadn't felt so trapped since . . .

. . . *his old bedroom, a line dripping suppressant into his veins, the soft chill of Lehrer's voice: "You know you only have yourself to blame."*

Dara's next breath crystallized like ice in his lungs.

He opened his eyes, just to prove to himself he wasn't there—that the ceiling was the cracked ceiling of this shitty apartment, not the ceiling of his old bedroom with the sticky glue leftover from the glow-in-the-dark stars he'd pasted there as a child—the stars he'd torn down and thrown away after that first time he'd stared up at them while—while—

Dara lurched out of bed and paced over to the window instead, pressing his brow against the cold glass and staring down at the sidewalk below.

Noam was long gone. Dara couldn't even tell which footprints in the snow were his.

He'd never wanted a drink more in his life.

Dara scrubbed his hands over his face, dragging fingers back through his hair. *Calm down.* It didn't do much good. Already he needed to leave, to break down that door and go . . . *anywhere*, anywhere he could feel the cold air on his skin and see faces that didn't belong in the spotty mirror over that dresser and touch objects that didn't live in this room.

Useless. He was useless, magic-less, good for nothing but sitting locked in a room while witchings went and saved the world.

He should have shot Lehrer when he had the chance. Even if it didn't work, even if Dara was the one who died.

Dying was better than doing nothing.

*Stolen from the digital records of Calix Lehrer:*

DATE: 6 March 2123

PHYSICIAN'S NOTE: Routine exam.

**Name:** Lehrer, Calix Markus

**DOB:** 2 January 2000

**Address:** Apt. 13, Carolinia Government Complex, Blackwell St., Durham, CAR

**Citizenship:** Republic of Carolinia

**Parents or Legal Guardian** (*if under 18*): Over 18

**Blood Type:** AB-

**Status:** Witching; *Antibody titer:* Present at 1:2; *Presenting power:* Not reported

**Height:** 6′ 10″ **Weight:** 220 lbs.

**Problem List:** None

**Previous Hospitalizations/Surgeries:** Red ward (3 wks, age 2); coercively hospitalized at St. George's w/ a number of exploratory and experimental surgeries (ages 12–16)

**Encounter Notes:** Patient presents for annual wellness check. No current complaints. Pt is healthy 123yo male who appears well nourished with good muscle bulk and adequate fat stores. Patient heart rate and respiration slightly elevated (HR 113, RR 25), blood pressure/temp within normal range (BP 121/70, T 37C). Suspect dehydration and fatigue have caused tachycardia and increased RR; recommended pt drink more water and pt agreed.

**Diagnoses:** *Primary:* Well patient; *Secondary:* None

DATE: 4 November 2122

PHYSICIAN'S NOTE: Mr. Álvaro is a recent admission to the Level IV training program.

**Name:** Álvaro, Noam Isaac Mendel

**DOB:** 30 July 2106

**Address:** c/o Colonel Sarah Howard, Level IV, Carolinia Government Complex, Blackwell St., Durham, CAR

**Citizenship:** Republic of Carolinia

**Parents or Legal Guardian** (*if under 18*): Ward of the state

**Blood Type:** AB-

**Status:** Witching; *Antibody titer:* Present at 1:2; *Presenting power:* Technopathy

**Height:** 6′ 2″ **Weight:** 165 lbs.

**Problem List:** Iron-deficient anemia (mild)

**Previous Hospitalizations/Surgeries:** Appendectomy (age 14, performed while inmate at Federal Juvenile Detention Center); red ward (1 wk, age 16)

**Encounter Notes:**

Patient is 16yo male presenting for well child exam. No complaints today, no concerns. Recent treatment for moderate protein malnutrition and recent acute magic viral infection, now chronic carrier. Recovering well. Gaining weight appropriately. Reports greater independence and increased exercise capacity.

Reports mood is good—interactive and engaging during clinic visit. Patient heart rate, blood pressure, temp all within normal range (HR 72, RR 16, BP 110/65, T 37C). Ordered routine blood tests.

**Diagnoses:** *Primary:* Well patient; *Secondary:* None

DATE: 6 May 2123

PHYSICIAN'S NOTE: Evaluation of fever, chills, joint pain.

Name: Shirazi, Dara

**DOB:** 25 October 2104

**Address:** c/o Minister Calix Lehrer, Apt. 13, Carolinia Government Complex. Blackwell St., Durham, CAR

**Citizenship:** Republic of Carolinia

**Parents or Legal Guardian**: Over 18

**Blood Type:** O-

**Status:** Witching; *Antibody titer:* Present at 1:2; *Presenting power:* Telepathy

**Height:** 5' 9" **Weight:** [unknown; patient refused]

**Problem List:** History of ventricular arrhythmia secondary to severe metabolic derangements (hypokalemia); iron-deficient anemia due to malnutrition

**Previous Hospitalizations/Surgeries:** red ward (2 wks, age 4); laceration repair (performed magically by CL) and intentional overdose requiring ICU hospitalization (age 16)

**Encounter Notes:** Consultation on request of C. Lehrer. Pt is an 18yo male. Generally resistant to providing history so information obtained from his father, CL. Father brings in pt due to fevers, joint pain and excessive fatigue, concern for acute viral intoxication syndrome. No history of viral intoxication syndrome in the past. Age of primary infection: 4, ab titer: 1:2. Pt enrolled in Level IV—typical daily magic expenditure substantial at baseline but father reports recent drastic increase due to "teenage angst." Father reports hx of polysubstance abuse, food restriction with self-induced vomiting. Last alcoholic drink 5–6 hours before presentation. History of withdrawal symptoms but no hospitalizations for withdrawal seizures or DTs.

Cachectic with temporal wasting. Tachycardic (heart rate 106, BP 92/40). QTc prolonged at 480, moderately febrile (temp 39C). No respiratory distress with clear lung sounds (RR 26). Abdominal exam benign. Fine resting tremor present. Diaphoretic. Moving all extremities spontaneously.

Hyper—almost intentionally exaggerated—patellofemoral reflexes. Examination revealed bruise on right lateral bicep.

Pt is a high-dynamics witching in a competitive training environment. Possible viral intoxication syndrome although symptoms likely multifactorial, including sequelae of moderate to severe malnutrition, polysubstance abuse with possible withdrawal syndrome. Differential diagnosis/rule out: systemic lupus erythematosus, acute infection, liver failure, severe hypokalemia, alcohol withdrawal syndrome.

Offered inpatient treatment for constellation of symptoms and physical exam findings suggesting multiple possible life-threatening conditions. However, patient appears to have decision-making capacity and he and his father, who is his legal power-of-attorney in any case, declined. I warned him about my concerns for life-threatening arrhythmia and withdrawal and strongly recommended close monitoring, preferably inpatient.

Recommend lab work today and close monitoring with repeat lab work in a few days: complete blood count, electrolyte panel, ANA with magic antibody reflex+SLE reflex, toxicology panel, liver enzymes.

Expressed concern to C. Lehrer regarding pt's suitability for further Level 4 training.

**Prescriptions:** Iron replacement, potassium replacement, eszopiclone (for insomnia), sertraline (for depression)

**Diagnoses:** *Primary:* Fever (idiopathic); *Secondary:* Substance abuse disorder; unspecified eating disorder; major depressive disorder

# Chapter Twenty-One

## Noam

Come by the apartment for dinner.

The text was waiting on Noam's phone when he got out of Swensson's Friday strategy class, Noam instantly tilting the screen away from curious gazes as he opened the messaging app. Lehrer never texted him anything incriminating, but even so the last thing Noam needed was Ames or Bethany catching his name on Noam's phone.

Not like they didn't already know, of course, but . . .

"I'm meeting a friend for dinner," he told them when he split off from the group at the stairs. "I'll see y'all later tonight?"

"Sure, if you ever make it back," Ames said—but this time, to Noam's surprise, it was Taye who elbowed her in the ribs and said: "Yep. Have a good time, Álvaro."

Noam took the stairs down and cut across the atrium to head through the west wing to Lehrer's apartment. He still wondered sometimes why Lehrer hadn't taken up the chancellor's residence outside downtown—although he supposed, on second thought, living in a mansion would probably harsh Lehrer's whole ex-revolutionary style.

Noam expected Lehrer to be waiting for him when he opened the door, presiding from his favorite armchair with a neat scotch in hand.

But although Wolf scampered up to nudge Noam's thigh for a scratch behind the ears, the living room was empty. Noam wandered deeper, into the kitchen—and that was where he found Lehrer with a match in hand, bent over a pair of candles at the table to light the flames.

"What's this?" Noam said.

Lehrer straightened, waving the match in the air to quench it. He gestured down at the table—white-tableclothed now, bearing the candles but also twin plates piled high with brisket and mashed potatoes and asparagus, a bottle of red wine and a kiddush cup, a loaf of challah resting beneath a drape of fabric. "Gut Shabbos," he said, one brow lifting. "Forgive me; I was feeling nostalgic."

Noam stared at him. *Nostalgic.* Despite knowing Lehrer was Jewish, both from history and from Lehrer's having told him, he'd very much gotten the impression that nominal Judaism was as far as that went. Lehrer had mezuzot on his doorframes, another gesture, but this was . . .

"Since when do you observe Shabbat?"

The slight smile that had curved Lehrer's lips flattened somewhat. "I thought you might . . . appreciate it. Was I wrong?"

Noam had no idea how to feel about this, actually. Lehrer preparing Shabbat dinner was the kind of surprise he would have found enchanting back when he and Lehrer first got involved. But now it felt manufactured somehow, like Noam could see the gears turning behind the construction of this whole scene, the intention behind bringing out what Noam assumed was Lehrer's family's own candlesticks—as if to say, *You're my family now.* As if to say, *Remember what I lost.*

"No," Noam said, a few seconds too late. "No, it's . . . thank you. It's nice."

He sat down in his usual chair, Lehrer taking the one adjacent. They ate in silence for a few minutes, the clink of cutlery and an awkward curtain hanging between them—one Noam wasn't sure he wanted to draw aside. Only when he stole a glance up at Lehrer's face, Lehrer's brows were still knit together; a pang of something grotesquely like sympathy shot through Noam's blood.

"It's delicious," Noam said, a peace offering. "I still can't figure out how you had time to learn to cook on top of everything else you have to do."

"I've had quite a few years to hone my skills."

"Still. Any other hidden talents I ought to know about? Are you a secret concert pianist? Marathoner? An expert at whittling?"

Lehrer laughed at last, his gaze meeting Noam's over the candle flames. "I did devote twenty years or so to mastering the violin, actually. It was quite the passion for a while."

"Do you still play?"

"Not as much as I should. I didn't have nearly as much free time after I—" Lehrer broke off. It was the first time Noam had ever seen him look so caught off guard, like he'd forgotten what he was saying and who he was saying it *to*. But after a beat he continued, voice tighter than before: "Raising a young child was effortful."

That flicker of sympathy sputtered and died.

Noam picked up his knife and cut into his brisket again, but it was too late now; he'd lost his appetite. His mind kept circling over all the things Lehrer used to say about Dara. How Dara was difficult. Dara was *troubled*.

"Maybe you should have hired a nanny," Noam said at last.

Lehrer snorted. "I hired seven."

The tension slid into the background once more, muffled by Lehrer's charm and a quick change in conversation, Lehrer guiding them out of dangerous waters and onto safer ground. After, Lehrer stood at the sink doing the dishes, and Noam reached for the half-empty wine bottle, spinning it in semicircles atop the table.

"Can I have the rest of the cab?" he asked.

Lehrer frowned at him over his shoulder. "Of course. You know you don't have to ask with me."

"Right. Sorry." And that was true—Lehrer'd never blinked at offering Noam anything from wine to his most expensive scotch, even when Noam was still sixteen. It used to make Noam feel so *adult*, enough that when he went to Leo's bar and Leo wouldn't serve him, Noam had actually been taken aback.

Noam refilled Lehrer's own glass and took a sip of the wine. He barely tasted it.

"Do you have the phone?" Lehrer asked, and it took Noam a moment to realize what he meant.

The phone was in Noam's pocket. He hadn't kept it any farther away than that ever since he killed the Texan. He'd even slept with it under his pillow last night.

He drew the phone out now and set it on the kitchen table. Twenty-four hours, and he still hadn't tried to read it. The most he'd done was write a script to elbow his way past the antiwitching tech protecting the phone from his technopathy. It had taken the better part of the day, Noam typing away at code in class and as he sat on the bus on the way back from Dara's apartment. Now, the wards were down. He could tangle threads of his technopathy up in the phone's cell drive, but all that data was still a buzz of electricity and binary code, uninterpreted. Because Noam hadn't decided—

He hadn't decided how much to tell Lehrer. Lehrer had the antiwitching tech schematics already, of course—doctored very slightly from the version he'd given the Black Magnolia—but the Texan's phone connected to Texan servers. That was a whole new wealth of information; probably not as much as they'd like, but Noam had at least been able to access his messages and emails. He'd know everything the Texan knew.

And so would Lehrer. The moment Noam started parsing the data, Lehrer would sense it. He'd feel Noam's magic, and he'd expect an answer.

Lehrer dried his hands on the dish towel and moved back to the table, resuming his seat and steepling his fingers.

Noam stared down at the phone, its unassuming black casing, the dark screen.

"Do you need a flopcell?" Lehrer asked eventually.

"No."

"Then what's the delay?"

Noam looked up. One of Lehrer's long fingers tapped the backs of his own knuckles in rhythm with the tick of the second hand on his expensive wristwatch. Was that suspicion flickering in his eyes or just a reflection from the Shabbat candles?

"I'm thinking," Noam said.

He couldn't stall any longer. At last, Noam focused on the binary and translated it into information. In his peripheral vision he saw Lehrer lean back in his chair at that, apparently satisfied that Noam was finally doing something—and he didn't speak again, even though it took Noam the better part of twenty minutes to find what he was looking for.

The blood drained from his face so immediately that a flush of dizziness crested through Noam's mind, and he jerked his gaze up to meet Lehrer's. Lehrer sat forward, his expression gone sharp as his suit collar.

"What is it?"

Noam didn't know how to put it into words. How could he possibly—how could he look right at Lehrer's face and *say*—

"There was an email," he said, the words like chunks of ice in his mouth, cold and painful. "And I don't—maybe I misunderstood—no. I didn't misunderstand. And it sounds like . . ."

"Spit it out, Noam."

Noam sucked in a narrow breath. "Texas has been locking up witchings. In . . . facilities. For study."

*Just like in the catastrophe.*

Lehrer's face went blank—not neutral, but *blank*, as if he'd extinguished all emotion in that single moment, quenching it as efficiently as pouring a bucket of water over coals.

Somehow this—more than the knowledge that Lehrer had infected and killed his own people, more than the adrenaline that shot through Noam's veins sometimes when Lehrer drew too close—*this* terrified him most of all.

After a moment Lehrer pushed back his chair and stood, tugging the cuffs of his sleeves down so a careful quarter inch showed below the hem of his suit jacket.

"I should have expected this," he said, voice tight and bitter. "Bad enough that they exile their witchings to the quarantined zone—but of course. Of course. How else did they develop antiwitching technology, without witchings to test it on? How else was a vaccine developed? Those labs in the QZ had to get their funding somewhere. Foolish of me to think . . ."

He turned on his heel, pacing away from Noam—toward the kitchen window. He paused there with the fingertips of one hand perched on the sill, gazing down into the courtyard at . . . something.

Noam stayed in his chair, both hands gripping the underside of his seat. It was like everything in his chest was crumbling slowly, an ancient structure falling into dust.

"I'm sorry," he said after a moment. What else was there to say? He couldn't fix this. He couldn't even imagine what Lehrer felt. It was an incomprehensible evil.

Lehrer faced him, bracing both hands back against the window ledge. "No. I don't need you to be sorry. I need you to be *angry*. Last year you would have torn the world up at the roots for Atlantian justice." Lehrer's gaze was still and dangerous as shattered glass. "So now I need to know: Will you do the same on behalf of witchings?"

A year ago, Noam would have answered without hesitation. A year ago, he wanted nothing more than to make his anger into something caustic and violent: a tool he could use.

And maybe he was still willing to burn half the world down if it meant justice for all those people Lehrer killed. For his parents. For Dara.

But last year he let Lehrer wield Noam's anger as a weapon to seize power, and it was a mistake.

Was he so willing to make that mistake a second time?

*Lehrer's right,* a different voice murmured in the back of his mind. *Hating him doesn't make him wrong. Hating him doesn't make Texas right.*

If Noam did nothing, he was just as much a monster as Sacha had been.

"Yes," Noam said. "Always."

Lehrer pushed away from the window and drew close again, resting his fingertips atop the back of Noam's chair, close enough his knuckles grazed the line of Noam's shoulder blade.

Noam held his breath.

"Good," Lehrer said. "Then I'll tell you what we're going to do."

Winter in Texas was snowless, but this close to the coast, the wind that blew in off the Gulf chilled to the bone. Noam drew his military-issue jacket a little closer around his shoulders as the icy air rippled through his hair and sent the evacuation notices fluttering against every window, every wall.

"These are the best thing I've ever eaten," Bethany announced when she emerged from the little corner store, the screen door falling shut behind her. The sound of her voice seemed to echo down the empty street. Her cheeks were a little pink, but that was the only sign she noticed the cold at all.

"You said that about taquitos."

"That was before I had these." She kicked his ankle with the edge of her boot and held out the open bag. "Go on—try one."

Noam peered at the label. "Cheese straws? We have cheese straws in Carolinia."

"These are jalapeño flavored. It makes them ten times better. Trust me."

Noam took a handful, popping one into his mouth. It was crunchy, cheesy . . . and Bethany was right: the spiciness did make it better.

"I'm going out on the lines tomorrow," he said after he'd chewed, swallowed.

He felt Bethany's gaze like the point of a blade pressed against his cheek. When he turned to look at her, she tilted her chin up. The bloody light of the late sun deepened her hair from blonde to red. "Are you going to . . ."

"No," he said with a heavy exhale, and he wished he wasn't holding so many cheese straws; he fought the urge to knot his hands in fists. "No. Not yet. We should wait for orders."

"*We* give the orders out here, Noam."

Noam pushed another cheese straw into his mouth to buy time before answering. "I meant from Major General García." *Or Lehrer.* "Believe me. I'd love to end it all tomorrow, but—"

"Field Commander Álvaro, sir!"

Noam turned. A private stood at attention, hand drawn to his brow in a salute.

"What is it, Private?"

"There's a call for you and Field Officer Glennis in the officers' barracks from the First Battalion, Twenty-Third Regiment."

Noam and Bethany exchanged glances.

"Thank you," Bethany told the private, and she rolled up the bag of cheese straws and stuck it in her pocket as they headed back.

The combat outpost had been a school before it was their base. Not Noam's first choice. He tried to avert his gaze as they passed by the corkboards posted full of children's drawings and framed awards: *Science Olympiad, Mathletes, Battle of the Books.* The town had been evacuated bloodlessly, empty by the time their battalion got here.

Even so.

Lieutenant Colonel Harris was in the comms room when they got there, sipping black coffee—burnt, Noam could smell it from here—and scrolling through something on her holoreader. She had the privacy settings on so no one could see her screen; not that it made a difference, with Noam around.

"We need the room," Noam said.

She shot him a narrowed glare over the edge of her holoreader, looking very much like she was considering snapping back. Harris hadn't taken well to the idea of Level IV cadets being afforded tactical command over her unit. Which, yeah, if Noam had his way, he wouldn't be in charge either. He was seventeen. But Lehrer gave the order when he sent them out here to organize the push toward Houston. All Level IV cadets were provisionally promoted for the duration of wartime.

Noam swallowed back his urge to add *please.* The moment he pretended subservience, he'd never claim his authority back.

After a moment the lieutenant colonel sighed and flicked her holoreader off, tucking it into her back pocket and heading out through the side door.

Noam took her vacated seat and put the phone on speaker. "Hi, Ames."

"Hey yourself," Ames's voice said back, crackly—they were using satellite signal to avoid getting tapped in Texan wires. Noam nudged the signal a bit with technopathy, and her next words came out crisp and clear: "Just checking in to make sure y'all haven't gotten killed yet."

"Not yet," Noam said dryly, and when he looked toward Bethany, she rolled her eyes.

"Taye's here too," Ames said. "Taye, say hi."

Taye's voice piped up through the speaker. "Hello, hello. How's the east side?"

"Cold," Bethany said, drawing closer and perching on the edge of the table near the phone. "Uneventful. *Especially* uneventful."

"Yeah, well, we'll see how long that lasts," Taye said, and from the muffled way he said it, he probably had candy in his mouth.

"They have to let us fight," Bethany said, tilting closer to the microphone like she was worried she wouldn't be heard otherwise. "Otherwise, why send us? It's certainly not for our prodigious strategic ability. They obviously want us to use our magic."

"Rules of engagement with Texas are always *no magic till otherwise ordered*," Ames pointed out.

"Only we're the ones supposed to be *giving* said orders," Bethany said. "If we all agreed to use our powers, we could have the airport under Carolinian control overnight. We'd take Houston in two days."

"Sixty-four percent probability," Taye piped up. "If we were gamblers, we'd have the best odds in the house."

"This isn't a math problem," Noam said.

"Everything's a math problem."

"Oh yeah? And where did you pull those figures, out of your ass?"

"Actually," Taye said. "I calculated it from—"

"You know what?" Noam said. "I don't want to know. The point is right now they don't know which regiments have witchings and which don't. That's our ace up the sleeve. If we play it too soon, they'll fix us with antiwitching units, and we'll lose our upper hand."

"What upper hand?" Ames said, and this time if her voice sounded tight, it had nothing to do with radio signal. "We're sitting ducks, Álvaro. Don't you think it's *weird* that Lehrer didn't give you better instructions than this? He put you on the front lines. He put *all* of us on the front lines. Be pretty convenient if we died here, wouldn't it?"

"*Ames.*" Noam's gaze flicked left, toward Bethany. "Get yourself together."

"Really? That's what you're gonna say? Get myself to*geth*—"

"Are you implying the chancellor of Carolinia would wipe out an entire Level IV cohort for no good reason?" Noam leaned on the last three words and clenched his jaw, hoping to god Bethany and Taye just thought Ames was drunk again. Not thinking clearly. "Is that what Lehrer would find convenient?"

A long silence answered. For a second Noam almost thought Ames would break right here and now, spill all their secrets over this line.

But then—

"I wish they'd just tell us if we're supposed to be waiting on high command," Bethany said, pulling out the bag of cheese straws again and crunching into a fresh handful of them a little too aggressively.

"Noam, what *have* you heard from Lehrer?" Taye asked.

"Not much, to be fair," Noam said. "If I had to bet, I'd say he wants us to use magic. But I'd also say he wants us to wait on orders."

"Okay, but he could send those orders whenever he wants," Bethany said with her mouth full. "What's he waiting for? Don't you think there needs to be clearer communication? This is dumb. We don't know how to wage a *war*."

"Only we do," said Taye. "What do you think all those strategy classes with Swensson were for, exactly? When we graduate Level IV, we aren't gonna be lieutenant colonels barking orders for a single battalion. That's not how Level IV works, and y'all know it. We're gonna be expected to actually *make* these decisions. Graduation isn't all that far away, for any of us."

"Exactly! And you think we should attack!"

"No, I said sixty-four percent chance of success if we did. Probably. I mean, obviously there's a confidence interval there, so the probability could be as low as forty or high as seventy percent . . . sorry. Point is, I think we sit back. Wait for more data."

"Listen, I want to fuck Texans up as much as you do," Noam said, more to Bethany; he looked directly at her as she wiped the crumbs off her mouth with the back side of her wrist. "I get it. Okay? But we should save that move for when it'll make the biggest difference."

"Cutting off their air supply route *is* a big difference! They won't have food, they won't have medicine—"

"It won't matter if we can't hold the city," Noam pressed. "Right now their army's divided up trying to defend too many different points at once. They don't have enough antiwitching tech to cover all their bases. But if they bring in reinforcements, well. We might have an airport, but good luck getting Houston."

Bethany's knuckles were white where she gripped the edge of the table. "I don't think the rest of you get it," she said. "I'm a healer. I'm the one who has to fix all our soldiers when they come back full of bullets and shrapnel from some skirmish on the ground. And I—I can't. I can't keep doing this. I can't keep watching our people die when we're doing *nothing* to end this. Not if there's another choice."

"There is," Ames said bluntly on the other line. "We stop fucking around like a bunch of Level I idiots, and we take charge of the situation."

Bethany turned toward Noam, almost beseeching, and for one reeling moment Noam was reminded of Dara—

Only they looked nothing alike, *were* nothing alike. Unless he counted the fact they were both perpetually disappointed in him.

"We *will* use magic," Noam promised. "I think that's implicitly obvious by the fact we were sent here. But we . . ."

No. He couldn't bring himself to say *We can't move too soon*—because Bethany was right. Ames was right. Every second they delayed, they allowed more Carolinians to die. Carolinians it was their responsibility to protect.

He wanted so badly to say *fuck it* and throw it all away, throw out everything he'd ever learned about strategy and forget the Houston mission and just—

But Taye was right too. And although waiting might lose them soldiers, if they lost the war, it wasn't just Noam's unit who'd be dying.

"For now, we wait," he said, mouth twisting into a grim knot. "I'll call Minister García in the morning to confirm. There's no point in us all arguing about what decisions we're expected to make when we can ask high command. Is everyone good with that?"

Bethany's face was a sickly shade of pink, but she huffed out a breath and made a rough gesture with one hand, a gesture Noam took as consent.

"Well, good luck with that," Taye said. "I'm gonna sign off, get some sleep while I can."

"I'll touch base tomorrow with an update after I talk to García," Noam said and hung up with a twist of his technopathy.

Bethany slid off the table. She pulled her hair out of her ponytail, but it was only to put it back up again in the same style, an anxious tic.

"I'm going to check on my patients," Bethany said, meeting Noam's gaze. He couldn't tell if it was an accusation.

But he let her go, and as the door closed behind her, he dropped into the nearest chair and pressed the heels of his hands against his shut eyes.

Fucking Lehrer. Fucking—no, fucking *Adalwolf* Lehrer. Because this was his fault. Because he was the reason Calix Lehrer thought it was totally appropriate to let a bunch of teenage Level IV students run their own battalions and make independent tactical decisions without oversight from high command.

Because if it worked in the catastrophe, it should work against Texas, apparently.

"Goddamn it," Noam muttered against his own wrists, and sighed, and told himself *tomorrow*. Tomorrow, he'd talk to Defense Minister García and get this all figured out, if only so he could report back to the others and definitively say the choice was theirs. Tomorrow.

But he didn't get a chance to wait that long.

He woke with a start, his heart pounding out of his chest—and for a moment he thought he was somewhere else, half expected to turn and see Lehrer there—

But it was Bethany, both hands gripping Noam's arms and the whites of her eyes glinting in the dark. "Noam," she said, voice taut and thin. "Get up. You have to get up."

He shoved himself upright, Bethany releasing him only to tug open the drawers of his dresser and start tossing clothes onto the foot of his bed—uniform shirt, wool socks, jacket.

"What happened?" he asked, already pulling his T-shirt off over his head.

"Ames happened," she said, and it felt like a shot of adrenaline right in his heart. And he knew, he *knew*, even before she said, "She didn't want to wait, I guess. She went and used her magic on the Texan encampment in B3—redirected a bunch of water to destabilize the ground beneath them. Earthquake. Bad one. Not bad enough."

"Shit," Noam muttered, telekinesis finishing the buttons of his shirt as he pushed out of bed and grabbed his trousers. "What did Taye say?"

"They're in retreat," Bethany said. "Trying to get across the river. But . . ."

But they were fucked. There weren't enough choppers to pluck a whole battalion off the ground and fly them out to safety. They might get across the river, but it'd just be to sit and wait for Texan antiwitching units to sweep in and burn them all to ash.

"How long?"

"I don't know. We aren't picking anything up on radar, but that doesn't mean anything."

Not with Texan technology. Although Lehrer had been content to freeze Carolinia in the twenty-first century, for the most part, that nostalgia hadn't extended toward weapons tech. Noam'd had plenty of time to compare specs between their weapons and those of the Texans barricading the airport. Their abilities were well matched—which, of course; Lehrer would never put Carolinia at risk by letting her military's capabilities fall behind the rest of the world's.

But that didn't mean the antiwitching units hadn't figured out some kind of cloaking tech Carolinia didn't know about. And with no way to code his way past the antiwitching shields, Noam wouldn't sense the enemy troops coming until it was too late.

He followed Bethany out of the barracks and down the hall to the tactical room. Lieutenant Colonel Harris was there already, alongside Major Xia, who looked very well composed for a man who must've been woken up not long before Noam had been.

"I strongly advise inaction," Xia said before Noam could get a word out. "Third Battalion is already headed to First Battalion's aid. We should hold here. We cannot afford to lose the ground we've gained."

Noam glanced toward Lieutenant Colonel Harris, but the woman had no words to add. She gazed back with flat eyes and thin lips.

Fine.

"We aren't abandoning this ground," Noam said, tilting his chin up and looking back to Major Xia. "But we aren't letting Texas massacre *both* First and Third Battalions either."

And—this might be too far; this might be *exactly* one step too far. If so, Noam had to hope Calix Lehrer's name was powerful enough to get him out of a court martial.

He wrapped his technopathy up in the nearest comm device and forced it to send an encrypted message straight to Major General García; let no one accuse him of acting in secrecy, at least.

The message pinged out into the night. Noam took in a shallow breath, one that did very little to steady his nerves.

"We're moving on the airport," Noam said. "Tonight. And we'll do it using so much magic they'll sense it all the way back in Houston."

They approached openly, emerging from the woods to the south of the airfield to move across the wide close-cropped grass bracketing the runways. The barbed wire fence surrounding the property was meant to keep out delinquents and wildlife; it was no match for Carolinian tanks. It crumpled like jewelry wire under their tracks.

The Texans retaliated fast—they had their soldiers in some kind of loose formation by the time Noam's boots hit tarmac, tanks rolling out from hangars and turning their turrets toward Noam's battalion.

Noam's blood felt like it was buzzing in his veins, his breath coming shallow and fast and this—

It was nothing like what Noam had experienced before.

Noam had trained in close quarters—fighting to stay one step ahead sparring with Lehrer, mock skirmishes drawn up in tactics class and acted out on constructed sets, Noam and Lehrer slipping through the close-grown trees of the quarantined zone in pursuit of a target. This wasn't a riot turned violent, tear gas and ballistic shields and the constant threat of police weapons.

The sky felt too big, splayed out overhead like a black sea. They were open on all sides, visible at all angles, and even if riots and QZ missions held the threat of death, they'd been nothing like *this*.

Texans up in the air traffic control towers froze their aerodrome beacons so the white light glared down in their faces. Noam squinted against the sudden glow of pain behind his eyes—and if he hadn't been ready for it, hadn't been waiting, the brightness might have been enough to distract him from the charge as it ignited in the chamber, the swelling heat and pressure against the metal body of the first projectile.

Noam flung his magic out and *pushed.*

It wasn't delicate. It was magnetism, a great humming pulse that jammed the round in its chamber and bent the fiercely strong ferromagnetic buckypaper that constructed their tanks.

*So that's why I couldn't detect anything on radar,* Noam thought grimly. The carbon nanotubes that made up the buckypaper were highly electrically conductive; they could block microwave electromagnetic interference. Their planes were probably made of the same shit—pretty damn effective for keeping Noam's technopathy off their computers and electrical equipment.

But the magnetism Noam had thrown against it was far more powerful than radar. All that advanced technology buckled and caved like paper crushed in a fist.

"Holy shit," Noam heard someone mutter behind him, and any other day he might've found the time to be flattered.

Tonight, all he could think about was how silent Texan planes would be when they dipped down to spill their antiwitching soldiers across the grass.

*Think about Ames,* he told himself, extending his magic again to tear guns from their owners' hands, knotting rifles up like ribbons. *Think about Taye.*

He *wanted* those antiwitching soldiers here. Because if Texas thought this was it—if they thought Carolinia was finally making its move, exposing the witchings among its units—well. They only had so many antiwitching soldiers. They couldn't send them all. Texas would have to send a battalion to deal with Ames and Taye, a battalion for Noam and Bethany. Then they'd want to hold the rest in reserve, defending Houston and Dallas and San Antonio, dancing in anxious anticipation of Lehrer's next move.

It was a gambit. But Noam didn't have another choice.

Not one that left Ames and Taye alive.

Behind him the sergeants shouted orders to their units; rounds of tank fire blasted out from the front Carolinian lines. Then they stood there and watched the Texan lines bloom with smoke and asphalt and shrapnel.

Noam should tell them to hold fire. They should march in and take the Texans prisoner. They were defenseless; it was . . . was capturing enemy troops any worse than slaughtering civilians?

Only if they did that, they'd all be sitting ducks when the antiwitching reinforcements came in. Their hostages would become weapons used against them.

So he stayed where he was, feet grown roots into the tarmac, and watched his soldiers kill thousands of unarmed Texans.

Was this how Lehrer felt? During the catastrophe, when he ordered the massacre of DC, all those dirty bombs injecting virus into the air and dirt. The wreckage he'd left in his wake, Lehrer's power pulling skyscrapers down to their knees until nothing and no one was left.

The decision felt like a steel shell closing round his heart. And then he felt nothing at all.

"Secure the infrastructure," Noam ordered once the dust had cleared.

They marched forward down the runway, picking their way through smoldering metal and bloody bodies. Some were still alive, trembling hands waving like poppies in a red field.

Later, once they'd swept the area for survivors and placed their own soldiers in all the buildings and towers, Noam found Bethany vomiting right outside the largest aircraft hangar. She wiped her mouth and lifted her head when he approached, her cheeks a mottled pink.

"Sorry," she said.

"Don't be sorry."

"It was the right thing to do," Bethany said, in the kind of firm tone that made Noam think she was trying to convince herself as much as him. "For Ames and Taye and their battalions. But for the war too."

Noam didn't say anything. He couldn't open his mouth. He felt certain if he did, he'd spill his stomach on the ground next to hers.

Bethany's hand caught his, her slim fingers lacing together with Noam's. She squeezed. "We're Level IV," she said. "That includes Ames and Taye. Like it or not . . . like it or not, we're too valuable to die here." She inhaled, as if steeling herself, and said: "Lehrer would have wanted you to do whatever it took to save them. You did the right thing."

And she was right. Of course she was. In Lehrer's perverse utilitarian calculus, a single Level IV cadet was worth four battalions of baseline soldiers.

Maybe more.

Noam wished he could promise her—promise himself—that he was still as good a person as Dara had always thought he was. Wished he could believe he'd ever truly been good.

"I don't know if it was right," Noam managed to say at last. He glanced toward her, then out again toward the sky—what he could see of it, anyway, past the light pollution of those aerodromes. "When those antiwitching units get here, we might not be able to fend them off. We won't have our magic. What if I . . ."

*What if I just damned us all?*

"You didn't," Bethany insisted, and she gripped his hand still harder, until the tips of Noam's fingers went numb. "Listen—*look* at me, Noam."

He looked.

"You didn't," she said again. "These are good soldiers. They'll do their job. This is what they trained for—it doesn't matter to them if those men have antiwitching armor. They can still get shot."

Noam made himself exhale slowly, and after a moment, he squeezed her hand back.

"We need a plan," he said. "Better than just waiting here. We need a plan."

"Okay," Bethany said. "Then let's make a plan."

The antiwitching units arrived two hours before dawn.

They swept down from the skies as silently as Noam had predicted, black birds that almost blended into the starless sky. Noam waited with one of his units in a dark hangar, staring out into the night with his pulse pounding in his throat.

Right now he wished he had Bethany back with him, there to whisper *it'll be all right*—but she was deeper in the building, sequestered away where she could focus on healing as many of their soldiers as she could. Noam only had these strangers. Strangers who watched him with glowing eyes, marking his every motion, every breath, looking for fear.

Noam *was* afraid. Noam was terrified.

But he kept his body steady, his expression set to neutrality. He kept thinking, *What would Lehrer do?* A horrible thing to think, a repulsive standard to aspire to, but at least Lehrer would've known what came next.

Noam had cut the power to the airport and to as much of the surroundings as he could reach. That was one thing he'd learned from reading the Texan antiwitching schematics, at least. They relied on electricity. If they couldn't charge up, eventually they'd run out of juice.

It was a dumb hope. Noam's battalion might not last long enough for it to make a difference. But at least it was something.

"Air defense systems," Noam murmured, not audible to anyone but himself. No one needed him to give orders now. They knew what to do.

Clusters of soldiers broke off from a far structure—unoccupied, in case the aircraft returned fire. Even from here Noam could make out the cylindrical missiles perched on their shoulders. He sensed their internal computerized mechanics: the command line-of-sight system that let the operator identify a target, the laser data link that would ensure the missile achieved its goal.

Missiles like that were notoriously difficult to operate. They'd even talked about it in Level IV, during Weber's tactics class—debated the relative utility of using less advanced systems in lieu of expending time and power training specialized forces to work the command line-of-sight. Half the soldiers carrying these systems on their shoulders right now weren't trained.

But they didn't need to be.

Noam's technopathy tangled up in those too-advanced systems, and he shut his eyes, focusing his attention down to nothing but data.

Aim.

Fire.

The percussive bursts of rocket fire followed a brief and rapid rhythm. Noam felt them make contact with aircraft not because his magic had breached the planes' antiwitching shields but because he felt the missiles themselves collide with something hard and solid, felt them blossom in fire and heat.

He opened his eyes.

The sky was aflame, rose-gold light flourishing against a dark field.

But that wasn't the end. Of course it wasn't.

Four planes made it to the ground, and although Noam's unit was able to take out some of the soldiers parachuting down from the damaged carriers, they couldn't get them all.

"Defend the structure," Noam repeated his own orders to himself. "Let them siege. Wait for reinforcements."

His soldiers fell into formation at the entrance to the hangar, and Noam sensed all the other units doing the same. Then the peppery rhythm of machine gun fire. From all sides—the antiwitching soldiers would have to split their efforts even more than they had already, would make themselves easy to pick off.

Noam hoped.

"Sir." Lieutenant Colonel Harris appeared at his elbow, her own gun in hand—although hopefully she wouldn't have to use it. "You need to get to a more defensible position."

Right. She was right. No matter how much every fiber of Noam screamed to stay in place, do his part to protect the soldiers he was responsible for, ultimately he was more useful applying his technopathy to their own side's weaponry and making sure the power grid stayed down. Couldn't do that if he got shot.

He nodded, once, and turned to head deeper in the aircraft hangar, under the shadowy wings of a dark-windowed Texan jet. The sound of gunfire retreated until the uneven gasps of his own breath were louder—and there, hidden behind forty-five tons of steel and fiberglass, Noam let himself tip forward and press his brow against the cold wall. He clenched his eyes shut and focused on his heartbeat, trying to slow the frantic patter of his pulse against his ribs.

*Calm down. You have to be in control.*

If he wasn't in control, all those people would die. And it would be all his fault.

*Pull it together, Álvaro.*

He pushed off the wall and headed toward the back stairs, taking them two at a time up to the third floor. He found a spot by a window in someone's abandoned office where he could see the battle playing out down on the ground and reached out with his power again—this time for the comms, repeating the message he'd been sending out since they came up with this fucking plan: *Urgent reinforcements needed at Houston airport; antiwitching units on the ground.*

Nobody answered. Not that he could sense.

That was the part he didn't dare tell the lieutenant colonel or the major—or even Bethany.

*What if we're alone out here?*

He couldn't watch the bloodshed. Couldn't watch his own people getting gunned down, see the way their bodies contorted when the bullets hit them, reeling back and then slumping to the ground. He turned his gaze toward the antiwitching planes instead, half planning to see if there was any way he could use magic on something *adjacent* to them to strand the soldiers on the ground, only—

Only there were more people coming out of the final plane. And although they were escorted by soldiers in that shimmering, iridescent armor . . . they weren't wearing it themselves.

"*Shit!*"

Noam lurched to his feet, but he didn't get a chance to run down-stairs, didn't even get a chance to send off a comm to the lieutenant colonel or the major.

One of those unarmored men lifted a hand, then brought it down in a heavy swoop.

The aircraft hangar began to cave in on itself, dust and plaster rain-ing down on Noam's hair a split second before he managed to shift his focus up and grasp the building with telekinesis.

And—fuck, god*damn* it, this building was heavy. Noam gritted his teeth against the effort of it.

He should—he couldn't hold this, he couldn't, he had to—*put* it somewhere. Only there were people here, people *in here*; he couldn't expose them to gunfire—

Even the floor under Noam's feet was unsteady as he staggered out of the room and toward the stairs. The whole building swayed like the deck of a ship, the metal grip on the stairs slippery and uneven under-foot as Noam made his way down. He almost reached for the handrail, but—no, that'd be worse. He'd probably tip over the side and fall, fall, fall . . .

He made it to the ground floor with sweat beading his brow. Half his magic was still tied up maintaining the Faraday shield on his mind; he barely—he could barely keep this building up, barely keep one men-tal finger on the Texan witchings' abilities in case they tried something new. Which of course they would.

"Noam!" Bethany ran toward him, white faced with blood on her neck. Someone else's, Noam assumed.

"Get people out of here," he managed through gritted teeth. "*Out.* I can't—I can't hold it. Watch them. Witchings. They'll try—"

He couldn't. Couldn't talk. Even breathing felt strenuous.

To her credit, Bethany didn't question him. She just wet her lips before she spun on her heel and dashed toward the lieutenant colonel and the front lines.

Noam's legs were shaking, little waves of dizziness cresting through his head. He gave up standing and dropped to his knees there on the floor, pressing both palms against the cold concrete and sucking in a narrow breath. He vaguely sensed Bethany's magic, pale pink and fiery, flashing out in reaction to something one of the Texan witchings did.

*Texan witchings.* Two words Noam never thought he'd think in a sentence together, but there was no mistaking it: they were . . .

Internment hospitals. Right. These weren't Texan soldiers; they were—they were *research subjects.* They were incarcerated just like Lehrer had been during the catastrophe.

Bile rocked up in Noam's throat, and he swallowed against it; if he vomited now, he'd lose focus and kill them all.

Fuck it. Lehrer wasn't here. Fuck it—

Noam released the Faraday shield around his mind.

Magic flooded his system, a wash of energy like cool water dousing him from overhead. The building stabilized—at least for now—as Noam pushed himself up again, dragging a shaky hand over his sweaty brow.

He had to get out. Before the building collapsed. Before those anti-witching soldiers—and their witchings—moved in on whatever was left of the hangar. Noam couldn't fight them, after all, not with that armor.

He should retreat with the rest of his unit.

A lot of *should*s. Noam'd never been much for those.

He went forward instead, through the glittering dust that still rained down from the fractured ceiling, toward the glowing white lights of the aerodromes. Toward the Texan soldiers and their prisoners.

Toward Texan witchings.

# Chapter Twenty-Two

## Noam

Noam sensed the last of his soldiers escape the crumbling building, the metal of their guns fleeing out a back door. He waited for them to get clear before he let go.

The hangar collapsed, a slow but immediate implosion, like an island caving into the sea. Noam didn't look back. He didn't need to; he *felt* it happen, the steel skeleton of the building crumpling like scrap paper and tugging on his magnetism like an electrical circuit. But he couldn't focus on that—because ahead, beyond the plume of dust and smoke, he also sensed the sizzle of strangers' magic.

And they'd sense him too.

Noam tasted his own fear in his mouth, hot and ferrous. It coiled down his spine like a snake: venomous.

Fear was as much a weapon as anger.

Noam acted first. He threw his magic out, tight and constricting as a web, sparking with as many volts of electricity as he could muster. Better to end this quickly, kill them before they could figure out a strategy.

Only, shit, at least a few of them managed to deflect the net—he felt their magic sizzling against his, an opposing magnetic pole that sent light striking up toward the dim sky. Noam's palms were damp already. But there was no time for that, no time to submit to the adrenaline searing through his veins.

The witchings retaliated almost instantly. All of them. A storm of magic, crackling with too much—*everything*. Fire, electricity, the threat of imminent pain. And—*shit*—Noam deflected the flurry of bullets just in time. It *hurt*, it physically hurt, extending his magic like this: blocking the witchings' attack, evading the bullets. He didn't even . . . god, he didn't even have an automatic weapon, only his service pistol.

He drew that anyway, flicking off the safety and reaching out with his power to sense—

He couldn't sense them. Of course. Antiwitching armor.

Noam's magic lashed out again, and he used the cover to step out from the smoke wreathing the collapsed hangar.

Four of them. Four witchings, *twelve* antiwitching soldiers . . . shit, *shit*.

Noam aimed his gun at them anyway and fired, over and over; he hit one in the neck, and the soldier in that armor collapsed like a broken doll. He squinted against the white flares of light as they held down the triggers on their machine guns, Noam's electromagnetic shield the only thing keeping those bullets from tearing into him like he was made of paper.

He couldn't shoot them all. He was gonna run out of bullets. He couldn't use his magic against that antiwitching armor, either; he had to—fuck, he had to be smarter.

Okay.

*Focus.*

It was taking almost all his focus fighting those damn witchings.

One of the witchings had their own electromagnetic shield up now, defending the antiwitching soldiers from Noam's bullets. Question was, which one?

Violet-colored magic—okay, trace it back to the source. *There.*

That one. Blond hair.

Noam redirected his magical attacks, using whatever he could spare from his defenses to assault that one witching. The others noticed, of course, and so he had to contend with *their* efforts to protect blond guy—

A shot of lightning zipped past him, uncomfortably close. Shit. He couldn't drop his guard.

Just. *Kill the blond guy.*

Noam threw as much power as he could behind the attack, yelling with the effort of it. It felt like magic was barbed wire ripping through his veins. Like it would tear him open and he'd bleed out here on this field, like he'd burn himself to cinder—

Fuck it.

He started running full tilt across the tarmac. He got the chance to see the blond guy's eyes widen a split second before Noam collided with him, and they both toppled to the hard ground.

He was inside their shield now, could have shot his own gun at the antiwitching soldiers if he wasn't so busy deflecting their bullets. Noam slammed his elbow against the blond guy's throat—it was bright, so bright, the night lit up with the pop-pop of automatic gunfire as the soldiers emptied their magazines on Noam.

He had the Texan witching gripped between his knees, the man's fingers pressing hard into Noam's thighs as he tried to fight him off with superstrength.

"Just *die* already," Noam growled and thrust forward with as much strength as he could muster.

The witching's skull crushed under the weight of Noam's hand. His blood sprayed out like paint. His insides splattered Noam's face. They tasted like red meat.

Some distant part of Noam was aware enough to know he should be horrified. But there was no time for that.

He swept out another wave of magic. And this time, his bullets found their targets, slipping into the vulnerable cracks between armor to bury deep in living flesh, the antiwitching soldiers dropping around Noam like puppets with their strings cut.

Noam couldn't move. He was frozen amid the carnage, gore dripping off his face and smearing his hands. Distant gunfire rounded off. Someone's magic tore a plane from the sky, and it crashed into the dirt, black smoke pluming toward heaven.

*I killed them.*

*I killed them all.*

His legs gave out, and he collapsed forward, pressing his brow against the hot tarmac. When Noam's eyes slid shut, all he could see was Dara. They were in the Level IV common room. Dara was curled up on the sofa, his bare feet tucked between the cushions and a book held against his knees. He was reading Tolstoy.

*I love Tolstoy,* Noam wanted to tell him.

Say it. He should say it.

*Have you read this one before? We can talk about it if you want.*

He'd been too afraid. Nervous Dara would fix him with that derisive glare and say something snide and dismissive that would make Noam want to vanish into the cracks between the floorboards.

He should have said something.

Why had he waited so long to say something?

A terrible wind ripped through Noam's hair and caught the back of his uniform shirt, whipping it against his spine. Another helicopter. Texan reinforcements.

*Get up.*

Noam didn't move.

*Get up. You'll die here.*

Noam stayed where he was. He breathed in the scent of smoke and death.

Gravel crunched under the weight of boots on the ground. Noam stayed where he was, his eyes shut, trying to remember Dara's face. The way Dara had looked up, just then, and met Noam's gaze across the common room, and the corner of his mouth lifted like he knew a secret Noam didn't.

"Álvaro!"

They knew his name. How did they know his name?

"Álvaro," the voice said again, and then a hand pressed against the nape of his neck and turned him over onto his back, the aerodrome lights careening overhead. Then a face slid into focus.

Major General García crouched over him, her hair tangling up in the helicopter wind. She had two fingers pressed to his neck like she was checking for a pulse.

"Oh," Noam said. His voice sounded like it came from very far away. "Hi."

"Are you hurt?"

Noam thought about it for a moment. "No. It's not my blood."

García's brows raised. "I can see that. Come on—let's get you up."

She curved an arm under his back and helped hoist him to his feet. It was only once Noam was standing, gazing back toward the destroyed hangar and all the wreckage he'd left in his wake, that he realized . . .

"Did we win?"

"You demolished them," she said, and her hand lingered on his nape a beat longer before falling away. "Come on. Time to go."

Noam was still staring at the smoke, his eyes watering with the heat of it. "Go where?"

"You've been called back to Dallas. The chancellor wants to see you."

*From an interview originally published in* Ariel, *a popular magazine in* Texas.

**Ariel:** Dr. Rathbone, you spent six years living in Durham, Carolinia, and studying at Carolinia National University. Can you tell us a little bit about how this was possible, given that you aren't a Carolinian citizen?

**Rathbone:** You're quite right: I'm not Carolinian. I was born in York, actually, and lived there most of my life. I studied biology at Cornell University—but what I was really interested in was genetics. Say what you will about Carolinia being stuck in the past; they have some of the best genetics researchers on this planet. When I was offered a fully funded PhD fellowship at Carolinia National University, I would have been a fool to turn it down. But . . . you're right. I was the only person in my program who wasn't a born Carolinian citizen.

**Ariel:** That must have been quite the culture shock.

**Rathbone:** It was. Not just the fact that I had to get used to using the kind of technology that was popular when my grandparents were university aged. Carolinians have a very peculiar political consciousness. Compared to York and Texas, they have relatively European social policies: single-payer health care, guaranteed housing, free higher education, a livable minimum wage, prolonged parental leave. And they're very much on par with the rest of the world when it comes to their progressive pro-LGBTQ attitudes, gender equality, and—forgive me, but I have to agree with them when it comes to witching rights. They are the only country in the world right now where it is safe to be a powerful witching.

**Ariel:** I'm sensing a *but* there.

**Rathbone:** *But* . . . well, I think we can all agree their immigration policy leaves something to be desired. It's all well and good providing affordable housing for Carolinian citizens, but there were neighborhoods you didn't go to at night. Atlantian refugees were left to cobble together shared housing in tenements and slums, with no government health care, no education . . . even the strictest quarantine laws in the world can't stop magic from spreading once it's taken root in one of the refugee communities. And of course that only created more xenophobia, more violence.

**Ariel:** We've all heard rumors, too, of the ironclad strength of the Carolinian propaganda machine.

**Rathbone:** Ah, yes. Well. All you have to do is look at historical records to uncover the truth. In Carolinia, children are taught that Calix and Adalwolf Lehrer almost single-handedly destroyed the former United States with the efforts of their Avenging Angels. However, outside of Carolinia, it is common knowledge that—although the Avenging Angels were responsible for the establishment of the nation of Carolinia and the destruction of Washington, DC—there were multiple revolutionary organizations working in concert to help bring down the United States.

**Ariel:** How aware, would you say, is the average Carolinian about how the present nations of North America were formed?

**Rathbone:** Reasonably aware, but with some caveats. It is widely known in Carolinia that the nations as they exist today were formed from the only land remaining on the continent that had not yet been infected with magic. What is less known, of course, is that in the early days after the US government fell, Calix Lehrer and the early Carolinian government detonated a number of biological weapons containing the magic virus throughout the continent. We could have had Chicago, Toronto, a great deal of California . . . instead, Lehrer infected as much of the continent with magic as he possibly could.

**Ariel:** Why did he stop? Why not infect the entire continent—the entire world?

**Rathbone:** It was a political ploy. He had the means to infect the entire planet. But Lehrer stopped the bombings as soon as he was granted the full extent of the demands he made from the rest of the world during the establishment of Carolinia. It would be one thing if Lehrer had died at a normal old age and been succeeded by someone else. But with Lehrer still alive, holding power in Carolinia, that same threat has sustained Carolinia into the modern day. No nation dares undermine Carolinian autonomy. It's why we have relatively open trade with the Carolinians despite limited diplomacy and sustained Carolinian isolationism. Lehrer has already established what he is capable of, how far he's willing to go to get what he wants. He only needed to make an example of us once. Now the world will never forget.

That is Calix Lehrer's legacy.

# CHAPTER TWENTY-THREE

## NOAM

A car waited on the tarmac when they landed in Dallas, black with tinted windows.

"I need to return to base," Major General García told Noam before he disembarked, leaning with one elbow braced against a seat back and her hand curled in a loose fist. "That car will take you to the hotel."

"Okay," Noam said, but she still didn't move—kept her arm where it was, blocking the aisle.

"Listen," she said after a moment, tone softening, and all at once Noam felt like he'd swallowed ice, because he'd never heard García use that tone. Not ever. "What happened in Houston . . . you did the right thing."

Those words curdled in Noam's gut like sour milk.

"Oh," he said awkwardly. "Thanks."

A small smile tugged at one corner of her lips, and after a beat she reached out and squeezed his upper arm. "We'll talk more, later. When we're both safely back in Carolinia."

She let him go, then, down the gangway and across the airfield toward the waiting car. For a moment, sitting there in the back seat with the doors shut and fresh air-conditioning blowing through his hair, Noam wondered if he was supposed to say something, tell the AI their destination maybe. But then, slowly, they rolled forward, and the front console navigation display switched to show a map into the city center.

Noam leaned back against the black leather seat and shut his eyes.

He must have been more tired than he thought; he dozed off somewhere between the airport and Dallas's downtown, lurching awake only when the car rolled to a stop outside the Wilshire Hotel.

And the Wilshire Hotel was . . . well, it was a goddamn *hotel* all right. The façade was all limestone and tall windows, and when Noam stepped through the old-fashioned swinging doors into the lobby, he felt like this whole damn place was designed to make it obvious people like Noam Álvaro didn't belong here.

So he took his time crossing that marble floor, trailing dust and dirt and soot in his wake.

The man at the front desk eyed him dubiously as he approached. It was only after he was in speaking distance that the man's gaze fixed on the surname patch on Noam's uniform.

"Mr. Álvaro," he said, with a lilted note of surprise. "We weren't expecting you so . . ."

"So dirty?"

"So *soon*," the man revised. "You're in room 904. And—Chancellor Lehrer wanted me to inform you he expects your presence as soon as you arrive. Suite 1200."

Of course he did.

"Thank you," Noam said, and he followed the man's directions toward the bank of elevators that stood past the desk on the other side of the lobby.

As soon as the golden elevator doors slid shut behind him, Noam exhaled a heavy breath. What would Lehrer do if Noam just . . . didn't show up? If he went to his own room and crawled in bed and refused to emerge for three days?

Only that was a dumb question. Lehrer would use electromagnetism to open the door and come in and drag him out. And he wouldn't be angry. Just *disappointed*.

Noam punched the button for floor 12.

Lehrer's was the only door on that floor, because of course it was. Noam knocked.

The sound of footsteps on a tile floor, and the door swung open.

Lehrer was in civilian clothes, shirtsleeves rolled up to the elbows and his collar undone. His gaze slid down the length of Noam's body, taking in the disheveled uniform and blood-smeared face, but he stepped aside to let Noam in all the same.

The penthouse was . . . massive, like the ground floor of someone's fancy house, all gleaming mahogany furniture and fresh flowers in crystal vases, the floor-to-ceiling windows providing a clear view of downtown Dallas. Noam didn't bother pretending not to stare; he twisted his head to take it all in, from the perfectly carved wall molding to the chandelier hanging from the ceiling.

"I told them I wanted a single room," Lehrer commented; Noam glanced back as Lehrer shut the door by hand, a dry smile twisting his lips. "Nevertheless, they insisted."

"It's very . . ."

"Ostentatious?"

"I was gonna say obnoxious."

Lehrer snorted and stepped farther into the suite, Noam frozen in place as he drew closer. Lehrer's fingers pressed into Noam's cheek, thumb curving under his jaw, and Lehrer tilted Noam's face toward the right.

Could he tell how Noam's breath went cold in his lungs? How Noam's skin felt too hot under Lehrer's touch?

He'd drawn his Faraday shield back up on the plane—but he'd been exhausted, drained. What if it wasn't enough?

"I wish you would've cleaned this," Lehrer said, and one finger slid up to graze Noam's cheekbone.

Noam sucked in a sharp gasp, a spark of pain flaring when Lehrer bore down. For one reeling moment he thought that was *Lehrer*—some sadistic punishment for walking in here covered in dust and mud—but when Lehrer drew his hand away, there was blood on his fingertips. Not the Texan's blood, presumably.

"Oh," Noam said, lifting his hand now to touch the laceration on his cheek. The flesh around it was bruised, throbbing. "I didn't even notice."

Lehrer wiped his hand on a nearby tablecloth, even though he could have evanesced the blood just as easily. "Do you want me to heal it?"

Once upon a time, Noam would have said no. *Had* said no, wanting to preserve bruises as trophies of war. Now he just thought about the people he'd killed.

About the bruises on Dara's thighs, the ones Noam had kissed.

"Yes," he said.

Lehrer reached for him again, but this time his grasp was firm and intentional; a shudder ran through Noam as he felt Lehrer's magic stitch through his torn flesh, doing the arcane work of regenerating cells and summoning lymphocytes to consume any early infection. When his fingers skimmed Noam's cheek again, this time it was painless and smooth.

But Lehrer didn't let go. Instead he curved that hand back around the nape of Noam's neck and tugged him closer, leaning down to press a kiss to Noam's lips.

Noam kissed him back, told himself it was just to maintain the illusion of interest—that there wasn't some part of him that still grew warm thinking how easy it would be to skim his touch down from Lehrer's waist to his narrow hips.

Noam was still trying to come up with a fresh excuse to stay out of Lehrer's bed when Lehrer drew back. He brushed his thumb over Noam's lower lip, that quartz gaze still fixed on Noam's mouth.

"Go clean yourself up. You reek of death."

Lehrer released him, moving away instead of closer—toward the bar cart, picking up a glittering decanter of scotch.

Noam's heart was still a trapped animal hurling itself against his rib cage. He made himself inhale, one hand—his right hand, the one Lehrer couldn't see—clenching in a fist.

"I don't have any other clothes," Noam said.

Lehrer turned toward him again, lifting that dram of whisky to his lips. He took a small sip, swallowed, then said: "I'll have some delivered. They'll be here long before we have to leave for dinner."

Noam blinked. "Dinner?"

"Yes. With the Texan president and his wife and some of their cabinet members." Lehrer lowered the scotch glass to hip level, finger tapping against its rim. "I've already told them you'll be attending, in your official capacity as Atlantian representative."

Noam didn't want to go to dinner. How the hell was he supposed to sit there and look right at the leaders of this godforsaken country and pretend he hadn't killed thousands of their soldiers just this morning?

He swallowed around something hot and leaden in his throat. "I can't. I'm not a diplomat."

Lehrer waved a dismissive hand. "Don't worry—I'll do all the talking. You're just there as window dressing." He arched a brow. "I want you to be able to make an easy escape. The dinner is hosted in the presidential residence; all their tech is protected by antiwitching technology. Find a computer—any computer—and program us a back door past their firewall."

Okay, well at least *that* was something Noam could do. He gave Lehrer a half smile. "All right. Consider it done."

Because, yeah, maybe Texas was siding with the Black Magnolia, but that didn't make them not a country led by antiwitching genocidal tyrants. If Lehrer managed to take Texas down before the resistance killed him, so much the better.

The en suite bathroom was as elaborate as the rest of the penthouse. Noam shed his ruined uniform and climbed into Lehrer's massive glass-walled shower, letting out a soft sigh as the hot water pounded down on his back and sluiced away all those layers of grime and blood. The water ran brown as it swirled round the drain, and Noam shut his eyes, scrubbing both hands over his healed face.

Only all he could see then was those lines of unarmed Texan soldiers falling like cut flowers as Noam's unit gunned them down.

His eyes flew open, and he tipped forward, pressing his brow against the wet glass as he sucked in a series of ragged breaths.

*It's okay. You're okay. Everything's okay.*

Repeating the litany didn't make it any less untrue.

How the—how the hell did Lehrer do it? Shut off his conscience and just . . . *do what had to be done?*

The shower steam was suddenly oppressive, dizzying as a sauna. Noam grabbed a washcloth and scrubbed off as efficiently as he could, rubbing a round of shampoo into his hair and rinsing off the suds. The nausea abated only when Noam pushed open the shower door and stepped out onto the plush white bathmat.

Lehrer was on the phone when Noam emerged from the bathroom, towel wrapped tight round his waist. Lehrer glanced over at him, mid-sentence talking about tariffs, and pointed left.

Noam followed his direction, padding through the formal sitting room and through a set of heavy wooden doors into what must be Lehrer's bedroom.

Lehrer—or someone else—had already unpacked his suitcases, all Lehrer's suits hung on neat hangers from the rack of his walk-in closet. Noam flipped past his military uniform and a series of tailored jackets to find a plain T-shirt and a pair of flannel bottoms. He had to roll the waist of those three times over to keep the hems from dragging on the floor, but it was a far sight better than lounging around Lehrer's room in a goddamn towel.

Lehrer was still talking when Noam emerged, pacing back and forth through the main living area and far more absorbed in that conversation than in Noam. Even so, when Noam made for the door, Lehrer broke conversation to say, "No, stay here."

Noam paused, arching a brow. Lehrer gazed back unblinkingly, and of course, Noam broke first. He dropped down onto one end of an antique-looking sofa and propped his bare feet up on the opposite armrest. He shot off a few texts to Bethany, Ames, and Taye via technopathy, but only Bethany replied immediately:

Everything's under control here, don't worry. All the Level IV students are being recalled to Carolinia until the peace talks are over.

Peace talks?

Noam looked toward Lehrer again, but Lehrer was at the bar cart pouring a fresh drink and didn't notice.

They're having peace talks? he sent back.

Guess so, Bethany responded. Who knows, maybe something'll actually come of it this time.

Something had come of it last time. Carolinia had refused to sign the treaty, refused to decimate its witching population, and had closed its borders. That was what passed for peaceful resolution when dealing with Texas.

Only . . .

*Peace talks.* Did that mean—

Lehrer hadn't said a word about Noam's performance at the airport. Did Lehrer consider that success or failure?

What if the only reason they were in peace talks at all was because Noam had failed to hold back his battalion—because they never took Houston?

"Feeling better?" Lehrer said, skimming long fingers through Noam's damp hair.

Noam hadn't even noticed he was off the phone.

"Yes." Noam tilted his head back to look at him, but Lehrer was already crossing round the sofa; he nudged Noam's legs aside and took the other cushion, settling himself in with one arm slung over the seat back.

"What are you thinking about?"

Noam put his feet back down on the floor, curling his toes in the thick rug. "Bethany said we're in peace talks with Texas."

"We are," Lehrer confirmed. But he didn't look angry. In fact, he *smiled*, hand dropping to Noam's shoulder to trace little circles on the knob of his collarbone. "You did very well out there. I'm pleased."

Noam's gaze snapped up to meet Lehrer's.

Lehrer laughed softly. "You ought to trust yourself more. When your classmate made a poor decision, you reacted swiftly and decisively. You saved two Level IV students from certain death. You secured the Houston airport. And with that, we almost don't need the city itself— they have no more supply chain. They're effectively besieged."

"We're winning," Noam said, the relief like cool water plunging into his veins.

"We're winning," Lehrer said. That hand on Noam's shoulder trailed down his arm; Lehrer laced their fingers together on the seat between them. "Thanks to you."

Noam had always loved the way Lehrer's eyes crinkled at the corners when he smiled. But he also knew, now, how easily that gaze went cold.

Noam wet his lips, his hand tightening around Lehrer's. "You never sent orders," he said. "I—we had to do something. Why didn't you give us *orders*?"

"You haven't figured that out already?"

Noam stared at him. Lehrer's thumb moved in a steady pattern against the back of Noam's hand.

"No," Noam croaked out eventually. "No, I haven't, actually. We could have died. All of us."

"If you'd died, then my trust in you would have been grossly misplaced," said Lehrer calmly. "But you didn't die. You survived. Noam . . . you showed great leadership ability today." He smiled, letting go of Noam's hand to graze his touch along Noam's jaw instead, fingertips lingering at Noam's mouth. Noam hardly dared to breathe. "I won't live forever, you know. Even with all my abilities, I am not immortal. I need an heir."

Noam's heart was beating too fast, something hot and liquid spreading beneath his skin. And maybe this was the wrong move, but it didn't *feel* wrong, it—

Noam caught Lehrer's lips in a kiss. He felt Lehrer smile against his mouth as Lehrer pressed Noam back against the sofa, and Noam . . .

Noam let him. One of Lehrer's hands found his hip; the other braced against the cushion to keep his weight from crushing Noam as his lips moved to Noam's cheek, his jaw, his throat. Noam's eyes fluttered open as he stared up at the ceiling and tried to keep his breathing steady. He could smell Lehrer's cologne, pine and vanilla; a strand of Lehrer's hair fell loose to graze Noam's overheated skin.

After a beat he remembered to put his hands on Lehrer, too, smoothing from his shoulders down to his waist.

"I love the way you look in that shirt," Lehrer murmured, already sliding his touch up under the hem to find bare skin. "I'll like it even better once you take it off."

*Five minutes,* Noam told himself. Just five minutes, long enough to make Lehrer think—believe—

But already he was grasping Lehrer's wrist, pushing his hand back down to the safer territory of Noam's hip. "I'm too tired," he said when Lehrer lifted his head to give him a questioning look.

A tight sigh, but Lehrer pushed up, withdrawing back to his own end of the sofa. He drew out a cigarette and lit it with a snap of pyromancy, exhaling smoke toward the window. "It's always something."

"I'm sorry," Noam said, curling back into a seated position. "It's not intentional. I just . . ."

Lehrer cut him a sharp sideways glance, his eyes as hot as the cigarette smoldering between his fingers. Noam's excuses died in his chest.

"I've been very patient with you."

Noam's stomach shriveled. "I know."

Lehrer took another drag from his cigarette. It had been five weeks now since Noam went undercover. And for a reeling moment Noam wondered if this was it—if Dara might prove his point right here and now. If Lehrer ordered him into his bed, Noam would have no choice but to obey, Faraday shield or no Faraday shield. If he lost his cover, it was over. But all Lehrer said was: "Go back to your room."

Noam didn't need to be told twice. He left his dirty uniform in Lehrer's hamper and took the service stairs down three floors to the room he'd been assigned. It was only after he shut the door behind him and turned the useless lock that he realized his hands were shaking.

# CHAPTER TWENTY-FOUR
## DARA

Noam kept his end of the bargain, even all the way from Texas.

Priya showed up every morning at eight with a plastic grocery bag of food and a pack of cigarettes. She'd stay an hour or so, pitying Dara enough to give him that small amount of human contact—but she always left, off to do whatever it was the Black Magnolia had her doing, and Dara was alone for the day to pace his narrow apartment and try to absorb himself in a new book before Claire arrived for the evening shift.

But not even *Crime and Punishment* could hold Dara's attention for long. His mind kept circling back to Noam and Ames—Bethany and Taye—all down in Texas fighting one of Lehrer's wars. Possibly dying for it.

Dara had never been claustrophobic before now. He used to love small spaces, in fact—had filled his room in Lehrer's apartment with dozens of houseplants with wide frond-like leaves, vines that dangled down from the ceiling like Spanish moss. It had made his bedroom feel like it was blocked off from the rest of the world . . . and Dara liked the way Lehrer had to navigate around all those plants every time he came in, an invader in unfamiliar territory.

This was different. This felt like being trapped in that same room—barren now of plants, of Dara's telescope, his books, and his ceiling stars—caught there with a line in his vein and his magic tamped down and bound. The rising panic of knowing he'd die between those four walls.

"War's on hold," Claire told him on the fifth night, the both of them perched on chairs shoved up against the window, blowing cigarette smoke out into the icy air. "Apparently Lehrer's got Houston in a stranglehold, and the Texans want to talk treaties. All action is suspended until there's word one way or the other."

"That's a good thing," Dara said, making Claire glance over at him in surprise. He tapped ash against the windowsill and shrugged. "If the war went on much longer, Lehrer might not make it back in time for Independence Day. We'd lose our shot."

Not to mention, the longer Noam was in Texas, the fewer chances he'd have to discover where Lehrer kept the vaccine.

"I suppose," Claire said after a moment. She stabbed her cigarette out and flicked it into the night air, then pushed herself up, dusting both hands on her jeans. "Either way, I'm still doing damage control with Texas for their spy's death in east Durham. Try explaining to a bunch of paranoid antiwitching freaks that random muggings happen in Carolinia just like they do anywhere else." She shook her head. "Fucking nightmare."

"Right," Dara said and swallowed down the truth.

"Anyway. We're meeting on Monday, as usual. I'll have Priya come get you beforehand. And Dara . . . maybe take a bath first?"

She left. Dara lifted an arm to sniff himself; he couldn't smell anything.

But now that he thought about it, he couldn't remember the last time he took a shower. Before Noam and Ames went to Texas, for sure—all the days following that blurred together, indistinguishable except for whether Dara managed to make himself eat.

So he made a point of cleaning off and changing into a fresh set of clothes before Priya showed up to escort him down to Leo's bar.

"Hey, where the hell've you been?" Leo asked, passing over a glass of club soda when Dara sat himself down at his usual stool. He'd added a twist of lemon this time; it bobbed up and down in the bubbles like a tiny yellow ship at sea.

"House arrest," Dara muttered. "Álvaro put wards on my apartment. He thought Lehrer might send someone after me."

"Wasn't that already a risk?"

"I suppose. But you don't know Álvaro." Once Noam got it into his head that someone he cared about was in danger, he stopped caring about anything else.

Unless that person was Ames, of course. Guilt still twinged in Dara's chest when she walked in, stripping off her parka and dumping it over the back of a wooden chair. Looking at her, all he could imagine was Lehrer's golden magic tangled up inside her skull like so much metal wire.

But if Ames was back, then that meant—

"Where's Noam?" he asked when she sat on the stool next to his.

"Texas," she said, raising a finger to get Leo's attention. "Can I get a whiskey sour?"

"What do you mean *Texas*?"

"I mean Dallas," she said, twisting round to look at him properly. "Lehrer had him flown in. Some business about him being Atlantian liaison—I don't know. Guess Lehrer wants him to reassure the Texans that Lehrer doesn't plan to annex them the way he did Atlantia."

"But he does," Dara said.

"Probably. But anyway, point is Noam's with Lehrer. So. It's just me."

A cold hand closed around Dara's heart. Never mind not having time to look for the vaccine. In close quarters with Lehrer, with tensions running high . . .

Dara had gone on trips with Lehrer before. When he was fourteen, Lehrer even took him to Paris on a diplomatic trip. They'd stayed at a beautiful historic hotel in the eighth arrondissement. The balcony had a perfect view of the Eiffel Tower, framed by the crimson flowers that grew thick and fierce in the window boxes. Dara had found a little used bookshop a few blocks away, would hole up there while Lehrer was in meetings and work his way through every book he could find, reading the entirety of *Les Misérables* in the original French. It was one of those rare early days, when Dara still saw this new arrangement with Lehrer through rose-colored lenses. Everything seemed bright and special. And Dara had felt so very adult drinking the glass of champagne Lehrer passed him, when Lehrer trailed his hand down Dara's spine, when Lehrer took him to bed.

But it didn't end well. A meeting didn't go Lehrer's way, and the glittering postcard-perfect façade shattered like mirror glass. They'd left early, Dara's bruises covered with an unseasonable sweater, and Dara never read *Les Mis* again.

"Lehrer will catch him," Dara whispered, clutching his club soda in one numb hand. "He'll—Noam can't fool him, he'll—"

Dara managed to cut himself off just in time, tipping forward to take a big swallow of his soda to wash down the words he so nearly let slip. *Lehrer will use persuasion, and Noam won't obey. And then he'll know.*

But anything he said in front of Ames, he might as well be saying to Lehrer's face.

"He'll be okay," Ames said, more gently this time. She reached over and found Dara's free hand, squeezing once. "Noam's smart. He'll figure it out. He's lasted this long, hasn't he?"

"Texas will be different," Dara said. And he couldn't explain how he knew that was true, just that it *was*. He knew that down to the marrow of his bones.

"Let's get started," Claire said after the last of them—Holloway—had finally shown up, unwinding his black scarf and settling in at an empty table. "Priya's got an update from Texas."

"Well, they aren't happy," Priya said, perching on one of the bar-stools and twirling her straw between her fingers. "But I think they're going to drop the murder accusation for now. They're blaming Lehrer, not us—that's the good news. The *better* news is that they might be able to get us a prototype of the vaccine."

*Oh thank god.*

A vaccine. If that was true—if Texas came through on their promise—Noam wouldn't have to stay with Lehrer. They could just *take care* of it, end all of this now before—

"Will they have it ready in time for Independence Day?" Leo asked, an innocent question, and dread plunged black into the pit of Dara's stomach.

*Shit.*

Ames.

He caught Claire's gaze across the room; even her black skin had gone visibly pale. Silence hung over the room, sharp-toothed and vicious.

"What?" Leo said, glancing between them all. "What did I say?"

"Nothing," Dara interjected swiftly and slid his empty glass across the bar. "Can I get a refill?"

Leo grabbed the glass and filled it up, stealing a couple looks at Dara like he thought more information might be forthcoming. Next to Dara, Ames kept kicking the toes of her shoes against the underside of the bar—she knew what had just happened. Her cheeks were flushed a dull red.

Behind her back, Dara gestured toward Priya. She drained the rest of her drink and got up, moving forward like she was headed to the bar to get a refill of her own.

Dara's blood was frozen in his veins as she set the glass down on the bar top. Ames lifted her head—and Dara met Priya's gaze right as Priya stabbed the syringe needle into the side of Ames's neck.

"What the fuck?" Ames leaped up, her barstool toppling over and her hand slapping against her neck. But it was too late; Priya had already pushed the plunger.

Dara caught Ames's wrist. "It's okay," he said quickly. Her eyes were wide and wild when she reared around to face him instead, a thin trickle of blood cutting down the side of her neck to stain her shirt collar. "It's okay. It's just suppressant."

"The *hell*, Dara!"

She must have reached for her magic, then, because Dara watched the color drain from her face from one breath to the next. And Lehrer must've ordered her not to let herself get caught, because she instantly broke to the right—but Dara was faster, hooking his arm around her neck to catch her in a clinch.

Either Ames was stronger than he remembered, or Dara had gotten weak these past months. She thrust her elbow back into his ribs, hard enough he wheezed and only just managed to keep his grip.

"Help me!" he managed to get out.

Priya tried to go for Ames's middle, but she couldn't get past Ames's knees. Ames had always been good at physical sparring, vicious and efficient.

"Dara!"

Dara ducked, and Leo broke an empty bourbon bottle over Ames's head. She slumped in Dara's arms and he staggered, struggling to hold up her deadweight. Leo dropped what was left of the shattered bottle in the sink behind the bar, and Dara and Priya heaved Ames's body between them, slinging one of her arms around each of their necks.

"What was all that?" Leo said, as Claire swept up the broken glass with a flicker of telekinesis.

"She's under Lehrer's persuasion," Dara explained, shifting to get a better grip on Ames's waist; her sweater was thick and made her hard to hold on to. "She didn't know about the Independence Day plot—that was our one secret from him, but now she knows, so . . ."

"So now he'd know," Priya finished grimly. "Or he would, if we let her go back there. Not that we have anything better to do with her. I don't suppose you'd let us stash a hostage behind your bar for the next several weeks?"

Dara shook his head. "Not that long. Just a few more days—Noam can do to her what he did to himself." He said it like he was way more confident than he felt. It must take substantial magical effort to sustain a shield like the one Noam had on his mind. Dara wasn't even sure Noam could manage to hold two at once. "We just need to wait for him to get back from Texas. We can keep her in my apartment."

Claire and Priya exchanged looks. It really *was* the best plan, even if Dara felt a little guilty suggesting the obvious selfish option. But at least if Ames was with him, he wouldn't be alone anymore.

"Sounds good," Claire said at last. "C'mere, let us help you get her upstairs . . ."

Lugging Ames's unconscious body to the second floor was a surprisingly rigorous undertaking. The stairs were narrow and uneven, and Ames's body had a habit of slipping too far one way or another, like she had weights shifting from limb to limb.

"You sure she isn't boneless?" Claire said through gritted teeth as they dragged her up the last step, Ames's head lolling uselessly back toward the floor.

Claire entered the code on Noam's wards, and Dara shouldered open the door to his apartment.

"Here," he said, hooking his foot round the leg of his sturdiest chair and dragging it over.

They dumped Ames on the chair. Priya had scrounged up some zip ties from the emergency kit she brought to every meeting; she used them to bind Ames's wrists and ankles to the chair.

"Every hour," Priya said, passing over the kit with all its syringes of suppressant. "You have enough for six hours—I'll be back in a few with a fresh supply."

None of them voiced the obvious: it might take far more hours for Noam to return home than there was suppressant on the black market.

Dara took the bag and nodded. After a beat Priya reached over and clapped her hand on his shoulder, allowing him a soft and almost understanding smile.

"We'll check in," she said.

They left, and although Dara couldn't sense the magical wards locking again in their wake, he could imagine them. He envisioned a silver-blue electric curtain falling around the apartment, a stage at the end of an act.

Dara turned toward Ames, still unconscious, and wiped away the trickle of blood running down from her temple.

"Just you and me," he said. "Again."

# Chapter Twenty-Five

## Noam

The Texan president's residence was a massive construction in white marble, obviously modeled after the relics of the former United States—all grecian columns and broad, smooth steps. But they didn't enter from the front. The motorcade took them round to the west side, to the more subdued private entrance meant for the presidential family themselves.

Noam rode in a separate car from Lehrer—for appearance's sake, he presumed, although a tiny twist in the pit of his stomach suggested that maybe, *maybe* . . . it was personal.

Maybe Lehrer didn't want to be alone with him now.

*Well, that makes two of us,* Noam thought as nastily as he could, and smiled and nodded as the Carolinian ambassador to Texas kept talking on and on about the winter weather like Noam gave a shit about whatever *El Niño* was supposed to mean.

"Ah, here we are," the ambassador said as their car rolled to a stop behind Lehrer's, as if Noam hadn't noticed. "It's a magnificent house. You're very lucky to have the chance to see it. There's nothing quite like it in Carolinia."

Noam was starting to think the ambassador liked Texas better than his own home country.

One of the Chancellarian Guard opened the door, and the ambassador emerged first, Noam following in his wake. The drive was composed of what must have been ten tons' worth of small white pebbles; they crunched and rolled under his feet as they walked up toward the house.

Lehrer preceded them all, a slim figure in navy blue trailed at great distance by two guards. Lehrer had told Noam once that he loathed the way the presence of the Chancellarian Guard undermined his power. *They should never forget how capable I am of defending myself,* he'd said.

And true to form, he eschewed bodyguards in Carolinia; the only time Noam ever saw them at all was in the wake of that assassination attempt.

But here they were. A muted presence to be sure, far back and armed only with handguns holstered at their hips, but *here.*

Lehrer must be worried.

Only, of course he was, Noam realized. Texas had the vaccine—that was the whole reason Lehrer had declared war in the first place. If the Texans found a way to inject him with it, they would win the war in a single stroke. Lehrer would be trapped here, impotent and in Texan power. Carolinian armies would be trapped within Texan borders.

Every country in the goddamn world would ally themselves with Texas. They'd crush the life out of whatever was left of Carolinia in the wake of Lehrer's neutralization.

*We shouldn't be here.* Adrenaline bolted up Noam's spine like a shot of lethal poison. Why hadn't someone warned Lehrer? Why didn't—

But they did. They did warn Lehrer. And if they didn't, Lehrer would've known anyway, would've figured it out the same way Noam had.

And he came anyway.

He brought Noam with him, *anyway.*

Because even with both their lives in the balance, finding that back door past Texan antiwitching shields was worth the risk.

Sickness crawled up the back of Noam's throat. They all stood there on the front drive, wide open to snipers, as the Texan president and his wife greeted Lehrer in the foyer. All smiles, that baseline man's hand gripping Lehrer's gloved one: *So very glad you could make it.*

Noam stretched out his magic, searching. He couldn't sense any sniper rifles, but that didn't mean anything in the country that invented antiwitching shields.

Lehrer and the president had finished their pleasantries. As they walked deeper into the residence, Noam and the ambassador followed through the front door.

The Chancellarian Guard stayed on the front lawn. Apparently Lehrer's ego was still too big to let them follow him in to dinner.

The ambassador was right about one thing, at least. The house really was one of the most impressive pieces of architecture Noam'd ever witnessed—second only, perhaps, to Duke Chapel. Nothing else in Carolinia was like this. The high ceiling almost seemed to float overhead, the herringbone parquet floor draped with plush imported rugs and all the furniture polished to a gleaming finish. It was an understated kind of beauty; in comparison, their hotel gave the impression of trying too hard for opulence.

It was annoying, because Noam actually *liked* it.

Discussions continued in the sitting room prior to dinner, tuxedoed servers supplying aperitifs from tiny pewter trays. Noam sipped his, a fizzy pomegranate-red drink garnished with a perfect round of orange.

"Harvey, this is Noam Álvaro, my student and the interim liaison for Atlantian affairs," Lehrer said, placing a hand lightly on Noam's back as he introduced him to the Texan president. The man had a slim bronze circlet resting atop his head—just like Sacha's, designed to keep Lehrer from influencing them with his persuasion. Come to that, everyone else here was wearing a similar crown, including the staff. "Noam, this is President Harvey Méndez."

"What a pleasure, Mr. Álvaro," Méndez said, shaking Noam's hand. He had a thick, drawling accent like sugar syrup. "I've been looking forward to meeting you. I was quite fond of your predecessor. We were all very sad to hear of his passing."

It took Noam a second to realize he meant Brennan. Whether Méndez knew Noam had killed him was unclear.

"Thank you, Mr. President. Tom was a close friend of my family's," Noam said. "He is deeply missed."

"I'm sure," Méndez said.

Lehrer's hand fell from Noam's shoulder, the gesture uncharacteristically short lived and chaste. Noam was anxious down to the blood; he kept expecting someone—any of them, perhaps even Méndez himself—to lunge forward to stab him and Lehrer both with syringes of milky-white vaccine. Every second they didn't was another fray on Noam's nerves.

"I hope you have the opportunity to see some more of our beautiful country while you're here," Méndez went on. "There's so much more to see of Texas than hotels and airports."

Noam's gut tightened. So Méndez knew, then, that it had been Noam who led the assault in Houston.

Noam smiled back, as mildly as he could. "I would love that. I've heard the backland prairies in particular are gorgeous."

Not *heard* so much as *seen photos in old books*, but it was neutral enough—and it provided Lehrer an easy route to change the direction of the conversation.

"Perhaps we can tempt you to visit Carolinia, as well," Lehrer said, resting a friendly hand on Méndez's upper arm. "You haven't lived until you see the Smoky Mountains during peak foliage. It's breathtaking."

And solidly within the quarantined zone—but none of them mentioned that, of course.

Somehow they all maintained inoffensive conversation topics for the next half hour; Lehrer introduced Noam to several other Texan officials in attendance, including their secretary of state and the secretary of homeland security. Noam wasn't entirely sure what the difference between the two was, really, unless Texas felt they needed two equivalents to Carolinia's minister of defense.

Finally a servant emerged to announce dinner, and they all filtered into the dining room—every bit as elaborate as the rest of the house Noam'd seen so far, set with gold charger plates and antique crystal water goblets. At least Noam had figured out dinner etiquette since that harrowing dinner party at General Ames's house, so he didn't look like such an idiot when the palate cleansers arrived between courses.

This was almost definitely the best time to see if he could figure out a way past the firewall. After dinner they'd all have to go have more drinks and launch into all the obligatory diplomatic conversation; it would be impossible for Noam to escape.

So after the main course was swept away, Noam made his excuses and slipped out of the dining room. Only then one of the aides caught him in the entryway, offering to escort him to the bathroom.

"Oh, no," Noam said. "That'd be awkward, don't you think?"

"It's my job, Mr. Álvaro," the aide said evenly.

"I can find it."

"I'll show you," the aide insisted again, and Noam couldn't keep arguing. He had to let the man show him through the carpeted halls of the residence, all the way back to a single-person bathroom with granite counters and an old-fashioned tile floor.

Noam forced a tight smile for the aide as he shut the door. The moment he turned the lock, he twisted his face in a silent scream.

God fucking *damn it*!

How the hell was he supposed to get loose and find himself a computer if he couldn't even go to the bathroom without a chaperone?

He used the toilet while he was there, buying time to think. But by the time he was washing his hands in that pretty gold-tapped sink, he still hadn't figured anything out. His best option was to jolt the aide with a shot of electricity and escape while he was unconscious, but while that might get him *to* the computer, he'd have a hell of a time getting out again. What happened when someone realized the aide was missing? Or worse, when the aide woke up and told them all that Lehrer's protégé had knocked him out and disappeared?

At that point, Noam was pretty sure whatever flimsy sense of diplomatic etiquette had kept Méndez from injecting them both full of the vaccine would evaporate.

He scrubbed damp hands over his face, dragging fingers back through his hair. Which, of course, only served to mess up the perfect pomaded style he'd spent ages fixing up to Lehrer's specifications. He made a face at his reflection and did his best to comb it back into place, mostly succeeding in making himself look more or less like he'd been kissing some stranger in the back closet.

Actually.

That was an idea.

Lehrer would fucking kill him, but what Lehrer didn't know . . .

Noam frowned at himself for a moment, then let his weight tip to the left, toppling against the sink and knocking the soap dish into the bowl. It was loud enough to earn an immediate knock on the door.

"Mr. Álvaro? Everything all right in there?"

Noam waited several seconds, pinching his cheeks until his skin was flushed pink. Then he opened the bathroom door, leaning against the counter as if for support. "I'm sorry," he mumbled. "I . . . dizzy, all the sudden."

Concern creased the aide's brow. "Do you need me to get a medic?"

"No—no, I'll be . . . I just. Is there somewhere I can sit? For a second?"

"Of course," the aide said immediately. He offered Noam his arm, and Noam hooked their elbows together, letting himself list in against the man's body as they made slow progress farther down the hall, into a new sitting area. This one was warmly lit by a few lamps glowing on end tables. Perfect.

The aide helped Noam down onto one end of a sofa, then hovered there in front of him, clearly feeling helpless. "Do you want water? I can ring for some."

"Oh—no. I'm. It's okay. I only need a moment."

Noam tipped his head down into the palms of his hands, breathing in the scent of his own skin. After a few seconds he looked up again, one hand lifting to grasp at the back of his own neck. "I'm sorry about this," he said, a bit self-deprecating. "I don't know what came over me. Usually I can hold my liquor a little better."

"Ah," the aide said, comprehension dawning on his face. "Yes, I understand. I used to be like that when I was your age too. You're . . ."

"Eighteen," Noam lied, because that was presumably the legal age in Texas same as it was in Carolinia. He shrugged one shoulder. "Yeah. It's probably the Aperol spritz from earlier. I wasn't thinking—with the wine, at dinner . . ."

"You'll feel better soon," the aide reassured him. "Especially if you've gotten some food on your stomach."

"I'm already feeling better," Noam said and gave him a soft smile. He reached forward and caught the man's wrist, fingertips pressing in against its soft underside. "Thank you. Really. I—from all I've heard about Texas, I wasn't expecting kindness."

"Not all of us hate witchings," the aide said. "I'm sure it's the same way in Carolinia. The government thinks one thing. Some people agree; some people don't."

That was not at all what Noam had been led to believe. After the catastrophe, Texas had hung up the bodies of dead witching militants around the walls they built bracketing them safe from the quarantined zone. A warning—to Adalwolf and Calix Lehrer's Avenging Angels and to anyone else. They'd declared themselves a witching-free zone, as if that were something to advertise proudly.

But the catastrophe was over a hundred years ago now. Things could change. And the longer Noam spent around Lehrer, the more he was starting to wonder how much of what Carolinians knew about Texas was propaganda.

"Texas keeps witchings in government hospitals," Noam said. "You experiment on them. You torture them."

"*No*," the aide said, and he tugged his wrist out of Noam's reach— but he didn't move away. "I don't know what you've heard in your country, but it isn't like that. The program is voluntary. And there's no torture."

Noam couldn't admit how he got the information, though. Couldn't say, *That's not how it seemed from the emails I found on the phone of the Texan spy I killed.*

Maybe Texas was just like Carolinia.

Maybe both governments did terrible things. Secret things. And the majority of the population continued on with their lives blissfully unaware, convinced of their own government's benevolence in contrast to the evil of everyone else.

"That's a relief to hear," Noam said. He pushed himself up, at last, taking his time, like he was still a little fatigued. "I have to admit I was afraid to come here at first. I'm glad there are some Texans who don't hate me just for existing." He gave the aide a weak smile.

"You're from Atlantia, right?" the aide said.

"My parents."

"People said the same thing about Atlantia before Carolinia annexed it," the man told him. "You know that, right? 'Atlantians are bigoted. Atlantians are closed minded.'"

"I think most Atlantians were a bit busy trying to stay alive to worry about being prejudiced," Noam said.

"That's my point, though. Just because something's a stereotype doesn't make it true."

It was . . . well. It *was* interesting to consider. But as illuminating as this conversation had been, Noam was getting real far off track. He had to get rid of this man, not launch into a fresh political debate with him.

"You're right," Noam said, conciliatory. "We hear all kinds of things about Texas that I'm sure are untrue. Like that you're all homophobic."

"Criticism of Calix Lehrer, a homosexual man, is not the same as homophobia."

Damn it. Noam had been hoping the man would say something he could work with, like, *How could I be homophobic if I'm gay?* But that was definitely a long shot. Texas'd never had a queer president. They still had plenty of antiqueer hate crimes too. Even if most Texans weren't homophobic, queerness still wasn't normalized for them the way Lehrer'd normalized it for Carolinians.

Ugh. This was pointless. It had been a stupid idea from the start. Seduce some random Texan aide and slip out after while he was still pulling himself together? It sounded dumb even in Noam's head.

This was the presidential residence. There was absolutely no way Noam was getting into those halls alone—this wasn't Gordon Ames's funeral, where Noam was a trusted wanderer.

He'd just have to figure out a way to explain that to Lehrer.

"You've given me a lot to think about," Noam said. "But I should be getting back. I've been gone awhile."

"Of course, Mr. Álvaro," the aide said, right back in that professional mode.

He guided Noam down the hall and to the dining room, where the others had started in on the dessert course: an elaborate-looking tiramisu.

Lehrer didn't attempt to catch Noam's eye during dinner. It would have been too risky trying to communicate anything here—too many malevolent eyes watching, too much suspicion with lethal stakes. Noam finished his tiramisu in silence; he wasn't important enough to be spoken to, at least not when Lehrer and the ambassador sat at the same table. Which was fine, anyway. Noam didn't have anything to say. He still didn't—

Well. He didn't *have* to have an opinion on Texas. Not yet. Right now the priority was getting rid of Lehrer. Until Lehrer was gone, every other evil was ephemeral.

But the Texans remembered Noam existed by the time they all retreated back to the drawing room.

Gregory Pulver—the Texan secretary of state—handed Noam a glass of bourbon and said, "So, Mr. Álvaro. Tell me about yourself."

At least the question was banal. It was the same one Noam was presented with every time he accompanied Lehrer to one of his stupid dinner parties. And that made sense, he supposed. Everyone was curious about Lehrer's new teenage protégé, the one who'd replaced infamous Dara Shirazi.

But Noam always got the impression the question boiled down to one thing: *Where did you come from?*

"There's not much to say." Noam's typical evasion. "I only joined Level IV a year ago."

"And yet already you've been named liaison for Atlantian affairs," Pulver pressed. "That's a lot of responsibility for an . . . eighteen-year-old?"

Noam didn't correct him. "I was qualified. I was mentored by Tom Brennan, who held the position before me."

*Never give anyone more information than you have to,* Lehrer had instructed him once, his palm heavy at the nape of Noam's neck. *Make them fight for everything they get, until they're grateful to learn anything at all.*

"So you consider yourself particularly well informed on the Atlantian response to annexation," Pulver said.

It wasn't a question, so Noam sipped his bourbon instead of answering.

Lehrer had been deep in discussion with President Méndez and the secretary of homeland security—but maybe he sensed the direction of this conversation, because he turned to face the room. "Shall we sit?"

They claimed their chairs, Noam intentionally picking one opposite Lehrer's. He didn't want to sequester them in a corner. There was something about having the minority side of a discussion clustered together that gave the impression of *easy prey*.

Not that anyone was liable to see Lehrer in a vulnerable light. Lehrer occupied that elegant armchair as if it were his chancellor's seat, legs neatly crossed at the knees and the hand that didn't hold his whiskey glass settled easy on the armrest—which was carved in the likeness of a growling lion. Lehrer's long fingers draped right over the chiseled lines of the lion's bared teeth.

Lehrer's smile was a knife being unsheathed. "Let's discuss the terms of Texan surrender."

Méndez and Pulver exchanged looks, the latter's mouth fixed in a straight line.

"This isn't a surrender," Méndez said. "It's a cessation of hostilities in both nations' mutual interest."

"Call it whatever you like," said Lehrer, expression unchanged. He set his whiskey glass aside, reaching for his jacket pocket. "Do you mind if I smoke?"

No one denied him.

Lehrer lit the cigarette with a snap of pyromancy and took a long drag, exhaling toward the fireplace. "This feels familiar," he commented.

"The last Caro-Texan war was before my time," Méndez said. "2074."

"Ah, right. I forget how young you all are. Well, let me give you a little history lesson: I've sat in this room with four presidents just like you, and the discussion was remarkably similar. I could practically script it." Lehrer swirled his whiskey round in its glass. "You'll demur and make empty threats, citing your antiwitching technology. I'll remind you of the losses you sustained in recent battles and how much more violent things will become if we take Houston. You will recall that I've never failed to deliver my promises where biological

warfare is concerned. Ultimately we'll come to an accord that reestab-
lishes our tradition of hating each other from a silent distance—until
next time, anyway."

Méndez lifted a brow. "You forgot one thing. We have a vaccine
now. If weaponized, it would decimate your witching population. You'd
be virtually defenseless."

"Even counting only baseline soldiers, we have the largest standing
army in the world," Lehrer said idly and finally sipped that bourbon
again. "I wouldn't call that *defenseless*. Besides—you're a long way from
weaponizing that vaccine. It's still only absorbed intravenously. Do you
really think your science will move faster than me? Than the virus itself?"

Noam used to imagine what it would have been like to sit in the
room with Calix Lehrer during the peace talks from any war in the past
hundred years. But now that he was here, he realized it was somehow
not at all and yet *exactly* as he'd imagined it. Somehow he'd thought
Lehrer would be less explicit about what he could do to Texas if they
failed to surrender. And yet . . . it was working.

And why shouldn't it? This was exactly why the rest of the continent failed to get Carolinia to reduce their witching population
back in 2019. Because of Lehrer. Because they knew what Lehrer was
capable of.

A thrill rolled through the pit of Noam's stomach, warm and alive.
Whatever else he might think about Lehrer, he was still *this*.

"If we agree to a cease-fire," Méndez said eventually, "you will need
to remove your soldiers from Texan territory. We won't make the same
mistakes Atlantia did." He glanced toward Noam at that; Noam kept
his expression impassive.

"Of course. And you will cease all research into the weaponization
of the vaccine."

This time, it was Pulver who interjected. "I'm surprised, Chancellor,"
he said. "I would have thought you'd be very interested in our vaccine-
development research. Surely you are eager to prevent more outbreaks

in Carolinia. Not to mention the challenges of sanitizing your newly acquired Atlantian territory."

"I fail to see how the weaponization of this vaccine plays into any of that."

"Don't you?" Pulver said. "If aerosolized, the vaccine could be dispersed across the entirety of Carolinia and Atlantia together. You'd eradicate magic within Carolinian borders. Surely you want that."

But Lehrer didn't. All of them knew that. And from the dissatisfied set of Lehrer's mouth, Lehrer was well aware.

"We have our own vaccine-development program," Lehrer said. "But unlike you, we are more interested in finding a way to eradicate magic's mortality rate—not eradicate magic itself. So I'm afraid our goals are not quite as aligned as you might think."

"And how many innocent people will you let die while you waste time on this fool's errand?" the secretary of homeland security snapped—and clearly saw her mistake a moment later reflected in Lehrer's pale gaze, which had gone cool.

"No fool's armies surround Houston," Lehrer said softly.

"I'm sure the secretary meant no offense," Méndez cut in. "My apologies, Chancellor. Our goal here is to work toward a constructive solution—not to get mired in insults on both sides."

Lehrer's answering smile was brittle. "Perhaps this discussion would be better held tomorrow, during the official meeting." He rose from his chair, downing the rest of his bourbon in one swallow and using telekinesis to float the glass down to its coaster. His cigarette had already vanished, presumably decomposed into its component atoms and scattered like dust.

The rest of them stood as well, ripples in the wake of Lehrer's decision.

"Mr. President," Lehrer said, shaking Méndez's hand. "I look forward to continued diplomacy."

Méndez escorted them to the front door, trailed by a pair of blank-faced aides carrying their winter coats. And Noam sensed the metal a second before he saw it, the syringe clutched in the grasp of one of those aides. That metal: an inch from Lehrer's neck as the aide helped Lehrer into his coat.

A low laugh escaped Lehrer's throat, and the needle ripped itself out of the aide's grip, flying neatly into Lehrer's instead.

"Nice try," Lehrer said, examining the syringe with an appraising gaze.

"Chancellor," Méndez gasped, his face gone the same sickly color as the wallpaper. "I—we—I'm so—"

Watching the Texan president fumble for some kind of explanation for the obvious assassination attempt was like watching a man beg for his life at the guillotine. Some of Sacha's supporters had begged that way at their executions. Lehrer had taken no mercy.

"Well," Lehrer went on, as if he hadn't heard the president's reply. A small smile toyed with the corners of his lips, and when he glanced up, it was to meet Noam's gaze. Noam felt something in his chest go cold, and Lehrer's mouth twitched. "One should always finish what one started."

Lehrer shrugged off his coat and dinner jacket and passed them off to Pulver, who accepted the burden wordlessly. He seemed incapable of looking anywhere but Lehrer's face, even as Lehrer flicked open his cuff link and rolled up his sleeve in quick, efficient movements.

And as Noam and Méndez and the others all watched, Lehrer slid the needle into his own vein and pressed the vaccine into his bloodstream.

"*Sir*," Noam managed to get out, the word breaking like thin ice.

Lehrer drew the syringe free and tossed it into a nearby houseplant. A slim line of blood cut down the length of his forearm.

"Are you satisfied?" Lehrer asked Méndez with an arched brow.

"Chancellor . . ."

"I suppose you thought I was an idiot," Lehrer said conversationally, rolling his sleeve down again and concealing the blood. "Have you heard of mithridatism? The term refers to an ancient king who poisoned himself with small doses of lethal toxins to develop an immunity. He feared his mother planned to assassinate him, apparently. Ever since an iteration of the vaccine surfaced in the quarantined zone . . . well, I could hardly let myself stay vulnerable to such a threat. I've been injecting myself with the virus for months. With the rate of evolutionary change in magic, it seems this vaccine is rather *outdated* for all the strains of virus that infect me these days."

*Shit. Shit shit shit shit shit—*

Lehrer held up his wrist, and a gold spark of magic lit through the air; his cuff link affixed itself to his sleeve. Telekinesis.

The vaccine didn't work.

Lehrer laughed softly and retrieved his jacket from Pulver's arms, draping it over his shoulders once more and slipping the buttons through their holes by hand. "I suppose this means there will be no peace treaty after all," Lehrer told Méndez, who stood there as if his feet had grown roots into the floor. "I wish you all the best . . . and my condolences, about Houston."

Noam followed Lehrer in a frozen daze as they departed the presidential residence. He drifted down the drive, a mind floating far above his body, which was tethered to Lehrer's as if by an invisible cord. He watched them both climb into the waiting government car. Watched himself lean into the far corner of the back seat like he could vanish into it, while Lehrer glanced down at his wristwatch.

"Only nine," Lehrer said, sounding pleased. "The night is still young."

*He knows.*

Nausea crawled up the back of Noam's throat and he swallowed convulsively, both hands clenching in fists against his thighs.

Lehrer glanced sidelong at him. "I apologize for all the theatrics," he said, as if that was what upset Noam. "But politics are just that—a play on the world stage. Better you learn that now."

Noam tipped forward and pressed his head against his palms, staring at the floor of the car. A tremor had started up in his gut, spreading fast like a virus. "I wasn't able to get in the Texan servers," he told his own shoes. "I couldn't get past security."

Only silence answered. Noam stayed there, holding his breath in his mouth, until at last he couldn't stand it anymore—he had to look up, twist around in his seat toward Lehrer.

Lehrer reached into his jacket pocket and drew out a slim silver cigarette case. He selected one and lit it with pyromancy, rolling down the window enough to blow his smoke toward the night sky.

"I'm sorry, sir," Noam ventured, and Lehrer's gaze met his again.

"I'm sure you are."

*He knows,* that voice whispered again: *He knows.* Noam dragged a hand back through his hair, twisting the short strands around his knuckles and wishing he were anywhere else—somewhere he could vomit into a convenient bush without earning Lehrer's false concern.

"Headache?" Lehrer said idly.

"Mmm."

Lehrer took another drag off his cigarette. "Perhaps we should consider suppressants," he said. "At least until these headaches subside."

Noam stared at him, something sharp and venomous shooting through his veins. "What? Why?"

"Don't forget I've been here before. With Dara. I can recognize the signs."

"I'm not fevermad."

"We'll see." Lehrer turned away from him now, focusing his gaze out the tinted window at the city that slid by outside, and left Noam to tilt his head against the back seat and count how many more days he could get away with this.

Whether it was still even worth it at all.

*Video footage stolen from the offices of the Psychiatric Associates of Carolinia.*

INT. DR. GLEESON'S OFFICE

Dr. Gleeson sits behind his desk, reading glasses perched on his nose, examining a file. He lifts his head at a knock on the door, but before he can rise, the door swings open, and another man enters.

Gleeson stands quickly, both hands braced atop his desk.

GLEESON: Mark? What are you doing here? Why—

Gleeson must have found the answer in Mark's mind, because he goes visibly pale. An instant later Mark draws a gun from the back of his jeans and points it at Gleeson.

GLEESON: Mark. Put down the gun.

Mark says nothing. His hand visibly shakes as his thumb pulls back the hammer.

GLEESON: You don't have to do this, Mark, you . . .

MARK: He told me to.

GLEESON: Who? (A beat later.) Calix? Calix told you to kill me?

MARK: I have to.

GLEESON: Mark. Mark, listen to me: he's trying to frame you, don't—

Mark pulls the trigger. A gunshot explodes, loud enough the audio crackles. Gleeson's body falls back against his chair, blood splattering his shirt and the window glass.

Mark stands there for a moment, staring at Gleeson's corpse and breathing thickly enough his shoulders heave with each inhale. Then he lifts the gun, as if in a trance, and shoves the barrel into his mouth. He shoots himself.

*The film continues, fixed on this silent scene, for another ten minutes before the bodies are found.*

# Chapter Twenty-Six

## Dara

Ames woke slowly, a dull, pained hum escaping her lips.

Dara abandoned his book, tossing it aside on the bed without thinking to mark his place. Ames blinked her eyes open, blurry gaze skimming the unfamiliar room before fixing on Dara and going sharp.

"Where am I? Shirazi . . . what the hell did you do?"

"I'm sorry, Ames." He gripped the edge of the bed with both hands, wishing he could reach for her but not quite daring to. "We couldn't take the risk."

Her mouth tightened, but she didn't deny it. Didn't admit it, either—although knowing Lehrer, he'd ordered her not to tell them the truth. And for a moment Dara almost thought she was angry, that Lehrer had pushed his persuasion so deep he'd convinced her she actually *wanted* this.

But the glint in her eyes wasn't rage. With her hands bound, she couldn't brush away the tear that escaped down her cheek or hide the way she shuddered when she took a breath.

"He's an asshole," she said at last, voice coming out tight and low.

"I think that's been established," Dara agreed. He slid closer to the edge of the bed and at last reached out to touch the barest tips of his fingers to her knee. "We'll figure this out. I promise. Noam'll be back from Texas any day now—he was able to get Lehrer out of his head somehow. He'll get Lehrer out of yours too."

He tried to sound more certain than he was.

"I wondered about that," Ames said, sitting a little straighter. "Lehrer didn't tell me he couldn't read Noam's mind anymore, obviously, but I kinda figured something had to have happened. Otherwise . . ."

Persuasion stole the rest of the sentence, but Dara got the gist: *Otherwise, why would he need me?*

A short laugh tore out of Ames's throat. "Although now that you've told me as much, I guess I'm not getting out of here anytime soon. Either Noam does his little trick, or you have to kill me."

"Ames—"

"No, don't worry about it. I bet Taye five hundred argents you'd be the death of me one day. I mean, I can't use five hundred argents once I'm dead, obviously, but it's the principle of the thing."

Dara managed a weak smile, one that did nothing to quell the waves pitching in his stomach. He drew his hand back into his lap.

Ames turned her face toward the ceiling, tapping her toes against the hardwood floor. "Well," she said, "since we're gonna be here awhile, I guess we should, like . . . figure out a topic of conversation or something. Just not astronomy, Dara—you know that shit's boring."

"All right." Dara drew his legs up onto the bed, crossing them under his body. "Tell me about Texas."

"Oh, *that*. That was . . . I fucked up. Basically."

"What do you mean?"

Ames exhaled. "I mean I didn't wait for orders. I attacked the enemy encampment on my own and brought all hell raining down on our heads. So then obviously Texas sent in all their antiwitching units, and Noam's unit had to attack the airport to split their manpower. We barely got out of there."

"How? With antiwitching units—"

"We retreated over a river, and I drew up all the moisture to make the ground soggy and swampy. Antiwitching armor was too heavy to get through. They went back for helicopters, but by that point we'd had reinforcements come in. Probably would've won, if the powers that be hadn't called for a cease-fire."

Clever. Ames's presenting power was influence over water. *So you're essentially a cartoon character,* Dara had said to her when they first met, Ames eight and himself nine—but she'd just come back with *I probably got it from watching too much anime.* It made her one of the first people Dara had met who seemed impervious to his insults. And that made them friends. Even so, it took a solid year of training and seeing the destructive strength of Ames's abilities firsthand before Dara learned to respect them.

Maybe Leo was right. Maybe he was a bully.

"Are you okay?" he asked softly. He didn't really mean it in the physical sense. Ames had always wanted to climb the ranks in the military.

That dream was probably dead now.

"I'll live. Whatever. It doesn't matter anymore, does it? Everything's fucked."

"I'm glad you're safe," he said. "Not that being locked up in here is all that much better."

Ames raised her brows. "Not better than getting shot at?"

Dara grimaced. "I didn't mean it like that. But you have to admit, this"—he gestured, encompassing the tiny apartment: the broken radiator, the protein bars Priya had brought him that he never ate, the unmade bed—"is not exactly where I thought I'd be by age nineteen."

"And where did you think you'd be? Lehrer was never gonna let you fly off and be a diplomat in fucking *Prague* or wherever—"

"Dead. I thought I'd be dead," Dara said. And for a moment they looked at each other, Dara's fingers twisting up in the bedsheets and

Ames strapped to that goddamn chair, messy hair casting shadows over her eyes. Dara sighed. "Not like that. Not . . . necessarily. But I never thought I'd make it this far. I was so sure Lehrer would kill me once he could prove I'd betrayed him—and if he didn't, Sacha would, the second I stopped being useful."

"Yeah, and if neither of them got around to assassinating you, you'd have taken matters into your own hands. Is that it?"

"For god's sake, Ames—"

She blew out a heavy breath and shook her head. "It's a fair fucking question, and you know it."

The words were punctuated with a long silence, both of them remembering the day after Dara got home from the hospital—the first time Lehrer let Ames visit, her sitting at the foot of his bed with both of them staring at each other and refusing to speak. She'd been so furious with him. He had seen it written in the line of her mouth, the way she dug her nails into her palms.

It was the first time Dara had thought Lehrer actually cared if he lived or died. He'd stayed home all week. Slept in a chair in the corner of Dara's bedroom, snapping awake every time Dara rolled over.

"No. Well—I don't know. I hadn't really thought that far ahead. It's not . . . it doesn't matter now, anyway. It's over."

Ames wet her lips. "Okay. So. I'm trying to trust you, Dara. But you have to promise me . . . promise you'd tell me if you ever felt. Like that. Again. Okay? Because I'm not doing that shit a second time, I . . ."

"I will. Ames . . . I will. I promise. I'd tell you."

"And eat your fucking protein bars."

He snorted and let his weight drop back onto his elbows, legs coming to dangle over the edge of the bed. "Your protein bars, too, now. We eat well at Maison Shirazi."

"Dara, this doesn't even count as a maison*ette*."

"Oh, I'm sorry—we can't all live in an art deco mansion in Forest Hills."

314

She made a face. "To be honest, I'd rather live here. That place is just . . . it was my dad's, not mine."

"So redecorate."

"Dara. I am *not* going furniture shopping with you."

"Who said anything about shopping ourselves? You can pay people for that."

"You are, in fact, the worst person I have ever met."

"Thank you." Dara grinned, but that second of happiness was chased by an immediate flicker of guilt. The same guilt that always laced his interactions with Ames because . . . he'd never told her about him and her father. He should have. Especially by now, he should have told her. If she didn't already know.

If Noam hadn't told her.

Only he didn't, he wouldn't have, and Dara knew it.

There was no reason to keep it secret anymore. The general was dead. Dara had watched him choke on his own blood, in his own bed.

But how the hell did you say that to someone? How was that merciful?

"I might sell the house," Ames said, shifting against her bindings. Her wrists weren't red yet, but they would be after a few hours. "I can't handle being there. Not . . . I mean, he got murdered *in that house*. And then I spent two hours sitting in this tiny room with Lehrer while he asked me question after question and *made* me tell the truth."

"I'm sorry," Dara said.

"Don't be. It's fucking . . . that was so long ago now. It doesn't matter. It just pisses me off that Lehrer went to all those lengths; then he *still* never bothered finding the actual killer. So like . . . what was even the point?"

Dara clenched his teeth so hard his jaw hurt.

While he was suppressed, he'd been susceptible to Lehrer's persuasion. Without his telepathy's interference, Lehrer had been able to keep him trapped in that apartment better than any locked door ever could.

315

That had been the first time Dara realized what it was like to have one's mind cut open and spread wide, fertile ground for the taking. And there'd been no way to tell what was persuasion and what wasn't. Every word out of Lehrer's mouth might have been a seed planted in dark soil. Every thought Dara had, potentially traitorous.

But he got his telepathy back in the QZ, at least for a while. Any influence Lehrer had gained over him deteriorated there. Ames, though . . .

Ames had spent weeks under persuasion now. Weeks reliving the trauma Lehrer put her through in that MoD cell, teasing her mind apart thread by thread.

"Me," he said, the word falling from his lips before he even realized he'd made the decision. "It was me. I killed him."

If some part of him had hoped the confession would make him feel better, well . . . it didn't. He felt like someone had wound a chain through his guts and drawn it taut.

Ames wasn't saying anything. She just sat there, her hands fallen still against their restraints. Her gaze was fixed on his face—he couldn't tell if she was angry, or . . . or *relieved*, or shocked. Or all three. She looked at him like she'd never seen him before.

"It was . . . Sacha asked me to do it, but that was . . . I'd talked to him. About your dad and what he did to your family. It was my idea. So."

Ames still didn't move. *How* did people survive without telepathy? Because Dara wasn't so sure he could.

All he could do was wait and will her to forgive him, to—to not hate him, at least, although he knew he didn't have any right to expect something like that. God. Ames had always . . . she'd always been there for him, kept all his terrible secrets, and this was how he repaid her.

He twisted his fingers up in the bedsheets beneath him. "Please say something."

"Like what?" Ames burst out at last. "Like . . . okay, Dara. You just told me you murdered my father. Forgive me if that takes a sec to sink in."

"He fucked me," Dara said. The words tumbled out before he could stop himself. And the second they were in the air, he pressed one hand to his mouth like he could push them back in—but it was too late. Ames's face had gone white, her staring at him and him looking back, wide eyed over the ridge of his fingers.

*Shit.*

Her tongue flickered out, wetting her lips. "What did you say?"

Too late. No taking it back now—no denying it.

"He . . . we were having sex." *General Ames raped you,* Noam had said, but Dara's mouth wouldn't work that way. Couldn't put it in those words. It felt like that word belonged to Lehrer.

"Since fucking *when?*"

"Since I was fifteen," Dara said. "But he . . . I could read his mind, so. I knew he wanted it. Before."

That had been one of the more awkward conversations he'd ever had with Lehrer: the night they both witnessed the same scene playing out in Gordon's mind, and Lehrer sat him down once they got home and tried to explain that sometimes people had certain thoughts, but that didn't mean they planned to *act* on those thoughts. As if Dara weren't a telepath. As if he didn't know that better than anyone.

Only less than a year later, Lehrer raped him for the first time—and then Gordon decided he wanted to act on those thoughts after all, and after eight months of Lehrer, Dara had been so desperate to blot Lehrer's touch off his body with someone—anyone—else that Dara didn't even try to stop him.

Ames's face twisted up, and for one horrible moment Dara was sure she was about to spit in his face—

"That's gross," she said. "He's—he *was* disgusting. I'm sorry. Jesus Christ, Dara."

Relief poured into him like ice water, shocking and cold. He let out a sharp, shaky breath. "It wasn't that bad," he said, tension still aching-tight in his shoulders; he lifted a hand to squeeze the side of his neck, trying to massage it out. "Relatively speaking. I don't know. It pissed Lehrer off, anyway."

Although that came later. At first Lehrer had laughed in his face and called him a *desperate whore.*

Lehrer's anger had emerged in subtler ways, seeping up like rotten groundwater to poison them both.

Ames twisted in her binds again, rubbing her wrists against the zip ties. "Still. Fuck. I wish you would've told me. I mean—I get why you didn't. But, like . . . ugh, I guess it shouldn't surprise me that my dad turned out to be a fucking pedo on top of everything else. I'm glad you killed him. What a creep."

Dara snorted. "That's one way of putting it, I suppose."

He'd never seen it that way. Maybe it was too much to bear, to think that Dara had let himself get put in this situation not once, but twice—that if it kept happening, that meant there was something wrong with Dara. Something fundamentally broken, just like Lehrer always said.

"I'm sorry," he said again. "Maybe Lehrer's right about some things. I *am* the common denominator here. Maybe I . . . can we really blame your dad for fucking me, if I—"

"Don't you dare say that, Dara Shirazi," Ames snapped. "It wasn't your fault. You didn't *do* anything to make Lehrer or my dad or *anyone*—you didn't. Okay?"

Dara tipped his head down to press his palms against his brow and shut his eyes, long enough to take a steadying breath. Ames had told him the same thing after he confessed what Lehrer had done. He'd tried to explain it the way Lehrer would have explained it: *I made Lehrer do it.*

But Ames had refused to accept that explanation. And she hadn't stopped fighting him on that point until Dara finally relented and agreed she was right.

If she was right then, she was right now too. Lehrer and General Ames were both grown men. Dara wasn't responsible for the choices they made.

His burner phone beeped on the bed next to him. Time for another dose.

"Sorry about this," Dara said, getting up and retrieving one of the syringes from atop his dresser. He made a face at Ames, and she mirrored it back but tilted her head to one side all the same, giving him easy access to slip the needle into her vein and depress the plunger.

"How many of those you got?" she asked.

"Not enough," he admitted grimly, tossing the syringe into the trash—no sharps container—and retreating back to the bed. "So we'd better hope Priya gets back to us with more soon—or that Lehrer sends Noam home from Texas to figure this out."

"Great." Her mouth twisted up, but there was nothing either of them could do.

Theme of their entire friendship, really.

They just had to wait.

# CHAPTER TWENTY-SEVEN

## NOAM

Holloway found Noam within an hour of his return to Carolinia—a message sent to his cell phone not fifteen minutes after Noam got back to the barracks: Come to my office.

And it was there, standing in front of Holloway's mahogany desk still wearing his tailored civilian clothes from Texas, that Holloway told him the Black Magnolia had Ames.

Noam skipped dinner to take the bus up to Geer Street instead, climbing the steps to Dara's apartment two at a time and tugging down the wards he'd erected in a single motion. Even so, he made himself pause long enough to knock, weight shifting from foot to foot as he heard steps approaching and Dara opened the door.

"I came as soon as I heard," Noam said, and he looked past Dara, over his shoulder and into the room—Ames was strapped to a chair near the window. His electromagnetism sensed a small pile of empty syringes in the trash can.

Ames shrugged one shoulder, presumably her best attempt at a wave considering both her arms were restrained. "Hi, Noam."

Dara stepped aside to let him in, and Noam shut the door, throwing the wards back up in his wake.

"So."

"So," Ames said, "as much as I wish this was some kind of kinky thing Dara's into now, it's really not. And I'd like not to die strapped to a chair in the shittiest apartment I've ever seen."

"You were able to get Lehrer out of your head, right?" Dara said softly, glancing sidelong at Noam. "Can you do the same thing for her?"

Faraday. It took enough effort to maintain that already—if someone attacked him, and he was supporting *two* shields . . .

But then again, the moment he'd implemented the Faraday shield around his mind, all his memories instantaneously came back—all those things Lehrer ordered him to forget. And when Lehrer suppressed him later, the persuasive orders hadn't automatically reactivated. Having the shield up, even briefly, had been enough to undo Lehrer's command.

Noam sucked in a shallow breath. "Yeah," he said. "Yeah, I think so. But I can't keep it up forever. We . . . we'll just have to hope Lehrer doesn't get suspicious and put persuasion on her again. As long as he thinks she's still under his control, she should be safe."

Ames shifted uncomfortably in her chair, hands gripping the seat. "Is it gonna hurt?"

"What? Oh, no. Don't worry. It'll be over in just a sec. You won't feel a thing."

She looked dubious, but Noam shut his eyes and concentrated, focusing on the way the geomagnetic field warped around her body, her skull, the same way it shifted to accommodate all physical objects. *Focus.* He gritted his teeth, and drew on his magic, and pulled a Faraday shield into being around her mind.

It wasn't—it wasn't *quite* as difficult as he'd expected. Yes, he could feel the strain on his magic like a weight added to the hem of an already heavy coat. But there was no instant exhaustion, no fever rising under his skin.

Even so. He released the shield almost as soon as he'd erected it. When he opened his eyes, Ames was still looking at him like she was waiting for something.

"That's it," Noam said.

"Wait, it's over?"

Noam laughed a little. "Yeah, it's over. You're all good."

"Oh thank god. Dara, release me from my chains."

Dara moved forward, pulling out a pocketknife to snip the zip ties binding Ames down. She immediately stretched her legs out along the floor and rubbed her wrists, which had gone pinkish over however many hours Dara'd kept her here.

"Shit," she said. "I really gotta pee. Dara, no offense, but guys' bathrooms are nasty. Is there—?"

"Turn left out the door, and it's the last room on the right," Dara said, collecting the discarded zip ties—like he cared so very much about keeping a tidy floor. Or maybe he wanted an excuse not to look at Noam as Noam tugged down the wards and Ames darted out the apartment door, leaving them alone again.

"So," Noam said, standing there with his thumbs hooked awkwardly in his belt loops.

Dara tossed the zip ties in the trash and straightened up, finally turning round to meet Noam's gaze. "So, what?"

Noam had to tell him. He couldn't just . . . he couldn't hide the fact Lehrer was resistant to the vaccine from the whole of Black Magnolia. But the moment those words came out of his mouth, he knew what Dara would say.

And Noam wasn't sure he was ready for that particular fight.

He wet his lips and shook his head. "I just. I . . . missed you, Dara. That's all."

Dara tilted his head to one side, and for a second Noam thought he didn't believe him—only, no, that wasn't it. There was a softness to Dara's gaze that hadn't been there before, a *consideration*.

"Ames told us you went to Dallas with Lehrer," he said. "Was that . . ." He didn't finish the sentence, but Noam couldn't help imagining what might've come next—*Was that okay? Were you okay?*

Although that might be wishful thinking on Noam's part. There were so many ways that question could end.

"Yeah," Noam said, lifting a hand to drag his fingers back through his hair. He dropped down onto the edge of Dara's bed, the spring mattress bouncing a little under his weight. "It was . . ."

*Terrible.*

Noam hadn't slept the entire flight back to Durham. Just paced the length of the plane, adrenaline shivering up and down his spine. And every time he shut his eyes, he saw the bodies of those soldiers crumpling as Noam killed them—killed all of them. Every time he stood still, he felt Lehrer's touch on his skin—heard Lehrer's voice: *We'll see.*

His mouth had gone dry. He licked his lips, or tried to. Shook his head. "I . . ."

Dara was staring at him from across the room.

"We saw combat," Noam said eventually. "Ames probably told you."

Dara exhaled, shifting his weight to the other foot. "She did," he said. "I . . . I'm sorry. I know that was . . ."

Noam tipped his head forward to scrub the heels of both palms over his face. "Thousands of people. I killed . . . *thousands* of people, Dara. For fucking—for what? For *Lehrer*? For this bullshit—this—"

"People die in war. It's not your fault."

"Yeah, well, these people died because of *me*. So it kinda is my fault, actually."

"You weren't you. You were—you're a soldier, Noam. You acted for *Carolinia*."

Noam laughed against his own hands, the sound muffled and low. "You know I'm an anarchist, right? I don't even believe in fucking . . . I don't believe in borders. I don't believe in *states*. But I just killed a whole lotta people in the name of one."

"What else were we supposed to do? Texas is locking up witchings—experimenting on them. I hate Lehrer more than anyone, but he's right. Something had to be done." Dara's footsteps were soft as they approached. The mattress dipped next to him—and after a long moment, Dara's hand settled light on Noam's spine. "Besides," he added, "I thought you were a communist. Wasn't that the point of your whole coup?"

Noam snorted and lifted his head. Dara was watching him with a small smile on his lips, soft and hesitant. "That," Noam said, "was before I really got to know Calix Lehrer. I've changed my mind now. All states are corrupt."

"Edgy, Álvaro."

"Says the guy who tried to shoot a head of state at a dinner party."

Dara's grin tilted a little wider. "I also killed Sacha for you, so I think I deserve *some* ancom street cred."

"Did you just unironically say the words *street cred*?"

"Is that not a thing people say anymore?"

"Dara, that is not a thing anyone has *ever* said." Somehow it felt as if a weight had lifted from Noam's chest; his next breath came easier, and Dara's hand smoothed against his back, dragging from his neck down his spine and then up again.

After a second Dara took in a breath—a sharp one, like he was girding himself for something—and said, "Noam. When you went to Dallas—"

But he didn't get a chance to finish the thought, as that was the moment Ames chose to return from the bathroom, pale but otherwise not much worse for wear. The conversation naturally refocused around her and what the hell she was supposed to tell Lehrer when he called her in to debrief, and how utterly fucked they'd all be if Lehrer persuaded her again.

"Maybe I shouldn't go back at all," Ames said, standing there by the window staring down at the radiator as it spat weak steam against the wall. She kicked it, but even the violence was half-hearted. "I know way too much. If Lehrer gets paranoid . . ."

"You could stay here," Dara suggested, gesturing at the room. "It's not exactly diplomatic accommodations, but it's better than the alternative."

"What would I tell Lehrer?" Noam said. "That y'all realized she was a spy? Then what—you killed her? Or should I say y'all have some massive stockpile of suppressants somewhere that he doesn't know about? I can't tell him about Faraday."

"You don't have to tell him either way. We could be using suppressants still, but we're running low. It would make us sound weak—that's beneficial."

Noam twisted his cuff in his fingers, looking for a loose thread to wrap round his knuckles—but his shirt was too new, too expensive. He clenched his nails in against his palms instead. "I don't think so. The whole argument for leaving Ames in place to begin with was that we could control the flow of information—let Lehrer think he has two functioning spies, corroborate our stories. If he knows we've made her, he'll have to act fast to mitigate the damage. And he won't expect me to be *fine* with it—I'll have to be . . . I'll have to be angry with him."

He bit back the rest of that narrative.

*I'll have to be angry. Which will make* Lehrer *angry.*

*And he's angry enough already.*

But it wasn't as if they'd be better off if Lehrer realized Ames wasn't persuaded. He'd know Noam must have figured out a way to evade his power. That would be a certain death sentence.

"Actually, you know what, I have an idea," Dara said, and they both swung their gazes round to look at him. "Neither of you go back. You both stay here. Seems as if that would solve the problem altogether."

Noam sighed and pushed himself off the bed. He immediately regretted it—without the press of Dara's body against his side he felt too cold, bereft. "Fine," he said. "Ames stays here. I'll . . . I'll figure it out." *Somehow.*

Because if he left Lehrer now, they'd be worse off than they started. Without suppressants—without the vaccine—

It was starting to seem more and more like Lehrer had no weakness at all.

And yet Noam still remembered sparring in the government complex—the sheen of sweat on Lehrer's brow, Lehrer's defenses always a beat too slow. The low heat in Lehrer's cheeks as he stood in the bathroom door and watched his doctor drain Noam's blood for the transfusion.

He did have a weakness.

And Noam was the only one, now, who stood a chance at exploiting it.


Lehrer allowed him two days.

Two days to steep himself in Level IV culture, two days to go to basic and curriculum classes and eat at the little table in the barracks kitchen—skipping their one-on-ones in favor of frigid runs through downtown, shoes tamping down snow that had already gone to dirt and slush. Two days without sleeping. Two days—long enough for Noam's anxiety to rise to a fever pitch.

Then the text message: You will attend our lessons today.

Noam stood outside the door to Lehrer's study, sucking in tiny gulps of air with damp hands clutching his satchel strap—imagining Lehrer winding that strap round his neck.

Lehrer had to sense him out here the same way Noam sensed him in return, Lehrer's golden magic a flickering net around his body as it moved from the window toward the bookshelf. Noam knocked.

The door swung open of its own accord, and Noam moved into the room. Lehrer had just selected a thick text—*Ethics in Virological Discourse*—and said, without glancing at Noam:

"Take a seat."

"I'd rather stand."

"Suit yourself." Lehrer took another book off the shelf and then, finally, turned his gaze to meet Noam's. His long fingers tapped against their embossed spines. "Where is Carter Ames?"

Noam suspected Lehrer already knew the answer. There was a cool, even set to his eyes that Noam didn't like. Dara's voice in his head: *You keep making the same mistake, Álvaro.*

"Have you really not figured that out?" Noam said, a laugh biting at the last of his words. He clenched his fists at his sides and hoped Lehrer interpreted that as anger and not what it really was. "They made you, Calix. They—we *all* know what you did."

A moment's pause, punctuated only by the tick of the clock on the wall. Lehrer set the books down on a nearby table and moved closer— not directly toward Noam, but curvilinearly, as if he didn't want Noam to realize his approach till it was too late. "And what is it," he murmured, "that I'm said to have done?"

*Dara,* Noam realized with a feeling like a dart in his chest. *He thinks I talked to Dara.*

Suddenly his heart was in his throat. Because why *wouldn't* Dara have told Noam the truth about what Lehrer did to him? Why would that not have been the first thing out Dara's mouth the moment they were alone?

Did Lehrer already suspect? Did he think Noam'd abandoned him a long time ago—that all these weeks were a last desperate attempt on Dara's part to kill Lehrer for good?

Shit. Goddamn it, *fuck.*

"You persuaded her," Noam said to buy himself time. The accusation came out tight and harsh: the first shot of war. "You made her your spy."

"And was that wrong of me, in your estimation?" Lehrer drew nearer still. "Two spies are better than one."

*Especially when you need one spy to spy on your other spy.*

"She's my friend."

"She's Level IV. Her duty is to this country—to *me.*"

Noam swallowed. The back of his throat was too dry, raw. "You fucked with her mind."

"Persuasion is hardly permanent."

"I dunno, seems plenty fucking permanent to me." Tears prickled at Noam's eyes now, traitorous heat threatening to spill down his cheeks. He scrubbed at them angrily, wiped the wet heel of his hand on his hip.

Lehrer was close enough now he could have touched Noam. Noam half expected him to—but Lehrer gripped the back of a chair instead, thumb pressing into the upholstery. "She's the same person she's always been," he said. "My persuasion ties to memory. The command will only last so long as she remembers the circumstances under which I gave it."

"And I assume you made damn sure the circumstances were memorable."

He couldn't stop envisioning Lehrer's fingertips pressing into skin instead of fabric. Driving bruises into bone.

"Is that what you really think of me?" Lehrer said softly.

*Yes.*

Noam gritted his teeth. He couldn't do it. Whether Lehrer thought he'd betrayed him or not, at least he'd let Noam live thus far. After all . . . for Lehrer, there were two possibilities. Either Dara had told Noam the truth, or—for some reason—he'd kept Lehrer's secrets.

*Lehrer doesn't have your conscience. And he isn't stupid.*

Noam had committed himself to this path, knowingly or not. Now he had to see it through to its inevitable end.

"I don't know anymore," Noam snapped. "You tell me. Did you torture her?"

Lehrer released the chair now, drawing closer. For a second Noam half expected Lehrer to reassure him. But the smile that drew along Lehrer's lips was thin and unbalanced. "Only a little."

It was as if Lehrer'd torn a rope of barbed wire through Noam's lungs. He couldn't breathe, couldn't—

"Fuck you," he got out, and he rocked forward, hit Lehrer in the chest with both fists—he wanted it to hurt, wanted to leave marks—knew Lehrer barely felt it at all. Lehrer grasped the back of Noam's skull, and Noam's own forward momentum sent him stumbling in against Lehrer, his brow hitting the center of Lehrer's sternum. Lehrer twisted one finger in Noam's hair, caressing it.

Ames. God fucking damn it, *Ames*, she didn't even . . . she hadn't said a thing.

Noam shoved at Lehrer's shoulders again, and this time Lehrer let him go, Noam stepping back quickly enough he bumped into an end table. The lamp on its surface rattled, Lehrer's magic catching it just in time to not-fall.

"You," Noam said in a shaky voice. "I did this—I've done all of this *for you*. I—don't you get that?" He was crying freely now, didn't even bother wiping his face clean. "All of it. Because I want to protect my friends. Like—like *Ames*. Because I don't want them to get hurt, because I thought you would be the one to keep them safe."

Lehrer watched without speaking, without flinching.

"I wanted you to protect—I didn't—not *torture them*."

Lehrer let out a soft huff of breath. "You've tortured plenty of people on my orders. Don't pretend you find it so immoral now."

"That's not how this *works*," Noam burst out. He very nearly stamped his foot—didn't, thank god, because Lehrer would never let him forget something like that. "It's not a zero-sum game! You don't make—moral evaluations aren't independent of context!" The phrase was dragged directly from one of the readings Lehrer had thrust upon him, early after Brennan's death. Probably Lehrer had seen the book as a peace offering.

"Nor is this independent of context," Lehrer said calmly. "Why shouldn't I cause one girl some brief, *temporary* pain to assure the safety of an entire witching nation?"

"This isn't a witching state, Calix. Three percent. That's not a fucking—"

"Not yet."

Noam made himself exhale long and slow, digging his heels down against the floor. "There was another way. You didn't have to torture her to protect *Carolinia*."

Lehrer tilted his head a fraction. "Didn't I? What other choice did I have?"

A horrible laugh tore itself from Noam's throat, and he flung both hands in the air. "*Me*," he shouted and jabbed his fingers in against his own breastbone. "You—have—*me*."

Whatever else Lehrer might've said to that—*for now*, perhaps, or *do I have you?*—he kept silent, watching Noam as if Noam were a particularly confusing museum exhibit.

Noam wanted to dig his fingernails into Lehrer's hairline and peel his face away from the bone. Crack open his skull and—*see*. Spread Lehrer's mind out on the table like the contents of a dissection.

"You just don't trust me," Noam said when Lehrer said nothing. He hated how uneven his voice sounded. How . . . weak. "You don't . . . have you ever? Trusted me?"

"Would I have made you my protégé if I didn't?"

"Let me rephrase. You don't trust me *anymore*."

Lehrer pressed one finger under Noam's chin, tilted his face up toward the light. "And why should I? You betrayed the man who all but raised you. You killed him in cold blood. I'm not under any illusion you care more for me than you did Tom Brennan."

"*Fuck* you."

Noam was shaking now, a dead leaf against Lehrer's unmoving touch.

Lehrer was . . . right. He was—Noam did kill Brennan. He shot his head open like a rotten fruit. He abandoned Dara to the quarantined zone. He let—his own mother killed herself to get away from him.

And who could blame her?

Noam was under no illusions that he was a good person anymore. Lehrer had been right, that night in the courtyard after the coup. They were the same, Noam and Lehrer: two faces of one coin.

"Fuck you," he said again, barely a whisper.

Lehrer shook his head slightly. "And yet," he said, "you won't even do that."

Noam jerked his face away, out of Lehrer's reach. Lehrer's hand retreated to his side, as if it meant nothing, and Noam stared at a vase on the far side of the room so long it blurred and bled in his vision.

"Go back to the barracks," Lehrer said. He reached out, and a book sped from across the room into his waiting grasp; he pushed *Ethics in Virological Discourse* into Noam's arms. "And read this. Return tomorrow prepared to discuss."

He stepped back, giving Noam space to grab his satchel from the floor and stalk away. Noam glanced over his shoulder at the door, his hand slippery on the knob, but Lehrer had already crossed back to the end table and retrieved the remaining book to flip through its pages. He didn't look up, although he knew Noam was there. Knew Noam watched.

So Noam left. He went back to the barracks, clutching the book and his own spared life, and the guilty weight of too many crimes.

# Chapter Twenty-Eight

## Dara

Living with Ames was a sight better than living alone.

Dara was still restricted to this building, but at least now Ames was here—both of them sitting cross-legged on the cold floor, Ames shuffling cards for poker; Ames eating all the high-calorie bits of Chinese takeout that Dara wouldn't touch; arguing about which sister from *Little Women* was the objective best (Amy March, said Dara, *obviously*). They managed to share the narrow twin bed. After all, they'd done it plenty of times back when Ames's father was still alive, both too drunk to go back to the barracks, tangled up together under Ames's childhood duvet with a convenient bucket on the floor by the pillows.

It was almost like those days again. Dara felt guilty for thinking that way—after all, it wasn't like Ames had a choice about being here—but he *did* feel better for having her around. She was the third living thing in this apartment, now—last week Dara had asked Claire to bring him a houseplant. She'd come back with a tiny little pothos vine in a ceramic pot. Dara had positioned it near the window, and he was embarrassed to admit he'd taken to *talking* with the plant, one-sided conversations to fill the empty hours. Now that Ames was here, though, Dara's social life expanded beyond vegetation.

Another bonus was that Ames, unlike Dara, still had magic. That meant that once Noam gave her the codes, she could undo and redo Noam's wards whenever they wanted to escape the studio apartment and head downstairs to Leo's bar.

This was perhaps the one downside to Ames's presence too. If Dara had gotten used to spending time in that bar for meetings—or alone with Leo—it was completely different with Ames around. Some part of his brain still implicitly associated Ames with . . . well, with getting trashed. Ames-and-bars was flickering club lights and loud music, gin and bourbon and pills tipped back, fucking strange men in grimy bathroom stalls.

It didn't make a difference that it was only four p.m. The sky was already dark this time of year, time blurring into time when Dara didn't have classes and meetings and basic training to track the hours.

He was pretty sure Leo would give him a drink if he asked. He might not approve, but he'd *do* it. Dara was nineteen; he was old enough. And maybe Dara could keep himself in control. One drink, or two. Then stop.

But that wasn't really true, was it? Dara didn't have control. Dara would drink himself unconscious—had, in fact, drunk himself to the point that Lehrer had started sending his personal physician to draw Dara's blood every week to check liver function.

If Dara had one drink, Dara would drink himself into the grave.

So Dara sipped his club soda as Leo passed Ames her third tequila cocktail, then used his straw to macerate his lemon slice against the bottom of his glass.

"You wouldn't believe the kinds of embarrassing stories I could tell you about this one," Ames was saying, jerking her thumb in Dara's direction. Dara grimaced at her, and she grinned back. "Like the time he was sick and Lehrer made him go to this big gala thing anyway, and Dara puked all over the Italian ambassador's shoes. Or how Dara went through like a zillion nannies as a kid—apparently none of them could stand him 'cause he'd read their minds and repeat all their worst thoughts back to them just to prove he could."

"Okay," Dara said.

Ames kept going: "*Or* how when he was fifteen, Dara got arrested for solicitation, like literally *solicitation*."

"That was a misunderstanding," Dara cut in quickly. "I was joking. How was I supposed to know he was an undercover cop?"

"Didn't we just talk about how you were a telepath?" Leo pointed out.

"I try not to read minds in public. There are too many of them. It gets . . . noisy."

"So . . . to be clear, you weren't *actually* asking a cop to pay you," Leo said.

"You two are both the worst." Dara tilted forward and tipped his brow against the edge of the bar counter. "No. I was not, in fact, a teenage prostitute. Despite evidence to the contrary."

A beat of silence answered that, stretching on long enough Dara could hear his own pulse in his ears.

"I didn't mean it like that," Ames said at last, her voice gone soft. He felt her hand on his arm, squeezing. "I'm sorry. I'm just . . ."

Drunk? Right.

Dara remembered what that was like.

"It's okay," he said on a heavy exhale, lifting his head and pasting a smile onto his lips. "Moving on now."

"Time for embarrassing Ames stories instead?" Ames said, a false note of levity lighting her tone. "I'm sure Dara has just as many."

Dara did, in fact, have plenty. He stuck to the palatable ones, though—told Leo about the time Ames crashed Lehrer's government car when she tried to take over from the AI, how Ames used to be pathologically afraid of the color orange because it, quote, reminded her of gas station hot dogs.

And, slowly, the embarrassment faded.

At five, someone knocked on the door. Dara and Ames and Leo exchanged confused looks—the bar didn't open till eight, and there was no meeting today. Leo held up a hand to tell them to stay in place as he crossed to the door, peering through the spy hole. But then, instead of waving for them to hide, he sighed and turned the latch.

"Did I miss the invitation?" Noam said as he moved into the bar, trailed a step behind by—

"Bethany?" Ames said, rising from her chair. If she'd been slurring her words before, that was gone now, each syllable crisp and sharp. "What are you doing here?"

"Wow, thanks, nice to see you too," Bethany said, pushing the door shut behind her with her heel. "Hi, Dara."

Dara slid off his stool as well, suddenly not at all sure what to do with his hands. She was staring at him, a brightness rising in her wide eyes—tears. After a moment she sniffed and laughed, shaking her head, wiping her face with one hand.

"Sorry," she said. "Noam already told me; it's just . . . seeing you. It's a lot."

"Why would you bring her here?" Ames snapped, turning on Noam instead. "What the hell, Álvaro? You of all people should know how dangerous—"

"I'm almost sixteen," Bethany interjected. "I can decide for myself, thanks."

"You've been gone five days, Ames," Noam said after a slow moment. "Everyone's worried about you. But . . ."

"Especially me," Bethany finished for him.

Ames's color was still high in her cheeks, one hand braced against the bar counter like that anchor was the one thing keeping her from launching herself at Noam. Dara lifted an arm, touched the tips of his fingers above her elbow.

Bethany sighed after several seconds. "I'll be fine. I really don't need a second mother, Ames."

Not that Bethany's actual mother took care of her at all—but both Dara and Ames knew better than to say that out loud.

"Fine," Ames grumbled eventually. "Just . . . sit down, I guess. Leo, can we—"

"Club soda?" Leo said archly. "Coming right up."

Bethany slid onto a stool near Ames, Noam taking a low seat at a nearby table. Noam's gaze followed Leo around the bar as Leo filled up a glass for Bethany at the spigot, like he still expected Leo to whip out a gun and a badge at any second.

"So," Ames said. "What's . . . new, I guess? Latest updates from the barracks?"

"Nothing, really," Bethany said. "Taye's working his way through all the original James Bond films, so we're all being subjected to that."

"Not the worst thing in the world," Ames said slyly. "I mean, that blond Bond was pretty fucking built, right?"

"I'm more intrigued by Vesper Lynd, actually."

"Fair. She *was* the most interesting of the Bond girls—"

"I'm interested in most of them," Bethany said.

"*Really?* You can't tell me Pussy Galore had character development."

"Not interested like that." Ames still looked confused, so Bethany added: "*Interested.* In a gay way. Because I'm gay."

"Oh."

Dara covered a laugh with a quick gulp of club soda. He'd known since—well, always, of course; telepathy didn't allow many secrets. But as far as he knew, this was the first time Bethany had put it into words.

He had, however, thought Bethany's being lesbian was a tiny bit obvious.

"Cool," Ames added lamely. "Like . . . no, I mean, it's cool. Of course it's cool. Dara's gay, so."

"Let's not make this weird," Bethany said.

"Nope, no weirdness here," Ames said, and after a second she reached over and grabbed Bethany round the shoulders, pulling her in for a rough sideways hug. Bethany yelped, and Ames laughed, said, "You're weird enough in other ways."

"Look who's talking." Dara quirked a brow at Ames, who let go of Bethany to flick some of her drink at him.

They managed to shift the conversation back to Taye and his movie preferences, which transformed into a lively debate about whether James Bond or the hero of a newer Carolinian spy movie would win in a fight, and Dara ate his way, *again*, through all Leo's bar snacks trying to fuel his argument.

*Pig,* said a voice in Dara's head. It sounded a lot like Lehrer's.

"I'll get more," Leo said, moving to get off his stool, but Dara stood first.

"No—I ate them all, so I'd better take responsibility for my own gluttony. Where do you keep the rest?"

"Back room." Leo gestured over his shoulder, past the bar, toward a shut door. "In a big box labeled, unsurprisingly, *bar snacks.*"

"I'll go with him," Noam said swiftly, pushing up from his chair and flashing a brief smile in Dara's direction. "I wanna check out your beer collection, anyway."

More likely he didn't want to send Dara into a room full of booze alone, but Dara didn't call him out on it. Noam trailed him into the back room, wandering past Dara as Dara searched for the snack box, both of Noam's hands thrust in his pockets, gazing up at the labels on all the beer crates. As if Noam had actually developed a nuanced palate for craft ales in the past six months on top of everything else.

"You and Ames doing okay?" Noam said eventually. He still had his back to Dara, was pretending to be fascinated by a box of IPAs. "Anything . . . do you need anything?"

"Not really," Dara said.

"Is she . . . I mean, she was kind of spiraling, back in Level IV. She's been spiraling ever since her dad. So . . . I don't know."

"She's okay," Dara said, which felt like an oversimplification, but he wasn't sure Noam would really get it even if Dara tried to explain. Dara and Ames had built a friendship out of mutual self-destruction, chasing oblivion because it was easier than facing reality. And sure, maybe Noam enjoyed a drink every now and then, but he wasn't like Dara. He wasn't like Ames. He didn't have that sickness inside him, constantly threatening to swell up and overtake everything.

Dara had talked to Ames about it a lot, lately. Sobriety, withdrawal, how difficult it was to face the emptiness that all the drugs and alcohol had been covering up for so long.

But . . . frankly, Ames probably needed more help than Dara could offer. Professional help.

Not that Dara would say that out loud.

It wasn't any of Noam's business.

And—there it was: *bar snacks*, scrawled in Leo's big blocky hand. Dara crouched down to drag the box out from its place. All those peanuts were surprisingly heavy.

He turned around and found that Noam was looking at him now, arms crossed over his stomach like he was defending himself from a blow. Two of his fingers pinched his shirtsleeve between them, twisting the fabric round.

"I think Lehrer's going fevermad," Noam said.

Dara's hands slipped on the box. He would have dropped it if not for Noam's telekinesis flashing out to grab it from him, floating it over to sit on a nearby crate.

"Excuse me?"

"I'm not positive," Noam added quickly. "But . . . there are signs. He's been feverish. Fatigued, too—he was weak when we sparred. I almost—" His throat bobbed when he swallowed. "Anyway. Maybe if I can convince him to spend more magic . . . he'll get worse."

Dara's lungs didn't feel like they were working properly. Each breath just burst out of him again the second he took it. His chest ached.

"Fevermadness doesn't kill you that quickly. Even if he spends a lot of magic—it could be months. And he'd take a steroid prescription before he'd put himself on suppressants."

He turned on his heel—away from Noam—and paced down to the far end of the storeroom. Back again.

"Besides," he added, facing Noam once more, "I'm not so sure you're right about that. Lehrer's a hundred and twenty-four years old—and he's been using magic that whole time, even if just to keep himself young. I went fevermad at *eighteen*."

"So maybe he figured out some tricks. Or maybe telepathy's more draining than eternal youth."

"Than *constantly healing* your own cells over and over?"

Noam gestured broadly with both hands. "I dunno. You're right—he's been fine so far. But something has clearly changed. He's sick now. Even if he was able to sustain himself for two lifetimes off his own magic before, maybe he's reached the end of that rope."

To be fair . . . it was bound to happen eventually. Lehrer must have known that. Living forever wasn't sustainable, not if you had to use magic. Dara just didn't get why it took this long. Why Lehrer could be so old, when Dara . . .

Dara got sick in a matter of months.

As with everything, Lehrer was just *that much better* than Dara.

"What are you going to do?" Dara said after that taut silence. "Make him perform all your telekinesis for you? Hurt yourself on purpose to make him heal you? That isn't enough."

"No," Noam said. "But on Independence Day—when we have to fight him—we'll have to get close enough to give him the vaccine in the first place. To make sure it . . . works."

"It'll work."

Noam made a complicated-looking expression, like he was about to say something else, then changed his mind last second. "Even so, it's to our benefit to weaken him as much as possible. We'll have to tempt him into spending a huge amount of his magic in one go. Then inject him. And then . . . we'll see, I guess."

Dara's mouth twisted. He didn't like it. He didn't like *any* of this, actually, but he'd made himself pretty clear on that front already.

"Okay," he said. "It's as good a plan as any, I suppose. If you think you can manage it without him just . . ."

*Just cutting you down like an inconvenient weed.*

"He's struggling," Noam said. "I can do it. I know I can."

Dara exhaled another soft sigh. It seemed like he was sighing all the time lately. And always because of Álvaro. "Okay," he said again. Gestured toward the box of bar snacks. "Carry those for me, then. Since you're so magically *ept* now."

Noam rolled his eyes, but he was still grinning as he heaved the peanuts off the table with telekinesis and floated them ahead out into the bar.

The others seemed to have moved on to a new conversation topic, so Noam and Dara ended up sitting at a separate table, sharing a little bowl of chipotle salted peanuts. Dara squeezed his lime over the bowl and tossed the remainder into his fresh glass of club soda.

It felt pointless arguing with Noam now. A part of Dara still wanted to, though, that need like tiny rodent claws scratching at the inside of his sternum.

Dara picked out a single peanut to roll on the table under his fingertip, leaving a trail of damp-looking salt in its wake. "Don't take this the wrong way—"

"A promising start."

"—but do you know what your problem is, Álvaro?"

Noam raised both brows. God, Dara would never get over how much he loved Noam's eyes: the perfect shade of tree-bark brown.

"You can't ever let it go," Dara said. "Once you get an idea in your head, that's it. You'll chase it way past the point of reason. Even when chasing that goal means you have to do things you never would otherwise."

Noam tossed one of the peanuts in his mouth, crunched down. "I don't know," he said. "I don't really think you're wrong. But you make it sound like that's a bad thing."

"It's not, necessarily. The way you do it, though . . ."

"The way I do it makes it bad?"

"This isn't coming out right." Dara grimaced. "I mean—yes, sometimes. I always respected how driven you were to fight for Atlantian rights, for example. Even if we disagreed on some of the practicalities, you were . . . it was impressive. It was one of the things that I . . ."

The word *loved* caught in his throat like a half-swallowed pill.

"Yeah, and you think I took it too far," Noam said, thankfully not seeming to have noticed the way Dara was gulping water all the sudden, washing old confessions down. "You think I took a good cause and made it violent."

Dara ate a peanut to buy himself time. "I suppose. You don't—you have to admit, Noam, you have trouble drawing the line."

"And you think I crossed it. With Lehrer."

"I don't want to talk about Lehrer."

"Okay. We won't, then. But . . . Dara, I'm not gonna apologize for caring about things other than myself."

"Oh, and I *only* care about myself? You—"

"That's not what I said," Noam interrupted. "I said I have an *ideology*. And there's nothing wrong with that. There's *nothing* wrong with fighting for something you believe in." He dropped an uneaten peanut back into the bowl and fixed Dara with a flat stare. "What are you doing here if you don't believe in this too?"

Of course Dara believed in the resistance.

He did.

He believed Lehrer needed to die.

. . . Only that wasn't what Noam meant. Then again, Noam wasn't asking because he didn't already know the answer.

"What do you believe in, Dara?" Noam pressed again.

Dara sipped at his soda. Swirled his straw round the glass when he lifted his head again. "I believe Vladimir Nabokov is the best novelist of all time."

*"Dara."*

Dara gazed back at him, Noam's incredulity written all over his face. Without telepathy, Dara couldn't quite tell if he was actually frustrated or just . . .

But then Noam snorted and said, "Yeah. All right. What else?"

The corners of Dara's mouth tipped up. "I believe in utilitarianism," he said. "I believe bourbon is the gentleman's choice in whiskey. I believe pineapple belongs on pizza. Oh, and the fact that goats eat everything you own just makes them more endearing."

"You are ridiculous," Noam said—but he was laughing now, leaning back in his chair and folding his arms over this chest.

And—god, Dara had missed this. The softness to Noam's eyes when he looked at Dara, and even without telepathy Dara still remembered how that expression had paired with a softness to Noam's thoughts too. Something warm curled up in Dara's chest.

He picked up a peanut and tossed it across the table. Noam leaned forward to try and catch it in his mouth and missed by a mile.

"And what are you doing with your life, when you aren't making terrible decisions in the name of the resistance?" Dara asked.

"Running," Noam said, bending over to retrieve the peanut from the floor. He—disgusting boy—ate it anyway, then smirked when Dara made a face. "And . . . I've been getting involved with the Atlantian nationalist movement."

"I saw," Dara said. "You've been in the newspapers."

"Not that. That's propaganda for Lehrer—I'm supposed to position myself opposite Holloway."

"I did think your whole argument sounded uncharacteristically flaccid."

"That's a terrible choice of word."

"*Soft*, then. Not the Noam Álvaro we all know and loathe."

"Well, as you so astutely pointed out just a few minutes ago, I can't let shit go." Noam tapped one finger against the table. "So I've been meeting up with community leaders in secret. Not encouraging riots per se, but . . ."

"You never quit, do you?"

"Never," Noam said with a self-satisfied grin. "The second Lehrer's finished, Atlantians are taking our country back."

Dara smiled back. "Good for you," he said sincerely. "But . . . so much for anarchy, hmm?"

"Well, letting Atlantia get absorbed into Carolinia isn't really congruent with anarchist values either, you know. Baby steps."

Dara kicked his ankle under the table and immediately wished he hadn't. The lines of Noam's expression softened further, and Dara knew, he *knew* Noam was . . .

Noam was still in love with him. And Dara had no idea what to do about it.

# Chapter Twenty-Nine

## Noam

Second Wednesdays of the month were for sparring.

The days leading up tumbled into each other like a fallen house of cards, Sunday into Monday, Monday into Tuesday—until it was Wednesday morning and Noam had to leave the barracks and go down to the empty room they'd been using these past months, water bottle clutched in one sweaty hand and his magic sizzling like static in his bones. He sensed Lehrer's own magic from a floor away, like some kind of primitive self-preservation instinct.

Noam paused in the stairwell and pressed his face against the brick wall, holding that cold water bottle to the nape of his neck.

If this was anything like last time . . .

If this was like last time, and Lehrer was weakened, Noam couldn't hesitate. He couldn't make that same mistake.

He had to follow through.

His stomach clenched and flexed, a feeling not unlike motion sickness. Noam swallowed against it, but his throat convulsed around his own spit; his short nails scraped at the mortar between the bricks.

*Calm down. You have to be calm.*

Lehrer would sense Noam's heart beating too fast, the electrical signals in his ventricles flickering like bad lights. He had to relax.

He couldn't relax.

He'd tell Lehrer he went for a run beforehand, Noam decided as he pushed off the wall and made himself go down the last flight of stairs. That's why he was late, and sweaty, and anxious.

But when Noam pushed open the door to the sparring room, Lehrer's gaze didn't so much as glance down at his chest.

"I heard the most interesting rumor today," Lehrer said, shucking off his tie and tossing it into a folding chair.

The razor edge to his voice wasn't reassuring. That sickness in Noam's gut pitched higher, his tongue suddenly sandy in his mouth.

Lehrer was waiting. For Noam to say something, clearly.

"What rumor?" Noam managed.

Lehrer's slim fingers undid the first several buttons at his collar. Rolled up his sleeves to the elbow. "I'm told you've been preaching some interesting ideas in Little Atlantia. Ideas that are . . . let's say, *incongruent* with the narrative we mutually agreed upon."

Shit.

It wasn't like Noam didn't think Lehrer would hear about all that. But maybe he kind of . . . hoped he wouldn't, anyway.

He lifted his water bottle, screwed off the cap, and took a desperate swallow. His throat stayed raw.

"Yeah," he said after a long beat. "About that . . ."

He didn't know what to tell Lehrer. He was too—he'd *prepared* something to say, but all those words had flown out of his head, chased off by the fever-pitch fear of standing here in front of Lehrer, Lehrer's anger like magic glinting in his pale eyes.

Lehrer stepped closer. Stopped two paces away, near enough Noam could see each individual strand of his hair.

"I'm waiting, Noam."

Noam fumbled to get the cap back on his water bottle. "I'm sorry," he said belatedly. "I don't . . . I know it's not what we talked about. But this—the whole story line about waiting, accepting what help we're given—it's not *true*, Calix. We both know that."

"And so you willingly undermined our plans," Lehrer said softly, "because you didn't . . . *personally* . . . believe in our message."

Noam twisted the cap on his bottle again, on-off, on-off—Lehrer made an exasperated sound and snatched the bottle out of his grasp, tossing it aside violently enough it burst, spilling water all over the vinyl floor.

*"Answer me."*

Noam took in a shallow breath, tilted his chin up even though every instinct told him to tuck his face down, retreat like a scared baby deer. "I couldn't do it. I can't say those things. It's not—I don't have it *in* me. You—"

"I what?"

"You know that about me," Noam finished, but it came out quiet, vulnerable. A childish plea.

Lehrer didn't blink. Didn't move. It was as if some switch inside him had shut off, the man in front of Noam as cold and soulless as a machine.

A slow bead of sweat cut down Noam's spine.

Then—at last, the moment cracking like thin ice—Lehrer turned away, pacing toward the other end of the room.

"I don't have time for this," Lehrer said. "Let's spar."

Noam didn't even have a moment to prepare.

Lehrer's first burst of magic snapped across the space between them like a bolt of lightning. Noam deflected it right in time to see it detonate against the wall to his back, soot like a black star against the paint.

The second followed almost instantly on its tail, the floor quaking underfoot; Noam stumbled, flinging out electromagnetism to keep his balance—and that was all the hesitation Lehrer needed to close the distance. Noam'd managed to blink the stars from his eyes, to reach for his own offensive play, when he glanced up, and Lehrer was *there*, he was *right*—*there*—and Noam shoved his knee up toward Lehrer's stomach too late.

The blow hit him on the cheekbone, powerful enough Noam stumbled back three paces. His skin was blazing with pain; he launched a volley of electricity back at Lehrer, but Lehrer tossed it away like a discarded cloak. Lehrer's long strides consumed the short space between them once more.

Noam lifted his arm against his face in a defensive posture in time for Lehrer's hook to catch his wrist, skipping away from his face.

Noam jabbed his foot forward, trying to propel Lehrer back, but Lehrer was too fast. He grabbed Noam's ankle and yanked him off balance, sending Noam crashing to the floor hard enough his breath whooshed from his lungs in one fell beat.

Fuck—*fuck*, Lehrer was—

*Weak* was the last word that could describe Lehrer now.

Noam's magic had gone dumb and useless, a blunt weapon—all he could sense was electricity, magnetism, as if every other ability had abandoned him right when he needed them most. He clung to those, tried to—

If he could sense the electrical signals in Lehrer's heart, or his brain, he could—

His power slipped off Lehrer like oil on water. Lehrer kicked him in the ribs, hard enough Noam cried out, curling forward reflexively to protect his organs. He flung out one hand, clawing at Lehrer's leg, trying to get purchase to—to what? To drag Lehrer down, or himself up, or—he didn't know, and Lehrer wasn't giving him time to think. The attacks came too fast, almost as if they weren't even in succession anymore—like Lehrer was somehow using more than one kind of magic at once: electricity but also strength but also something else, a pain unlike anything Noam had ever felt in his life. Fire chased down wires inside him, a conflagration of his—

*Nerves.*

Lehrer had seized control of Noam's own nervous system and twisted it toward agony. Because Lehrer might not be able to manipulate Noam's brain, but he sure as fuck could manipulate the tiny bright neurons in Noam's fingers and muscles and bones.

A shifting sound of cotton on cotton, barely audible above Noam's own broken voice—was he screaming? Crying?

A cool hand pressed against his throat. Lehrer's fingers tightened very slightly, almost but not quite enough to cut circulation.

"Do you want me to stop?" Lehrer murmured.

Noam was past the point of pride. "Yes," he groaned, both hands clutching at Lehrer's. His nails scratched uselessly against Lehrer's knuckles, Lehrer's skin breaking and repairing all in the same breath.

"Yes, what?"

A hitching sob tore out of Noam's throat. "Yes, *please*—"

Lehrer's grasp tightened further, and something black cut in at the edges of Noam's vision, his mind gone fuzzy.

God, he couldn't die like this, he couldn't—not now, not here, not with . . . *him*—

"Please stop—please . . . sir."

A moment later that hand let go. The pain vanished.

Normal sensation returned in slow pulses, a prickling like a thousand needles over his skin. Noam shuddered and rolled onto his side, dry heaving against the pool of spilled water.

All he could see was Lehrer's legs, the shifting fall of his trousers as he stood. "Pull yourself together," Lehrer said. His shoes paced away.

Noam sucked in another wet sob. The water against his cheek had gone lukewarm. It soaked into his uniform shirt.

"Get up," Lehrer said again, more impatiently this time, and Noam could do nothing but push himself upright with trembling arms. The bruises along his ribs screamed in protest. His arm was an angry mess of dark color.

Noam wiped one hand over his face and dragged himself up under Lehrer's unyielding gaze.

Only then did Lehrer turn and retrieve his tie from the chair where he'd left it. Somehow that felt so long ago now.

*What the hell just happened?*

Lehrer wasn't . . .

Dara was right. Noam couldn't defeat him. Not so easily.

He'd been a fool to ever think he could.

"Go," Lehrer said, flapping one hand dismissively.

Noam clenched his jaw hard—which also hurt—and made himself say: "Are you at least going to . . ."

*No, not like that.*

"Will you . . . heal my ribs. Sir."

Lehrer glanced toward him, still buttoning up his shirt. "Why?"

"I have basic on Monday. I can't—I won't do well. Like this."

Lehrer finished with the buttons, left his tie hanging loose around his neck as he paced back toward Noam once more. And Noam instinctively flinched back, recoiling when Lehrer touched his fingertips to Noam's cheek.

"This won't leave a mark," he said after a moment's consideration. "As for the rest . . ."

Noam's breath was a trapped bird in his chest.

"I don't think so," Lehrer said.

"*Calix*—"

"You know the rules," Lehrer said, his hand falling away. "Act and consequence. Mistakes made sparring should live with you until you learn from them."

"This wasn't—this is different, you were—that was past my skill level. It's not fair. I couldn't defend myself."

Lehrer let out a low laugh. "Then I suggest you practice. I won't tolerate such a pitiful performance a second time."

Noam stared at him, sweat and fatigue glazing his eyes until Lehrer's face was an indistinct blur. Because one way or another, he was pretty sure . . .

There wouldn't be a second time.

*A heavily revised handwritten draft stolen from the desk of C. Lehrer. Dated ca. coup of 2123.*
*Notes added by N. Álvaro.*

It is with ~~reluctance~~ a sense of great responsibility that I stand before you today, ~~citizens people of Carolinia~~ fellow Carolinians, ~~representing as a representative of the military junta~~, to accept provisional interim ~~command~~ authority over ~~our this~~ our government. ^As a representative of the military junta and ~~As~~ a patriot, I accept this duty readily ~~willingly~~; but as a man, I must admit I take on this role with a heavy heart. I, like many ~~in this government~~, considered Harold Sacha ~~an ally~~ a friend. **(Lehrer has a long and documented animosity toward H. S., see appendix C § 8.)**

But as the report of Attorney General Holloway's investigation is made public, ~~you will soon realize~~ it will become clear that ^Chancellor ~~Harold~~ Sacha's treason not only constituted an aggressive act against ~~Atlantia~~ a foreign government, but ^was violence against all Carolinians. **(Lehrer refers to an aggressive act** against Atlantia here; records from the former Atlantian government and from the chancellor's office show Atlantia was preparing to declare war against Carolinia before Lehrer's junta ordered occupying soldiers in Atlantia to enforce annexation; see appendix D §§ 7–9. The members of the Atlantian government who were party to this decision—incl. Pres. Mary Tran, VP Fredrick Henderson, Maj. Gen. Jeremy Swyers, Maj. Gen. Amanda Shaw, Maj. Gen. Bert López, Maj. Gen. Jamie Kim, among others—all conveniently died of magic infection within two weeks of the annexation, excepting Maj. Gen. Shaw, who survived the virus only to be found dead by apparent suicide four days later; see appendix D § 10.)

This will not be the first time I have been given authority over the government of Carolinia, and neither time was I elected to that authority. The first time I was appointed king by a committee. This time, I have been afforded power by mere virtue of being the highest-ranking ~~military official~~ commander ~~in~~ ^of the Carolinian armed forces. I do not believe anyone should be <u>bestowed</u> (**Emphasis sic**) power; power should ~~always~~ only be granted by the people. This is ^the principle on which ~~why~~ I abdicated as king and abolished the monarchy~~, and~~. I stand by ~~this belief~~ this conviction ~~now~~ ^now. ~~Therefore my goal is to keep t~~The interim authority of this military junta ^will be limited to no more than two months' time~~., sufficient period~~ ^In the next two months, we will ~~to~~ hold a special election to replace Chancellor Sacha and his ~~administration~~ circle of traitors. (**See appendix A** for evidence of fabricated charges against many of the officials in Sacha's administration who were speedily executed by guillotine the day following this speech.)

*Remaining pages missing.*

# Chapter Thirty

## Dara

Ames and Dara were halfway through watching a nature documentary on her phone—the kind of film that was mostly an excuse to watch wolves stalk their prey across pale winter landscapes, an exercise in hoping the elk would live but pretty much knowing it wouldn't—when a knock at the door interrupted the film midhunt.

They exchanged quick looks, and Dara glanced down at his watch.

"Oh," he said. "It's already six twenty. I didn't realize it got so late."

Ames pushed herself up and tracked over to open the door and let Noam in. He had bags slung over both arms, heavy with contents that turned out to be groceries when Noam unpacked them onto the dresser. Nothing that had to be cooked, of course; the apartment didn't come furnished with a stove.

There was something unnatural about the way Noam moved, the back of his neck too stiff—like he was uncomfortable being watched.

"It's a lot of fruit," Noam said, half an apology. He glanced back over his shoulder; his lower lip was red and chewed on.

"I like fruit," said Dara.

"Some protein bars."

Ames met Dara's eye when Noam turned his back again, her brows knitting together as she tilted her head in Noam's direction. Dara shrugged.

"You know what," Ames said. "I actually just realized I forgot something downstairs. Think Leo'll let me sneak in and snag some snacks while I'm at it?"

"Always worth trying," Dara said and allowed her a brief smile of gratitude as she slipped out the front door.

Noam kept unpacking, arranging the food atop Dara's dresser in little clusters by type: fruit, protein bars, styrofoam cups of dried noodles. Dara drew his legs up onto the bed and watched as the back of Noam's neck flushed a slow, dull pink.

"Do you need any help?"

Finally Noam turned around. "No. Sorry. I'm done."

"You don't need to apologize. We appreciate the help. Takeout was getting repetitive."

Noam drummed his fingers against the top dresser drawer and said nothing. He was biting his lip again.

Dara didn't like the feeling that was curling up in his chest. It itched, just out of reach.

At last Dara drew up the nerve: "Did something happen?"

"No. Not really." Noam's gaze skittered away from Dara's to stare at a spot on Dara's bed like it had suddenly become the most fascinating thing in the world.

"I don't believe you."

"Okay, well, you don't have to."

God. What was Dara supposed to say to that? The thing in his chest twisted tighter, and he gripped the edge of the mattress, sheets mussing under his palms.

How had they ended up here?

It was several seconds before Dara was able to speak again. "I don't . . . I don't want you to think that just because I—because I don't want you there . . . with him . . . that you can't talk to me at all."

Noam's gaze darted back to meet his. When he took in a breath, his shoulders trembled, visible even from across the room.

"It's not anything he did," Noam said slowly. "It's . . . I'm . . . starting to worry. A little."

*And you weren't worried before?* Dara bit back those words right in time. "Worry about what?"

"I'm worried he knows," Noam whispered. And he looked so young just then, no longer the cold killer Dara had met in the meetings, an assassin in tailored suits. He was just a seventeen-year-old kid caught deep in something he no longer knew how to escape.

Dara pushed himself up off the bed and paced closer—not close enough to touch, but near enough he heard the wood creak when Noam braced himself harder against the dresser.

"Did he say something?" Dara asked. He tried to keep his words quiet, nonconfrontational.

"He said he didn't know if he could trust me. And he—he's angry. Because I won't . . ."

Noam didn't have to finish that sentence, and Dara didn't want him to. Cold fingers knit around his heart. It hurt.

"You have to get out of there," Dara said in a low tone. "It's been six weeks—you're out of time, Noam. He'll hurt you."

Noam was breathing fast and shallow, his pupils dilated like they couldn't take in enough light. Dara slipped his hand around Noam's wrist, fingertips pressing in against his pulse. It, too, beat quick and erratic.

"I should have left with you," Noam confessed, softly enough it was barely audible at all. Dara tipped in closer to catch the last words. Noam twisted his arm under Dara's grasp to catch Dara's hand with his own, tangling their fingers together and squeezing hard. "I'm sorry. I should never have—I let you go out there alone. I'm sorry. I'd give anything to go back and . . ."

"Leave?"

Noam swallowed, nodded.

"You still have that choice," Dara said. "You can leave him. Right now. You don't have to go back."

Already the words felt dead in his mouth. Dara had said that before, and Noam always gave the same answer.

Noam stared at him, his throat convulsing, clearly trying to figure out how to tell Dara no—how to tell him, for the hundredth time, that staying with Lehrer was more important to him than Dara was.

"Don't say it. Don't even . . . don't bother."

Dara tried to extricate his hand from Noam's, but Noam gripped tighter, keeping him in place. "It's not that," Noam said. "It's—I was going to say . . . you're right."

Dara's gaze flicked up. Noam wet his lips.

"It's . . . what you said, in the bar the other night. About how I can't let things go. You're right. And maybe—I don't know. Maybe it's because I've been so—my whole life, people do things to, they . . . they *hurt* the people I love. And there was never anything I could do about it. Not until I got magic." Noam's hand slackened against Dara's, but Dara didn't try to pull away again. He rubbed his thumb against the backs of Noam's knuckles, and Noam said: "I can do something, now. And maybe I . . . maybe I'm afraid of being powerless again."

The moment that followed was heavy and silent, thick enough between them Dara could've twisted it in his grasp like fabric.

"You aren't powerless." Dara's voice wavered. "You—Noam, even if you didn't have magic, you wouldn't be powerless. You're so . . . you're the bravest person I know. The stupidest too." That earned a broken sort of laugh from Noam. "But. You're strong. He won't break you like he—"

His throat closed around the rest.

357

Noam's inhale was sharp, audible. He lifted his hand and slid chilly fingers into Dara's shorn-short hair. "You aren't broken, Dara."

A soft noise pulled itself up from Dara's chest, not quite a sob, and Noam's fingertips pressed in against the back of his head, his breath warm on Dara's lips—and whatever that sound was, it was muffled against Noam's mouth when Noam kissed him.

Dara's heart couldn't possibly keep beating this fast. It wasn't sustainable—and yet he never wanted to stop feeling this way, like something was finally opening up in his chest . . . blooming, a flower he'd thought wilted long ago.

He stepped closer, pinning Noam between himself and the sharp edge of the dresser, one hand finding Noam's hip as he kissed Noam back—more, harder, like he could make up for lost time. Noam's body felt solid beneath Dara's hands in a way nothing had in years. He couldn't get enough.

If the kiss after Dara's return had been messy and needy and desperate, this one was all of that in a different way. This was stained with hurt and betrayal and resentment—but there was affection, too, a deeper and more vibrant kind of love. Dara had worried he'd lost the capacity for that when he lost his telepathy. That without the ability to read someone's mind, he'd never know them well enough to want them like this.

But god, he wanted Noam. He wanted him *so much*.

He slid his hands under the hem of Noam's shirt; Noam's telekinesis kicked in a second later, undoing the buttons so Dara could push the fabric off his shoulders. The shirt dropped to the floor behind them, Noam kicking it out from underfoot.

Dara's breath froze in his lungs.

"Noam—"

His touch skimmed along Noam's ribs, skirting the inflamed skin along his flank. Bruises burst like so many dark nebulae, darting down toward his hip. More, on Noam's arms and shoulder.

"It's nothing," Noam said, both his hands back on Dara's face, cupping it between them so Dara had no choice but to meet Noam's eyes again. "Sparring. I swear."

*Sparring.* As if a thin guise of pedagogy made the violence any easier to swallow.

Dara shook his head roughly, fingertips digging in at Noam's wrist, but Noam just said again—"I swear"—and kissed him, and Dara . . . Dara couldn't. He couldn't push him away. Not anymore.

Noam took a step forward, and Dara stepped back, letting Noam press them across the narrow room until Dara's calves bumped up against the edge of the bed. Noam stripped off Dara's shirt slowly, like he wanted to remember every inch of skin he revealed. He kissed the line of Dara's collarbone and murmured against Dara's neck, "I love you."

A shiver unwound in Dara's stomach. He caught Noam's mouth with his, kissed him hard enough to press his answer into Noam's lips, his body, his skin.

The bed felt smaller when they fell onto it, limbs tangled and Dara's hands combing through Noam's hair. He couldn't stop needing more—not when Noam tracked kisses down his chest, his stomach—not when they'd both shed their trousers and it was skin on skin, friction and heat.

In the lamplight, Noam's body glowed gold. Dara trailed his touch along Noam's unbruised shoulder. Noam's eyes were half-lidded, shadowed beneath his lashes.

Dara shifted beneath him, curling a leg around Noam's waist and drawing him down close. Noam's lips parted with a soft exhale.

"Do you have a condom?" Noam asked. "Lube?"

Dara nodded, but Noam still hesitated, one hand hovering over Dara's hip.

"I've never done this before," Noam said—then his cheeks flushed, and he added: "Well, that—I mean, I've never—not like—"

Dara didn't want the details.

"It's okay," he said, pressing a finger to Noam's lower lip to shut him up. Then Dara grinned, the dangerous kind of grin that used to turn Noam's thoughts dark and liquid. "I'll teach you."

Still—knowing this was new, at least for Noam, that there was one thing Dara could give him that Lehrer hadn't—it tasted, fiercely, of victory. That coal burned in Dara's chest as they moved together, Noam whispering in Dara's ear the kinds of words Dara had always wanted him to say. On Noam's voice they were soft and low, rough like Noam's kisses became, and later—when they were both lying still and spent on that slim bed—they smoldered in Dara's mind like they'd never go out.

Noam's brow tucked in against Dara's chest, each exhale hot against Dara's overwarm skin. His hand had gone still on Dara's stomach; Dara wanted to memorize the sight of his fingers against Dara's ribs.

After several moments Noam lifted his head. "It just occurred to me . . . ," he said. "What happened to Ames?"

Dara laughed. "Oh, she got the picture, I think. She probably won't come up until you go down there and tell her it's safe."

Noam's face scrunched up. "Fuck, that's embarrassing."

"Are you really under the delusion that it wasn't obvious to everyone what happened in the barracks that time? Noam. This isn't news."

Noam groaned. "Right. Telepathy. I really didn't need those fears confirmed, thanks."

"I'd say I'm sorry, but . . ." Dara grinned.

"You're awful, and I hate you."

It was so close to being like it was before—or how their relationship should have been, if Dara hadn't spent that year terrified and traumatized and slowly going fevermad. He pushed up far enough to snag the edge of the quilt at the foot of the bed, tugging it up to wrap them beneath the blanket, together. In the warm cocoon built by that blanket, it almost felt like they'd never have to leave. They could wind the hours out longer and longer until time lost all meaning, the rest of the world vanishing into an ever-expanding black hole.

"Don't leave," Dara said against the heat of Noam's skin. He squeezed his eyes shut—the way he used to shut his eyes when he wished on shooting stars, as if not looking could make his dreams come true. "Stay here, with me."

Noam's hand drew a slow motion along Dara's back, up and down.

"I want to," Noam said. "I wish I could. But . . ."

Dara clenched his jaw. And after a moment he pushed back, sitting up and letting the quilt fall around his hips. "But you're going back to him. Again."

"I'm—no," Noam said, and he sat up too. "I'm going to the barracks. There's basic tomorrow."

"Fuck basic—*Noam*. Please. Please don't go."

It was pathetic, it was . . . begging, and Dara knew that, but he had one hand on Noam's thigh anyway, grip digging in. Noam's fingers curled loose around his forearm, but he didn't push Dara away.

"Dara. I can't stay here. I—I have to go back."

"You don't *have* to do anything."

Noam pressed his lips in a tight line. "Think about it. Think about—you said yourself Lehrer's smart. Do you really think he doesn't know where you are? That he hasn't figured it out?"

*No. No. He—*

Dara's blood had gone still and cold in his veins. He couldn't breathe all the sudden, his lungs laboring to take in air.

"The only reason he hasn't killed you yet is because I keep going back," Noam said. "Because I tell him what happens here. If I don't show up tomorrow, he'll come. He'll find us."

Dara swallowed against the thick bile in his throat. "So we go somewhere else. We—we can stay with someone. Holloway, maybe."

"Holloway's a government official; Lehrer will be watching him the same way he's watching *everyone*. I can't stay. And it—I'm sorry, Dara, because I know. I *know* it fucking kills you. And I wish . . . I wasn't able to be there for you last year, when Lehrer was—and I wanted to. I want to be there for you, now. But—"

"But you can't be here for me," Dara said tightly, "because you're still *with him*."

Noam was the one shaking now, a low tremor in his limbs that Dara only noticed because they were touching. "Not for much longer," he swore. "Not—it'll be over soon. I promise."

Dara inhaled through his nose.

He didn't want to fight.

Not again.

"Fine," he said. "All right. Go."

Noam nodded. Then he leaned in and kissed Dara, an unsteady hand on Dara's neck. Dara stayed in bed as Noam got dressed, pulling on pants and sweater and jacket, covering up all that bruised flesh. And when the door shut behind him, Dara sank low and pulled the covers up over his head, building a fortress around himself in the dark.

# Chapter Thirty-One

## Noam

"I'm coming with you," Taye said that next afternoon, catching Noam at the bedroom doorway right as Noam was about to head out on his daily run, water bottle already clutched in hand.

"What? Why?"

Taye's brows went up. "I mean, I don't have to, if it's like . . . a personal-time thing. I just figured you might want the company. And I could use the workout; I've been dying in basic with all those sprints Li's been making us do. I swear that woman hates me."

Noam only realized he'd been staring at Taye in silence for several seconds when Taye added:

"So . . . can I come?"

"Oh. Yeah. Sure. Let's go."

Noam waited for Taye to get changed and guzzle a truly inhuman amount of water at the kitchen sink before they headed out. Noam set them along his usual six-mile route—the route that had gotten longer and longer lately, Noam circling certain loops twice, three times to delay having to go back to the government complex.

Taye, at least, was fast. He kept up with Noam easily enough even though he was at least two inches shorter. Noam sensed Taye's orange-red magic doing something to the soles of his shoes every time his stride landed, keeping himself from slipping on the ice even without crampons.

"Man," Taye said once they'd covered the first couple miles, only slightly out of breath. "It's so weird to think the year's almost over. I mean . . . it's almost *March*. I've been in Level IV half my life. Hard to believe that's gonna end."

"You're graduating this year?"

"Yep. Turn eighteen in three weeks. Then I'm out of here, soon as the semester's over."

Noam had known on some level that Taye was about to age out of the program, but he hadn't really *thought* about it before. Not really.

"It'll just be you and Bethany," Taye said. "I mean, unless Ames comes back and they make her redo spring semester, since she's missed so much class."

Lehrer had, ultimately, invented a story for Colonel Howard and the rest of the Level IV administration about Ames going to rehab for her addiction issues. Noam wished that were actually true.

But there was something about the way Taye said it, his voice too light, too careful, that made Noam think Taye hadn't bought that story either. The addict part might be right, but Taye probably knew Ames well enough to know she'd never put herself in rehab voluntarily.

"I'm sure they'll let her graduate," Noam said, trying to sound confident.

"Do you know what program she's in?" Taye asked. "I was thinking I might send, like, a postcard or something, but nobody seems to have a forwarding address."

Noam shook his head. "No idea."

"You could ask Lehrer."

Noam looked at him too quickly. Taye noticed, judging by the way his gaze lingered on Noam's before he turned his attention back to the horizon.

"Yeah," Noam said. "Yeah, I'll ask. Good idea."

They ran another quarter mile, the soles of their shoes hitting pavement punctuating the rapid pound of Noam's heartbeat.

"Do you have plans for after graduation?" he made himself ask to fill that silence.

"Yep. Got a job waiting for me and everything."

"You don't sound very excited about it."

Taye shrugged, the gesture comical when performed in motion. "I mean . . . it's fine. I'm gonna be working in military engineering. Turns out math magic's pretty good for building really big weapons."

Noam grimaced. "Oh."

Taye laughed, a little more breathless than before. "I don't know, man. I've always been pretty lucky, you know? My parents are both still alive. They're well off. I basically grew up surrounded by all these smart university professors who were only too happy to teach me everything they knew about anything. My parents still actually *talk* to me, unlike Bethany's mom. And I guess I just . . ."

For several long moments, Noam thought Taye was gonna trail off and leave it at that. But then he shook his head and said:

"I wanted to do something useful with myself. Find a way to take all that good luck and use it to like . . . change the world, you know? Like maybe I could run for Congress or start a nonprofit or something. But looks like that's not in the cards."

"You could turn down the weapons engineering position."

"It doesn't work that way, dude. You know that. We're Level IV— we do what they tell us to do."

They ran the next five miles in silence. On mile eight, Taye knocked Noam's shoulder with the heel of one hand, and they both stopped, Taye hunching forward to grasp both knees as he struggled to suck in a proper breath.

"Think we've gone far enough?" Taye asked, after Noam had dropped down onto a nearby bench and scrubbed the sweat off his forehead with the sleeve of his shirt. "Like . . . Jesus, there's only so far a human being was built to *run*."

"I think I might keep going a little farther," Noam said, once he was confident he could say that much without gagging on his own arrhythmic inhales. "Gonna try to get to thirteen."

"You," Taye said, "are an absolute madlad."

Taye always did love his vintage slang. But that didn't make him wrong, Noam thought a half hour later, after Taye had jogged back in the direction of the government complex and Noam was dry heaving with his head thrust into the bowels of a public trash can. Maybe he'd been pushing himself too far, too fast. But at least when he was running, there was no thinking about Lehrer, or Dara, or anything else. Just the cold and the pain.

More pain today than usual, though. Noam finally managed to gulp down his nausea and carefully draw his head back out of the opening on the side of the covered trash can, even if he couldn't quite make himself straighten up again. Instead he draped himself over the lid and tried not to think about the pain in his chest or the way his limbs felt like they were about to give out. He was still two miles from the government complex—that was another two miles at least that he'd have to run to get home.

But when he tried to stand, his balance wobbled, and he ended up clutching the trash can for dear life as successive waves of dizziness swam through his head. *Shit.* He'd never reacted like this before, never felt *this* exhausted after a run. Maybe it was too much, trying to go for distance after the shitshow that had been sparring with Lehrer the other day.

Noam had almost asked Bethany to heal him after that, but he'd been afraid Lehrer would notice—and Lehrer would take that as insubordination, Noam's refusal to obey his order. *Act and consequence.* Lehrer and his perfect syllogisms, spelling out the logic behind his casual cruelty.

Noam lifted a hand and touched hesitant fingertips to the spot on his ribs that still hurt, his abdominal muscles clenching up on reflex like his whole body wanted to flinch away. When he closed his eyes, he could still see the way Dara had looked at him when he'd seen the bruises. That memory, more than anything else, sent another ripple of sickness through him.

Goddamn it. No way was Noam going to make it back in this condition. He could barely keep himself awake, never mind force his body to run again.

Lehrer would be informed, of course, that Noam ordered the car. But at this point, Noam didn't care. He pulled out his phone and called the government complex valet and had them send a sedan to pick him up. Noam collapsed in the back seat and drifted there, halfway between consciousness and unconsciousness, the rest of the way home.

Noam had come to expect it now: the ten p.m. text, the moment after one of their private lessons when Lehrer would trail his fingertips along Noam's cheek and say, *Come over tonight.*

It felt like so long ago that Noam had responded to such invitations with a low thrum of heat in his belly, drunk off a lethal mix of the sexual and illicit. And Lehrer had been . . .

Not kind. But something close to it.

*Fond*, perhaps.

And Noam had eaten it up. All those late nights, both of them staying awake even though Lehrer had meetings in the morning—Lehrer reading terrible poetry out loud and Noam laughing so hard his stomach hurt. Lehrer catching his wrists with one hand and pinning him down, Noam intoxicated by the thrill of losing control.

God. Noam had been such an idiot.

Tonight was no different than all the rest. Only this time Noam felt like he didn't belong here, in Lehrer's apartment, surrounded by all the accoutrements of a long life lived—Lehrer's antique carpets and cozy sofas, the smell of the old book in Noam's hand, the taste of expensive whisky on his tongue. Now Noam was an actor on an unfamiliar set, fumbling to remember his lines.

He would rather be in Dara's tiny broken-down apartment than among all this antique finery.

Being here was like being close to Dara in a different, darker way. He could imagine Dara sitting in that chair or gazing out that window. Could see him curled up on the rug by the fireplace with *Ada* in hand.

Lehrer had been in the kitchen cleaning up dinner—boeuf bourguignon and glasses of dry red wine—but he came back into the living room now. Noam heard his footfalls on the carpet as much as he sensed his magic like a controlled firestorm to Noam's back.

Noam didn't dare look. He kept his gaze fixed on the page, although he was no longer processing the words written there. Lehrer drew closer, closer—until he was standing just behind the sofa, near enough Noam smelled his black vanilla aftershave. Suddenly it took all Noam's concentration to keep his breath coming slow and even, to turn the page on cue.

*Don't be paranoid,* he ordered himself—but all he could think as Lehrer slid his fingers against the nape of Noam's neck was whether Lehrer was about to tighten that grip, to snap bone.

Could Lehrer tell? Could he see Dara's touch written on Noam's body, the way Dara had seen Lehrer's?

"You seem tense," Lehrer murmured. And then he did press in, but it was just to massage the place where Noam's neck met his shoulder. "Perhaps I should have gone easier on you the other day."

Noam let the book fall shut in his lap.

Lehrer's fingers kept working that muscle, his other hand rising up to grasp Noam's other shoulder. This time he dug into the aging bruise; Noam hissed between his teeth, and Lehrer's touch dropped.

Noam shouldn't start a fight. He should play easy and innocent, put Lehrer at ease.

But what came out was: "Yeah. You should have."

Lehrer moved round the arm of the sofa now, into Noam's line of view. His face was still set in a mask of false concern. "You know I only ever do what's best for you, Noam. Such experiences are educational."

Noam stared back at him with a flat gaze.

Lehrer tapped his tongue against the backs of his teeth, an admonishing sound. "This petulance is unbecoming. You should have grown out of that by now. You must, if you ever hope to gain real power."

Noam's answering anger was too quick, too waspish to control: "And how much power is left to go around, Chancellor?"

Lehrer's expression stilled—and when he tilted his head, the light from the hearth cast long shadows below his cheekbones, at his temples, transforming his face—however briefly—into something terrifying and macabre.

But when he spoke again, his voice was soft, even paternal. "What brought this on?" he murmured. He moved closer, away from the flickering fire and into the lake of yellow light that fell beneath the lamp on Noam's end table. His steps were slow and sure, movements steady as a ship cutting through cold water. "It wasn't so long ago you still believed in what we can achieve together. What have I done to convince you to abandon everything we've worked for?"

Really? He was really asking that question?

Noam shoved his book aside and stood. Not that it did him much good; Lehrer still towered over him, same way he towered over everything.

"Maybe I'm sick of your methods."

Lehrer drew nearer still, until Noam had to take a step away, putting the coffee table between them. "It's Dara, isn't it?" Lehrer said softly. "You've been going over there . . . letting him put ideas in your head . . ."

"It has nothing to do with Dara."

"Of course it does. Everything does, with you—with both of us. Don't lie to me, Noam."

*Persuasion.* God, it was—had to be.

Dread fell like a heavy stone into Noam's gut.

Noam shook his head once, roughly. "I'm going," he said. "I'm leaving. I need to—I'm going back to the barracks. We can talk about this tomorrow."

Something crossed Lehrer's face then, a shadow far deeper than any the fire had cast. Noam turned and headed for the door, quick strides—he needed distance, needed a shut door between the both of them—

But Lehrer was faster. Always faster.

He caught up with Noam in the hall, hand grasping Noam's wrist and tugging him back hard enough Noam stumbled.

"Don't," Lehrer said. Their gazes met; Lehrer's glittered with something unseen and dangerous. "We aren't finished here."

"Let go of me."

Lehrer didn't let go.

"Where is it you have to go so quickly?"

"I told you, the barracks—"

A smile twisted Lehrer's lips. "And that's where you'd rather be, is it? Not here. Not with me."

Noam pulled his arm against Lehrer's tightening grip. It accomplished nothing. "Calix. Let—"

He didn't finish. Lehrer's mouth crushed against his, swallowing up the words in a kiss. Lehrer pressed him back, pinning Noam against the wall with one hand braced over his shoulder, Lehrer's teeth catching his lower lip, Lehrer's other hand abandoning Noam's arm in favor of sliding down from his waist toward his thigh.

"Don't pretend you don't want this," Lehrer said against Noam's numb mouth. "Don't act like you don't—"

Noam twisted his head aside, forcing Lehrer's kiss to graze his jaw instead—and somehow that was what it took to make Lehrer release him, taking a sharp step back toward the opposite wall.

Noam's pulse was a wild thing between his ribs, his skin alight with chills as he pushed himself upright. He and Lehrer stared at each other for a moment, Lehrer gone still like he was actually *surprised* for once in his ancient life.

Not that Noam was gonna stick around to enjoy it.

There was nothing left to say. He spun on his heel and started off toward the front door once more—made it two steps before Lehrer's hands found his bruised ribs, drawing him back.

"Stop," Noam said—gasped, really, because his lungs barely had the capacity for speech. All he could think was Dara's voice in his head, *He'll hurt you.* "Stop," Noam said again, twisting enough to look Lehrer in the eye, both his hands balling into fists. "I—"

"—have a headache?" Lehrer finished for him.

Noam's protests were dead leaves in his throat. And Lehrer still hadn't let him go, Lehrer's magic sparking off his skin and against Noam's, tiny oscillations of pain.

A sharp breath, and Noam jabbed his heel against Lehrer's instep, missed. Lehrer's hand abandoned his ribs to twist in Noam's hair instead. He used that grip to shove Noam forward, Noam's feet stumbling under his own weight as Lehrer slammed him headfirst against the wall.

White light exploded behind Noam's eyes, bright and loud as a gunshot. The agony cascaded from his face to his skull, down the rope of his spine to tingle in the tips of his fingers. He barely choked in a breath before Lehrer thrust him forward again.

The second impact was like shattering every bone in his body. Something hot and wet coursed down Noam's cheek, tasted like metal in his mouth.

Noam's legs gave out. Lehrer caught him with a quick arm around the stomach before he could hit the floor, heaving him upright and pressing him there between Lehrer's ember-hot body and the cracked wall. His breath on Noam's neck was uneven, Lehrer's chest heaving against Noam's back.

Lehrer's lips were dry as they moved against Noam's ear, his voice dark like ash.

"I bet your head hurts now, doesn't it?"

He let go. Noam sagged against the wall, blood dripping off his throbbing face and speckling the hardwood floor. Noam stared at it without really seeing, his hands flat against the plaster and his mind a haze of impenetrable fog.

Lehrer moved away, a shadow on the fringe of Noam's awareness. But he was back a moment later, the edge of his coat sweeping through Noam's peripheral vision as Lehrer pulled it on.

"I have an interview off-site," Lehrer said curtly, as if they were discussing this over breakfast and not here in the hall with Noam blinking back tears and Wolf padding down to nudge a worried nose against Noam's leg. "Go to the meeting tonight. Nowhere else."

Noam sniffed. That, too, tasted like blood.

Lehrer's footsteps retreated down the hall toward the door—but stopped halfway there.

"I will see you back here tonight at ten sharp." Noam imagined persuasion whipping around Lehrer's words like gold fire. "I expect you to have your priorities in order by then."

Even after Lehrer left—after the door had fallen shut in his wake and the wards reconstituted themselves around the apartment—it took a long time for Noam to push himself up off the wall. Wolf's pink tongue darted out to lap the blood off the floor.

"Good boy," Noam mumbled. His mouth felt dumb and useless.

Wolf sat on his haunches and let out a soft whine.

Noam dragged a shaky hand through the fur atop Wolf's skull and started off back down the hall toward the living room.

The whole apartment looked different now: like a reflection of the one he knew, blurry round the edges and surreal. Noam moved as if he'd been programmed to do so, toward the kitchen for ice—only then he diverted course by the door. Didn't want to drip water on Lehrer's floor, after all.

But when he got to the bathroom, he had to face himself in the mirror, and that more than anything else brought him careening back to earth.

The bruise on his brow was already purpling—a second mark on Noam's cheekbone was still red, but it would darken quickly enough. The blood came from a cut on his eyebrow and a split lip, coursing down over the inflamed skin; speckled stains marred his uniform collar.

The other half of his face was pristine and unmarred, all smooth skin and sharp bone.

"Shit," Noam whispered.

He tipped his head down and turned on the faucet, but the first splash of water on his face stung badly enough he had to grit his teeth against a scream. He thrust Lehrer's hand towel under the stream instead, dampening it enough to press the cold terry cloth against his injuries.

Even when he lowered the towel, his face didn't look much better. The bruises seemed angrier somehow, blood and water mixing to a pinkish fluid that dripped off his jaw and into the sink.

Noam didn't recognize himself like this.

He should have learned healing magic. He should go to the barracks; Bethany knew healing—

Only he couldn't go to the barracks. Couldn't be seen like this.

But he would be seen. Because it was already—*shit*, it was eight thirty; the meeting was at nine.

*Ten sharp,* Lehrer had said.

Noam touched shaking fingers to the edge of one bruise. It had already started to swell. He should get ice, figure out a way—he couldn't

373

go to the meeting with these marks on his face. Couldn't look Dara in the eye when he . . . he . . .

He grabbed a comb from Lehrer's drawer and scraped it through his hair, trying to coax it to fall just so over his brow. Useless; his hair wasn't long enough.

And—god, but now he was remembering the day he met Dara, how Noam had glimpsed a bruise hidden by Dara's carefully tousled curls. Only then he hadn't thought, hadn't even *considered*, and . . . and now . . .

"God fucking *damn it*!" Noam slammed the comb down against the counter hard enough Wolf darted off and leaped onto the safety of Lehrer's bed, curling up to watch Noam with liquid eyes. Noam hadn't even realized Wolf was there. "Sorry, boy."

He had to leave soon. But he couldn't go out looking like—

Noam crossed to Lehrer's closet, tugging open the doors and flicking through the hangers for some of the spare clothes he kept here. He found them hanging in long plastic bags; Lehrer had them dry-cleaned. Because of course he had.

Noam changed into something fresh, kicking his bloodied uniform into the far corner of the closet and emerging to find Wolf still tracking him with his gaze, head resting on his paws. Noam could almost convince himself Wolf understood what had happened somehow.

And maybe he did. He'd been here with Dara, after all.

Back in the bathroom Noam attacked his hair with the comb a second time, adding a sweep of Lehrer's wax to coax it into a controlled style. At the very least, he could walk into that meeting with some kind of . . . *dignity*, as Lehrer might've said. He could walk past the guards in the atrium, all those government officials, with his face bloodied but held high.

It occurred to him, then, how incredibly fucked up it was that he still cared what Lehrer's people thought about him.

Before he left, Noam leaned over the bed to press stinging lips to the crown of Wolf's head. Wolf lapped at the flat of Noam's wrist, his cold nose damp against Noam's palm. "Be good," Noam murmured against his fur.

The walk through the government complex was every bit as bad as Noam imagined. He felt the stares stick to him like molasses, dragging along in his wake. All those whispers behind hands.

What story would Lehrer invent to explain this?

Whatever story it was, Noam was sure it'd be a great one.

"Geer Street," he told the government car the guards called for him outside. For once in his life he couldn't muster the courage to take the bus.

But as he stood on the icy sidewalk outside Dara's building—it was snowing again, the flakes accumulating on his shoulders and cold against his bruises—whatever nerve he still had dwindled.

Maybe he shouldn't. Maybe he should turn around and go back to the government complex—back to the apartment to wait for Lehrer in the bedroom with the lights down low, and . . .

*And what, Álvaro?*

He tightened his jaw and took a sharp breath. He was already late.

The meeting was well underway as Noam let himself in, Holloway midspeech about the security plans for Independence Day; Ames was drinking a red cocktail, Leo perched atop a nearby table with Claire and Priya at the bar, and Dara . . .

Dara caught his gaze the second the door fell shut in Noam's wake.

He was on his feet in an instant, the chair legs scraping against the floor loudly enough Holloway fell silent. All gazes swung round to look at Noam, Priya's gaze going wide as Ames muttered, "Shit."

"Sorry," Noam said, trying for a self-deprecating look and waving his hand. "Didn't mean to interrupt. Keep going."

Victoria Lee

He knew how he looked. He could still see that reflection in the mirror, how—*grotesque*, how obviously violent. But he didn't want to imagine that through any of their eyes. Through Dara's.

Noam never should have come here.

"What the hell happened?" Claire asked, rising to her feet, too, slower than Dara.

For his part Dara still stared, mouth parted and his eyes gone wide. It was like Dara had been shot but hadn't realized yet, was bleeding out.

"I'm Level IV," Noam said by way of explanation. "Sometimes training gets rough."

Ames's mouth closed so hard her lips had gone white. She wasn't going to contradict him. But Dara . . .

Dara didn't look capable of speech.

Noam made himself move closer, pull out a chair at Claire and Priya's table and sit down. He wasn't sure he was fooling anyone. Claire and Priya had fallen silent, and from the way Leo was looking at him, Noam knew he was reconstructing the blows in his head the way only a soldier could. Even Holloway had an odd expression on his face, eyes narrow and considering.

It was several seconds after Noam had settled in that Dara slowly, slowly sank back down into his chair. Holloway picked up where he'd left off, shuffling the notes on the table before him and licking his thumb to flip to the next page, lecturing on about camera angles.

Not that any of that mattered when there was a technopath on hand.

Noam let Holloway talk. Now that Noam was here, it was like all that terror from the hallway of Lehrer's apartment had finally seeped into his bones, a sickness that spread like mildew through his marrow. One hand curled round the seat of his chair, hidden by the table, gripping it so hard a splinter caught under his nail.

He wasn't any better by the time the meeting was over, and he couldn't remember a single thing they discussed. Noam's mind was a jumbled cacophony of meaningless words. His head hurt like a motherfucker. *Lehrer was right about that much,* he thought and nearly laughed.

Noam tried to leave quickly, but Dara called his name from across the room before he even made it to the door. And then Noam had to turn and look at him.

Dara had one hand braced against the tabletop, his skin gone the sickly color of old photographs.

"Can I talk to you?" Dara said, and Noam had no choice.

He nodded.

Dara led him out into the alley behind the bar—the same alley where Noam lit his cigarette once, Dara's hair dusted white with snow.

"I have everything under control," Noam said.

Dara shook his head. The sound he made next was half a laugh and half a hitched breath, pitch falling low. And now that they were out here, it seemed like he couldn't even look at Noam. His gaze flitted from the ground to the brick wall to Noam's coat to the end of the alley, anywhere but Noam's mangled face. When he finally tilted his head toward the sky, the streetlights reflected in his eyes, off unshed tears.

Noam took a tiny half step closer to Dara, expecting Dara to move back to regain distance. He didn't. That clenching feeling in Noam's gut twisted tighter.

"I can—we're so close, Dara," Noam said, insisted. Already his hands were going numb in the cold; he pressed them into his coat pockets. "It won't be long now. I've been taking pictures of anything I can in the apartment—old letters, journal entries. Hacking video files. And he must keep the vaccine nearby. I know it."

Dara still wasn't speaking. A single tear had fallen free of his lashes, slid down his cheek.

"Independence Day is in two weeks," Noam said.

"You won't last two weeks."

Dara lowered his gaze at last, and with the redness in his eyes—the way he fixed them on Noam like he could pin him down with sight alone—made him look as furious as he did heartsick.

"Dara—"

"I keep telling you these things. You keep not listening. Just like last time."

"I'm—Dara, you know I believe you. It isn't about that—"

"He won't stop," Dara cut in. "He'll keep hurting you. He'll do more than that. He'll—"

Something cold crystallized in Noam's heart, the certain knowledge of what came next; and he didn't think he could survive hearing it said on Dara's lips, after everything.

"Don't—" he started, but Dara pushed on, a fierceness twisting his features as he said it.

"He'll rape you."

A fresh wave of pain crested through the bruises on Noam's face. He was crying, Noam realized belatedly. The salt from his tears had gotten in the open wounds.

"He won't," Noam said, but he barely recognized his own voice.

A terrible sound tore out of Dara's lips. "You can't possibly—you can't believe that, Noam! Do you really think you're that fucking special? Do you think you're so very different from me?"

"I . . . no, but—"

"You think I deserved it, then?"

"*No*—god, Dara—"

"Then what? *What*, Noam? Do you even hear yourself?"

Noam wet his lips; it just stretched Lehrer's cut open wider. He grimaced. "That's . . . here's the thing, Dara. I consented from the beginning."

"You're *seventeen*, he's—you can't, you told me yourself you can't— when he—"

"You know what I mean," Noam snapped. It came out angrier than he meant it to, and he flinched, fingers curling up toward his wrists. "Sorry. But . . . I wanted it, Dara. You have no idea. I—"

"*So did I,*" Dara snarled. "Or he told me I did, anyway, and he never fucking let me forget it either. But when you stop wanting it, you don't get that option. You *won't*. You don't get to *change your mind* with him." Dara was crying freely now, the tears slipping down his cheeks; his eyelashes had already gone to frost. "You told me that the first time it happened, you were drunk—so drunk you don't even remember it. Don't you hear yourself, Noam? Don't you get it? If it were anyone else . . . if it were *me*, you would be telling me that was rape."

Every breath Noam took felt labored, like it cost immeasurable effort to keep himself alive.

No. Dara was wrong, it wasn't—Noam hadn't—

Calix wouldn't do something like that.

Noam hated himself the moment he thought it. Because . . . because Lehrer *had*, to Dara. Only Noam couldn't help the voice that whispered back: *But he'd never do that to* you.

He shouldn't think like that. Dara would kill him if he could overhear it. But . . .

But it was true. There was something special about what Noam and Lehrer had—or used to have, maybe, and yes, Calix—*Lehrer*—hit him, but did that erase everything else?

"Two weeks," Noam said again. "I only have to make it a little while longer. And he—that's all he wants, isn't it? He's afraid he's lost me. So. I'll just. I'll prove he hasn't."

Dara had been midway through wiping his face; his hand fell away at that, his gaze flicking back to seize on Noam's. "What the hell are you—what are you saying?"

God. God. Noam wanted to vomit. Didn't have anything in his stomach to throw up.

"I'm saying I . . . I'll give him what he wants. I'll sleep with him."

In the silence that responded, Noam thought Dara was crying again. His shoulders were shaking, his lips quivering. Noam realized too late that wasn't grief.

It was rage.

"That's your solution?" Dara said. "That's what you'd rather do than stay with me? Even after this—after he *hurt* you—you'd rather be with him."

"No. Of course not. But I—"

"Then go." Dara spat the words out like acid. "Do it. Go back to him, and—and fuck him, and whatever else you want. But if you do that, you don't come back."

Those words ricocheted through Noam, leaving electricity in their wake.

He didn't mean it.

He couldn't—he *wouldn't* mean it, not something like that. Only Dara had his chin tilted high, and although Dara's eyes shimmered with tears, they were cold in a way that had nothing to do with the ice in his hair.

Noam drew his hands out from his coat pockets and reached for him; Dara took a step back, keeping Noam at a distance. Shook his head.

"Dara. Please. I—you know I don't want this, but I have to. We don't have any other—"

"Choice?" Dara's mouth twisted in a sardonic knot. "But you do have a choice, Álvaro. You've always had a choice. And if you walk away from me right now, you're choosing him."

He wasn't.

Noam would never choose *him*.

But if he stayed here with Dara . . .

They still didn't know how to defeat Lehrer. The vaccine was probably worthless. And fevermad or not, Lehrer was still strong enough to kill Noam easy.

If Noam stayed here, he might live another few weeks. But then they'd all die, every one of them. Including anyone else Lehrer had infected or killed in the name of the Carolinian cause.

"I'm sorry," he whispered, but Dara wouldn't look at him now. Wouldn't say a word.

Dara pushed past Noam and flung open the door to the bar, retreating back into the warmth. The door slammed shut behind him, and it felt like the last cannon fire at the end of a long battle.

Lethal.

# Chapter Thirty-Two

## Noam

Noam barely remembered the trip back.

He knew he took the government car. He knew he must have gotten out of it at the entrance to the government complex, shown his identification to the guards. Must have taken that mirrored elevator up to the fourth floor and walked down the hall and into Lehrer's study and taken down Lehrer's wards.

And yet, toeing off his shoes in Lehrer's hall, he couldn't remember how he got here.

It was 9:57 p.m. And judging from the fluttering firelight at the end of the hall, Lehrer had already returned.

Noam followed that light into the living room. He didn't know what he'd expected—more violence, perhaps, or Lehrer with his shirt already half-unbuttoned. But what he found was Lehrer standing by the hearth and gazing down into the flame. He had a drink in hand already, still full.

Or refilled, perhaps.

Lehrer lifted his head and looked at him. Then he sighed, pushed off away from the fireplace, and beckoned Noam closer.

Every step Noam took was another key turned in a lock.

Once Noam was in reach, Lehrer lifted that same hand to skim his touch over Noam's damaged face.

"I'm sorry about this," Lehrer said, and he *looked* sorry—his lips gone thin as his magic flickered to the tips of his fingers, healed Noam's bruised flesh. "I lost my temper. It was unacceptable. It won't happen again."

Noam didn't know what to say to that. His tongue was heavy in his mouth, wordless.

Even with Noam's face healed, Lehrer's hand lingered—slid farther back, fingers tracing the shell of Noam's ear. Lehrer took in a shallow breath—but then he shook his head, said, "Let me get you a drink."

It felt bizarrely *familiar*, watching Lehrer pour the scotch from the bar cart—that faceted crystal decanter poised over the tulip glass, Lehrer lifting the dram and carrying it back to press the drink into Noam's limp hand.

Lehrer took a sip of his own whisky while watching Noam—and after several seconds Noam made himself drink as well. This time he barely felt the burn on the way down.

"I was afraid you wouldn't come back," Lehrer said in a quiet tone. He was still so close. His gaze flickered between Noam's eyes, like he couldn't quite read him. "I didn't . . . when I told you to be here at ten . . . I didn't use persuasion." His mouth twitched up, however briefly. "I admit I hoped you'd return. But I was equally certain you'd run."

*Say something.*

Noam had to say something. He swallowed against the taste of liquor in the back of his throat.

"I thought about it," he said. His grasp felt slick around the tulip glass. He shifted his fingers closer to the base for a better hold. "But. I just . . . I guess I couldn't, in the end."

Lehrer let out a soft breath, one Noam felt whispering through his own hair. "You have no idea how much of a relief that is to hear," he said. His hands were on Noam, skimming light along his ribs—those, he hadn't healed. Noam stayed very still, so still he thought Lehrer might feel Noam's heartbeat pounding against his chest as his touch wandered down Noam's sternum. Lehrer's fingers caught on one of Noam's buttons, and he rubbed the pad of his thumb against the mother-of-pearl.

But he didn't push it through its hole. For all Lehrer had made himself clear this afternoon—after everything—he didn't move to undress Noam. Not yet.

"I don't want to hurt you, Noam," Lehrer murmured. "You're . . . important to me. And perhaps I've not done the best job of showing that lately."

Noam's hand lifted—he wasn't sure if he was moving to push Lehrer away or draw him closer, and in the end he just grasped Lehrer's wrist and did neither. Just kept him there, held in space, the backs of Lehrer's fingers still brushing Noam's stomach.

Lehrer's cut-glass gaze traversed Noam's face like he'd never seen him before. Like he couldn't get enough of him. "After my brother died . . . I didn't think I'd ever care about anyone again. I didn't want to need anyone, or anything. And I didn't think I'd ever meet someone else who could be my equal."

The words felt like water in cupped hands—powerful, lifesaving, but impermanent. Trickling away.

Lehrer touched Noam's cheek, his mouth. "Tell me you won't leave me," he whispered, lips a scant inch from skin.

And as hard as Noam searched, he couldn't sense Lehrer's magic.

It wasn't persuasion.

*Now or never.* Noam had to make a decision.

The hand on Lehrer's wrist shifted, knocking Lehrer's touch from his shirt. But it was just so Noam could move into the space left behind, rising up on the balls of his feet to press his mouth to Lehrer's.

Lehrer's inhale was quick, audible. He kissed Noam back without hesitation, grasping his hips with both hands and keeping him in place as he leaned closer, pressing their bodies together. And for a second it felt like it used to, both of them impatient and desperate for more; Lehrer's teeth dragged along Noam's lower lip, and dizziness answered in Noam's mind, spun-sugar euphoria.

Lehrer pushed him back, driving them both down the hall toward his bedroom with Lehrer's telekinesis already tugging his tie off from around his own neck, Noam's hands lifting to draw the silk free and toss it aside.

The back room was pitch dark, although when Lehrer's magic flared, the lamp answered—a dawn of golden light. Lehrer was breathless when he drew back, gaze drifting down the length of Noam's body. He held Noam like he was fragile, like Lehrer had never realized how precious he was before now.

When he kissed Noam again, it was gentler, uncharacteristically so. Lehrer's hands slid down to Noam's hips and untucked his shirt, palms sliding up and along Noam's bare skin.

"We're so good together," Lehrer said against Noam's mouth as he tipped him back onto the bed. His weight on Noam's chest made it hard to breathe; panic reared its ugly head and clawed at Noam's insides as Lehrer kissed his cheek, his neck. "We belong together."

*No.*

No, they didn't.

Something in Noam snapped, a horrible tension and a worse release. He shoved Lehrer back with both hands, and Lehrer went easily, confusion shifting into his expression as Noam pitched upright, Noam's knees drawing defensively toward his chest.

"What is it?" Lehrer said, concern creasing his brow as Noam struggled to take in a fresh breath. His nails dug in against his own shins, and suddenly everything in this room was a threat—the heaving shadows and soft mattress beneath him, the smell of cigarette smoke and the bladed lines of Lehrer's face.

"I can't," Noam said.

He tasted salt. His lungs felt shredded and bloody.

Lehrer moved back, off the bed. Noam crawled forward after him, limbs weak and shaking as he pushed off the bed and onto his feet. Lehrer hadn't moved—hadn't said a word, the lamplight glinting off the whites of his eyes.

Noam dragged a hand back through his own hair.

"I'm sorry," he said, voice wavering. "I can't do this anymore."

Lehrer's voice was low, barely audible but laced through with ice. "What did you say?"

He was so close, a slim cut of darkness silhouetted against the dim light. Noam took a reflexive step back—toward the door.

Lehrer moved in his wake, slow but inevitable.

"I don't want this." Another step. Noam's veins were burning, and when he dug his fingers into his palms, his skin felt thin as paper. "I don't want you, Calix. It's over."

"It's not over."

Noam's breath fluttered in his throat. Suddenly his Faraday shield felt heavy in a way it never had before, like it took effort to maintain. Lehrer's persuasion was a weight leaning against his mind, threatening to break through.

Noam was in the hall now, the living room to his back and Lehrer standing in the bedroom doorway, tall enough he consumed the whole length of the frame. Backlit, Noam couldn't make out Lehrer's face. Couldn't see him at all.

"Come back here, Noam." No mistaking the magic that ignited the air between them. "You aren't going anywhere."

Noam was frozen in place, feet grown roots into the floor. Only it couldn't be persuasion—he had Faraday, Lehrer couldn't—

No. This was fear.

Lehrer held out his hand for Noam to take. "Don't test my patience." This was the moment. If Noam disobeyed him now . . .

Noam drew his magic to the tips of his fingers, the surface of his skin. "I said no."

Silence fell. For a terrible second they were both locked in place, Lehrer dark and unreadable, Noam's very blood on edge as the realization sank in.

As Lehrer knew, all at once, that Noam was no longer his.

Hadn't been, for months.

Lehrer broke first.

He surged forward, inhumanly fast; his touch grazed Noam's throat for one reeling beat before Noam recoiled out of reach. Noam's magic surged out from him all at once, seething with electricity to slam into Lehrer's hastily erected defenses.

And suddenly all Noam could think about was the way it felt when he was on the floor of the sparring room, broken and screaming—how easy it would be for Lehrer to bring him down again.

"I knew it," Lehrer rasped. He sent something white hot and deadly lashing across the space between them; Noam stumbled back and slammed himself against the wall just in time. The conflagration lit into the floor, flames arcing toward the ceiling in the brief moment before Lehrer quenched it. "You think I didn't know, Noam? You think I didn't *figure it out?*"

Noam shot magic back toward Lehrer like a dozen poisoned darts; none of them struck home. Lehrer was a force of nature, a storm bearing down; Noam barely had time to distinguish one attack from the next, every defense hurled into place at the last second. His mind buzzed, static roaring in his ears. He was distantly aware of Wolf scurrying down the hall to hide in the bedroom, an odd thing to notice at a time like this, and yet—

He couldn't keep this up. Couldn't focus hard enough for long enough. Soon he'd break, and Lehrer's magic would swarm through the cracks to devour him.

"You're transparent," Lehrer said. "That Faraday shield on your mind—who gave you that idea? Who fed it to you like honey on a spoon?"

Lehrer's next blow caught Noam in the knee, and he fell, crashing to the floor heavy enough the ricochet sent a vase flying to shatter against the fine rug. And Lehrer was there before Noam could recover, his knee bearing down against Noam's sternum and his hand at Noam's neck, crushing the air from his windpipe.

Noam choked and scrabbled at Lehrer's arm with both hands as Lehrer leaned in close, closer, until a fallen strand of his hair grazed Noam's brow. Lehrer's face was contorted with fury, eyes pale fire.

"You gave them to me. Every one of your . . . compatriots. You betrayed them—and yourself. For *nothing*."

Noam jabbed his knee up, slamming it in against Lehrer's ribs. Lehrer didn't move, wasn't even fazed.

Lehrer pressed down with the heel of his hand, and Noam's vision flared to white.

"We could have been great," Lehrer whispered. His breath was fast and shallow, air bursting in beats against Noam's skin. "We could have changed the world, you and I."

Noam's mind had gone lax and liquid, unconsciousness seeping up like groundwater. He fumbled for his magic; it slid and slipped through his fingers.

*Last chance.*

He hurled as much power as he could muster into Lehrer's gut. Lehrer flew back, slamming into the opposite wall.

Noam didn't wait for his gaze to clear or for Lehrer to rise. He scrambled to his feet and dashed toward the living room, panic blinding him to the corner of the rug he tripped over, the end table he banged his hip against.

Lehrer's magic caught up with him halfway across the den.

Pain exploded in Noam's chest, three sharp snaps splitting the air as his ribs broke. Noam cried out and threw forward a lash of electromagnetism to anchor himself in place. His telekinesis flung a chair at Lehrer—a table—a lamp. They crashed against him like waves breaking upon a rock.

Lehrer progressed through the wreckage without misstep.

"There's nowhere to run," Lehrer said. "Dara can't protect you now. The rest of your team is . . . impotent. Weak." A thin smile cut across his lips. "And as for Minister Holloway . . ."

Another crack of magic split against Noam's face, a laceration opening along his brow, slicing down toward his mouth. Blood splattered the carpet underfoot.

"He's been mine since the beginning."

And then there was pain.

It seared through Noam's nerves like a nest of lightning, rocking him back on his heels—only Noam's magnetic anchor kept him upright. He heard screaming, echoes of someone yelling in his ears.

The same trick Lehrer used in sparring. It burned a path down to his core, unstoppable wildfire.

Distantly Noam was aware of Lehrer drawing closer. He didn't realize how close until Lehrer's fist slammed into his stomach, sending him lurching back and heaving air from his lungs. Lehrer's grip on his shoulder held him in place for a second blow.

"I wish I could say I'd make it quick . . . ," Lehrer murmured in his ear.

He pressed a chaste kiss to Noam's temple.

"But I want it to hurt."

Lehrer's grip found Noam's wrist and tightened until the bone cracked. Kept squeezing, grinding it to dust.

Noam couldn't think, couldn't see. Could barely even feel the pain anymore. It was too much, all encompassing, an ever-expanding universe and his mind floating free in black space.

*No.*

No, he couldn't give up.

If Lehrer left this room alive, he'd go straight to Dara.

Noam dragged up the dregs of his magic and focused again—as ever—on magnetism. On electricity. On finding the frequency of Lehrer's magic as it seethed through his nerve endings and playing the opposite tone.

All at once, the pain vanished.

Not all of it, not the agony of broken bones and something deep in his gut that felt as if it had split open.

. . . But enough.

Noam flung the rest of that magic against Lehrer, screaming with the effort of it—every ounce of power he could bring to bear, until all he had left was agony and exhaustion and the dull throb of fever in his skull.

Lehrer fell, and Noam bound him down with an impossible gravity.

It wouldn't last.

But it might last just long enough.

He staggered down the hall toward the study door, legs weak and shaking under his own weight. Behind him he felt the cords of his magic snap, Lehrer struggling against the tide holding him back and escaping.

Noam left a trail of blood in his wake, magic leaking from the soles of his feet and the palms of his hands in a spray of silver-blue light.

He shoved open the door with his shoulder. Lehrer was right behind him, right *there*—

His hand brushed Noam's shoulder, injecting pain like venom into vein, before Noam slammed the door shut between them. And in the same gesture he yanked Lehrer's wards out of the way like old curtains and threw up his own in their place—the same wards he'd constructed around Dara's apartment, tight and bled-through with technopathy.

Noam was out of breath, his lungs screaming with the agony of taking in air. Every inhale was like puncturing them with his own broken ribs—and maybe that's exactly what was happening, Noam thought dizzily as he faltered toward the next door—maybe he was collapsing inside.

He didn't have much time. The technopathy might baffle Lehrer for a minute or two, but he'd get past it quickly.

Lehrer was too clever to be restrained for long.

Noam had to get out of here. Had to get somewhere public, somewhere with . . . witnesses.

He couldn't make it down the stairs on his own. The hardwood was slippery underfoot, each lurch down its own exquisite torture.

Noam grabbed onto the railing with one sweaty hand and heaved himself up, bracing his heel against metal. The stairwell weaved before him, his vision just oil paints running together.

He hissed in a breath and heaved himself over the ledge and into free fall.

Noam mustered enough magnetism to catch himself mere feet from the ground floor, slowing his fall enough to keep the collision from being lethal. Even still, judging from the wretched scream that tore from his throat and the sharp-split pain in his side, he'd broken another several ribs.

His head was on fire. Noam crawled across the landing to the door, hand slipping on the handle once, twice, before he managed to drag himself back up onto his feet and pull down.

Very distantly, he sensed the wards on Lehrer's apartment crumble and fall.

Noam stumbled into the atrium. At this hour the crowds were thin, most of the tourists and government employees having gone home for the day. But there were still enough people weaving between the separate wings of the complex that Noam felt—

Not safe. But.

He was *so close*.

He kept his gaze locked on the doors to the back street, dragging himself step by step across the marble floor with his broken wrist clutched to his chest. Already people had started to stare. Noam gritted his teeth and tried to lift his head, to walk a steady gait. It was all but impossible.

A familiar glint of magic cut into Noam's awareness right as he made it to the far side, the guards pushing open the doors. He looked back, over one shoulder.

Across the atrium, Lehrer was a still figure in a gray suit, a solitary pillar around which the hubbub of evening traffic swirled and eddied and passed by. Their gazes met as Noam stepped out onto the street.

Lehrer lifted a hand—not farewell.

A promise.

# Chapter Thirty-Three

## Dara

After Noam left Dara—*left*, on purpose, left for good—Dara had gone back into the bar and slapped a handful of argents onto the table for Leo and taken a bottle of bourbon in trade.

Ames at least knew to leave well enough alone.

Dara paced the short length of his apartment, that bottle waiting on his dresser and his shirt buttons torn half-open—it was too hot in here, *too hot* for midwinter, for all snow still fell outside the window and the radiator spat useless steam against the plaster wall. Dara circled his thumb and forefinger around his wrist and dragged it up his forearm, checking how far he could get.

Not far enough. He'd gained weight.

Dara wished he could strip off his skin, his life. Shed it like spent currency and fade into oblivion.

Oblivion was what that bottle would buy him, when he finally gave in.

And he would give in. He knew it. The bottle knew it. It stood there on the dresser and reveled in that knowledge, mocking him.

Damn it.

Dara broke pace, crossing to the dresser and tearing the foil from around the bottle's neck, yanking the cork free. He poured himself a sloppy dram and stared down at the whiskey that spilled over the rim of his glass and wet his fingers. He'd played a terrible game and won an even worse prize.

This was Álvaro's fault. So much in the ruins of Dara's life was Álvaro's fault.

He left the bourbon there and spun on his heel to pace another lap.

Outside the snow blanketed the city inch by inch, silencing it under so many layers of cold and ice. Dara pressed his brow to the frigid windowpane and stared down at the grim street, darting like a sooty line toward downtown.

He didn't know why he kept making the same mistake.

Or maybe the problem wasn't other people at all. The problem wasn't trusting in traitors. It was Dara. Dara, the common denominator at the end of the function, the first glinting chunk of superdense matter at the start of the universe.

All his fault.

*Born broken*, as Lehrer had told him so many times.

He twisted round again, back toward the dresser. Picked up the glass and hurled it against the far wall.

Crystal shattered, shards spraying across the hardwood floor and spinning underneath his bed. Dara screamed until his throat ached, until the neighbors pounded on the ceiling, until he had nothing left but air and anguish.

Then he made himself sweep up the broken glass and pour the whiskey out his window, sat on his bed, and glared at the opposite wall until his pulse slowed again.

A practical person would have picked up his burner phone and called Claire or Priya, told them everything Noam had said, everything Noam had gotten himself involved with.

They'd call the mission a failure. Pack up and flee back to the quarantined zone, regroup to try again some other day.

But how many people would die in the meanwhile?

Dara gripped his phone in one hand, staring down at the blank screen.

Maybe he was as bad as Noam, though, because Dara couldn't bring himself to dial. He couldn't walk away and leave Lehrer here, still living.

Dara had come to Carolinia to burn Lehrer's kingdom down. He wouldn't leave until he stood on its ashes.

He was about to go downstairs to get Ames when the burner phone buzzed against his palm. Dara glanced down, and his heart slammed to a stop.

Noam: downstairs, come get me. fast

Dara pitched himself up off the bed, shoving his feet into shoes and grabbing his coat from the hook by the door. He was still pulling it on as he clattered downstairs, running into Ames on the way. She caught his elbow and said, "Where are you going, mister?"

"It's Álvaro," Dara said. "He just messaged me. I don't know why, but it sounds—he's outside."

Ames let go. They both dashed down the last flight of stairs and tumbled out into the snowy night. An unfamiliar car idled on the curb, something ancient and barely functional puffing exhaust into the dark.

The windows were tinted. It could be a trap.

Dara didn't care if it was.

He yanked open the passenger-side door.

Noam lay slumped in the driver's seat, blood dripping from a gash on his face and one arm—the one resting in his lap—so red and swollen it had ripped the seams of his shirtsleeve.

"Shit," Dara gasped. He crawled into the car, bracing his knees on either side of the gearshift to slide a hand onto one of Noam's cheeks, tilting his face toward him. Noam's eyes cracked open, fluid-clumped lashes fluttering like it took effort just to look at Dara. "What did he do to you?"

Only Dara already knew the answer to that question.

Ames had moved round to the other side of the car, opened the driver's door. Noam's weight dropped back, and Ames braced against him just in time, looping both hands under his arms to keep him upright. She didn't say a word, but her eyes were wide and her face gone pale. A muscle twitched in one cheek.

Dara wondered if this was how she'd looked with him, every time she dragged him home too drunk to stand. Too out of it to keep from aspirating his own vomit when withdrawal hit.

"Get his seat belt," Ames got out. It sounded tight, like her teeth were clenched.

Dara jabbed his thumb against the latch and leaned forward to grab Noam's ankles from the floor, pulling his legs up and onto the seat as Ames dragged him bodily out of the car. Noam cried out when they did that, his whole body arcing forward like he'd been shot through with an electric current.

"Don't," he mumbled when Dara had finally made it back out, grabbing one of his arms to take the burden off Ames. "Not . . . we have to go. Away."

"What's going on?"

Leo had emerged from the bar, messy haired and with a towel still thrown over one shoulder—he'd left midshift. He blew out heavily when his gaze fell to Noam, taking a halting step forward across the icy sidewalk. "Jesus Christ."

Noam said something incomprehensible against Dara's chest, his face tilted in against Dara's shoulder. Dara nudged him up enough that Noam's mouth wasn't blocked.

"What did you say?" he whispered.

"He's coming."

It was like a blade fell, cutting through Dara's spine and severing it in two. He stiffened, fingers clenching around a handful of Noam's shirt.

"Get him in the car."

Ames helped Dara drag Noam to the back door, Leo on the other side of the car pulling Noam in by the shoulders to sprawl across the back seat. This time, Noam didn't scream. He barely even moved at all.

"Do you live around here?" Dara asked Leo, meeting his gaze across the seat, Leo's fingers pressed against Noam's neck like he was checking his pulse.

"Yeah. But I have a roommate."

At least he didn't suggest they go to the hospital.

Ames took the front seat, pulling the door shut in her wake. Then: "*Shit!* It's not driverless."

"Figure it out," Dara snapped back, climbing into the back seat and dragging Noam's limp legs up onto his lap, shifting over enough to see his face. Noam was looking paler by the minute, his eyes shut and still.

"Don't you remember me crashing Lehrer's car that time? I can't fucking drive!"

"*Ames!*"

"Fine, fine—hope I don't kill us all—"

She tossed something back toward him, and Dara caught it on reflex. It was surprisingly slippery; he glanced down—Noam's phone, the screen covered in blood.

The car lurched out of park, Ames's knuckles blanching around the wheel as she pressed the gas. Across the back seat Leo had his head tilted down to keep his ear near Noam's mouth.

"Are you some kind of doctor or something?" Dara snapped, irritation rearing up in him—as if, in the absence of a better target for all that fear and anger, his temper had latched onto Leo instead.

"I got trained in basic life support while I was in the army," Leo said. "Not much good without equipment, but . . ."

Dara wished he had Noam's head in his own lap instead. That he could brush his fingers over Noam's brow and tuck his hair back behind his perfect ear.

Instead he was useless. Always, *always* useless now.

Dara blinked his eyes hard against the tears that threatened to spill down his cheeks and patted Noam's leg like that would make the slightest difference.

Noam wouldn't die. He couldn't.

Dara wouldn't let him.

"Where are we going, exactly?" Ames said from the front seat. They turned onto Magnum Street, headed back downtown. Dara blinked against the glittering city lights as they rose to meet them, his pulse erratic. He kept expecting to see a black government car peel around the upcoming corner to block them in.

"Not your place," Dara said. "Go to . . . Holloway. Go to Holloway's."

Holloway was a government official—Noam had been right about that—but it was the best choice they had. They couldn't check into a hotel, not with Noam in this condition.

Ames nodded in the rearview mirror, and Dara turned his attention back to Noam, whose chest rose and fell more slowly now, the slightest of motions. Leo dabbed at the blood on Noam's face with the bar towel, not that it did much good.

"Stay with me," Dara murmured, knowing Noam couldn't hear him. He wished he dared text Bethany, but he couldn't guarantee Lehrer didn't already have someone watching her phone. Watching *her*.

All Dara could do now was tangle his fingers around Noam's clammy palm and hold on tight.

Holloway lived in Forest Hills, in a house not far from the one Ames had grown up in.

In comparison, though, Holloway's home was more subdued: a white clapboard front, colonial-style, with black shutters and a painted-blue door. Holloway's butler was already out on the front step by the time Ames managed to coax the vintage car up his drive and put it in park.

Ames ran up the gravel to talk to the butler, explaining the situation far better than Dara could have right now, no doubt. He and Leo carried Noam between them, up the steps and into Holloway's wood-floored foyer. Holloway himself met them in the sitting room, sweeping newspapers off a chaise so they could set Noam down.

"He needs a healer," said Holloway, crouched down on the floor with one pale hand gripping the corner of the seat cushion. "This doesn't look good. Can I ask what happened to him?"

"Lehrer happened," Ames said grimly. She paced back and forth in front of Holloway's tall windows, arms crossed tight over her chest. "He'll probably be here any minute, looking for us."

"I'll call around for a discreet hotel," Holloway said, rising to his feet. "For the time being, my personal physician can examine him. He's well compensated for his discretion."

Dara and Ames exchanged looks.

"Fine," Dara said at last, looking back to Holloway. "If he can get here fast."

"We're so fucked," Ames muttered after Holloway had left the room. She was chewing on her thumbnail, all the way down to the quick. "Once Lehrer realizes we aren't at yours or my dad's house, this is the next place he'll check."

"We shouldn't move Noam again too quickly," Leo said. He'd taken a seat on the ottoman, legs bunched up to fit between that and the armchair. "He's in shock."

All their gazes swung back round to Noam again, who'd gone the same taupe color as the upholstery beneath him.

For better or for worse, Leo was right.

Holloway returned soon with a sachet of ice and pillows to prop up Noam's head. The ice went on Noam's wrist—and his ribs, which were bruised and contorted beneath his skin when they lifted up Noam's shirt. But that was all they could do until the physician arrived, a thin older man carrying an antique black bag that must have been bigger on the inside, judging from all the equipment he pulled out of it.

The doctor kicked the rest of them out of the sitting room while he worked. Holloway had his cook make up a cheese board for them to snack on as they waited—although for his part all Dara could manage was to peel the leaves off one of the little wild strawberries and swallow hard against his rising nausea. Ames rummaged through Holloway's cabinets and pulled out a bottle of tequila, stared at it for a solid five minutes, then put it back unopened. They all waited in silence.

The doctor emerged after an hour or so, peeling latex gloves off his hands and dropping them in Holloway's kitchen trash. He drew Holloway into a separate room—that in itself was enough to make Dara's heart knot—but Holloway returned quickly enough.

"Noam's spleen has ruptured. It will probably heal on its own, but for now . . . he needs a blood transfusion," Holloway told them. "Dara, Leo . . . are either of you AB negative?"

Leo shook his head. "A positive."

"I'm O negative," said Dara.

"Perfect. Do you object to . . . ?"

Dara dropped his demolished strawberry. "Let's go."

Holloway led him back into the front room, where his physician rolled up Dara's sleeve and tied off the tourniquet, instructing Dara to squeeze his fist tight as he slid the needle in.

Afterward, Dara dropped down into his seat at the kitchen table with the others, a bandage wrapped thrice round his elbow and a low dizziness coursing through his head. He dropped his brow into his hands.

"Should've eaten something first," Ames said archly, and Dara kicked her under the table.

He found Holloway in his study later that night, the room lit only by a single lamp atop Holloway's desk. Holloway lifted his head when Dara came in—he'd been hunched over some papers on his desk, reading glasses perched on his long nose.

"Did you need something?" Holloway said.

"No. I wanted to say . . . thank you." Dara stood in the center of Holloway's rug, trying hard not to twist his hands in front of him like a nervous child.

He'd known Holloway since he *was* a child, of course, although Dara wasn't sure he'd ever been nervous. He wasn't raised to be nervous.

Holloway was elected attorney general when Dara was twelve. He'd been so young when Dara met him—was still young, in truth; had grown a mustache in an effort to look more dignified.

Holloway's mind had been an interesting place.

"Of course," Holloway said, drawing off his glasses and setting them aside. "Might I offer you a drink?"

Dara shook his head. "No. Thank you."

One of Holloway's dark brows went up. "Good. Although surprising, coming from you."

Holloway gestured for Dara to take one of the chairs near the window of his study and rang for tea instead. "Peppermint," he specified over the line with a knowing grin for Dara; clearly Holloway still remembered Dara's tastes.

"How's he doing?" Holloway asked once they'd both settled in with their drinks, Holloway's long legs stretched out before the sofa and crossed at the ankles.

"I don't know." Dara stared down at his own tea. His reflection was visible on its surface, if only in fractured pieces obscured by the billowing steam. "He hasn't woken up."

Holloway hummed. "Perhaps we shouldn't move him tonight, after all. I haven't been able to arrange a hotel yet—and if Mr. Álvaro is still so weak . . ."

Dara nodded.

Holloway took a sip of his tea, set the cup down in its saucer with a clink of porcelain on porcelain. "I thought he'd be safe," he admitted. "Lehrer seemed to . . . care about him, in his own way."

"That's not how Lehrer operates."

"Relatively safe," Holloway revised. "The real risk, of course, being if Lehrer realized he was being double-crossed."

"Noam was always at risk."

The silence that followed that comment was heavy, laden down by implication—although Dara still couldn't tell if Holloway had realized . . .

Dara curved his hands closer round his teacup, tipping his face down into the steam.

"Did you know?" he asked his tea. "About Lehrer. About what he did to me."

He'd never checked. He'd been so cautious reading minds, especially in those later years.

He hadn't wanted to have his fears confirmed—that everyone looked at him and saw his own victimization written on his skin like fresh bruises. Only perhaps that was giving high society too much credit. No one would have thought Calix Lehrer capable of such things.

When he finally dared to glance up again, Holloway watched with wary eyes, his own cup held in hand as if he'd forgotten to take his sip.

"No," Holloway said at last. "But perhaps I should have guessed. I'm sorry."

A tight smiled pressed at Dara's mouth. "It's fine. No one did."

And the people he'd told outright hadn't believed him.

They stayed at Holloway's that night. With Noam still in poor condition and Holloway playing it safe with the hotels, staying in place was starting to seem increasingly optimal. Lehrer hadn't shown up yet, after all, and Holloway had plenty of guest rooms—but Dara eschewed his in favor of sitting curled up in a chair in Noam's room, staring at Noam's face in the dull moonlight.

He still hadn't woken up.

A lot of that was sedation, Dara knew. The physician had injected Noam with some pain medication, had left bottles of pills for later—bottles Dara shoved under the bed so he wouldn't see them and be tempted.

But it still worried him. If Noam would come to for a moment—long enough for Dara to say *I love you* and *it's okay* and *I forgive you*, then . . . maybe . . .

Selfish, of course. Noam was asleep for a reason, and here Dara wanted to drag him back to consciousness—to agony—just to get this guilt off his chest.

Leo found him later in the night, long after Dara's watch had ticked past three a.m. and he'd torn it off his wrist and thrown it across the room—couldn't stand looking at it anymore, couldn't keep remembering the day Lehrer gave it to him.

"You okay?" Leo settled down on the floor by Dara's chair.

"Essentially."

Dara's gaze didn't shift from Noam. He didn't want to miss the slightest movement.

"Can I get you something? There's leftovers from dinner. Or even just . . . a coffee, maybe?"

Dara shook his head.

"Maybe some company, then?"

The next shallow breath burned in his lungs, Dara opening his mouth to say no—but he ended up nodding instead, both hands fisting up against his knees.

Leo shifted his position, stretching his legs out along the floor to get comfortable. "Y'all were pretty close, weren't you?" he asked. "Have you been friends a long time?"

"We hated each other," Dara said with a low laugh. "For most of the time we've known each other, we . . . I couldn't stand him, actually."

He could imagine the look on Leo's face without having to see it. "Really? Why?"

"I don't remember now." Dara sank lower in his chair. "Well. That's a lie. I do. It's . . . well, it makes me sound horrible to say it out loud."

"There's no judgment here."

Dara turned his head enough to catch Leo's gaze. Leo flashed him a small smile, and Dara sighed.

"He showed up during a . . . well, I don't want to say it was a *good* point for me and Lehrer. But it was . . . fine. It was okay. I was working with Sacha by then, and I . . . I'd convinced myself I had everything under control—"

*I have everything under control,* Noam had said in that alley, scant hours before Lehrer nearly killed him. Dara shoved the memory away and shut his eyes, long enough to focus on the rough fabric of the upholstery of the chair he sat on, the way his clothes fell against his own body.

"Anyway," Dara said, making himself keep going. "Then Lehrer told me one night there was a new student coming to Level IV. A recent survivor, someone with magic dynamics high enough to rival both mine and Lehrer's—someone clever enough, perhaps, to use it. And Lehrer wouldn't say a word about him when I asked. He just gave me this pitying smile, like he already knew I was damaged goods."

"That's . . ."

"That's Lehrer," Dara finished, opening his eyes again and tossing Leo a self-deprecating look. "Nothing new there. But then Lehrer canceled a dinner reservation he'd made for us—I never got to spend time with him, you understand, not *proper* time where we could actually . . . *talk*, instead of lessons, or . . . and he canceled it. To meet Álvaro."

"Doesn't sound like that's Álvaro's fault."

"Oh, none of this was Álvaro's fault. Maybe you haven't realized it yet, but I'm not a very good person."

Leo didn't say anything to that, just kept watching Dara until Dara continued.

"Lehrer started bringing Álvaro to our meetings. Our private lessons. And—I've had a lot of time to think about why that bothered me as much as it did. I've pretty much decided it's because I was afraid of what Álvaro might notice between me and Lehrer. That he might take one look and realize that I was . . ."

*Desperate.*

Only that was Lehrer's word. Dara refused to own it.

Not anymore.

"I thought Álvaro would realize what Lehrer did to me. I was so self-conscious of everything that happened in that room. I hated Álvaro for witnessing it. I hated him for stealing Lehrer's affection from me. I hated him for adoring Lehrer so completely—for trusting him more than he'd ever trust me."

"It was a difficult situation."

Dara laughed bitterly. "Well. What made it worse, of course, was that I was madly in love with Álvaro from the moment I met him."

Leo arched a brow.

"Not *at first sight* the way you're thinking," Dara said before Leo could get worse ideas. "I used to have telepathy. That was my presenting power. So from the moment I was in Noam's mind, I *knew* him—and it didn't take long until I knew him better than anyone else could ever hope to. Better than he knew himself, in some ways; most people have shockingly poor insight into their own thoughts and desires."

"*Oh*," Leo said, but it was in a tone that made Dara think he understood, perhaps, what Dara meant.

How overwhelming it had been to encounter a mind like that.

Noam had been equal parts fascinating and infuriating—brilliant but stubborn, passionate but misguided, full of so much emotion and intensity and vibrance that it . . . scared Dara.

Still did sometimes.

He'd wanted so badly to be the subject of all that fire. For Noam to take the fervor he had for philosophy and politics and focus it on Dara instead.

Even if it terrified him.

Dara pushed one corner of his mouth up, then glanced back to Noam, who hadn't moved since Leo got here. Dara wanted to slip onto his knees at the edge of Noam's bed and press Noam's hand between his, kiss his motionless fingers.

"Besides," Dara said, "he didn't see me the way other people did."

And that had been worth more to Dara than anything else life had given him.

When Leo left, Dara got up out of the chair and shifted to sit on the edge of the bed by Noam instead. Noam squirmed in his sleep, his face twisting up in a mask of discomfort. Dara pulled one of those pills out from the bottle under the bed and parted Noam's lips with his fingers, tossed it toward the back of his tongue. Held Noam's jaw shut until he swallowed.

Then he pushed the covers down and settled on his side, curled in close against Noam—close enough to lend Noam his heat. Dara tipped their brows together and let their noses brush, Dara's hand a knot against Noam's chest.

"Be okay," he pleaded, demanded.

He wished more than anything that he could force Noam to obey.

# Chapter Thirty-Four

## Noam

The pain veined through him like thousands of threads drawn taut. And for a moment Noam was suspended in space, trapped somewhere white and gauzy—and he couldn't muster the energy to remember where he was, if he ever got out of that apartment or if this was the limbo between life and death, if he still lay on Lehrer's living room floor with his blood seeping into the carpet.

Then he blinked open heavy eyelids, and a dim room swam into view.

He was under a thin sheet, the bed beneath him unfamiliar and dull early-morning light streaming in from the window. There was a chair drawn up near Noam's knees, and Dara was curled up in it, his head tucked in against his elbow and his lips parted in uneasy sleep.

Noam stared at him for a moment, mind slow to piece together what was happening.

Then he remembered.

"Dara," he said. It came out thin and wispy, barely audible. He swallowed against a gritty throat and tried again. "Dara."

Dara opened his eyes.

And then Dara pushed himself upright, dragging that chair closer to the edge of the bed and leaning forward to grasp Noam's wrist with one hand. "Noam," he breathed out, wide eyed and close enough Noam could count the cinnamon-dust freckles on his nose. "How are you feeling?"

Noam considered the question. "Like shit."

"That sounds right," Dara said, a tremulous smile crossing his lips. "You were—we were all worried about you. You were out for a while."

"Who's we?"

"Me and Ames. Leo. Holloway too."

Something twinged in the back of his mind, a realization that made it all the way to the tip of Noam's tongue before he forgot what he'd been about to say. "Ugh," he groaned, dragging up a hand to press its heel to his brow.

"You're on a lot of narcotics," Dara said. "It'll take a while for that to wear off. Or—is it . . . do you need more?"

Noam shook his head. "I'm good. But . . . thanks."

Dara caught Noam's hand as he lowered it from his head, lacing their fingers together atop the bed. "You don't have to talk about it if you don't want to," he said. "But if you—if you want to, I . . . you know I'll understand."

Noam did know that. Even if he wished it weren't true.

It was starting to hurt, staying propped up on his elbow like this. His gaze drifted down to that wrist, which had been bandaged up in some kind of splint. He vaguely remembered Lehrer breaking that wrist.

Not breaking. *Crushing.*

He settled himself back down again, a low moan escaping from between clenched teeth. Dara's hand tightened on his.

"I didn't fuck him," Noam said, once he was sure he could speak without vomiting from the pain. "For the record."

"I wasn't going to ask," Dara's words were low and cautious, like he thought Noam might flinch if he spoke too loud. "But . . . I'm glad. Not for my own sake, but—"

He didn't finish that sentence, but he didn't need to. They understood each other.

"You had a lot of injuries," Dara said, when it became clear Noam wasn't going to say anything else. "The broken ribs and wrist—a burst spleen. Punctured lung too. Holloway's physician came and fixed you up, mostly. We're hoping Bethany will come over this afternoon to heal the rest. Holloway's working on making that happen without Lehrer wising up."

"Good," Noam said, a little breathlessly now; the pain was rising up faster as the dull weight of the opiates began to fade.

"I was able to be useful for once, you know," Dara told him. "I gave you a blood transfusion. I'm type O negative—a universal donor . . . in fact, it was the one time my not being a witching anymore will ever come in handy, I suspect."

"What do you mean?"

"Witchings can't donate blood to baselines, of course—the infection risk—but we can't donate to each other either." Dara cocked a brow. "As long as the other witching's blood stays in your system, you can use their magic. People have *died* because a recipient was draining their magic and they didn't realize it."

A sudden hollow feeling bloomed in Noam's chest. "They go fevermad?"

"So I've heard."

Shit. *Shit.*

Noam shoved himself upright again, ignoring the way the room pitched as vertigo swam black into his vision. Suddenly he found it impossible to catch his breath, ruined lung straining against his bandaged ribs.

"What is it?" Dara asked, already on his feet. "Are you—should I get someone?"

God, Noam was such—such a fucking idiot, how could he have . . . he . . .

Noam fixed Dara in his gaze and made himself just . . . *say* it. "Dara. Lehrer's fevermad. He's . . . he's *fevermad*, I told you. I—I was right, and he—"

Dara was looking at him with those ink-black eyes, confusion still traced in his expression. Noam's stomach pitched.

"I gave him a blood transfusion."

"You *what?*"

Noam swallowed hard. "I know. I know, it . . . terrible fucking idea, it—"

"When?"

"Right after the assassination attempt. I—I'm—it was stupid, I never should have done it, and I regretted it immediately afterward, but now. He."

"Shit," Dara said on a thin exhale. He tangled a hand up in his hair and spun on his heel, pacing toward the dresser and back again. "Shit, Noam."

"I know."

"He's probably draining your magic *as we speak*. How are you supposed to fight him when he can end you, when he can just—just *burn you out* in a single—"

"I don't think he can," Noam said. "In . . . yesterday, at his apartment, he said he was going to kill me. But he didn't try that. Not that I could tell, anyway, and—"

"*Not that you could tell* being the operative phrase, Noam!"

Dara was right. Lehrer was dragging this out on purpose. There was no good reason to think he wasn't capable of snuffing Noam out like a quenched candle with a single massive burst of magic. Just because he hadn't tried it last night didn't mean he wouldn't try it in the future.

And—and, in all likelihood, that was what Lehrer had done to Dara as well. He'd gotten his hands on Dara's blood somehow—Dara was O negative; Dara's dynamics had been strong enough to rival Lehrer's—and he must have been injecting himself with Dara's blood for months.

Perhaps even years. Lehrer had drained Dara's magic bit by bit until all that was left was a rotting husk, days from death.

"Fuck."

"Correct," said Dara, and he dropped his hand from his hair at last. "God. Anything else you want to share, while we're at it?"

Guilt twisted like a poisonous vine through Noam's guts, tangling around his still-bruised throat.

"Lehrer's immune to the vaccine."

Dara's lips drew into a thin line. "Are you serious, Álvaro?"

"I didn't see the point in . . . listen, okay, you're right. I should have told you. But let's not argue about that right now, okay?"

For a second Dara looked like he was gonna blow right past that anyway, but after a beat he sighed and said: "Fine. Fine . . . so, that's it, then. It's over."

Noam didn't know what to say to that.

He didn't have any better ideas.

Except . . .

"What if he couldn't drain my magic?"

Dara huffed in exasperation. "Yes, that would obviously be ideal, but—"

"Suppressants."

Dara's words dropped off midsentence. He was still breathing too fast, shoulders trembling as they rose and fell, but he sat down in the chair again with a heavy drop. "Suppressants."

"One vial for me, one for Lehrer. We go to the Independence Day thing; we get Lehrer to spend a lot of magic at once somehow. And then before he can draw on my magic to recuperate, I inject myself with suppressant. He'll have to suffer through it on his own. He'll be weak. Fevermad."

"And then . . ." Dara grinned as the realization dawned. "We inject him. His body won't be able to fight the suppressant off if he's already—"

"Exactly."

It was a shitty plan, and both of them knew it. But it was better than the alternative.

Neither Noam nor Dara could let Lehrer walk away from this.

A knock came at the door.

"Come in," Dara said, twisting round in his seat just as Holloway stepped into the room.

Holloway's gaze fell to Noam first. "You're awake."

"Barely." Noam tried to smile, but it quickly became a grimace when he tried to push himself upright again.

"Careful," Holloway said. "Don't overdo it. Even aside from the physical injuries, you came here dangerously close to fevermadness. You need rest."

"Thank you," Noam said sincerely. "For letting us stay here. For . . . everything."

"Don't thank me yet."

Dara pulled his legs up onto the seat cushion and turned more fully in his chair to face Holloway. "Have you found a hotel?"

"Still a work in progress, I'm afraid," said Holloway. "Temporarily abandoned, as I've arranged for your friend Miss Glennis to meet us here and heal the rest of Mr. Álvaro's injuries."

"Bethany," Dara said with a clear note of relief. "That's good—she'll know what to do. She always . . ."

He kept going, elaborating on some of Bethany's more impressive healing feats, but something inside Noam had gone suddenly, horribly still.

Holloway.

*He's been mine from the beginning.*

Noam had forgotten—that memory buried under the weight of everything else that happened last night, driven from his mind by pain and terror. It emerged now, horrible and fully formed, and Noam jerked his gaze away from Holloway's face so he wouldn't be tempted to stare.

Fuck.

Of all the safe houses they could've fled to, of course they chose this one. Of course they'd hidden themselves away with Lehrer's *third* goddamn spy.

Dara was still talking, an easy smile on his lips—relieved that Noam was awake, that Holloway had kept them safe, that they'd figured out a way around Lehrer's secret strengths.

What if Dara gave it all away? Holloway already knew about the Independence Day plan, but he still believed that plot involved the vaccine. If Dara told him the new order of events, it really would be over.

If Lehrer wasn't halfway here already.

"Dara," Noam croaked.

Dara didn't hear him at first, kept talking to Holloway—they were on the subject of breakfast now, Dara listing a shockingly long number of dishes he was apparently intending to force-feed Noam—

"*Dara*," Noam said again. This time Dara's head swung round to look at him. Noam hated seeing the way worry etched the lines of his face so instantly, as if Noam were just . . . *that*, now. Something to coddle and protect.

A burden.

"Are you okay?" Dara asked, salt in the wound.

"No," Noam said. "Actually, I'm starting to feel kind of . . . dizzy, and I think I might try and . . . sleep. Some."

"Oh!" Dara was on his feet a beat later, glancing toward Holloway like waiting for his permission to leave. "Okay. We can—we'll leave you be, then."

Noam caught Dara's wrist. "No. Stay with me. Just . . . for a little while."

Dara flinched, and guilt immediately rose up dark in Noam's stomach. God. He kept forgetting Dara hated being grabbed like that.

He let go. "Sorry."

But before Dara could respond, there was another knock on the bedroom door. Panic surged up into Noam's mouth, sharp and briny— Lehrer, what if it was Lehrer?—but when Holloway opened the door, it was Ames and Bethany on the other side.

Bethany was pink-cheeked and wearing a dress that looked like she'd retrieved it—wrinkled—from her bedroom floor. She was across the room and at Noam's side almost immediately, blonde hair fraying loose around her face, like some kind of disorganized mad scientist.

Noam grinned despite himself. "You made it."

"*Barely.*" She made a face. "I had to make myself sick to get out of Swensson's class. It was disgusting."

"Wait," Noam said, holding up a hand. "Does this mean the time you fainted during basic and conveniently didn't have to go out with the rest of us on that QZ obstacle course was—"

"Turns out healing magic's more useful than people give it credit for," Bethany said with a crooked smile. "Now lie still—I have to concentrate."

Holloway politely loaned them some privacy while Bethany worked. After his footsteps had retreated down the hall, Noam gritted his teeth against the pain—Bethany was focused on knitting together his fractured ribs, which hurt like a *motherfucker*—and waved for Ames to shut the door.

"We gotta get out of here," he managed to choke out once Ames had turned the latch.

"Tell me about it," Ames said. "Honestly, it's shocking Lehrer hasn't sent someone to check Holloway's house—he *knows* Holloway's resistance. This is like the most obvious place in the world we could have gone."

Bethany moved on to his spleen, and that agony was one Noam felt deep and visceral, a broken sound ripping itself out of his chest as he twisted under the light press of Bethany's hands. "Sorry," she said, and Noam rubbed the sweat from his face with the flat of his palm.

"Yeah," he said, a little breathlessly now. "Well, Lehrer hasn't checked for a reason. He knows we're here already."

Dara and Bethany exchanged looks, Bethany's magic still weaving through Noam's gut.

"Lehrer told me. While we were fighting. He told me Holloway's . . . he told me Holloway's a spy."

Ames drew closer, the color drained from her face. "Did he mean— I mean, Lehrer *thinks* he owns a lot of people, but—"

"Do you really wanna take that risk?"

"I should have guessed," Dara said, voice gone tight. "I should have—of *course*. Because why didn't Lehrer kill Holloway the second he realized? Or at least put him under persuasion—stupid. We were so stupid to think—"

"We all assumed it," Noam said, turning his gaze up toward the ceiling now and trying to slow his heart rate as Bethany moved on to his broken wrist. "We all thought he'd save the magic, use Holloway as bait to draw out any other sympathizers. And that was exactly what made sense, given everything else Lehrer was saying at the time—letting the resistance stay in place, waiting for a critical mass to strike. But."

But they were wrong.

Lehrer didn't have to persuade Holloway, because he'd been bad from the beginning.

Lehrer and Holloway's twisted little alliance was stronger than ever. Probably the first political deal that either party had stuck to long term.

"Okay," Ames said, ruffling her hair badly enough it stuck out from her head in all directions, scarecrow-like. "Okay. So we gotta leave. Right? But where?"

Noam flipped through the list of options: Migrant Center was out, of course; that was too obvious. Same with Ames's house. The QZ was too far away. And Holloway had probably already warned every hotel in Durham to turn them in to the MoD if they showed up wanting rooms.

Goddamn it, why couldn't Independence Day be *tomorrow*?

Bethany had finished with Noam's wrist; she sat back on her heels as Noam pushed himself gingerly up to a sitting position. He still didn't feel great, but he'd spent a lot of magic fighting Lehrer. Maybe that was to be expected.

He dragged both hands over his face and blew out against his palms. Looked up at the others again, gathered round the bed and staring at him like they expected Noam to have the solution.

And he had one, all right. He was just pretty sure they weren't gonna like it.

"How do y'all feel about squatting?"

Noam was the one who found the house, listed online as *for sale*—had confirmed the present owners were out of town for the holiday week and that there were no showings or open houses scheduled until after Independence Day. Still, they had to wait till nightfall to flee, slipping out of Holloway's house in the early hours like fugitives—which, Noam supposed, they were.

The escape was easy. *Too easy,* Noam had thought, and it was only after they'd broken into that house and Noam had set up the wards—after they'd unpacked their bags and claimed rooms and Dara had Claire and Priya on the phone, Bethany safely back in the barracks—that they realized how fucked they really were.

They'd been lying to themselves, thinking Holloway didn't know they knew. Thinking Lehrer wouldn't have warned him. This whole time Holloway must have been waiting for them to leave, because when Priya checked their supplies, everything was gone.

Holloway had stolen the suppressant.

It wasn't like they couldn't get more on the black market—and Noam did, of course; he had the package shipped to the mailbox of an empty house, and Ames picked it up early in the morning, backpack on like she was headed off to school. They tested it on Priya—*You don't need my magic as much as you need Noam's,* she'd said. Well, it was true. They couldn't afford for Noam's magic to fail before they confronted Lehrer.

Independence Day was out, obviously. Now that they knew about Holloway—now that Holloway knew they knew—they couldn't follow through with the same plot as before. Problem was they didn't have a better plan.

Or: they didn't at first.

Lehrer made the announcement four days after Noam'd escaped. Noam was making tea in the kitchen when Claire called them into the living room, where she had the news playing on TV, Lehrer's face blown up larger than life on the huge flat-screen. He stood on the steps of the government complex, the Carolinian flag rippling huge and blue behind him, illuminated by spotlights and city glow.

"In the years following the catastrophe, shortly after Carolinia was founded, our nation was besieged from all sides," Lehrer said. He wore his military uniform, not the tailored suits he'd adopted as chancellor— and that had to be intentional. That was a message every bit as much as the words coming out Lehrer's mouth. "Peace was hard won . . . but in the end, we convinced Texas and Japan and England and all the other nations that Carolinia is stronger than they imagined. Stronger than they *could* have imagined. Our message was heard and understood: Carolinia is a nation of witchings, and we will always fight back."

Applause answered those words, a roar so loud that if there was any- one in that audience who had read all those files Noam leaked online, anyone who doubted Lehrer's authority, their voices were completely subsumed.

Noam slowly sank onto the sofa next to Dara, whose gaze was locked on the screen. Dara didn't even spare him a glance as Noam's hand found his leg, squeezing above the knee.

"The time has come to fight back once more. Texas has played their gambit. Now, we decide how Carolinia will respond. Tomorrow afternoon, at five p.m., I will be speaking live from Duke Chapel—a message for Texas, and for Carolinia . . . and anyone else who cares to listen."

Lehrer's gaze met the camera at that, and ice plunged into Noam's blood because for a second—just for a second—it felt like Lehrer *knew* somehow. Like he sensed Noam watching there on the other end of that live feed. Like these words were for him.

"This is it," Dara said from Noam's left. "We have to go tomorrow."

"Tomorrow?" Priya echoed sharply. "We aren't ready. We only just got the suppressant. We haven't had time to assess the security at the event—figure out where Lehrer's supposed to be and when—we have no *plan*."

"Waiting for Independence Day isn't any better," Dara snapped. He'd gone straight-backed, one of his hands in a fist against his knee. "He's still weak from fighting Noam. We can't give him time to recuperate—we have to strike now."

"I agree," Noam said, and all their gazes slid to fix on him.

"This is a terrible idea," Ames warned.

"All our ideas are terrible. But we can't do nothing."

After all . . .

With enough IV steroids—enough transfusions, even if from less powerful witchings, witchings who'd burn out and die in hours—Lehrer might regain his strength. He might recover.

It was now or never.

Even after their meeting dissolved, anticipation hung over the house like a building storm. None of them spoke to each other after the decision was made, splitting off in separate directions to separate rooms, all coming to terms with the possibility this might be their last night alive.

Downstairs, Ames was probably drinking herself unconscious in the kitchen. Leo had locked himself in his room with the lights off— asleep already, perhaps, or awake in bed staring into the yawning dark.

Noam and Dara shut themselves away after dinner, Noam crouched down on the floor and struggling to start a fire in the stone hearth. Even with pyromancy it was difficult; he couldn't get the wood hot enough to catch. The newspaper burned itself out, over and over, and Noam kept thinking about Lehrer doing that to *him* tomorrow—and at last he snapped, "*Fuck* it" and dropped back onto his heels.

"Can I help?" Dara asked from his perch on the edge of the bed. He looked thinner than ever, shadows deepening beneath his cheekbones and fingers like spider legs clutching bony knees.

"You're welcome to give it a shot."

Dara pushed up and crossed to retrieve the poker from where it leaned against the wall, used it to stab at the coals and dig the newspaper deeper under the logs. Noam shifted aside to make room as Dara crouched down and blew on the embers, sparks flaring up toward the chimney.

They'd debated the various risks and benefits to lighting a fire in an unoccupied house, but after the second night with no heat—the homeowners had turned it off in their absence, and Priya'd expressed concern about their fancy smart-tech system alerting them if the squatters turned it back on—they'd decided it was worth not freezing to death before they could defeat Lehrer. Ground rules, of course: no turning on the lights—and they only burned fires at night, when dusk would conceal the rising smoke.

Dara and Noam sat back and watched as the pale flames licked at the underside of the dry wood. Slowly, slowly, the bark began to smolder and—at last—to catch.

"We can add fire starting to your list of hidden talents, I suppose," Noam said as Dara stood and offered Noam a hand to pull him to his feet.

"A rare benefit of living in the QZ for six months." Dara hadn't let go of Noam's hand; his thumb rubbed a pattern against Noam's skin, warm and steady. "Come on. Let's sit down."

He drew Noam back to the bed, both of them climbing up to sit cross-legged facing one another, knees bumping. They hadn't had sex since that night in Dara's apartment. They'd tried, the first evening, but when Noam touched Dara in the darkness, kissed him, Dara had gone taut and still, and nothing Noam said—no number of reassurances spoken in a low voice—had been enough to remind him Noam wasn't someone else.

Noam had his own tiny terrors. They rose up sudden and silent in the middle of the night when Dara shifted in bed next to him, every one of Noam's nerves thrown on edge waiting for long fingers at the nape of his neck and Lehrer's voice whispering in his ear.

"I like this house," Noam said after several moments without either of them speaking. He lifted Dara's hand to press his lips to Dara's knuckles, glancing up between his lashes to meet Dara's gaze. "Maybe we can buy it when all this is over."

"We?"

Noam lowered Dara's hand but didn't let go. "Imagine it, Dara. We could have a life together—we could start over and do it properly this time. We'll get a dog. I could learn to cook, and Lakewood's close enough to downtown that we wouldn't be far from other options if we got bored playing domestic."

At first he worried Dara might say no—tug his hand away and tell Noam that was too fast, or that he wanted something different once they were free. But instead his grip tightened on Noam's, a tremulous smile flitting across his lips. "That sounds nice."

"I want to choose you," Noam said softly. "Every day, again and again."

Dara kissed him, Noam's lips parting under the pressure of Dara's mouth and his hand lifting to Dara's cheek. And for that moment Noam let himself believe in the future they'd spun together, all its brightness and its flaws, something so magnificently mundane it almost felt unachievable: late mornings waking up together, Dara perched on the kitchen counter while Noam made dinner, trading work stories over tea in the early evening, Wolf curled up in bed between them while they slept.

After the fire had died down, Dara drifting in a doze curled up on his side of the bed, Noam still couldn't sleep. He stared at Dara's face in what was left of the ember-light, every muscle in his body clenched up hard enough it almost hurt.

Noam wanted that future. He wanted it so fucking much.

But in less than twelve hours they would be at Duke Chapel—both magic-less, defenseless, hoping past the point of reason that their terrible plan would work.

That Lehrer hadn't outsmarted them even now.

Noam hadn't put voice to his fears, and neither had the rest of them, although he knew they all felt the same way: like criminals on the eve of execution.

*An encrypted email exchange between C. Lehrer and his personal physician, sent using a private server.*

**To:** Lilian Hillary, MD

**From:** Calix Lehrer

**Subject:** [Time-Sensitive] Require new dose

Monday, March 11, 2124, 10:23 p.m.

Dr. Hillary,

Please bring an additional two units of Álvaro's blood by my apartment tomorrow morning before 7 AM.

C. L.

**To:** Calix Lehrer

**From:** Lilian Hillary, MD

**Subject:** Re: [Time-Sensitive] Require new dose

Monday, March 11, 2124, 10:31 p.m.

Dear Chancellor,

Unfortunately, as we discussed at our last appointment, I must advise against taking another dose of witching blood so soon after the last. Although Mr. Álvaro's dynamics, like Mr. Shirazi's, are comparable to your own, excessive use of Mr. Álvaro's magic will eventually burn him out. Perhaps he would not go fevermad as quickly as the original, weaker witching donors. But as we saw with Mr. Shirazi, death of the donor is ultimately unavoidable.

Again, I recommend you conserve your magic expenditure for the sake of your own health as well as the donor's. You should remember to drink water and to rest.

Yours sincerely,

Dr. Hillary

**To:** Lilian Hillary, MD

**From:** Calix Lehrer

**Subject:** Re: re: [Time-sensitive] Require new dose

Monday, March 11, 2124, 10:32 PM

This matter is not up for debate.

**To:** Calix Lehrer

**From:** Lilian Hillary, MD

**Subject:** Re: re: re: [Time-sensitive] Require new dose

Monday, March 11, 2124, 10:34 PM

Dear Chancellor,

Yes, sir. I will bring two vials of Mr. Álvaro's blood first thing tomorrow morning.

Dr. Hillary

# Chapter Thirty-Five

## Dara

The next day dawned bright and sunny, a stark shift from the frigid gray clouds that had gripped the country for the past several weeks. It was a poor omen, Dara thought—like the universe itself granting approval to Lehrer's speech later today.

Alternatively, of course, the government had discovered another meteorpath and paid them to improve the weather just in time for a patriotic event.

They arrived at the Carolinia National University campus expecting a wildly different security scenario than the one they encountered. Armored tanks, maybe—hundreds of antiwitching units in their iridescent armor, undercover police skulking through the shadows. With all secrets revealed, now, why would Lehrer let them waltz into Duke Chapel so easily?

"This isn't an oversight," Priya murmured from the front seat of the car as they rolled slowly past the line of cars queuing up for entrance onto the event grounds. "It's a threat."

"Or a trap," said Ames.

Next to Dara, Noam was gripping his thighs so hard his fingertips blanched with the pressure. Dara reached over and placed his hand atop Noam's; Noam shot him a small appreciative smile.

It felt like they had to rely on so many assumptions for this to work. They assumed Claire's contacts in the security detail were still loyal. They assumed they wouldn't get recognized the second they set foot onto the grounds. They assumed all Dara's physics calculations were correct, and they could avoid killing hundreds of innocent people. They assumed the suppressant would work on Lehrer if he was weak enough—that they could even get close enough to use it.

Early this morning, before Noam was awake, Dara had sat at the corner of the sofa downstairs with his brow tipped against the cold windowpane and stared at the ice as it cracked and melted off the tree outside. He'd tried to imagine death: a quiet dark embrace welcoming him home.

Such dreams had come easily, once. When Dara was sixteen, he'd chased after death with both arms outstretched—and death had felt like warm bathwater and drugs in his veins, had smelled like spilled blood.

He couldn't reclaim that feeling now. He couldn't imagine stepping out of this life and leaving Noam behind—or Ames, or Leo, or even Priya. That story Noam wove last night about their future had sunk deep into his bones, and he couldn't excise it.

Dara *wanted* that.

For the first time in years, Dara wanted to live.

"Equipment check," Claire said, and they all counted off: no guns, of course, but earplugs—a weak defense against Lehrer's persuasion—and two vials of suppressant.

It was almost time.

At least one assumption held: they made it onto campus without being stopped. It was next to impossible to secure the entire Carolinia National University grounds, but even so Dara's heart was in his throat as they parked the car and walked right by all those guards in uniform, all the soldiers with guns and magic in their veins.

The quad was a mass of people, citizens and journalists and security murmuring into their walkie-talkies. The whole of Black Magnolia blended in almost seamlessly—Claire and Priya and Ames in street clothes, Noam and Dara both wearing press badges around their necks.

"Time to split up," Priya said when they reached the center of the quad, cordoned off by white ropes that kept a path clear from the drive up to the chapel itself—the path Lehrer would ascend when he arrived. The same path he'd walked on his coronation day.

Lehrer always did have a flair for symbolism.

"Good luck," Ames said to them both, extending a hand to shake Dara's first, then Noam's. "See you on the other side."

*I hope.*

The three of them—Ames and Priya and Claire—faded into the crowd, quickly consumed by the anonymity of three hundred unfamiliar faces.

And Noam and Dara made their way toward the chapel.

"Over there, maybe?" Dara asked as they drew closer to the front doors—which were well guarded, a dozen soldiers in antiwitching armor checking identification with guns at their hips.

Noam nodded, and they split off, weaving against the current of the crowd as it filtered into the narthex.

As they passed one of the chapel's side entrances, Dara was suddenly very glad they'd decided against positioning themselves inside the chapel itself. The Chancellarian Guard was already here, wearing dark suits and lining the arched walkways; soldiers in antiwitching armor stood watch by the doors.

They were early enough to get a good position near the portal at least, flashing press badges when they needed to elbow in closer. Dara leaned out over the path, peering down toward the drive where Lehrer's car would pull up. His stomach curdled; it was a long walk. Plenty of time for Lehrer's gaze to scan the crowd and see two familiar faces staring back at him.

"It's going to be okay," Noam said from over his shoulder. His hand caught Dara's, their bodies pressed together by the mob. Dara turned to look at him—and for a moment it was like nothing else existed. He tipped his face forward and rested his brow against Noam's. He focused on Noam's eyes, on the little threads of gold weaving through Noam's irises like striations in marble.

"I'm scared," Dara admitted, softly enough he couldn't even hear himself say it.

But Noam must have, because he curved an arm around Dara's waist and drew him in, burying his own face against Dara's hair. "Me too."

Noam smelled like the shampoo they'd borrowed in the Lakewood house, like vetiver and smoke.

"How much longer?" Dara asked against Noam's leather jacket. *Leo's* leather jacket, technically.

Noam must have checked his watch using magic, because he didn't let go. "Fifty-six minutes."

Those next fifty-six minutes dragged by slowly, the quad filling up with still more people—god, there were *thousands* of them. It wasn't as if Dara hadn't attended public government events before. But usually he was shuffled from place to place by someone bureaucratic and self-important, pausing only long enough for someone to shield his face from photos—the one good thing Lehrer had done as a parent was to keep Dara out of the public eye.

Dara had never been part of the crowd.

And then a ripple spread through the audience, a sudden ramping up of tension. Dara knew before he even looked:

Lehrer had arrived.

The car was sleek and black—vintage, not driverless; a relic from the early years of Carolinia. Modeled, perhaps, to look similar to the one from which Lehrer had emerged at his coronation.

The driver opened the back door. Dara whipped away before Lehrer could emerge, air gone to frost in his lungs. He stared at the sea of other people built up behind them, all craning to see—lifting phones overhead to film—and hearing the slow crescendo of delighted screams as Lehrer presumably made his first appearance.

"What's happening?" Dara asked tightly, finding Noam's hand again without looking and gripping hard.

"Nothing," Noam said. "He's just standing there, waving. It's a photo op."

Knowing Lehrer was still two hundred feet away didn't stop Dara's mouth from going dry. Two hundred feet was far closer than he'd been to Lehrer in—

Well. Since the gala.

Dara had insisted on coming today. Everyone tried to talk him out of it—Claire, Priya, even Noam. *Leo's staying back*, Noam had told him. *We can't bring weapons onto the grounds; they'll be looking for that kind of thing. Without magic to defend yourself, you'll only be in danger.*

It wasn't even as if Dara thought he was wrong.

But the thought of staying home—watching the speech from his phone and praying, *praying* they all made it out alive—

No.

"He's walking now," Noam murmured. "The Chancellarian Guard is ahead of him . . . he doesn't look happy about that."

The crowd roared louder, all those Lehrer groupies screeching just for the privilege of being heard by him. Dara wanted to press both hands over his ears. Wanted to tape their mouths shut.

"A hundred feet," Noam went on. Then: "Fifty."

Dara turned to look.

Lehrer was close enough the proximity sent Dara's heart slamming against his ribs, his breath coming in abortive little gasps he muffled behind clenched teeth.

He looked the same as he always did. Age hadn't touched him. Nor, it seemed, had fevermadness—there was no characteristic brightness to his cheeks, no glassy gleam in his eyes. It was as if he'd been constructed from alabaster and bone.

Unbreakable.

But not all the cries of the crowd were of adoration. A low rumble of dissatisfaction echoed far beneath all that devotion—there were those here today who had read all the material Noam leaked online this morning. All that evidence of torture and injustice.

Dara and Noam both averted their gazes when Lehrer drew closer, letting others in the crowd move in to take their coveted spots by the guard rope. Crammed between unfamiliar bodies, they both just stared at each other, neither one speaking—as if even breathing too loudly would lead Lehrer to them.

But Lehrer passed without incident. The crowd kept shouting his name until he had ascended the chapel steps—Dara glimpsed a brief shot of Lehrer waving from the portal before he stepped into the narthex and the heavy wooden door fell shut.

The crowds relaxed after that, attention turning toward the large screens that had been erected for viewing the proceedings within. Dara had always thought it an odd choice, giving this speech from *inside* the chapel instead of on its steps, where the public could see—but now that he was watching the live feed from the chapel itself, he was beginning to understand.

Duke Chapel was a massive feat of architectural design, all tall gothic arches and long stained glass windows. To reach the chancel, Lehrer had to proceed down the length of the entire nave—almost three hundred feet, flanked by eighteen hundred people filling the antique pews. With the late-afternoon light glittering in through the painted glass and lighting gold on Lehrer's hair, it was not hard to imagine Lehrer as a saint . . . to see this whole ceremony as the apotheosis of man to god.

The speech began, broadcast out to the crowd—streamed live to millions of holoreaders and phones and tablets and televisions all over the country. The world.

Noam and Dara stood side by side and listened, Lehrer's voice the same smooth baritone that had defined Carolinian rhetoric, carried on the same accent Lehrer had spent a hundred years perfecting. An accent he could easily have lost in the 116 years since Lehrer and his family left Europe and came to the former United States.

*I hate him.* The thought was almost like a realization in some ways. Dara had said it before, thought it a thousand times. But it had never been entirely true. There was always that part of Dara that still hoped Lehrer would change his mind. That he'd find some room in his blackened heart for his adopted son, after all—that Dara might arrive at some nebulous future point where Lehrer decided he was, finally, a peer.

All that was gone, dried up and blown away in the wake of these past eight months.

Dara never imagined losing hope would feel so . . . *liberating.*

" . . . with a grave and cautious heart that I am announcing the temporary suspension of term limits for all elected federal positions," Lehrer's voice said. "Until such a time as we can be assured of this country's safety from Texas's heinous War on Witchings."

Dara and Noam exchanged looks, Noam's mouth twisting in a furious knot. Dara could have told him this was coming. Dara had told him a dozen times that Lehrer's seizing tyrannical power should come as no surprise.

Not that it mattered. Not if they finished what they came here to do.

A shiver ran through the crowd at that. It seemed they weren't the only ones who were unhappy with such a declaration—although it seemed like there were just as many people shouting their support.

*What if everything Noam released isn't enough? What if we defeat Lehrer, but no one believes us about what he's done?*

The fear dropped like acid into Dara's stomach and roiled there. He dug his short nails in against the back of Noam's hand.

They had to believe. They *must.*

Dara couldn't keep screaming the truth again and again, and never being heard.

He barely paid attention to the rest of the speech. All he could do was stare over the heads of all the people gathered here as dusk dropped like a slow curtain, transforming gold light into silver. Near the end Noam pressed a hand to the small of Dara's back and said, "You should get out of range. You don't want to get caught up in this."

He was right. But Dara didn't move.

"I'm staying with you," Dara said. "Until the end."

Noam bit down on his lower lip, but eventually he nodded and used that pressure on Dara's spine to draw him along as Noam started trying to shift his way back to the front line.

"Excuse me," Noam said, raising his voice to be heard. "Excuse— press, let us through—"

Only the crowd closed ranks, shifting tighter as if to hold them back on purpose. As if making room might mean giving up their own vantage point.

*"Shit!"* Noam's cheeks were already coloring as he looked back toward Dara—flushing dark enough that some part of Dara reflexively twinged toward concern. Noam was too close to fevermadness already.

Dara glanced around, trying to find an easier route forward; there was none. All he could see was an ocean of unfamiliar faces, speckled with the gleaming screens of cameras and phones.

Dara nudged Noam's elbow. "Can you watch through someone's tech?"

Noam didn't look any less angry, but he nodded once and turned his face upward—as if staring at the darkening sky would help him focus. He had the first syringe of suppressant in hand, thumb poised on the plunger.

The crowd's cheers were almost as perfect a signal of when the chapel doors opened again. Dara caught a glimpse of what was happening on the phone screen of someone in front of him—of Lehrer standing there on the steps, his hand raised in a diplomatic wave.

And Dara heard the sharp intake of Noam's breath as he drew on magic, Dara tasting blood on his own tongue—a beat before the stone cathedral tower of Duke Chapel collapsed.

# CHAPTER THIRTY-SIX

## DARA

Panic erupted.

It took what felt like minutes for the entire tower to crumble, although Dara knew it must have been mere seconds—the stone caved *inward*, the demolition restricted to as narrow a space as Dara's calculations could manage given the sheer height of the thing. Because there was no time for Noam's telekinesis to force the wreckage down on Lehrer alone.

Noam's wide eyes met Dara's as he lifted the syringe of suppressant to inject himself.

He never got the chance.

The crowd was already reeling, stampeding. Someone slammed into Noam too hard, and the syringe fell from his hand.

"No!" Dara shouted, lunging.

The syringe rolled over the cobblestones, its clear contents sloshing in its vial. Dara scraped his knees on the rock; someone's foot caught him in the shoulder, and Noam was shouting something up above him, but Dara couldn't make out the words, couldn't think about anything but the suppressant. He flung out a hand, grasping a beat too late.

The syringe was crushed underfoot, broken glass ground into the street and the vial's contents a slick stain on stone.

Someone grasped Dara's arm and hauled him up—and for a split second Dara was reeling through blind space, terror climbing up his throat, before Noam's voice in his ear said: "It's me—Dara, it's me," and his vision refocused on Noam's familiar face.

"It's gone," Dara said, clutching at Noam with both hands. "Noam, it's—"

All at once the color drained from Noam's face, his body gone still against Dara's grip.

"No," Dara gasped, faltering forward to catch Noam's weight as he listed to one side. "No—"

Too late. They were too late. Noam's skin already felt hot against Dara's palms, his head lolling against Dara's shoulder as Dara tried to heave him back onto his feet.

The first part of the plan had worked perfectly. They'd collapsed the tower on Lehrer, forcing him to expend a massive amount of magic to keep himself alive.

The rest of the plan—cutting off Lehrer's power source—had gone desperately wrong.

"Is he okay?" someone asked, their hand grazing Dara's arm. The voice sounded familiar.

Dara looked up.

"*Taye?*"

Taye, in his Level IV uniform—Taye with the bright grin and the omnipresent red candies, Taye the mathematics genius—was staring at Dara like he'd never seen him before in his life.

"Wow," Taye said. "You're, like . . . alive and shit."

"Old news," Dara said. "What are you—how did you *find* us?" He grunted as Noam's legs gave out.

"Tell you later. Grab his left side."

436

Taye hooked an arm under Noam's other shoulder, and between them they heaved Noam up enough to drag him forward over the stones. "What the hell are you doing here? Why is Noam in a leather jacket? Why is Noam unconscious? And why are you not dead?"

"That's a lot of questions," Dara got out through a tight jaw. "Right now, we need to get Noam . . . somewhere else. Not . . . here."

The fallen boulders were already shifting in front of the chapel, dust blooming toward the dusk sky like a cloud of ash. Noam made a low, pained sound.

"Inside," Taye suggested. "That building, there?"

No. Too obvious. They had to go somewhere defensible, somewhere with limited entry points. Somewhere Lehrer could find them, but where they wouldn't be taken by surprise. Somewhere like—

"The crypt," Dara said.

For once, Taye didn't argue. He did some complicated bit of magic—likely involving math and gravity—and suddenly Noam was much lighter against Dara's shoulders. Light enough Dara could bend down and grab him under the knees, hoisting him up into his arms like a child.

"Who are we running from?" Taye asked as they shoved their way through the pandemonium. "The people who brought down the tower, or the other people?" "The other people," Dara said grimly.

"Yeah. Kinda figured, after half of Level IV disappeared under mysterious circumstances."

"You won't turn us in, will you?"

"Are you serious? I'm not a snitch, Shirazi." Taye looked deeply offended by the suggestion, so Dara let it go.

They burst free of the crowd closer to the chapel. All the guards and soldiers had abandoned the area—or been crushed under the falling rock, more likely. Not that it helped that much—the army was already setting up a barricade on the far end of the lawn, a helicopter's blades cutting through the air somewhere overhead. That's where Priya and Claire and Ames would be now, preventing those soldiers from searching the grounds for Dara and Noam before they finished their job.

The wreckage of the tower had started to shift more visibly now, stone and brick tumbling toward the quad as Lehrer slowly forced his way free. They had to run right past it to get to the chapel.

If Lehrer got loose before they got to the chancel—if he wasn't exhausted, wasn't fevermad enough when he finally caught up with them—

With every bit of magic they forced Lehrer to use, Noam got weaker.

Dara glanced down at Noam's pallid face and steeled himself. He knew what choice Noam would've wanted him to make.

"Taye," he said. "Can you make the debris . . . bigger?"

Taye followed Dara's gaze to the ruins of the tower. A beat later the stones were already multiplying in size, growing exponentially larger, heavier, requiring that much more magic to move.

Dara stopped short for a second, pressing his fingers to Noam's neck, his heart twisting in his chest—

Noam had a pulse.

Noam had a pulse, and was breathing, and he—he didn't actually look any worse than he had a moment ago.

A shudder ran through Dara's entire body, and he squeezed his eyes shut. *It worked.* Lehrer had drawn as much power from Noam's blood as he could, and now . . .

Now, all the magic Lehrer used would be his own.

The chapel was still and empty when they crawled through the half-collapsed side door and into the cool interior. Shattered glass littered the floor like lethal jewels, those gorgeous stained glass windows in pieces now.

Dara and Taye carried Noam up to the chancel, Taye shoving open the small wooden door next to the iron grate barring off a smaller private chapel. A short flight of stone steps led them down into shadow, into the crypt.

The space was smaller than Dara remembered, claustrophobic under a heavy rounded ceiling and lit only by a single swinging lantern—the rest had gone dark, shattered as ricochets from the tower's collapse echoed through the chapel.

Dara settled Noam on the floor, propping his head and shoulders up against the altar. Noam's head tipped forward, chin slumped against his chest.

"What can I do?" Taye asked, crouched down next to them as Dara dug through Noam's pockets, fumbling until his fingers closed around the second vial of suppressant.

"Go up there and hide," Dara said, glancing at him as he tucked the syringe into his own pocket. "And—hold on, give me your phone."

He entered his burner number into Taye's contacts.

"Text me," he said, pressing the phone back into Taye's hand. "Stay out of sight, and tell me when Lehrer gets closer."

*"Closer?"*

"He'll look for us," Dara said, and it came out sounding far braver than Dara felt. "He knows we're here. And I'm pretty sure it won't take long for him to find us."

Not with this proximity. If there was anything left of that blood connection between Noam and Lehrer . . .

They couldn't hide.

"You got it," Taye said, and he squeezed Dara's shoulder once before pushing to his feet and disappearing back up the stairs and into the church.

Alone, Dara's own breath was far too loud in this confined space—gasping on each inhale, like he was choking on his own air.

He was almost out of time.

The earplugs were in his back pocket; Dara fit them into his own ears and held them down while the foam expanded, the noise of the crowd outside retreating to a dull hum, and then silence.

He glanced down at his phone screen—still dark, for now.

Dara looked at Noam, sagging against the altar, motionless, like he belonged in the crypt already. Dara brushed a hand over Noam's damp, fevered brow.

"I'm sorry," he whispered. "I'm sorry."

He crawled up the steps, stone slippery and cold under his hands—but he had to stay low, in case something had happened to Taye, some lethal explanation for why he hadn't texted yet. But when Dara emerged into the nave, it was still empty, still dark.

Silence pressed down against his skull, a feeling like being very deep underwater. Dara hugged his arms around his own chest as he straightened upright, but he doubted the shiver in his limbs had anything to do with the cold.

He pulled out his phone and looked. The screen had gone white, a message from Taye. *He's out.*

Dara's heart seized. Abruptly it was very difficult to walk, as if all the bones in his legs had gone to liquid. He staggered left, deeper into the chancel. He had to . . . hide, he had to get out of sight. But where?

The altar was out. That was the obvious choice, would be the first place Lehrer checked. The smaller pews off to the side also seemed less than ideal, but—

Taye: he's going inside

The pulpit.

Dara darted across the chancel, up the few curving wooden steps that led to the carved stone pulpit perched there at the corner. He huddled himself deep against the chilly limestone and clenched his eyes shut, willed his breath to come soft and steady. Inaudibly.

He couldn't hear anything. God, he couldn't—he couldn't hear *anything.*

Lehrer could be anywhere.

Dara opened his eyes to stare down at his phone again, at Taye's last words. *He's going inside.*

He was here. He was in the chapel now, near enough that if Dara weren't wearing earplugs, he would hear Lehrer's footsteps on the wooden floor. Would hear his voice, perhaps, low and silken and laden with magic.

Taye: halfway up the aisle. he's checking the pews as he goes

Dara stared at the wall opposite him, at the long strip of carved wood that ran like a ribbon between pillars of smooth stone.

He should have chosen a better hiding place. He should have hidden in the choir pews after all, should have—

Taye: he's at the chancel

Dara pressed a hand against his mouth. He couldn't tell if it did any good. He was shaking now, violently. Was that audible? Could Lehrer hear?

A tear slid down his cheek, catching at Dara's knuckle, and he bit down on his own palm to swallow back a sob.

God, he could be anywhere. He could be walking up the lectern steps right now, might round the corner and fix his colorless gaze on Dara's face and say—

He couldn't stand it. He couldn't, he had to—

Dara crept forward onto his hands and knees, moving inch by agonizing inch until he was able to peer around the edge of the pulpit.

Lehrer stood at the altar, one long-fingered hand resting atop its surface, looking down at it as if the wood held a secret it might confess if he waited long enough. Lehrer lifted his head. Adrenaline seared through Dara's veins, blinding-white, and for a moment his mind was full of buzzing static—but Lehrer wasn't looking at Dara; he wasn't drawing closer. He was just gazing at the broken windows beyond the altar, out into the fast-falling night.

And . . . even from here, Dara could see he didn't look well. Lehrer's skin had gone the sallow color of candle wax, and the hand atop the altar was trembling.

Dara watched as Lehrer turned away from him, moving across the chancel and toward the iron grate that barred off the smaller side chapel.

That grate crumpled like paper with a wave of Lehrer's hand. But as it fell, Lehrer swayed on his feet, reaching out to brace himself against the wall.

It was several seconds before Lehrer was able to move forward again, drifting into the small chapel and examining its altar, trailing his fingertips over the cold wicks of the prayer candles.

He turned, and Dara lurched back behind the pulpit just in time.

God, he wanted to take out his earplugs—just to hear the moment Lehrer moved into the crypt—he couldn't miss that moment, couldn't abandon Noam down there to be trapped and killed in close quarters—

Dara dug out his phone and typed a message to Taye: now?

Taye responded almost immediately.

Taye: at the crypt door. just looking at it, hasn't gone in

What the hell was he waiting for?

Dara edged forward again, glancing out from behind the pulpit. He could barely see Lehrer from here now, just a slice of dark suit and tawny hair before Lehrer finally turned the knob and vanished down the stairs to the crypt.

To Noam.

Dara dragged himself to his feet, grasping the edge of the lectern for balance. He was shaking badly enough it was hard to walk—but he made it, clinging to the wall as he moved down the wooden stairs again and stole across the chancel to the open crypt door.

The stairs led down into shadow, cut only by the slightest glint of flickering amber light. Dara grasped the banister and moved down slowly, slowly. His heart was a live thing in his mouth, wild and broken as all those animals Lehrer used to kill in front of him, trying to force Dara to bring their minds back to life.

Dara peered around the edge of the stone wall that blocked the stairs from the rest of the crypt.

Lehrer knelt on the floor before Noam, tipped forward with one hand pressed against the center of Noam's chest.

It was all Dara could do to keep from launching himself forward, the immediate surging panic that Lehrer was killing him already, was reaching magic into the electrical signals inside Noam's heart and drawing them flat.

Dara pulled out the syringe instead, gingerly tugging the cap off the needle and slipping it into his pocket.

He crept out into the crypt itself, step by cautious step, approaching Lehrer from behind.

Lehrer didn't seem to hear him, didn't seem to notice, too focused on seizing whatever magic Noam had left.

Closer.

Dara could see the way the back of Lehrer's collar puckered away from his neck, the faint sheen of perspiration on his spine. Lehrer's suit was discolored now, layered in a thin patina of stone dust. From this angle Dara could make out the line of his jugular, the sharp edge of one cheekbone.

Noam beyond him, ashen and so, so still.

Dara was right behind Lehrer, close enough he smelled the sickly scent of his black vanilla aftershave, when Lehrer shifted, turning his head toward—

The needle sank into flesh, and Dara pressed down on the plunger as their eyes met, Lehrer's pale and furious as Dara stumbled back, fear like unfathomable agony burning through his blood.

Lehrer rose to his feet and yanked the needle from his neck. Threw it aside.

His mouth was moving—he was saying something, and all Dara could hear was the low rumble of wordless noise. Lehrer lifted a hand, gestured, and . . .

. . . nothing happened.

For a moment they stared at each other, Lehrer's shoulders still heaving with the effort of so much magic. And then slowly, unsteadily, Dara's hands lifted up to pull the earplugs free.

Sound rushed in to fill the void of silence. Lehrer's breath came in ragged bursts, the distant roar of battle far away but drawing closer. Dara's own pulse pounded in his skull.

"You have no idea what you've done," Lehrer said, the words dragged out of him hoarse and rough, as if over broken glass.

He took a step forward, and Dara held up both hands. "Stay there."

A cruel smile twisted Lehrer's lips. "Or what, Dara? You'll kill me?"

Another step; Dara stumbled back, the limestone floor gone slippery underfoot.

"You have no weapons. No magic." Lehrer drew closer still, his cheeks coal-bright and his gaze glowing with some terrible internal heat. "But I don't need magic to destroy you, Dara. I think we both know that."

"Stop," Dara whispered, knowing it was no good, his throat full of gravel and his heart sunken in his chest.

There was nowhere else to go. Dara's back hit the rough wall of the crypt, Lehrer advancing with slow, deliberate steps.

The dead watched with indifferent eyes as Lehrer lifted a hand and slid his fingers along the line of Dara's jaw. And Dara was fixed in place, unable to move, unable to breathe. Lehrer's touch drifted downward, along Dara's throat, and he said, "You've always been such a disappointment."

Something silver and blazing exploded in the cramped space, blinding as a dying star. Lehrer flew back, crashing against a pillar with enough force dust rained down from the ceiling above.

Ames stood at the foot of the stairs, one hand still outstretched and her face a lurid mask, magic glittering between her fingers. Taye was right behind her, service weapon drawn and the collar of his Level IV–issue dress uniform gone askew.

"*Fuck*," Ames shouted, and Dara had never seen her like this, luminous with rage. She hurled another burst of magic at Lehrer when he tried to get up, this one violent enough to crack his skull against the stone. Lehrer fell still.

For a moment they all stared at the sight of Lehrer—unconscious, a slow trickle of blood seeping down his brow, rendered abruptly and unmistakably human.

"I was just gonna point the gun at him," Taye said, "but okay."

Dara's legs couldn't hold him anymore. He sank down the wall, still staring at Lehrer's body. "How did you . . . how did you know I was . . . ?"

Taye holstered his weapon. "I was watching, remember?"

Ames moved closer to Lehrer—gingerly this time, like some part of her still expected him to rise up and kill them all. She nudged him with the toe of her boot. Lehrer made a soft, pained noise and didn't move, so Ames braced herself against the column for leverage and kicked him in the ribs with the full force of her body weight.

The heat was finally draining from Dara's head, thoughts reconstructing themselves in his mind shard by shard, and—

"Noam," Dara breathed.

He dragged himself upright, staggering across the crypt. The force of Ames's blow had sent Noam sprawling aside, fallen next to one of the bronze memorial plaques. Dara hunched over him and turned his face toward the dim light overhead. He was still breathing, but barely.

"Shit," Ames said, when she finally stepped over Lehrer's unconscious form and saw Noam. "Is he—fuck—"

"He's alive," Dara said, but it felt like a plea—*Let him stay that way.*

Noam was the gray color of bone dust, his skin so hot it hurt to touch.

"I'll get help," Taye said, and he dashed up the steps out of the crypt as Ames knelt down next to Dara and helped him tip Noam's head back to keep his airway open, stripping off Noam's jacket as if that'd be enough to cool his fever.

When Taye returned, it was with medics—but also with the army, antiwitching soldiers who escorted them up into the chapel, guns trained at their napes. But as they stepped out into the evening air, Dara curled his cuffed hands into soft fists and turned his face toward the sky, each breath a staggering reminder that he was alive.

*Audio-recorded interview clips with suspects in the March 14 CNU terror attack.*

INTERVIEWER: This is Investigator Price, badge number 0420-319, interviewing Dara Shirazi at the National Intelligence Agency headquarters, interview room number 4. Mr. Shirazi has waived his right to an attorney. Mr. Shirazi, can you tell me again what happened in the crypt?

DARA: Is Lehrer here?

INTERVIEWER: Don't worry about that right now.

DARA: Answer the question first. Is he still suppressed?

INTERVIEWER: Chancellor Lehrer is still in the hospital. Your friends could have done serious damage.

DARA: But is he suppressed?

INTERVIEWER: The chancellor is still unconscious. Suppressants are illegal.

DARA: You should make an exception.

———

INTERVIEWER: Those are very serious allegations, Miss Glennis.

BETHANY: It was a very serious crime.

INTERVIEWER: Do you have any proof that these acts occurred?

BETHANY: You really should be talking to Noam about this.

———

CLAIRE: I'm a Texan citizen. Before I answer any questions, I want to speak to a representative of my embassy.

———

DARA: For the hundredth time, no. We weren't trying to kill him. We're Level IV–trained cadets, and he was suppressed. If we wanted to kill Lehrer, he'd be dead.

———

AMES: You know what? I wish I had fucking killed him. Would serve him right.

———

BETHANY: No. I'm not thirsty. Thank you. Does my mom really have to be in here?

INTERVIEWER: You're fifteen years old.

BETHANY: Yes. So they keep telling me.

DARA: You should at least keep him suppressed for his own sake. He's going fevermad now. I'm sure the doctors have already told you.

INTERVIEWER: That's none of your concern.

DARA: If Lehrer gets his power back, it'll be all of our concern.

———

LEO: I won't say anything without a lawyer present.

INTERVIEWER: You know, it always helps to look like you've been collaborative. Juries like to see collaboration. Only guilty people won't talk without their lawyers.

*[Leo does not respond.]*

INTERVIEWER: Mr. Zang . . .

LEO: Zhang. Can you at least get my name right?

INTERVIEWER: Mr. Zhang, will you collaborate?

LEO: I'll happily collaborate. With my lawyer.

———

DARA: Did you put Lehrer in the same hospital as *Noam*?

———

INTERVIEWER: Mr. Washington, how did you even get tangled up with all of this? You seem like a good kid, from a good family.

TAYE: Constantly underestimated. *Constantly.*

INTERVIEWER: Can you elaborate?

TAYE: Um, yeah. Thought you'd never ask.

Like, I mean, half of Level IV disappeared. Dara was dead, Noam was constantly gone. Then Ames disappears. Bethany starts acting shady. I figured it had something to do with Lehrer—he's the common denominator. Something's up with him and Noam, Ames hates him, Dara hated him. But if I could find Noam, I could get to the bottom of it. It seemed like a safe bet Noam'd be at the CNU speech, what with Noam and Lehrer all attached at the hip these days.

INTERVIEWER: So you just came to the speech *hoping* to run into Mr. Álvaro.

TAYE: I was on security detail. My parents are both professors at CNU, heard the team was looking for more witchings. And I mean, I'm Level IV. My security clearance is *bomb*.

INTERVIEWER: I don't know what that means.

TAYE: It's an idiom. It's vintage. Means I'm the best.

INTERVIEWER: Okay. And how did you find Mr. Álvaro and Mr. Shirazi in the crowd?

TAYE: I watched TV.

———

BETHANY: Is Ames okay?

INTERVIEWER: She's fine.

BETHANY: I want to see Ames.

INTERVIEWER: Once we're finished with this interview, I'll see what I can do.

———

INTERVIEWER: I think you need to stop worrying so much about Chancellor Lehrer and start worrying more about yourself, Dara. You were missing for six months. Then you come back . . . you hook up with these terrorists . . . and you try to assassinate your own father. This could end very badly for you if you don't start talking.

DARA: He's not my father.

INTERVIEWER: Why did you try to kill your father, Dara?

DARA: He's *not—*

INTERVIEWER: Where were you the past six months?

DARA: Does it even matter?

INTERVIEWER: You might as well start being honest with us, Dara. Your friend Noam Álvaro already told us everything. Noam's a very cooperative young man.

*[Dara starts laughing. He can't seem to stop.]*

———

INTERVIEWER: You're obviously a very sweet girl, Bethany. It's clear you just got in over your head. Maybe if you can help us clear up a few of these questions, we—

BETHANY: Oh, shut the fuck up.

BETHANY'S MOTHER: *Bethany Glennis*, language!

BETHANY: You too, Mom. All you care about is whether my arrest is going to reflect badly on your medical career.

INTERVIEWER: Let's all take some deep breaths. Bethany, maybe—

BETHANY: Go to hell.

———

INTERVIEWER: Why would you throw away such a potentially illustrious career in the military . . . for *this*? I understand Dara was your friend, and that he and the chancellor didn't get along. But most family feuds stop short of murder.

AMES: Yeah, Lehrer still seemed pretty alive when we last saw him, so I dunno about this whole murder business.

INTERVIEWER: Attempted murder, then.

AMES: Is that what we're calling it?

INTERVIEWER: You tell me. What would you call it, Carter?

AMES: Retribution.

———

INTERVIEWER: . . . with Noam Álvaro at Carolinia National University Medical Center intensive care unit. Mr. Álvaro is a minor ward of the state; therefore, an advocate as well as Erin Chen, Mr. Álvaro's attorney, are both present. Mr. Álvaro, would you like to explain the events of March 14?

NOAM: I'm happy to explain everything.

CHEN: Noam—

NOAM: Under one condition. There are over a hundred files on this flopcell. Read them first.

# Chapter Thirty-Seven

## Noam

The investigation stretched out for weeks, the media consumed in a sudden storm of rumor and speculation—and then facts, testimonies, a headline in bold black type:

**THE INDICTMENT OF CALIX LEHRER**

> After reliable information emerged proving Calix Lehrer was himself responsible for infecting Carolinian and Atlantian citizens with a weaponized strain of the magic virus, Lehrer was indicted today in international court on charges of war crimes . . .

None of it felt real. Fifteen days in the hospital blurred into a featureless landscape of pain and suppressants and steroids washing through Noam's veins. Then the deafening *emptiness* when he woke the eighth day and reached out with his power, and all that equipment keeping him alive, all the computer screens at the nurses' station, the phones and holoreaders and security cameras—it was all blank space, an open wound where Noam's magic used to live.

Even now, three months into the aftermath, Noam's memories of winter were fragile and fragmented. Sometimes he wasn't sure he even wanted to piece them together again—even if Ashleigh, his therapist, said one day he'd have to face what happened and reckon with it.

Dara was a constant: there every night Noam was in the hospital. Holding his hand on the long drive home. A quiet presence every time Noam tried to draw on his magic, not remembering; when he broke down at the kitchen table and Dara's hand at the nape of his neck was the only thing keeping him anchored to the ground.

When they were together, it didn't matter what the rest of the world thought—if they saw Noam as a victim or a traitor, if they even deigned to consider Dara at all. Noam didn't want them to be defined by the worst things they'd survived. He wanted *this*: the jungle of houseplants in their living room, college applications on the counter, Dara singing along to Queen on vinyl—he wanted Shabbat candles, the smell of fresh paint and Dara's mouth tasting like coffee and long lazy mornings in bed.

He wanted what they built together: a new life.

"Telepathy or not, Dara is definitely *still cheating*," Ames declared as she lost another round of Saturday-night poker, Dara's grin bladelike as he leaned over the table to sweep the chips into his corner.

"Want me to watch his cards?" Noam offered, resting his hands on the back of Dara's chair. Dara made a face, and Noam swooped down to peck his cheek and steal one of the cheese cubes off Dara's plate.

Cheese cubes that were, he noticed, half-gone. Dara had been doing better about eating more, if begrudgingly—and Noam was trying to be patient. Ashleigh had said it might take a while before Dara was willing to gain real weight.

So Noam would take what he could get.

Bethany dealt out the next hand, and when Taye glanced down at his, he shook his head and sighed. "I fold. Y'all are a tough crowd."

Leo won the next round, and Dara finally excused himself from the table. "Let someone else win for a change," he added airily, earning himself a pelting of chocolate-covered raisins from Ames.

"How's the new house?" Bethany asked later, when the game was finally abandoned and they'd all drifted into their own separate knots of conversation. She was perched on the edge of Ames's kitchen counter, heels knocking against the cabinets below.

"Really big," Noam said, at the same time as Dara said, "Minuscule."

They exchanged glances, and Noam broke first. "Big enough for Wolf at least," he allowed. "Plenty of spots to claim as territory. No one is allowed to sit on the far right end of the sofa anymore, for example. It's just piled up with dog toys."

"Not enough closet space," Dara said.

"Maybe you should donate some of your clothes."

"I like my clothes."

Noam suppressed an eye roll and made himself turn back to Bethany. "It's a nice house," he said with a note of finality. "You should come over sometime. Dara cooks now."

"*Our* Dara?"

"Why does everyone always act so surprised?" Dara said, but he was grinning all the same, and when Noam slid an arm around his waist, he leaned into the touch.

"Hey," Ames said, breaking into the conversation with her mouth full of sugar cookies and someone's pink lipstick blotched against her cheek. She had a glass of water in hand; she'd stayed sober since getting out of rehab a month ago. "Not to like, interrupt or anything, but don't you two have somewhere to be?"

Noam glanced down at his watch—it was already past nine. "Oh—right. Thanks. We'll see you tomorrow at graduation, right?"

"Yep. Can't wait to see you in that stupid hat, Álvaro. Now get out of here."

They made their rounds, waving goodbye to Leo and Taye in the living room before heading down the steps and out into the warm early-summer night. The car took them south, past the suburbs and into the open wilderness—away from the glittering city lights and the glow of so many human lives intersecting and intertwining behind lit windows and under streetlamps.

Dara carried the blanket and basket; Noam took the rest, the pair of them hiking down a short curving path through the woods, then breaking out onto the rocky lakeshore.

"Conditions are perfect," Dara said, setting down his load and gazing out across the still-glass water. "It's so clear tonight."

Noam unrolled the quilt and weighed down the corners with stones. He opened his mouth to say something—*come here* or *sit down* or *help me with this*—but Dara was silhouetted against the indigo horizon, moonlight a low sheen on his hair and skin, and Noam stayed silent for a moment. Just watched him.

He was everything Noam wanted. Had always been.

At last Dara turned, gaze lighting on the unopened aluminum case Noam'd set down next to the picnic basket. "Want me to show you how to put it together?"

"Sure."

Dara constructed the telescope piece by piece, positioning the tripod and identifying true north, mounting the optical tube and attaching the finder scope and its mount. He made it look so easy, all smooth, quick movements of his hands. And when he peered through the lens, the wind picking up over the lake and ruffling through his hair, Noam thought Dara had never been so beautiful.

"There," Dara murmured, sitting back and trading Noam a tiny smile. "Look now."

Noam leaned forward, pressing his brow against the scope and squinting one eye.

And what had been a black sky transformed into a sea of glittering lights, a galaxy bursting from the fabric of space in vermilion and violet, all those stars and planets spinning inexorably inward toward a brilliant core.

Noam's breath went still in his lungs, the rest of the world falling away until in that moment it was just him and Dara and the infinite universe.

"What is that?"

"Messier 31," Dara said from near his shoulder. His chilly hand slid along Noam's forearm, laced their fingers together. "Better known by its Greek name: Andromeda. After the myth."

"It's . . ."

Words seemed insufficient to describe it. Noam stared a beat longer before drawing back, his gaze flickering over to focus on Dara's face instead.

Dara's eyes were wide, mouth parted, his weight drawn up on his knees as if to lean in closer—like he wanted nothing more than to see as Noam saw, to wind their thoughts together and share the same mind.

Noam touched his face, fingertips slipping back into Dara's hair. "Thank you," he said. "It's . . . incredible."

Dara tilted forward, and their lips met. His nose was cold against Noam's cheek, but where their bodies pressed together, he was warm.

Noam wanted to live in this moment over and over—again, and again, until it was written in his memory and bone.

When the kiss broke, Dara was smiling, a true broad smile that split across his face and was impossible not to match.

They lay back, facing the sky that curved overhead with their heads tilted side by side, and together they watched the night deepen toward dawn.

# CONTENT NOTES

This book contains depictions of sexual assault and child abuse. It also contains domestic violence, references to suicide, and depictions of eating disorders and substance abuse. For more detailed information, please see the author's website: http://victorialeewrites.com.

# Resources

National Sexual Assault Hotline: 1-800-656-4673
National Drug Hotline: 1-888-633-3239
National Domestic Violence Hotline: 1-800-799-7233
National Suicide Prevention Lifeline: 1-800-273-8255
National Eating Disorders Association Helpline: 1-800-931-2237

Many of these resources also have online webchat programs available for people living outside the US.

*To learn more about . . .*
. . . sexual assault and abuse: www.rainn.org.
. . . drug and alcohol addiction: www.abovetheinfluence.com.
. . . posttraumatic stress disorder: www.ptsd.va.gov.
. . . intimate partner violence: www.thehotline.org.
. . . suicide and suicide prevention: www.afsp.org.
. . . eating disorders: www.nationaleatingdisorders.org.

# ACKNOWLEDGMENTS

When I wrote the acknowledgments for *The Fever King*, I listed my dog last. So it is only right and proper that for the sequel, my dog is listed first. Aska: you are a very good boye.

I wrote this series for survivors. I wrote Noam and Dara for anyone who has been forced to question their own perceptions of reality—who doesn't fit the stereotype of what a victim "should" look like or act like, who fears they won't be believed. This was my story for so many years, and if this book makes even one survivor feel seen and understood, then it will all have been worth it. You are so much stronger than you know.

Thank you so much to my agents, Holly Root and Taylor Haggerty, for championing this story from the very beginning. I remember I was so nervous to describe the sequel's plot to you both. But when I did, y'all just responded "sounds about right" and told me that you trusted me. That meant everything to me. I still hope we can go to aerial yoga someday!

Thank you to my incredible editors at Skyscape, Jason Kirk and Clarence Haynes, without whose herculean efforts this book would not exist. Thank you for your thoughtful comments and for understanding the heart of the story I was trying to tell. To the rest of the incredible team who worked on this series—my publicists, Brittany Russell and Megan Beatie; cover designer, David Curtis; art director Rosanna Brockley; marketers Kelsey Snyder and Leonard Sampson; production managers Le Pan and Laura Barrett; copyeditor Stephanie Chou; proofreader Susan Stokes; and Kristin King—I'm so grateful for everything you've done. I'm also very lucky to have seen *The Fever King* made into a webcomic—thank you, Quinn Sosna-Spear and David Lee, for seeing the promise in this idea, and to Sara Deek for bringing it to life with your art.

Emily Martin, my Pitch Wars mentor and best friend: Hey, remember when we were sitting in your kitchen and I was trying to convince you that Something was a good idea and you were *so against it* and we talked for like ten more hours and now it's your favorite concept in the entire universe? Yep. Also, one day I will move back to Boston and we will essentially live at Aeronaut, and I promise you will get so, so sick of me.

I know I've been a nightmare to be around for the past year while working on this book and slowly dying, so thank you to Ben, to my parents, to my sister Ashlyn. Thanks also, again, to Aska—and to our new cat, Squid. I promise I will try to cut down on the sleeping pills now.

The writing community has been so welcoming, and I really feel like I've found a home here. I'm so deeply appreciative of all the writing sprints, the BookCon meetups, the fancy whisky and late-night texts and big queer energy. There are far too many names to list here, but to start with: Marina Liu, Brittney Morris, Zoraida Córdova, Victoria Schwab, Natasha Ngan, Mason Deaver, Casey McQuiston, Tracy Deonn Walker, Kaitlyn Sage Patterson, Ashley Poston, June Tan, Emily Duncan, Rebecca Kuang, Tes Medovich, Rory Power, Grace Li, Christine Herman, Andrea Tang, and Jeremy West. Thank you to all the bloggers and bookstagrammers who loved this book—I'm so honored by your support. Specifically thank you to Ashleigh B., Camille S., Lily H., Vicky C., Felicia K., and Grace T. P.—y'all killed it.

Thanks to everyone who read *The Fever King* and everyone who preordered *The Electric Heir*. I hope this book lives up to your expectations.

I also somehow managed to survive doing a PhD while writing this series, and for that I have to thank my adviser, Daryl; the whole rest of the department; and my friends Katie, Mary, Julian, Jon, Nathaniel, Bethany, Ellie, and literally everyone from Café Lemont (but particularly Seth, Natalie, and Bagmi).

If I forgot anyone in this list, I promise I didn't forget you in my heart.

# ABOUT THE AUTHOR

Victoria Lee grew up in Durham, North Carolina, where she spent twelve ascetic years as a vegetarian before discovering that spicy chicken wings are, in fact, a delicacy. She's been a state finalist competitive pianist, a hitchhiker, a pizza connoisseur, an EMT, an expat in China and Sweden, and a science doctoral student. She's also a bit of a snob about fancy whiskey. Lee writes early in the morning and then spends the rest of the day trying to impress her border collie puppy and make her experiments work. She currently lives in Pennsylvania with her partner.